A Christmas Tail

Cressida McLaughlin

The Complete Primrose Terrace

Cressy was born in South East London surrounded by books and with a cat named after Lawrence of Arabia. She studied English at the University of East Anglia and now lives in Norwich with her husband, David.

Cressy's favourite things include terrifying ghost stories, lava lamps and romantic heroes, though not necessarily all at the same time. She doesn't (yet) have a dog of her own, but feeds her love vicariously through friends' pets, and was once chased around a field by a soaking wet, very mischievous border collie called Wags.

When she isn't writing, Cressy spends her spare time reading, returning to London or exploring the beautiful Norfolk coastline.

To find out more about Cressy, visit her on Facebook and Twitter. She'd love to hear from you!

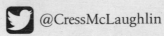 /CressidaMcLaughlinAuthor

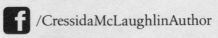 @CressMcLaughlin

A Christmas Tail

Cressida
McLaughlin

HARPER

Harper
An imprint of HarperCollins*Publishers* Ltd
The News Building
1 London Bridge Street
London SE1 9GF

www.harpercollins.co.uk

This paperback original 2015

1

First published in Great Britain as four separate ebooks in 2015 by HarperCollins*Publishers*

First published as one edition in 2015 by HarperCollins*Publishers*

A catalogue record for this book
is available from the British Library

ISBN: 978-0-00-813524-9

Set in Birka by Born Group using Atomik ePublisher from Easypress

Printed and bound in Great Britain by
Clays Ltd, St Ives plc

MIX
Paper from
responsible sources
FSC™ C007454

Acknowledgements

Huge thanks to my fantastic editor, Kate Bradley, who took a chance on me and has been an amazing supporter, guide and friend from our very first meeting.

Thank you to Mary Chamberlain and Juliet Van Oss, my copy editors, for making sense of my words with patience and precision.

Thanks to the whole HarperCollins team: to Charlotte Brabbin, Amy Winchester, Kim Young, Katie Moss, Martha Ashby, Ann Bissell and Charlotte Ledger

Thank you to the designer of my wonderful covers, Alexandra Allden.

For what is supposed to be such a solitary business, I have had a bucket-load of advice, encouragement and general brilliance from lots of authors along the way. I have to mention Alexandra Brown, Lucy Robinson, Miranda Dickinson, Holly Martin, Lisa Dickenson, Belinda Jones, Hannah Beckerman, Sarah Perry, Ali McNamara, RJ Ellory and Elly Griffiths. I am in awe of you all.

Thank you to Team *Novelicious* – I'm pretty sure I wouldn't be here without you. Especially Kirsty Greenwood and Cesca Major, who should also be in the previous paragraph, and who have been better cheerleaders than Kirsten Dunst.

To all the book bloggers I've chatted and squealed and tweeted about books with, thank you for chatting and tweeting about mine.

Thank you to Katy Jones, who set me on course.

Thank you to my friends and family – to Emily and Joe for all the advice, to Tina, Debbie, Judy and cousin Rachel for being so enthusiastic about my stories, and to Tom, Sandra, Jon, Lisa, Tim and Suzanne. To Lynsey, who has been a huge support and a great friend! To Kate and Tim for all the laughs, for Crete and the Hibiscus. To Kate Gaustad, my BFF for over 20 years, who will disown me for calling her that.

To the best teamies ever – Chris 'The Rottweiler' Williams, Well Done Ben Dunne, and Anne (bah) Tansley Thomas – who all put up with my aspiring author stories on a daily basis, and now have to cope with all the published author ones too. This is BONKERS.

To Katy Chilvers, for being possibly more excited than me, and for helping with my romantic hero research. Aramis has a lot to answer for.

To anyone who reads my book – you have helped make my dream come true. Thank you, and I hope you enjoy it!

Thank you to my sister, Lucy, who wrote the best murder mystery (aged 12) and gave me something to aspire to. Thank you to Mum and Dad for their unfailing support and inspiration; for reading everything and giving me unbiased, constructive feedback and entirely biased encouragement. I feel very lucky that I get to be your daughter.

Thank you to David, who has believed in me from the very first word, through all the hard bits and the fun bits and the champagne, and who is the most amazing person I have ever met. I wouldn't have the opportunity to write these acknowledgements without you.

And finally, to the dogs I have known and loved: to Max and Timmy, who let me share their basket; to Huey and Ella and Humph; to beautiful, mischievous Wags and to Pete (Worst Dog) and his fear of the wooden hippo. You won't be able to read this, but you're all in there somewhere.

To my family: Mum, Dad, Lucy and David.

Wellies and Westies

PART 1

'Now, just stay in the bag until I say so, OK? This could go one of two ways.'

Cat pushed the furry head back into her cavernous turquoise handbag and hoisted it up on her shoulder, pushing a strand of her pixie-cut chestnut hair out of her eyes. The sun was hesitant, the early March day too cold to be called balmy, but it was trying hard, and the thought that they were at last leaving winter behind gave Cat a spring in her step. She approached the main doors of Fairview Nursery, nodding and smiling at the clutches of parents, some with older children on their way to primary school, most with pushchairs, hoping that none of them would notice her bag's unusual bulge. Alison was already in the office, printing off the day's register and listening intently to messages on the answerphone; parents calling to say their child was ill and would be absent from nursery, someone wondering about the Easter opening hours.

Cat lifted her bag off her shoulder and placed it carefully on the chair next to the coat hooks. It wriggled, her keys jingling alarmingly, and Alison flashed her a questioning look, her neat, dark brows knitting together below her glossy fringe. Cat shrugged off her coat and scarf, hung them up and filled the kettle.

'Good morning,' Alison said when the messages had finished. 'Did you have a nice weekend?'

'Yes, thanks. A couple of nice long walks, a lie-in, a meal out with my friend.'

'Polly?'

'That's right.'

'The one you're living with?'

'Yes, and her brother.' Cat stirred milk into her tea, and put a single sugar in Alison's coffee. 'I've known her for years, and when this job came up, they . . .' she stuttered, 'they had space so . . .' Her words trailed away, and she wondered how her boss, a few years older than her and about three inches shorter, could make her feel as if she was always on trial for something. Or maybe it was just today, because looking at Alison, and listening to the muffled sounds coming from her handbag, Cat knew that she had made the worst decision since her move to Fairview.

She blew on her tea, attempting nonchalance. 'How was your weekend?'

'Good.' Alison nodded once. 'Can you come and help me get the children's coats off? I'll be letting them in shortly.'

Cat rolled her eyes. As ever, she was denied a glimpse into her boss's personal life, any titbit of information that might help Cat understand why a woman in her early thirties could be completely devoid of warmth, and yet be in charge of a nursery. Cat prided herself on her ability to get to know people, but Alison was an impossible case.

She followed her into the classroom. Miniature chairs and

tables were set out in front of a whiteboard, and there was a soft red carpet with scattered beanbags laid out for story time. The craft area, with a sink, bottles of squeezy paints and a jumble of brightly coloured aprons, was in the far corner.

'We'll take the register on the carpet, then move into the first activity, exploring different sounds.'

'Sure.' Cat knew all this. Alison planned out her lessons in minute detail, and gave Cat a briefing every Friday afternoon on the following week's plans, ensuring there was no room for error or spontaneity. Cat longed to say something, but as the assistant, and only two months into the job, she had tried to stay in line. Until today, anyway.

In the playground a couple of children, Peter and Tom, were pressing their noses up against the glass. Cat waved, and they waved back, their hands fingerless in woolly mittens. Behind them, Emma, four years old and one of the most mature children, waited patiently, her long hair in plaits, while her mother pushed her baby brother's pram backwards and forwards. Emma was holding onto Olaf's lead, the cocker spaniel puppy smelling the shoes of everyone around him, his tail wagging constantly.

'I'm letting them in now,' Alison said.

Cat's wave froze in midair and her stomach lurched. The small dog brought her thoughts back to her bag, and what was inside.

'Won't be a sec,' Cat called as she hurried out of the room.

Alison sighed loudly and flung open the double doors.

Cat's handbag was on the floor, halfway across the office, and making progress towards the door.

What if Alison had seen it first? Would she have called the police? Thrown it outside? Cat knew then that her plan hadn't just been stupid, it had been mind-numbingly ridiculous. She scooped the bag up, undid the zip further, and a black button nose snuffled to the opening, followed by a fluff of grey fur and then two dark eyes, looking up at her. Her heart stopped pounding and started to melt, as it always did when she saw Disco, her neighbour Elsie's miniature schnauzer puppy.

'Shhhh, Disco,' she whispered. 'We're going into the other room now, so you're going to have to be *really* still and *really* quiet.' Cat followed her instructions with a treat from her pocket, knowing how futile they were. You didn't have to be a dog expert to know that being still and quiet were two things that did not come naturally to a puppy. She put her handbag over her shoulder and, as casually as she could, went back into the classroom.

Alison was removing coats and hats, assisted by parents who were reluctant to let their young children go, even for a few hours, and she gave Cat a meaningful backwards glance. Cat placed her handbag at the back of the craft area, as far away from the carpet as possible. The bag emitted a tiny yelp, and Cat stuck her hand in, ruffled Disco's thick, warm fur and zipped it half closed.

'Cat?' Alison called, her voice high and tight. 'Any chance of some help?'

Cat hurried to the door and welcomed the children in, taking their outer layers off and helping them to hang them on the multicoloured coat hooks. Emma bent down to say goodbye to Olaf, and Alison appeared next to her, her short frame still imposing for a four-year old.

'Come on, Emma,' she said, 'leave the dog now. Time to go inside.'

Emma's mother put her hand on her daughter's shoulder. 'He's called Olaf.'

'Right,' Alison said. 'Well, we can't have dogs inside – some of the children are allergic.'

'You mean *you're* allergic to fun,' Cat muttered under her breath. Behind her, Peter, three years old, let out a bubble of laughter, his blue eyes bright with mischief.

'Shhh,' she said, 'don't tell on me.' She gave Peter a grin and sent him off to the carpet. Emma took off her coat and Cat could see she was blinking furiously, trying to force the tears back to where they'd come from. Cat resisted the urge to give her a hug – she knew Emma wouldn't want that – and a stronger urge to let Disco out, delight all the children and send Alison into meltdown. She watched as the nursery owner let the last of her charges in, closed the door and ran slender hands over her hair and skirt, before turning to face the children and clapping her hands.

They assembled on the carpet, Alison at the front on one of the beanbags, Cat cross-legged in the middle with children clustered around her. She was wearing a red and white flower-print dress over leggings and boots, and had painted her nails the colours of Smarties, knowing that the children would love them. Sure enough they were soon pulling her hands towards them, running their fingers over the smooth, bright surfaces.

Alison took the register and explained that their activity was called 'What's that Sound?' She started shaking a pair of pink plastic maracas. The children squealed and giggled and reached out towards the box of instruments.

'No, children,' Alison said, holding up a finger. 'I'm going to give you a musical instrument each, but you have to help me say what sound it's making first. Right.' She shook the maraca again. 'What's this?'

'Snakes!' Andrew shouted.

'It sounds a bit like a snake's rattle, doesn't it? Excellent.'

A few of the children mimicked the noise. 'Wwwhhsssssshhhhh.'

'Good.' She handed out maracas to some of the children.

'It sounds like sand,' Emma said.

'That's excellent, Emma,' Alison said. 'Can you think what might be a bit bigger than sand?'

Emma thought for a moment. 'Stones?'

Alison nodded. 'Small stones or seeds.' She handed Emma a maraca. 'Well done. The maracas are filled with seeds, or sometimes tiny stones, so that when you shake them they make a rattling noise. Now, everyone, what's this?'

There was a chorus of 'Drum!' as Alison took out a tiny bongo drum and started tapping it. 'And what do you do to a drum?'

'Bang it! Hit it!'

Cat thought she heard a small yelp from the other end of the room, but a quick glance told her that her handbag hadn't wandered. She began to relax, joining in with the drumming and handing out instruments.

Alison pulled the next item out of her box, and Cat froze.

'Does anyone know what this is?' Alison asked. She held the small metal item out in front of her.

The children looked perplexed, then Emma let out a gasp, her hand shooting up, fingers trying to touch the ceiling.

'Yes, Emma?'

'A whistle?'

Alison smiled. 'That's right, it's a whistle. And what sound does it make?'

Emma shaped her lips into a tight 'O', preparing to whistle, and Cat shot from the carpet, nimbly jumping between the children to get to her handbag.

'Cat? Where are you going?' Alison's tone was pleasant, but Cat heard the steel in it.

'I – I just need to . . .' She edged towards her handbag.

'Please come and sit down,' Alison said sweetly. 'We're having *so* much fun.'

Cat looked despairingly at the bag, then returned to the carpet and sat down slowly, wondering if she could delay the inevitable by freezing time. She planted a grin on her face.

Alison continued. 'What sound does the whistle make, Emma?'

Emma made the shape with her lips and blew as hard as she could. What came out was a soft, wet raspberry noise. Emma looked surprised. 'My mummy can do it,' she said.

Alison nodded. 'It takes a bit of practice, but you're very close. Now this –' she held up the whistle '– does it for you.' She pressed it to her lips and blew.

Children shrieked, a couple put their hands over their ears and Tom shouted: 'Dog!'

Alison frowned and gestured her palms towards the floor. 'Dog?'

Cat risked a glance at her handbag. It was in the same place.

'Dog!' Tom shouted again, his bottom bouncing up and down on the carpet. 'Dog!'

'Well, yes,' Alison said slowly, 'lots of people use these to train dogs, but—' She was interrupted by a quiet but determined yelp.

'Dog!' Tom shrieked again, and other children joined in. 'Dog, dog, dog!'

Cat got onto her knees. If she crawled quickly, maybe she could get there in time. Children were imaginative; it would be dismissed as overexcitement. But then the little black nose, the grey fur and next the whole fuzzy, inquisitive head pushed out of the handbag's opening, forcing the zip, and Disco was out. The puppy ran on her tiny legs towards Cat, knocking over three bottles of paint, and into the middle of the children, who erupted into delighted squeals.

9

Disco leapt and bounced and yipped and snuffled, exploring the sounds and smells and warm bodies around her, her little paws clambering on knees, small hands reaching out to stroke and tug her. Cat tried to gather the puppy to her, but Disco and the children were having too much fun, and so instead she turned to see her boss's reaction, wondering fleetingly if she'd be pleased that Cat had made the children so happy, and realized she was doomed. Alison was standing with her arms folded, staring at Cat with eyes that burned right into her conscience. She gestured towards the dog, words unnecessary.

Disco was standing with her front paws on Peter's knee, and Cat watched in horror as the patch of carpet around her back legs turned a darker shade of red.

'Wee!' Peter squealed.

Cat picked the puppy up and held her wriggling body tightly. The children reached out towards her, and as Cat left the carpet she caught sight of Emma. The young girl was grinning with undisguised satisfaction.

'Right, children,' Alison said, her voice as sharp as ice, 'that's enough sounds for today. If you'd all like to go to your chairs, we can do some colouring-in until fruit time. Cat, go to the office and wait for me.'

'Alison,' Cat tried, 'shouldn't I clear up—'

'I'll be through as soon as I can.' Alison turned back to the children. Peter was tugging on her skirt, his face bright and open. 'Yes,' she said, 'what is it, Peter?'

'Allergic to fun,' Peter said, pointing up at her. 'Achoo!'

'How could you do that to me, Catherine? After *all* we've talked about? All the rules we've gone through.'

'I'm sorry, I didn't think.' Cat was leaning against the table in the office, Disco tied to a bench outside the back

10

door, because Alison *couldn't stand to look at it for a moment longer; not after the havoc it had caused.* Cat didn't think that reminding her that Disco was a she, not an it, would add weight to her cause.

'You never do, not about the safety of the nursery. You're imaginative, full of bright ideas, but you never stop, for one moment, to think of the *consequences.*' Alison was walking backwards and forwards in the small, windowless space, her long plait swinging, her limbs tight with anger. 'What part of you thought bringing a dog into my nursery would benefit anyone? The children could have been injured, infected – anything!'

'I was helping out a friend,' Cat murmured. 'But I know, *now*, that I shouldn't have done it.' She shuffled her feet and looked at the floor.

'Do you?' Alison shot. 'Really? Because I think that given half the chance, you'd do it all over again. You're not a *completer finisher*, Cat, and that's the kind of assistant I need. It's not going to work out, but I think you already knew that.'

Cat's stomach shrivelled. 'If you could give me one more cha—'

'No.' Alison shook her head. 'No more chances. I'm surprised you stayed in your last employment for as long as you did. You're not reliable, you're not supportive and, frankly, you're downright disruptive. Your time at Fairview Nursery is over, and if I wasn't so angry with you, I'd pity you. I can't imagine you being successful anywhere else with this kind of attitude. Go out of the back door, and take that *thing* with you.'

'Can I say goodbye—'

'No. You'll get a formal letter confirming my decision and a record of your final payment through the post.'

11

Cat stared at the floor, unable to respond as Alison left the room and slammed the door behind her. She pushed herself off the table and, swallowing down the sob hovering in her throat, collected her coat. Outside, Disco had managed to tie her lead round and round the leg of the bench, and was sitting with her nose pressed into the wood, as if she'd been told to sit in the naughty corner. It was exactly how Cat felt.

The sun had fully emerged by the time Cat left the nursery, the sharp frost melting into crystal drops under its rays. She wouldn't be going back, unless Alison had a sense-of-humour transplant. She was no longer welcome, and therefore no longer employed.

'Oh well,' she said to the small puppy who, now free from her handbag cage, bounced along the pavement at Cat's feet, sniffing the grass verges, straining at her short lead. 'At least we escaped with our lives. At one point I wasn't so sure, were you?'

Disco yipped in response and Cat changed course, walking along the edge of Fairview Park, running her hands along the black railings. She still couldn't get over how idyllic her new home was. She had the beach, the park, and wide, quiet roads that demanded strolling rather than hurrying. Fairview wasn't large – it perched on the sea edge of the south-coast town of Fairhaven – and Cat was already getting to know the area's different charms. In Fairview Park she felt as if she could be anywhere. The wide expanse of verdant grass criss-crossed with paths, the oval pond and the Pavilion café were sheltered from the surrounding Georgian terraces and the sound of the sea, only two roads away, by tall evergreens.

At this time of the morning it was busy with dog walkers and couples strolling in the spring sunshine. Disco wasn't old enough to walk for long periods yet, her short legs getting tired easily, even though the rest of her seemed to have endless energy. The puppy stopped, sniffing enthusiastically at the base of one of the railings, and Cat stopped to let her – there was nowhere she needed to be.

She had already begun to recognize a few of the park's regular visitors, and she could see Mr Jasper bustling close to the trees, head down, as if he'd just put up one of his protest signs and didn't want to be spotted by any of the dog owners he despised. Cat felt her shoulders tense; she'd had enough of dog haters for one day and, while Alison was within her rights to protest about dogs in her nursery, Cat couldn't understand how Mr Jasper could ever think that getting rid of dogs from the park was a possibility.

A tennis ball landed heavily inside the railings, and Disco yapped loudly as a glossy Border collie raced up to find it. The larger dog stuck its shiny black nose through the bars to greet Disco. Cat crouched and stroked the dog's muzzle, then looked up to see someone watching her. The man was tall, with broad shoulders and a mass of dark brown, untamed hair. He had sharp, handsome features, and even from a distance Cat could feel the weight of his stare. His hands were shoved deep in the pockets of a leather jacket, the collar turned up against the cold.

The man continued to look steadily at her, not the dog – which she presumed was his – and Cat realized she was holding her breath.

Then Disco barked, sank her teeth into the sleeve of Cat's purple jacket, and pulled. 'Sorry, Disco,' she whispered. She carefully extracted the puppy's jaw, and when she looked up the man was striding away from her. He whistled, and the collie picked up the tennis ball and raced after him. Cat watched him go. 'Was that weird, puppy, or am I making something out of nothing?' Disco wagged her tail. 'That's what I thought.'

She was still thinking about the strange near-encounter when they turned into her road.

Primrose Terrace was an elegant crescent moon of tall, stately town houses, some in better repair than others, but all with their own charm. Each of the houses was painted a different pastel colour, their large front doors raised up from the pavement, reached by three wide front steps. The grass verges were peppered with primroses in the spring, and old-style street lamps made Cat feel she was in a Dickens adaptation whenever there was a hint of fog.

She'd moved from nearby Brighton just after Christmas to be closer to her friend Polly, further from the well-meaning prying of her parents, and to start as assistant at the nursery. Well, that had been short and not at all sweet, and Cat was suddenly jobless, directionless and desperate not to have to ask Joe for an extension on her rent so soon after she'd moved in. She tried not to let panic rise up inside her like champagne bubbles after the cork has been popped. She lived with Polly and Joe at number nine, and Elsie Willows, Chalky and Disco were at number ten, the street numbers running concurrently rather than as odds and evens. Despite being smaller than many of the other houses, without the customary attic conversion, number ten Primrose Terrace was one of the prettiest. It was pale blue with gleaming white window frames emphasizing the large sash windows, the front door was pillar-box red and Elsie had placed pots of budding hydrangeas at the edges of the steps.

Cat let Disco prance up ahead of her, then rang the bell. It took a long time for the door to open, and when Elsie stood in the doorway, leaning on a crutch, her short white bob, cardigan and long skirt as neatly presented as her house, Cat felt her cheeks redden.

'It didn't go as well as you'd hoped, then?' Elsie said, looking at Cat's face before opening the door wide and ushering her in, then hobbling after her into the airy living room.

Cat let Disco off the lead, and the puppy bounded to the basket under the window, where Chalky, Elsie's older miniature schnauzer, was having a mid-morning nap. Disco nuzzled Chalky's face, yipped and picked up a heavily chewed cuddly pig, then stood expectantly in front of the older dog. Chalky lifted his head, looked balefully at the puppy from under tufty eyebrows, and closed his eyes. Cat laughed, but Elsie was watching her expectantly.

'No,' Cat sighed, her smile fading. 'It was even more disastrous than my worst-case scenarios.'

'I told you that Alison wouldn't stand for it.'

'I had hoped she would come round to my way of thinking.'

'That, Catherine, is a triumph of optimism over common sense, and I'm being kind.'

Cat stroked Chalky and ruffled Disco's fur. Elsie lowered herself slowly into an armchair.

'I didn't want Disco in the house while you went for your check-up,' Cat said. 'Puppies get lonely, and then they get disruptive.' *Just like me,* she thought. 'I was going to see what mood Alison was in and then, at break time, bring Disco out to meet the children.'

'But you didn't get that far?'

Cat shook her head.

'You know what Alison's like,' Elsie said, 'and you know that dogs are her pet hate – no pun intended. She's probably more upset that you actively went against her wishes, rather than for any disruption you – and my dog – may have caused. But I am sorry, because you were doing a favour for me.'

'How was the check-up? I'm surprised you're back already.'

'Oh, it was fine.' Elsie waved her hand dismissively. 'The knee's healing, but slowly. I have to stay off it as much as I can for another few weeks. Nothing I didn't know already. What's the damage to you? Suspended? Cut in wages?'

'Fired,' Cat said. 'No second chances, no room for manoeuvre. Do you want some tea?'

She left Elsie gawping in the living room and busied herself in the kitchen, making tea and finding chocolate biscuits. Her insides felt hollow with panic, but already, talking it through with Elsie, she was beginning to feel better. It had only taken four days for Cat to become friends with her neighbour once she'd moved to Primrose Terrace, and what Elsie didn't know about Fairview wasn't worth knowing. She'd gone into hospital for a long-awaited knee operation at the end of February, and Cat was helping out, taking Disco and Chalky for walks when she could, cooking for her sometimes, keeping her company.

'I am so sorry, Cat,' Elsie said when she returned with the tray. 'I didn't think she'd go that far.'

Disco was on the sofa, performing a thorough hunt for any treasure that might be hidden between the cushions. Cat poured the teapot and scooped the puppy onto her lap. Disco wriggled, licked Cat's hand and settled down; a warm, breathing comfort blanket.

'She was furious,' Cat said. 'It was a stupid idea, I know. But I just thought that once she'd met Disco she'd realize how wonderful dogs can be. I mean, how could *anyone* be annoyed at this little thing?'

'Not everyone loves dogs, and some people actively dislike them. They can be smelly and messy and very badly behaved.'

'Yes, but look.' Disco was breathing softly, her small ears flopped over her eyes, her head resting on her front paws.

'You don't have to convince me,' Elsie said softly, 'but I don't think you'll be able to convince Alison. Stop worrying about her – what's done is done. You have to focus on yourself and what you're going to do now.'

Cat stared out of the window, watching as the man from a few doors down walked past, wetsuit on, a surfboard under his arm. Cat thought it must be pretty cold in the water today, despite the sun. She stirred her tea.

'Cat?' Elsie prompted.

'Sorry, what?'

'What are you going to do now that you have no job?'

Cat saw the challenge in the older woman's eyes and knew that she wouldn't get away with feeling sorry for herself. 'I have no idea,' she said. She stared at her hands and noticed that the varnish on one of her nails, the one that was orange like a tangerine, had started to peel.

'What about your old nursery? Would they have you back?' Elsie wouldn't give up, that was one of the great things about her. Solutions must be found and agreed on, in this case before the sun set.

Cat thought of the tiny nursery on a sloping hill over-looking the Brighton seafront. It had been energetic and spontaneous, and her ex-boyfriend Daniel, a teacher, had recommended her to the owners because of her creativity. It had been all the things that Alison's was not, and with its hippy attitude probably not a typical nursery. But Cat didn't want to go backwards.

'Yes, they would,' she said. 'But I moved here because I wanted to try a new view and new scenery and new people.

17

I like Primrose Terrace, and I love living with Polly. I need to find something here.'

'Right.' Elsie stroked Disco's fur. The puppy had transferred herself from Cat's lap to Elsie's and then conked out. 'You're very spirited,' Elsie said. 'You could set something up yourself, if that was a more appealing idea than shop work or waitressing in the short term.'

Cat ran a hand back through her short hair. 'I don't have the patience for waitressing. And I don't have my mum's artistic talent so I can't do greeting cards, or knitting, or making hats.'

'What can you do?' Elsie waved her hand away when Cat gave her a sharp look. 'I don't mean it like that – I know you've got a drama degree and that you're qualified as a nursery assistant, but what can you *do*? What do you enjoy? What about Fairhaven theatre? I'm sure they're looking for volunteers, even if it's just front of house.'

Cat laid her head against the sofa. 'But I need to pay rent, and the problem with theatres is they never have any money. I could volunteer, but it would be years – maybe decades – before there was the possibility of paid work.'

'So what else do you enjoy?'

'Long baths, cooking – sometimes – fresh air, walking on the beach. I'm interested in people.' She was beginning to run out of enthusiasm. The initial shock had worn off, and now all she wanted to do was to climb into one of those long baths and hide from her own stupidity.

'That sounds like an online dating profile, and not a very original one.'

'I can't help it if I have the most boring CV,' Cat said. 'Fairly OK at most things, not exceptional at anything, good with pretending and children and animals – except that animals are Polly's thing.'

18

'Just because Polly's training to be a veterinary nurse doesn't mean you can't. No misery, young lady. And it's not a boring CV. You've had a blow – almost entirely of your own making – but a blow nonetheless. You're bright and enthusiastic – you could do almost anything you put your mind to. What would you, Cat Palmer, like to do with your life? Take this as an opportunity.'

Elsie sat forward and poured more tea. At the movement Disco sat up, her eyes alert, then jumped to her feet and knocked Elsie's arm, forcing her to pour tea over the remaining biscuits.

'Rascal,' Elsie chided gently.

'But still adorable,' Cat said. 'More than anything, I'd like to spend time with Disco. I'd like to bury my head in her salt-and-pepper fur, take her for walks and watch TV with her on my lap. I could do that for the next few days at least, couldn't I?'

'You know you can borrow Disco any time you want. But I thought Joe wouldn't let you have a dog in the house?' Elsie frowned.

'No,' Cat said quietly, unexpelled emotion rising in her throat. 'No, he won't let me. He's got a cat, so no dogs allowed, apparently. I'm sure if we found the right one they'd get along fine, but he's adamant.'

'He's always seemed like a very pleasant young man to me, and I know people can be very sensitive about their pets – often rightly – but I'm surprised he won't let you have a dog.'

'Sometimes he's nice, but most of the time he's a grumpy sod. But I love living with Polly, and I love being here, on Primrose Terrace, and I want to stay.'

'Oh, chin up, don't get all teary.'

'I'm not.' Cat swallowed and blinked. 'It just seems like when one thing goes wrong, it magnifies all the other little niggles into giant, immovable barriers.' Her voice wavered at the end.

'That's why you need to be proactive. Keep moving forward, and have another biscuit.'

Cat looked at the plate, now swimming in tea. She shrugged and popped one into her mouth before it covered her hand in chocolate. 'At least I can *see* Disco and Chalky, and I'll still take them out twice a day while you're getting back on your feet.'

'That's the spirit!'

'Lots of spring sunshine and your two perfect pooches is exactly what I need while I'm working out a plan.' Cat clicked her fingers and Disco bounced across the carpet and started licking her wrist. Cat laughed as the dog's whiskers tickled her hand.

'You might be right.' Elsie drummed her fingers against her lips, her gaze fixed on the thick verge of grass outside the window, where the primroses were just starting to peek through. 'I think, Cat, that you may have come up with your own perfect solution.'

'Dog walking? As a job?'

'Yes, Polly. Taking other people's dogs for walks. It's a growing market – people who work all day, busy families, people like Elsie who might be temporarily unable to take their pets out. I bet there are loads of dog-owners out there who don't even know it's an option. Now it will be, because of me.'

They were sitting on the over-squashy, faded blue sofas in the living room of number nine Primrose Terrace, sharing a bottle of wine. Polly had come back late from Fairview vet's, where she was doing the work placement for her veterinary nursing degree, and had changed into blue cotton pyjamas, her bare feet up on the coffee table.

'And you're sure Alison won't have you back at the nursery, even if you grovel?'

'I wouldn't go back, even if *she* grovelled. I don't think it's the right job for me, not in a conventional nursery, anyway. Elsie's right, this is *perfect*. Between the beach and the park this must be a prime doggy neighbourhood, and I can't think of anything I'd like more than spending time walking other people's dogs.'

Polly scrutinized her, her wide blue eyes unblinking in a way that Cat had almost got used to, despite the effect, along with her long blonde hair, of being a bit *Midwich Cuckoos*. 'I'm sure you can do it,' she said slowly, 'but there are lots of things to consider. *Lots*. How much you'll charge, how many dogs you can walk at a time. Do the owners let their dogs have treats? If so, what kind and how often? Will you pick them all up from their houses? Will they get on with each other? And think of all the poo you'll have to pick up. It won't be a walk in the park.'

'Ha ha.'

'What, I – oh!' Polly grinned. 'It's true, though. I know you'll think things through, but you can be . . .'

'Impulsive, spontaneous?'

'Excitable, a bit like a dog.'

Cat threw a cushion at her. 'I get that I need to think about it like a business, but I'm excited, Pol. As excited as I was about moving here, finally getting to live with you. I think I can do this, and at the very least I can test the water, see if anyone nearby would be interested in a dog walker – other than Elsie, of course.'

'You won't charge her, will you?'

'I said I wouldn't, but she insists on it. She'll be my first client and I'll give her a special OAP rate.' Cat sipped her wine and beamed, feeling a swell of something like accomplishment, even though all they'd really done was come up with an idea and the hard work was ahead of her.

'Well, I think it's pretty inventive,' Polly said. 'Inspirational, almost.'

'Really?'

'Yes. You may not have intended to leave your job today—'

'Get booted out, you mean?'

'*But,*' Polly continued, holding up a finger, 'this could be better. And you'll have a nearly trained veterinary nurse on hand, should anything go hideously wrong.'

'What's going to go hideously wrong?' Joe sloped into the room, sat next to Polly and poured himself a glass of red wine. He was in his usual work outfit of jeans and a hoody, the current one navy with an orange goldfish on the front, his short hair sticking up in unruly tufts as if his day had involved a lot of head scratching.

'There's a tsunami heading towards Fairview beach. Think of the carnage it's going to cause.'

Joe sat up, almost spilling his wine. 'What? Who said anything about a tsunami?'

'Calm down,' Polly said, pushing gently against his chest. 'Cat was having you on. No tsunami.'

'Right.' Joe glared at Cat and she grinned. Joe and Polly could almost be twins. They were both blond-haired and blue-eyed, Polly's frame almost as slender as a boy's, but Joe's blond was more strawberry than ash. Cat had never found him unnerving, only annoying. 'So what's going to go wrong?' he asked.

'Cat's new business venture – except it's not, but if it does, then I'll be on hand.'

'To offer moral support?' Joe noticed Polly's feet up on the coffee table, and gently nudged them onto the floor.

'To provide medical assistance.'

'Are we going back to the tsunami? Why would you need medical assistance? Do your techniques work on people as well as animals?' Joe rubbed his forehead.

'Not for the people, silly,' Polly said, 'for the dogs.'

'Dogs?' Joe sat up again, this time keeping careful control of his wine. 'What dogs?' There was an edge of panic in his voice that Cat might have found amusing, except that it was his aversion to dogs that was stopping her from having one of her own at Primrose Terrace.

'All dogs.' Cat threw her arms up. 'I'm going to walk the dogs of Fairview. I'm going to look after them all, from chihuahuas to Great Danes, give them exercise and love and the freedom they deserve, and I'm going to get paid for it!'

Joe took a sip of wine, his movements slow and measured. Cat had, in the two months she'd been living there, discovered that this meant he was formulating an argument, considering his point carefully before he expressed it. Spontaneity was not Joe's thing. Cat was expecting a carefully crafted attack on all things canine. It didn't come.

'So your time at the nursery,' he said softly, 'it's . . . come to an end?'

'How did you know?'

'I didn't. But . . . it seemed slightly inevitable.'

'Why?'

Joe gave a quick smile. 'Because every time I asked about your day, you gave me an elaborate description of all the things you wished you'd been doing with the children – some of which would have got you sued, by the way – because the real answer was too boring to talk about. I guessed that you weren't that happy there. Sorry if I've got the wrong end of the stick.'

'Stick,' Polly said. 'Ha ha!'

'What?'

'Y'know, dog walking, stick . . . we're collecting dog puns.'

'Not intentionally,' Cat said. 'But you're right, I didn't last at the nursery.'

24

Since she'd been living there, it had become an evening ritual. Cat would tell Joe all the things she wished they'd been doing at the nursery, and Joe, a freelance illustrator, would go on about how wonderfully cooperative his clients were to begin with, and how it would take him half a day to lovingly create a drawing of a single person, only to be told by the client that they looked too angry, or too insipid, or too posh. Joe was currently working on websites, marketing and branding for small companies and, at the moment, a local magazine that was probably the cause of the hair pulling.

'Whose decision?' Joe asked.

'What?'

'Did you jump, or were you pushed?'

The room fell into silence, thoughts drifting up towards the high ceiling as Cat tried to conjure up the best way of explaining what had happened. She didn't need to.

'Cat took Disco to the nursery in her handbag, and she escaped during music time. It gave the children more excitement than Miss Knickers-too-tight could handle.' Polly poured more wine, put her feet back on the table and took them off again at Joe's instant glare.

'You took a puppy into a nursery in a handbag?' He narrowed his eyes.

Cat nodded.

'And expected chaos not to rain down upon you?'

'I was hopeful.'

'You were deluded. No wonder she fired you.'

Cat pressed her lips together and gave a small nod. 'Maybe. But look where it's led me.'

'What, to a bottle of wine and some pie-in-the-sky idea about becoming the local Dr Dolittle?'

'Hey!'

'Joe,' Polly chided, 'that's not fair. If Cat sets her mind to it, then I think she can do it.'

'Well, I'm looking forward to seeing how it turns out.' He raised his glass, and Polly and Cat did the same, though Cat could see amusement glimmering behind Joe's serious expression. His rather large ginger cat, Shed, took the opportunity to stalk into the room, shaking out his back feet in turn as if discarding distasteful footwear, and positioning himself on the coffee table. He nudged the bottle of wine close to the edge with his tail.

'How come Shed's allowed on the table and not my feet?' Polly asked. This was not a new argument, and Shed gave her a look that said just that: *I'm allowed, you're not. Get over it.*

Joe shrugged. 'It's harder to get him to behave than you.'

'So your battles are based on the effort it takes to achieve the required results? That's a hopeless way to live your life, Joey.'

'Yeah, well. I'm older than you are.'

'But not wiser.'

'It's my lease, so I get to make the decisions.'

'I'm paying the same amount of rent.'

'Do you always have to be so argumentative?'

'Only when I'm standing up for my rights.' Polly crossed her arms.

'Your rights to have your feet on the table?'

'I had a shower when I got in, so they're perfectly clean. Cleaner than Shed's, I bet. And he's got his bum on the table.'

Joe looked sideways at his sister. 'Fair point. Come on, Shed.'

He prodded Shed's back, and the cat glared at him and stepped onto his knee, kneading his paws into Joe's jeans.

'Ahhh – aaaaaaaaaah, not there, Shed!' Joe tried to move the cat but he refused to budge, and Cat hid her laughter behind her glass. She made the mistake of catching Polly's eye, and they both shook silently while Joe tried to rescue his private parts. Small portions of near-harmless revenge were very satisfying, even when they came from an unlikely source.

The bottle of wine was empty, Cat's eyes were blinking sleepily and Joe had long since disappeared to do more work or fume, silently, behind his office door. Polly switched off the television and drummed her fingers on the table.

Cat sat up. 'What?'

'He's not always been like that, you know.'

'Who, Shed?' Shed was asleep in Joe's place on the sofa, a big orange fuzz, his face buried under his tail. Cat imagined he was secretly plotting ways to get her into trouble, playing the perfect pet against her role of irritating new housemate.

'Joe,' Polly said. 'You've got the worst of him at the moment, that's all.'

'The two-month bad patch?' Cat raised an eyebrow and grinned at her friend's exasperation. 'Sorry, I know things weren't that great for him before I moved in, but I – I mean, I don't know the whole story.' She spoke gently, thinking of all the times she'd tried to get the truth out of Polly, knowing that it wasn't fair to level her curiosity at her new landlord, but unable to help it.

'It's probably time to tell you. He was really stung by Rosalin. No, not stung, that's not fair. Sometimes it's easy to think of Joe as a grumbling, emotionless lump, but he's not like that. He's broken-hearted.'

'She left him?'

Polly nodded, hesitated for a second, and then sighed. 'For his business partner,' she added. Her tone suggested she still couldn't believe it, and Cat could understand the incredulity.

'Alex did the first break-up. They'd been running Magic Mouse Illustrations for nearly five years, and he told Joe he'd been headhunted by a company in London, some global corporation with a fat salary and all the extras, and he was going to take it. That was hard, not only because Alex was leaving, but because Joe thought he wouldn't be able to do it without him. Alex was always better at the graphic design – Joe's skills are mostly straight illustration, which he's worried is a dying art. It's crushed his confidence to think Alex got poached, even though I'm pretty sure Alex wasn't telling Joe the whole truth.'

'What do you mean?' The temperature had dropped, and Cat put a cushion over her feet, too wedged into the sofa to go and get warmer clothes.

'I think Alex was exaggerating. I think he wanted out – he was about to steal Joe's girlfriend – so he applied for the job and got it. I'm sure there was no headhunting. Anyway, a few days after that Rosalin told Joe she was leaving him, that she was moving to London with Alex Duhamel, smooth and French and, from that moment on, no longer Joe's friend. It's put him off French things for ever – Brie, Paris – and women, and . . . some other things.'

'That's horrible.' Cat felt instantly guilty, felt the usual sweep of shame at her curiosity.

'He lost everything in a few days,' Polly continued. 'He's kept Magic Mouse going, he's got his head down, but he's not coping as well as he'd like us to believe. I'm sorry I didn't tell you earlier. I don't like introducing him as "my heartbroken brother". People shouldn't be judged on their back story, so I didn't fill in the blanks.' Polly sat forward, elbows on her knees. 'Also, I didn't want to worry you. It used to be me, Joe and Rosalin here. Joe was fine about you moving in – or he claimed he was – but you've still replaced Rosalin in this house, so you might be getting a harder time of it than you should.'

'He's not being actively mean to me.'

'But he's miserable, sarcastic, pessimistic. I thought it was about time I explained. I don't want you thinking I've mis-sold you the Primrose Terrace experience.'

Cat laughed. 'You haven't, and I'm really happy here, I promise. If I wasn't then I'd be in Brighton trying to get my old job back. But I'm really going to give dog walking a go. I don't know why I didn't think of it before – it's perfect for me! And your brother may be down in the dumps, but he sometimes makes an effort to be nice to me, and he's definitely got his uses.'

'Like what? Scooping up unfinished wine? Being gullible about natural disasters?'

'Those too,' Cat said. Her mind was whirring – it hadn't stopped since Elsie had suggested that she could strike out on her own and do something she really believed in. 'But I've also heard he does quite a good job of prettying up websites.'

'Ah.' Polly's thin, pearly lips lifted at the corners. 'Yes, he does have that going for him, whatever his insecurities are. And he is throwing himself into work to take his mind off things.'

'So his heartbreak could play to my advantage?'

'It could, but I wouldn't start your negotiation with that. "Hi, Joe, seeing as you no longer have a girlfriend to spend time with, could you just . . ." Maybe focus on his skills as a designer, his great visionary mind, his intellect in general.'

'Good plan.' Cat leaned forward and fist-bumped Polly. 'The two of us could really make a go of this dog-walking thing!'

'Two of us?'

29

'Of course. If you want to be a part of it?'

Cat and Polly had lived together at university in York ten years earlier, and discovering that they had grown up only a few miles apart had made their friendship stronger. After graduating, life had inevitably got in the way, but they'd remained firm friends, meeting up regularly. Cat had jumped at the opportunity to move the short distance from Brighton to Fairview and move in with Polly, and including her in her business idea was the logical next step. Polly was calm, measured and organized. Cat thought they would be a perfect match.

Polly chewed her lip. 'I – I'd love to, but at the moment I have so little time. Studying, the work placement. I'm so close to graduating now, I can't mess it up.'

'Just get involved when you can. And it's not all about the walking. There'll be admin, marketing, accounts. There's loads of things to consider – it's not going to be a walk in the park. Now,' Cat raised her eyes to the ceiling, 'which clever person told me that?'

'All right,' Polly laughed, 'you're on. I'd love to be involved. And first, the most important decision for any new business.'

'What's that?'

'A name. What, Cat, is your dog-walking business going to be called?'

'"@PoochPromenade. For all your dog-walking needs in the Fairview area of Fairhaven. No dogs too small (or big)." What do you think?'

'Sorry?' Joe turned over a page of the newspaper, his head bent towards it as if trying to block out the rest of the world. He was sitting at the dining table which, along with the sofas, was in the house's one giant living space. Cat thought it must have been two rooms that had been knocked through by some previous owners, or maybe the landlord Joe rented the house from.

'For my bio, for Pooch Promenade. I'm setting up Facebook and Twitter accounts.'

Joe took a moment – Cat thought he was probably counting to three – before looking up at her. She was sitting cross-legged on the sofa, her laptop balanced on her knees. 'Read it again,' he said.

She did. 'So, what do you think?'

He nodded, lips pressed together. 'I'm impressed. Hardly any flippancy at all, a bit of humour, striking the right balance between friendly and businesslike.'

Cat grinned. 'Thank you.'

'Apart from the name, of course, which could still do with some work.'

'But your suggestions were worse than ours!' Cat said. 'This one feels right.'

It had been a week since Pooch Promenade had been born, though it had taken a further four days to come up with the name. Polly had texted her suggestions from work: Doggy Daycare, Wonderful Walkies, Puppy Perks. They had interrupted favourite television shows, and Cat had woken in the middle of the night when an idea pushed its way to the surface. Joe had even got in on the act, though Cat wasn't sure the Post-it note he'd left for her to find when he'd gone out for a run had been a serious suggestion. It said *Bitchin' Walks*, next to a brilliant cartoon of a dog, lead in mouth, looking pleased. Cat had stuck it on the wall above her dressing table.

Polly had come up with Pooch Promenade while they were watching a period drama, the main characters strolling in the grounds of a grand stately home, parasols shielding them from the sun.

'Does Magic Mouse have a Twitter account?' Cat asked Joe.

'Yup.'

'So you've got lots of local followers?'

'Yup.' His head was back down, his fingers wrapped around his coffee mug. Cat made a face at him and started searching for it online.

'I saw that,' Joe said.

'Good,' Cat murmured, her attention drawn to the 2,500 followers Joe had managed to accumulate. 'Wow.' She began scrolling through them, clicking 'follow' on any that were obviously local to Fairview or Fairhaven. She recognized a couple of names, businesses mostly: Spatz Restaurant, the local library, Capello's Ice Cream Parlour – *Not Just for Sundaes*. She found the nursery, hovered over the 'follow' button and then clicked on it. Alison could find out how proactive she was being.

She scrolled down through photo avatars and the occasional cartoon picture. Magic Mouse Illustrations was represented by a simple cartoon of a mouse – half computer, half cheese-eating. It made Cat smile every time she saw it, and she wondered if she could convince Joe to draw something for Pooch Promenade. Her company would be so much more recognizable if she had a cute cartoon dog as the logo.

'You can't just follow people,' Joe said, 'you need to say something useful.'

'I will. But there's no point saying it if nobody's listening.'

'Very philosophical.'

Cat was trying to come up with a witty reply when her eyes snagged on a familiar name. Jessica Heybourne. Why did she know that name? She clicked onto her page, where there was a photo of a glamorous blonde, probably a few years older than Cat, smiling warmly at the lens with a confidence reserved for the frequently photographed. She had pale skin, heavily lined eyes and fair hair piled and teased like a cloud of candyfloss around her face. She had 22,000 followers, and her bio read: *Bestselling cookery writer, total foodie, love my Westies and living by the sea. THE HEART OF FOOD out now.*

That was it! Westies.

Elsie had told Cat that Jessica Heybourne should be at the top of her list of potential clients. She was a well-known author, popular in the community as well as further afield, and had three West Highland terriers and the potential to provide Cat with more word-of-mouth custom than the *Fairhaven Press*. And, as Elsie had told her gleefully, she lived at number one Primrose Terrace.

Cat had walked past it often, her eyes lingering over the elegant primrose paint, the large porch and the gleaming glass extension that was just visible from the side of the house. Cat sat back and sipped her tea, wondering how she should approach her. Jessica would never notice a general tweet – she probably didn't have much time to read Twitter, though she used it to promote her books and hook her adoring public. She'd have to send her a direct tweet. She could always follow it up with a personal visit.

Abandoning her laptop, Cat walked to the window. The rain was falling in a solid sheet, the terrace barely visible beyond the raindrops slaloming down the glass. It was a typical March day, and Cat didn't mind it – she would have to embrace all weathers if she was going to be a successful dog walker – but she wouldn't give a good impression if she knocked on Jessica's door looking like a bedraggled Great Dane.

She returned to her computer, followed Jessica and began composing her tweet. Half an hour and two bitten nails later she clicked the 'tweet' button, sat back and waited.

'What are you looking so nervous about?' Joe picked up her empty mug.

Cat shrugged. 'Nothing. Just . . . looking for some clients.'

'Inside your computer?'

'That's where it's at these days,' Cat said breezily, just as she remembered Joe's insecurities about traditional illustration being sidelined by digital design. He disappeared into the kitchen and Cat heard the mugs hitting the sink with excessive force. 'Shit,' she whispered, then called out, 'but how do you do it? You've got so many followers.'

Joe appeared and leaned against the door frame. He shrugged, his blue eyes fixing on Cat. 'I put stuff out there – what I'm working on, links to clients' websites and work I've done for them, chat to people when they ask a question. Just be open, friendly and professional, funny sometimes. And always talk about key things – mention Fairview a lot, and dog walking. Gradually people will pick it up, find out about you through searches or retweets.'

'Oh,' Cat said, surprised by Joe's openness and lack of sarcasm. 'Thanks, that's really helpful. Funny?'

'Funny's good. Funny will get noticed much more than a straight tweet. And I know you can be funny.'

'But . . . funny to you, maybe. Not intentionally.'

'I don't think you give yourself enough credit. Try it, see what happens. I've got to get to work.'

Cat listened to him pad gently up the stairs. His office was at the front of the house, above the living room, as it had the biggest windows, the most natural light for him to work with.

Once he'd gone, Cat felt the silence like a weight. She wasn't used to being at home during the morning. And Joe thought she was funny? She rubbed her forehead, reached out for her mug that was no longer there, and hit the 'load new tweets' button.

Jessica Heybourne had followed her – and replied! Cat bit her lip. *@PoochPromenade: A dog walker in Fairview? Are you new? I need to know more! Message me.* Cat's triumphant squeal filled the room, echoing off the high ceiling, and she thought she heard Joe's office door open, wait a beat, then click shut.

Twenty minutes later, against a darker sky and even heavier rain, the doorbell rang. It was a high, optimistic trill and Cat rushed to answer it. In a series of direct messages, Jessica's enthusiasm for Cat's new business had almost surpassed her own, and the celebrity author had insisted on visiting her personally, right away. Cat had changed out of her dressing gown into a cream ruffle-collared shirt and smart jeans, run a brush through her short hair and framed her large dark eyes with mascara.

She opened the door to see Jessica – even more attractive than her photo – smiling up at her from beneath the hood of a wide-belted navy trench-coat, a cloud of white, soggy fur at her feet.

Cat glanced behind her, listened for a second and then welcomed them in a little way. 'Hi, Jessica, thank you so much for coming. I'm Cat.'

'Lovely to meet you.' Jessica slipped off her hood, and her blonde hair cascaded down her back. 'And this is Valentino, Coco and Dior.' She gestured to the Westies in turn as they snuffled at Cat's bare feet, their wet noses tickling her skin, and explored the new space with enthusiasm. One of them took hold of Joe's running shoe, and Cat gently prised it from the dog's mouth, checked it for tooth marks and put it on the stairs. She prayed that Shed wouldn't appear, that Joe wouldn't decide he needed a top-up of coffee. If he realized she'd let three dogs into the house . . . she pushed the thought away and stroked each of the dogs in turn. They responded without a hint of shyness, all keen to lap up the extra attention.

35

They were wearing different-coloured velvet collars dotted with sparkling stones, which Cat thought probably weren't made out of glass. One of the dogs – was it Coco? – had his right ear bent over, as if affecting a slight vulnerability. Cat stroked the ear; the fur was unbelievably silky. They were friendly, pure white bundles of love, and Cat could feel her heart giving way.

'They're beautiful. How often do you walk them?' Cat stood so she was back at eye level with Jessica.

'Well, at least once a day, and it's easy having Primrose Park so close by, but I do sometimes run out of time, and I'm sure they'd like more.' Jessica's voice was low and breathy, even though she'd only walked a few hundred yards, and Cat wondered if it was deliberate, along with her ditziness – she'd lived in the area long enough to know what the park was called – as part of a persona. 'I'm on my own, you see,' Jessica added, 'and it's hard sometimes.'

Cat nodded. 'I know what that's like. Is it . . . recent?' She held her breath, wondering if she'd pushed it too far.

Jessica studied her dogs for a moment. 'Quite recent. I . . . I've had a bit of a time of it, but I'm coming out the other side, emerging, slowly, from my chrysalis. Things are looking more positive, exciting almost. But I couldn't have done it without my designer dogs. They've kept me sane, and they deserve the best.'

'Well, I can definitely help with that,' Cat said softly. 'I'll treat them as if they were my own. I – I'm sorry I can't invite you in. My housemate's working.' She gestured towards the living room.

'Oh, no, of course. I can't stay long anyway, but I did want to meet you. And I wanted you to meet my boys.' She gave an exaggerated flourish, but her smile was warm, her pale eyes meeting Cat's easily.

'They're lovely. Really, really lovely. I'd be very happy to walk them as frequently as you needed – on a trial basis, and then more permanently if everything works out. I can't see why it wouldn't, but the trial is just so we're all happy – you, me and your Westies.'

'What other dogs do you have?'

'Two mini schnauzers at the moment, but I've only been going . . .' She stopped, thinking about Joe's insistence that she be professional. 'We're a very new business, so we're still building our client list.'

'Sounds perfect! I love mini schnauzers.'

'They belong to Elsie, next door.'

'Oh, I think I've seen them – one's still a puppy.'

'That's Disco,' Cat said. 'She's a handful, but worth every bit of trouble.'

'They all are.' Jessica's beautiful face broke into a grin, and Cat felt herself warming to her. 'So, how about tomorrow?'

'Tomorrow?'

'I have to go to London, and these poor poppets will be left alone. Your tweet has come at the perfect time! Could you collect them about eleven? I've got a spare key.' She pulled it out of her pocket and dangled it on an elegant finger.

'Of course.' Cat took the key, surprised that Jessica was so instantly trusting. 'And they're OK with treats?'

'They're smothered in treats,' Jessica confirmed. 'They'll be very put out if you don't give them any. Won't you, darlings?'

Valentino looked up at his owner, waggled his hind legs and let out a short, loud yip.

'Fantastic!' Cat squealed, glancing behind her, and Jessica took a step backwards. 'That's brilliant. Thanks so much for coming, Jessica. I'll pick up Valentino, Coco and Dior tomorrow.' She grinned, hoping her words would have the

37

desired effect. 'We can sort out payment and a proper schedule after that.'

'Perfect,' Jessica said softly. 'Lovely to meet you, Cat.'

'And to meet all of you.' She bent, ruffled each of the Westies behind the ears, then felt her shoulders relax as Jessica put her hood back up and opened the door. The dogs trotted happily out into the rain and Jessica turned, planted a highly perfumed kiss on Cat's stunned cheek, and stepped into the shallow porch leaving a trail of Coco Mademoiselle behind her. She made her way carefully down the front steps, and Cat saw that she was wearing boots with four-inch heels. Cat gave the author a final wave, closed the door gently behind her, leaned against it and shut her eyes. She exhaled loudly, and felt her breath catch as the landing floorboard creaked.

She opened her eyes.

'Joe.'

He had his arms folded, his blond brows lowered. 'Was that dogs? In here?'

'Joe, I'm so—'

'You know how I feel about them, Cat. And what do you think would have happened if Shed had come in? For God's sake, don't you ever *think*? How many were there? More than one from all the snuffling and the – the smell.' He came slowly down the stairs, and Cat could almost feel his fury growing.

'Three,' she said. 'They belong to Jessica Heybourne and she – she wants me to walk them. I'm sorry they had to come in, but it was raining, and it was only for a few minutes. She's my first proper client.'

He was one step above her, looking down, and Cat could see more than just anger in his expression. She felt her excitement shrivel, Joe's disappointment crushing her more than she had thought it could. He nodded, and for a second Cat thought he was going to back down, to agree that yes, it had been justified, and hooray for her new client.

'Don't bring dogs in here,' he said instead. 'I don't ask too much – I think I'm pretty reasonable – but please, *please* don't bring dogs into this house. If you think that's going to be hard because of Pooch Promenade, well then . . .' He glanced away, looked back at her and then slid past her into the living room, his shoulder grazing hers.

Cat stayed where she was, feeling hurt and wronged and indignant, and pretty sure that she understood what Joe's unfinished sentence meant: work out a way to run Pooch Promenade without bringing dogs here, or find somewhere else to live.

3

Cat set out early into weather that had been summoned to test her resolve, wearing a black double-breasted jacket and skinny jeans, neither of which was waterproof enough. But not even the rain could dampen her spirits. She had done it. She had got two clients besides Elsie, and she was officially walking dogs. It was the first step, but hopefully the first of many with her four-legged friends.

As she'd picked up Disco and Chalky, Elsie had given her a shoulder squeeze and a meaningful look as if she was heading into battle. Then she'd collected the three Westies. Jessica had answered the door wearing a coral dressing gown, and had been much less forthcoming than the first time they'd met, her mind on an upcoming event or her editor's latest notes, she supposed. Cat imagined her leaning on a marble countertop, ingredients laid out around her, typing on a sleek MacBook Air as she created a delicate, exquisite dish, the dogs lying at her feet. It was an elaborate daydream, but one which Jessica fitted perfectly into, and Cat preferred thinking about that than the sadness she'd seen in the author's eyes as she'd hinted at a less than happy past.

Cat buried her head in her collar as she negotiated the dogs past a woman with a pushchair, the hood pulled low to prevent the baby from being splattered with rain.

Cat's second client was a man called Terry, who lived in one of the large seafront houses, and his Rhodesian ridgeback Bertha. He wasn't likely to be a frequent customer, but while his mother was in hospital he was having to spend a lot of time in Dorset, and couldn't keep dragging Bertha backwards and forwards only to leave her outside the hospital, confused and alone. Cat knew it was a risk, taking such a large, strong dog out with five smaller ones, but she wasn't going to turn down business so soon. Once she had a few more dogs she could stagger her walks, match the pets up like a dating agency – who was most suited to walk with who.

With all six dogs on their leads, she turned away from the churning, foaming sea, the seaside car park all but deserted, and towards Fairview Park. The Westies were very well behaved, only occasionally straying into the path of a passer-by, and Bertha was at the back, gliding on her long legs, with Chalky trotting along beside. Disco was causing Cat the most trouble, but only because – with five other dogs to be excited by – she had reached maximum bounce. She was yapping constantly and bounding in all directions, barging into Valentino and getting under Cat's feet. The Westies were good-natured, but Cat didn't think they would ignore her for ever.

The sky was low, the spring colours muted as she turned into the park, and it took Cat a moment to realize that her control would be short-lived. All six dogs recognized this as their stomping ground, and Cat knew that Bertha and Chalky were often allowed off their leads within the gates. Not today though. Cat was hoping – on her first walk at least – to return with the same number of dogs she'd started with.

Suddenly Bertha was at the front of the pack, the other dogs skittering along behind. Only Chalky remained alongside her, and when she glanced down he looked up at her with dark, mournful eyes. 'Don't look at me like that,' she whispered, quickening her pace to try and keep up with the pack. 'It's going to be fine. Doggies,' she called, 'come on, doggies! Slow down a bit.'

They ignored her.

Cat trotted down the path, past a young family, the eldest boy riding a bike with stabilizers, and an old couple walking hand in hand, wearing matching woolly hats. She could see a pair of red setters in the distance, their sleek coats standing out against the gloom, and a sprightly collie chased a tennis ball across the grass.

She took a deep breath and pulled on the leads. 'Bertha! Valentino, Coco, Dior! Slow down!' And then, hopeful of receiving some loyalty from the dog she knew best, 'Disco, treat time!' Disco's bounding changed direction and her little paws were suddenly on Cat's shins, her tail wagging. Cat came to a halt and grinned at the puppy, her breathing calmer. The other dogs slowed and then stopped, and she suddenly had the attention of six pairs of eyes.

'Good, good dogs,' she panted. 'Excellent dogs. Phew, thank God.' She reached into her pocket and gave each dog a treat. They chewed them down and looked expectantly up at her, ready for another.

'Having a bit of trouble, are we?' Cat froze at the words which, while perfectly friendly, came in a voice that was not.

'I'm fine, thanks, Mr Jasper.' He was standing a few feet away, his arms folded across his short, rounded frame. He was smiling, and only his dark eyes and the tone of his voice betrayed what he thought of her and her dogs.

'Did you know that over one hundred people a year are injured in accidents that can be directly attributed to dogs, within Fairhaven alone?'

Cat gritted her teeth. The dogs strained at their leads and Dior whimpered softly. 'I didn't, but I don't really have time—'

'Dog walkers are a *menace*,' Mr Jasper whispered, leaning in towards her, his features contorted like a gargoyle. 'You can't keep control of that many dogs. They'll get loose and they'll terrorize people. *You* are a menace, and I will put a stop to this.'

'To what? To people earning a living, dogs getting exercise?' Mr Jasper turned and strode quickly away. She called after him. 'Are you going to stop people using the park altogether, so you can preserve it as some kind of natural relic?' He didn't turn, but picked up his pace.

'OK,' she said to her pack, 'ignore him. Let's try again. But I'd like you all to take a moment to consider how difficult this is for me, how I'm prepared to admit that I've bitten off more than I can chew, and that you can either hinder or help me. And we don't want to give Mr Jasper any more ammunition, OK?' They stayed where they were. 'That's it for now. One treat now, one at the end. Those are the rules. So . . .' She waited. The dogs stayed still, apart from Disco, who was trying to destroy her left boot. 'So . . . *GO!*'

The moment she said it, she realized it was a mistake.

Now she wasn't walking, or even trotting, but was running to keep up with the dogs, the leads rubbing against her palms, wearing the skin sore. Chalky, his older bones not used to the pace, started whining. The Westies looked like summer clouds at her feet, Bertha like a small pony tearing out in front, and she couldn't even see Disco. And then, like a flock of birds, their direction changed, and their barking got louder. They pulled her past the Pavilion café, and Cat thought she saw George staring at her, a tea towel in his hand, but she couldn't be sure because she was focusing on not getting dragged behind the dogs like one of the tin cans on a wedding car.

They pulled her towards a clutch of trees at the edge of the park, and Cat saw the reason why. Was it possible for your heart to sink and beat out of your ribs at the same time? Cat thought it must be as she watched the grey, furry target bouncing across the grass like a Slinky, its tail a giant dandelion clock.

A squirrel.

Of all the bad luck in all the world, she had to find a squirrel on her first outing as a professional dog walker. 'Come ON!' She dug her heels into the grass, but they slid in the mud and she narrowly avoided ending up on her bum. 'Come on, puppies, please!'

They'd reached the trees. The squirrel had hopped up the trunk of a large oak, so at least Cat could try to get her breath back while all the dogs – Bertha included – tried to climb up after it. Cat could feel the disapproving gaze of every other person in the park burning through her coat, tickling the back of her neck.

'Please,' she coaxed, 'please stop. The squirrel won't come down while you're here, you can't get up there and I promise you – I *promise* you –' holding the leads in her left hand, her arm muscles burning, she managed to pull the bag of treats out of her coat pocket – 'squirrel does not taste as nice as these.' She shook the bag. The dogs didn't notice.

Cat swallowed down a wave of despair.

'Look, Disco! Chalky! Valentino, Bertha! Squirrel meat is tough, and it's all gristle with no flavour at all. Treats are *better* than squirrel.'

'Are you speaking from experience?' a voice said. 'I'd love to know when you've eaten squirrel.'

For a second Cat thought that Mr Jasper had followed her, but the voice was different and the strain on her arm disappeared as a hand gripped the leads, taking all the pressure. She risked turning her head, and found herself staring into the eyes of a man who, it seemed, had come to rescue her. Cat felt a jolt of recognition. She'd seen him and his dog before, had seen him watching her through the park railings the day she'd lost her job.

'How else do you suppose I get them to stop trying to climb the tree?' She should be grateful, but his flippancy when she was so flustered made her instantly defensive.

'You think that they're going to listen to your culinary advice?'

He was walking backwards, forcing her to move with him as the leads were still wrapped round her hand, and as he did so, the dogs, resisting at first, realized the game was up and turned away from their conquest. Disco bounded up to Cat's rescuer and put her paws on his jeans. He let go of the leads and lifted Disco into his arms, just as his collie dog, tongue lolling, trotted up and sat at his feet.

Cat felt her annoyance rise. His dog didn't try and antagonize Bertha or the Westies who, tired out by their chase, gave the new dog a cursory sniff and settled down on the grass. Here, they were sheltered by the trees, the rain still falling beyond their natural canopy.

'What are you?' Cat asked. 'Some kind of dog whisperer?'

He laughed, and while Disco struggled in his arms, Cat had the opportunity to look at him up close. His black-brown hair was expertly dishevelled, just asking to be ruffled, and his leather jacket – the same one as before – was worn at the elbows. He had the beginnings of stubble and there was amusement in his dark eyes. Was that amusement aimed at her? She was sure he'd been watching her before, and now here he was again, stepping in to help her.

Her irritation was swiftly replaced by curiosity.

'I'm Cat,' she said, holding out her hand. 'Thank you for . . . for that, back there. With the squirrel.'

'No problem.' He smiled at her and took her hand. 'I'm Mark. And this –' he nodded towards the collie – 'is Chips. We're new to the area.'

'Chips?'

'After Chips in *Dawn of the Dead*. The remake, obviously.'

'You named your dog after a zombie? That's not very kind. How long have you been in Fairview?'

Mark blinked at her and ran a hand over his jawline. It was quite pointy, quite determined, Cat thought, if jaws can be determined. 'A few weeks. You've not seen it, then, *Dawn of the Dead*?'

Cat shook her head.

'Chips is the dog, unsurprisingly, rather than a zombie. She's a hero – she saves the main characters from certain death. I'm splitting my time between here and London – it's lovely round here, very . . . peaceful.'

'Are you training your dog to survive a zombie apocalypse? What happens to her when you're in London?'

'Chips wouldn't need training, she'd know exactly what to do.' He grinned at her with white, even teeth.

Cat decided his jawline wasn't determined, it was smug, but he was a potential punter all the same. This was too good an opportunity to miss. 'I'll take your word for it,' she said. 'I could always look after Chips for you when you're back in London – feed her, take her for walks.'

'That's a very kind – and unexpected – offer. She's fine with me – she can cope on her own for a few hours if I'm working. Do you always go around offering to look after strangers' pets, or am I special?'

'Oh, oh, no, I mean . . .' Cat felt heat rush to her cheeks. 'It's what I do. I wasn't just . . . offering.' She shrugged.

'Ah.' Mark nodded. 'So all these dogs aren't yours, then?' Disco was burrowing into the crook of his arm, her stumpy tail wagging as if her life depended on it.

'No,' Cat said. 'I'm walking them.'

'Sure it's that way round?'

Cat gritted her teeth and gave him a tight smile. 'This is just . . . I'm still working out the best combinations, the easiest way to run things. Big dogs and little dogs together are a bit of a handful.'

'They are,' he agreed. 'I'm not sure Primrose Park knows what's hit it. And who's this little guy? Come out, buster.' He lifted Disco up, and the puppy started licking his chin. 'Hey.' Mark laughed and put her on the ground.

'She's a girl. Disco,' Cat said. Something flashed in her mind, making her do a double-take. She looked at Mark, but he was intent on the puppy and all the love she had to give. 'And Chalky's the older mini schnauzer and the Westies are Valentino, Coco and Dior. That's Bertha.' She pointed at the largest dog, who was staring out across the park, looking noble.

Mark pressed his lips together and looked at the ground.

'I didn't name them. God, I wish I'd never said anything now.'

'It's an impressive outing,' Mark nodded, unable to hide his smirk. 'And you've done well, considering.'

'Considering?' Cat shot back.

'Considering how unruly they are.'

47

'Well, I'm glad I've met with your approval.'

'I'm very happy to give it.' He was entirely unruffled, which had the opposite effect on Cat.

'Are you always like this?'

'Like what?'

'Incredibly patronizing.'

'I wasn't aware that I was being. I saw you were struggling, came over to help, and—'

'Yes, thanks for that, I appreciate it, but I'll be fine now that squirrelgate's over. Nice meeting you.' She tried to walk coolly off, but Disco was intent on spending more time with her new friend, and Valentino had managed to get his lead wrapped round Bertha's, so her aloof departure didn't happen. Mark bent down to untangle the leads. 'Thanks,' she said shortly. 'Again.'

'No problem . . . again.' She could hear the amusement in his voice.

Cat turned in the direction of the park gate. Within moments Bertha was once again in front, and Cat's sore hand stung in the wind. The rain was coming down harder now, running in rivulets off her jacket, her short hair plastered to her forehead. She risked a glance behind her, and saw that Mark was still watching her, Chips sitting at his feet, the tennis ball in her mouth. He was attaching a lead to her collar, but raised a hand when she turned. Cat looked quickly ahead and tripped over Disco, only just managing to catch her balance and prevent herself falling, sprawling, into the middle of her pack of pets.

Cheeks burning, she picked up her pace. She had to admit that, despite her best efforts, her first proper outing as a dog walker had not gone smoothly. Still, she would learn from her mistakes, and next time she strolled into Fairview Park she'd be completely in control, as serene as a swan, even if the bloody squirrel made another appearance. She was torn between never wanting to see smug Mark and Chips again, and hoping that he'd be there to see her moment of triumph.

'I'll show them,' she said to her suddenly well-behaved pooches. 'I'll show them just how effective I can be with my dogs. *Fairview* Park won't know what's hit it. I mean,' she said to Bertha, who was padding alongside her, her short golden coat rubbing against Cat's leg as they walked, 'he acts all smug but he doesn't even know what the park's called. It's not *Primrose* Pa—' She stopped, the spark she'd felt earlier exploding into clarity. 'Oh! That's very strange.' She glanced behind her, but Mark was no longer there. 'What's going on there, I wonder? What do you think, Bertha? Do you think I should try and find out?' She took the dog's easy silence as assent, and with her curiosity radar once more set to high, Cat made her way back to Primrose Terrace.

'It wasn't as bad as all that,' Cat said. 'It was a . . . lesson in dog management.' She was sitting on Elsie's sofa, brushing Chalky's fur. She'd dried each of the dogs with a towel as she returned them, and the mini schnauzers looked like they'd been through a spin-cycle. 'They saw a squirrel, and I'm sure the most experienced dog walker would have struggled to control a braying mob like mine.' Chalky looked up at her and pressed his cold nose against her chin. 'I wasn't talking about you,' Cat whispered. 'You were a gentleman – almost.'

'But you made it back, at least, no harm to any of them.'

'They didn't bite each other. They all seemed to get on fine, it was me they ganged up on.'

Elsie shook her head and stroked Disco. She was wearing a raspberry-coloured cardigan, her neat white bob perfectly in place. 'Dogs do sense emotions in humans, much more than I think we realize. I expect they knew that you were nervous, and thought they could have a bit of extra fun at your expense. You need to be more confident.'

'I need to be left to get on with it, is what I need.' Cat took a long swig of tea. It burned her throat, but she enjoyed the warmth after such a cold, wet walk.

'I thought this man rescued you?'

'He did. But he was smug about it. Ooooh, *so* smug, Elsie, you wouldn't believe. Everything about him is smug, his trendy frayed leather jacket, his stubble, his jawline.'

'He has a smug jawline?' Elsie looked sceptical.

'It's the most smug thing about him. *But . . .*' Cat narrowed her eyes.

'But?'

'What do you know about Jessica?'

'Jessica the author? Owner of your Westies?'

Cat nodded. 'Is she married?'

'Divorced, a couple of years ago now. She's clearly unsettled, because the house has been up for sale several times since then, but it always comes off the market again. I suppose she might not be around for much longer.'

'She did say she'd had a hard time recently. She was quite honest about it, considering we'd only just met.' Cat thought of Jessica's sad eyes, and then the Westies. Their soft white fur, their open, eager expressions. They hadn't been *that* bad today, and who could hold a grudge against such pretty dogs? Already she would miss them if they weren't there. 'What about now?'

'Came off the market again two weeks ago,' Elsie said with a smile, clearly happy that she had the answers to Cat's questions.

'Which means . . .?'

'She's found a reason to stay in Fairview?'

'*Exactly!*' Cat leaned forward, her voice rising, making Chalky jump. She held onto the old dog, unprepared to relinquish his warmth.

'What do you mean?' Elsie asked.

'Mark.'

'Smug Mark in the park?'

'If you have to use his full title. He said he was new here, and the "To Let" sign recently came down outside number four.'

'Good detecting,' Elsie said. 'But why do you suppose he's the one who's moved in there? Have you seen him?'

'No, I've only seen him a couple of times, in the park. But he said something that makes me think he and Jessica know each other.'

'Which was?'

'He called it Primrose Park. Have you ever heard anyone call it that? I mean, it's not even *on* Primrose Terrace – it's a road back – so why would you give it the wrong name?'

'No idea. What has this got to do with Jessica?'

'Guess who else called it Primrose Park.'

Elsie's eyes widened. She sipped her tea thoughtfully. 'That does seem quite coincidental. Good for Jessica. I don't know her well, but by all accounts she's had a rough time – there was a lot of speculation in the press about her ex-husband. She deserves some happiness.'

Cat nodded, her hands going over Chalky's ears again and again. He was asleep now, his breaths turning to snores, his back leg twitching as in his dreams he caught the squirrel. 'And Jessica said things were looking up – she hinted that there might be someone else. But then he didn't seem to recognize her dogs, or maybe he was pretending not to. I wonder . . .' she murmured.

'Wonder what?'

'Well, Mark seemed *so* smug and flirtatious. He seemed like he'd be . . . I don't know. If she's had a bad break-up, if she's had her heart broken . . . Maybe I should – should find out a bit more about him.'

'Cat.' There was a warning note in Elsie's voice.

'She seemed so lovely and trusting when I met her. She gave me spare keys to her house after five minutes. You'd think someone in the public eye would be more cautious and I just . . . I don't want her to get hurt.'

'You barely know her.'

'But I'm going to, if I'm going to be walking her dogs, and I think that Mark might . . .'

'Might what? Not be right for her? Cat, how on earth can you think that after having met each of them for five minutes? You're inventing things.'

'I'm trying to be helpful.'

'Don't you want to focus on building up your business *walking dogs* to begin with, rather than inserting yourself into your clients' private lives?'

Cat sat back on the sofa, her mind whirring. 'But I'm in the right place to find things out. I can easily do a bit of investigating . . .'

'No, Cat.'

'Why not?'

'Because, as I'm sure you already know, it'll end in tears.'

With the relaxing warmth of an extra-long bath working its magic on her limbs, Cat was in her rose-print pyjamas on the sofa, struggling to stay awake. She'd spent the afternoon plotting out the pages for the Pooch Promenade website, and now just needed somebody expert to create it. She wasn't sure after yesterday that Joe would want to be that person.

Darkness had descended, and the front room of number nine Primrose Terrace was cosy. Cat loved this time of year: the early sunsets, chilly in the evenings so that you could wrap up, but with vibrant flowers peeping up through the soil, the promise of summer around the corner. Her wrists and shoulders still ached, but her initial dismay at the disastrous walk had faded, her thoughts focused on how she could prevent it from happening again.

Shed padded into the living room, eyed Cat suspiciously and walked towards where her toes dangled enticingly over the edge of the sofa. Cat whipped her feet under her just as the front door banged open and Joe, breathing heavily and in full running gear, went straight past her and into the kitchen. Cat pretended to look at her website notes, listened to the cold tap running, the washing machine door opening, and tried not to feel so uncomfortable.

'Hey,' she called. 'Good run?' It felt lame, but she had to say something.

'Cold,' he called back. 'But that wasn't unexpected.'

'Still raining?'

'Yup.'

Great. Making an enemy of Polly's brother was not on her to-do list. She took a deep breath.

'Joe, I'm sorry I—' She stopped as he appeared in the doorway stripped down and bare-chested in just his shorts. Cat could see that underneath his jeans and hoodies, Joe clearly kept himself very fit. 'I shouldn't have let the dogs in yesterday,' she said quickly. 'Jessica sprang the visit on me, and I didn't realize she was bringing her dogs, but I . . . I couldn't turn away – t-turn her away.' Cat wasn't sure where to look; there was something about Joe's ripped torso that was making her feel a bit hot under the collar. She fumbled awkwardly as he stood there half-naked, fixing her with a steady gaze. His blond hair was dark from the rain, his blue eyes bright after his exertion.

She tried again. 'What I'm saying is . . .'

'I know what you're saying. I know it was an awkward situation, and I'm sorry if I seemed unreasonable. But I don't want dogs here, and I was surprised you'd let them in.'

'I am *really* sorry.'

'I know,' he nodded. 'Apology accepted.' He gave her a hint of a smile, retrieved his glass of water from the kitchen and sat down opposite her, his elbows on his knees. His breathing had just about returned to normal, but Cat found herself fixated by the rise and fall of his chest, his slender but toned arms, and the six-pack. She looked away, thought of Mark, of his dark, amused eyes, his easy charm. She studied the individual orange hairs of Shed's tail. She should go upstairs.

'You looked a bit soggy when you came in earlier,' Joe said eventually. 'Were you walking the dogs?'

Cat nodded, reached for her cold cup of tea. 'My first official walk as Pooch Promenade.'

'And how did it go?' She sensed him thaw a little, felt the slip back into a familiar routine.

'Well,' she said, trying to ignore Joe's bare chest. 'It started out well enough. I had a Rhodesian ridgeback, Elsie's mini schnauzers and the three Westies—' She stopped.

'Jessica's three,' he confirmed for her. 'It's in the past. Go on.'

'Right, thanks. We were trotting happily along, and then they spotted a squirrel, and then I might as well have been a rag doll at the mercy of a pack of huskies, I was that effective.' She felt a flash of the panic that had engulfed her earlier and shuddered. 'Ugh. Anyway, I had to be rescued by a handsome stranger.'

'Oh? Someone you know?'

'No, due to the fact that he was a *stranger*.'

'Fair enough.' He gave a sheepish smile. 'So he was your knight in shining armour?'

'Complete with collie.'

'He has a dog? Of course he does.' Joe scratched his jaw and glanced out of the window. Neither of them had got round to pulling the curtains, and Cat realized they must be clearly visible from the road, the lit room glowing like a beacon in the dark. 'And have you recruited his dog?'

'No. Well, not yet. But I think he must live close by, so I'm going to see if I can find out a bit more.'

'Oh, no.' He turned back to her. 'What are you up to?'

'Nothing at all.' She kept her tone light, knowing he would see through it in an instant.

Joe put his glass on the table. 'It took you two months to wreck your job at the nursery, and that was because you decided to upset the natural order. You knew what was allowed, and you did the opposite.' His voice was rising, his blue eyes hard. 'You're not even one week into your new job – *your* business, I might add, nobody to lose out except you – and already you're plotting something. You're going to mess it up before it's even got going.'

'I'm trying to get more clients, that's all.'

'You're after this guy?'

'I'm intrigued by him.' That was true, and she wasn't after him, especially not if he was already with Jessica.

'If you like him, why not just invite him for a drink? Then you can find out more by *asking* him.'

'It's more complicated than that. I need to know some things first.'

Joe took his glass into the kitchen. 'Not everything has to be complicated,' he called. 'And sometimes, *often,* in fact, simple is better.' He dropped his voice so Cat had to strain to hear him. She got the impression he was no longer talking to her. 'Most of the time, simple is far less bloody trouble.'

'Poor Joe,' Cat said to Shed, who was still at her feet. 'Not a happy bunny, is he?'

'Who's a bunny?'

'Nobody. I was just saying to Shed that he'd probably quite like to chase a bunny.'

Joe narrowed his eyes. 'Shed's far too lazy to go after a rabbit. Sometimes he finds going after a bowl of Whiskas too taxing.'

'Joe, would you like me to walk him for you?' She grinned. 'Walking cats isn't *that* weird – I bet quite a lot of people do it.'

'I'd love that.'

Cat frowned. 'Seriously?'

'Yes, I would love to see you try and walk a Rhodesian what's-its-name, three Westies and my fat cat. I would video it, and it'd go viral in about three days – three hours if a squirrel got in on the act.'

Once he'd gone for his shower, Cat put the kettle on. She felt a small glow of satisfaction. Maybe she hadn't completely ruined her relationship with him, maybe he could be worked on, made cups of tea, chipped away at until the real Joe – the Joe before Alex Duhamel and Rosalin – came back, emerging from the layers of misery. Maybe she could have her cartoon dog and Pooch Promenade website after all.

As March turned into April, Fairview Park transformed into a carpet of colour, of daffodils and marigolds and bluebells, the sea had more blue days than grey, and Cat and Pooch Promenade gained more confidence and more clients. Elsie's recovery was slow, and while she had begun to take Chalky and Disco around the block, they still needed more exercise. Along with Bertha and the Westies, Cat had a couple of poodles to walk twice a week, and a Border terrier called Huey whose owners worked full time. Meeting new clients and picking up the dogs, she was learning different routes, getting to know Fairview better, and finding that she liked the cheery seaside town more and more.

This morning she was doing a simple, three-Westie walk. Jessica was off to Brighton to do some filming for a regional ITV programme about this year's summer flavours, and had asked Cat to take her 'little darlings' out for an hour. Cat loved picking them up, loved the titbits of Jessica's life that she was given, allowing herself to fill in the gaps. She knew that Jessica was 'most definitely' staying in Fairview, but had yet to establish what had made her change her mind – if it had anything to do with a certain dark-haired man. It was none of her business, but she couldn't help trying to join the dots.

Did they know each other? Was Mark the reason for Jessica's recent enthusiasm? Did Mark just have a flirtatious nature? Cat had been told on many occasions that her curiosity only ever got her into trouble, but it was a switch that was set permanently to on. And while she kept telling herself that she was only looking out for Jessica, it had been a long time since a man as attractive as Mark had shown an interest in her. If she discovered that they were only friends, or didn't even know each other, what possibilities did that open up?

She left number nine, strode out into a bright, blustery morning and drank in the elegant terrace, the verges which were a sea of delicate primroses, the wide pavements drying quickly after the night's rain. As ever, Cat slowed her pace as she reached number four. It was a rented property and didn't look as polished as Elsie's or Jessica's houses or the boutique bed and breakfast at number three. The paint on the windowsills was cracked, and the front steps were beginning to crumble at the edges, but the front door was a bright, seaside blue with a gold number '4'. As she approached, a sleek-looking Audi pulled up outside, and the object of her curiosity climbed smoothly out of the driver's seat.

Mark opened the back door and Chips bounded up the front steps. Cat found herself coming to an automatic halt. She'd been right, at least, about where he lived.

'Cat,' he said, folding his arms and leaning against his car, amusement in his barely-there smile. 'The Cat who loves dogs.'

'It's Catherine, actually. But my friend Polly said that – that Cat was easier.' Mark didn't need to know that her best friend had given her the nickname because she was so endlessly curious. 'How are you?'

He was wearing dark jeans, sturdy boots and his leather jacket, this time with a dark grey scarf wound tightly round his neck. It looked incredibly soft. Cat had daringly decided to embrace spring and dig her royal blue bolero jacket out of the closet. She was feeling the wind at her throat as a result.

'Good, thanks. I've just taken Chips to the cliffs above the lighthouse. Lots of grass to run on, incredible views, clear, fresh air.' He breathed in deeply. 'Do you ever go there with your dogs?'

'No, I don't have a van, and it's too far to walk.'

'And dogs falling off cliffs is harder to recover from than dogs up trees?'

She narrowed her eyes. 'The park does provide fewer obstacles.'

'But today you're dogless.'

'I'm on my way to Jessica's. To take her dogs to the risk-free park. Do . . . do you know her?' Chips barked from the porch.

'Who?' Mark frowned. He took a step closer to her, and Cat could smell his aftershave. It was subtle, it smelled expensive. Cat swallowed.

'Jessica Heybourne. She lives at number one. I thought you might have bumped into her.'

He was staring at her, his lips curved into a smile. 'I just need to let Chips in, hang on.' He climbed the steps, unlocked the door, waited as the collie raced inside, then turned to face her. 'I don't know many people in Fairview, I've not been here very long.'

'Right.' Cat couldn't ask him again without it sounding obvious. 'But you like it?'

Mark nodded and descended the steps. 'It has many plus points, many striking views. Lots of things to recommend it. Primrose Terrace seems like a great place to live. Are you near here?'

'I'm at number nine,' Cat said. 'It's a very friendly road. I know Elsie at number ten, the owners of the bed and breakfast seem lovely, and of course there's Jessica.'

'Of course,' Mark said. He took Cat's upper arm and pulled her towards him. Her breath caught in her throat until she heard the pushchair rumble past and a woman calling 'thank you'. But by then her face was inches from his, and her stomach had discovered it could do somersaults. Never mind her finding out if Mark was being unfaithful to Jessica, she was about to *be* the unfaithfulness. 'We're blocking the pavement,' he said, not taking his eyes from her face.

'We should move.' She stepped backwards, swallowed and put what she hoped was a breezy smile on her face. 'I have to go and pick up the Westies.'

'Do you ever think about things that aren't dog related?'

'Of course,' Cat said, 'lots of the time, but this is—'

'What about right now?' He raised an eyebrow, and Cat found herself looking at his lips. The half smile, the jawline. She was thinking about his lips, and what they would feel like pressed against hers.

'I'm thinking about . . .'

'What?'

Her mind had stopped cooperating.

'Those big brown eyes are like saucers,' he said. 'You're panicking.'

'I'm not.'

'You really can't think of anything else, can you?' He looked satisfied, as if he'd proved his point.

Cat folded her arms. 'I wasn't thinking about dogs, actually.'

He leaned towards her and whispered in her ear. 'I know.'

Cat gawped and Mark looked away as a car started further up the terrace. When he turned back, his smirk was firmly back in place. 'So it's going well, the dog walking?'

She knew he'd thrown her a lifeline, but she was too flustered to do anything but take it. She was on much safer ground with dogs.

'It is. It – it's better. Disco's getting bigger, she's lots of fun still, but not quite so haywire, and I've been working out schedules, planning the walks around size, number and type of dogs. Squirrelgate was a one-off.' It was true. She'd sat down with Polly and drawn up a rota – there weren't enough dogs to fill it yet, but Cat could do three walks a day, two at weekends when the demand was less, and shouldn't run into any more problems if she spread out her clients efficiently.

'Glad to hear it. Although I'm not too disappointed you were having a bad day when I found you.'

'Do you take pleasure from other people's misfortunes, then?'

'Only if it means I can rescue them.'

'Are you a wannabe Superman?' Cat knew where this was going, and was trying to work out if she liked it or not. She was kidding herself – of course she liked it, but *should* she like it? She had never been a cheater, and if Mark and Jessica were together . . .

'I think Superman was less picky about who he rescued. He was an all-round, genuine superhero.'

'And you?' Her mouth was drying out.

'I'm not as squeaky clean as Clark Kent. I only rescue people I want to get to know better. Sod the rest of them.'

'OK.' She swallowed.

'That was a hint. Quite a big one, I thought.'

'T-that would be lovely,' she gushed. Why did he have the ability to turn her into a stuttering schoolgirl? Could what he had in mind be described as 'lovely'? And she was going to be late for Jessica. God, Jessica. She couldn't do it. 'Look, sorry, I really need to get going.'

Mark nodded and smiled, unperturbed by her sudden change of direction. 'Of course. Good to see you, Cat.'

'You too.'

'I'm already looking forward to the next time.'

She gave him a quick smile and hurried away, pulling her jacket tightly around her. And realized that he had neatly avoided answering her question about Jessica.

'Oh, gorgeous Cat −' Jessica flung open the door, the dogs at her feet − 'come in for a moment. I've lost Dior's lead, and he won't wear the black one.'

Cat hadn't been invited in before, and stepped tentatively over the threshold, wondering how clean her boots were − they were dog-walking wellies, not suited to polished wooden floors. Jessica's wide hall was magnificent, with walls covered in a cream and pale-green floral print, and a vase of fresh daffodils and a vintage telephone sitting on a cream dresser. Pistachio-coloured rugs on the floor picked out the detail of the wallpaper.

Cat couldn't imagine how a house with three dogs could cope with pale-green rugs but, like everything else, they looked pristine. A wooden staircase curved elegantly towards the upper reaches of the house, where skylights let in lots of sunshine. Jessica must have had the house completely remod-elled when it was extended, because it looked nothing like where Cat lived.

'I won't be two ticks,' Jessica said. 'If you could truss these ones up while I find Dior's?' She gave Cat the leads, red and blue velvet to match the jewelled collars, and Cat crouched to attach them to Valentino and Coco, giving them each a cuddle. The dogs barked and nuzzled her, and Coco, with his floppy ear, licked her cheek. Cat knew she would never tire of this, would never get over the warmth and friendship a dog could give, and the desire to have one of her own was stronger than ever.

'It was in the fruit bowl, can you imagine?' Jessica returned, holding the lead up, elegant as always in a navy skirt suit and dangling silver earrings, her blonde hair swept high off her forehead. Cat could never spot a single dog hair on Jessica, and wondered if she walked through some kind of vacuum closet before she went anywhere.

When the three dogs were ready, Cat hovered in the hallway while Jessica applied coral lipstick in the mirror. 'Is it in a library, then, your event?'

'Oh, no, not at all.' Jessica laughed, then cursed, blotted her lipstick and started again. 'It's in the Silver wine bar. Do you know it?'

Cat had walked past it, but had never gone in. She nodded. 'I didn't realize author events happened in wine bars, but then I suppose it makes a difference if you write about food.'

'Oh, they happen anywhere. But I do prefer these ones, a select few fans and journalists, a bit more sophistication. Lunch – one of my favourite recipes from the latest book, goat's cheese and tangerine salad – then questions. I should say it gets tiresome, but it never does. I lap it up, don't I?' She bent and gave each of her dogs a kiss on the forehead. When she stood, Cat looked for a white hair on her navy suit. Nothing.

'Now, Cat.' She turned and smiled, and Cat felt the full force of her glamour. 'Three weeks from now, at the end of April, I'm having a small gathering here. Nibbles, obligatory fizz, music. It's nice to do something as the evenings get lighter, I think, and it can get a bit . . . quiet in here sometimes. You'll come?' She thrust a shiny card into Cat's hand. It had silver writing on a white background, a spray of blossom in the corner, inviting her to Jessica Heybourne's spring party. A Friday night. Smart dress code.

'Really?' Cat's mind was racing, thinking of all the potential clients, the introductions Jessica could give her. Would Mark be there? What would she wear?

'Of course. And bring friends – it's Poppy, isn't it?'

'Polly. And . . . and I also live with her brother.' Would a party be Joe's kind of thing, or would he hate it? She wasn't sure, but she didn't want him sitting at home while she and Polly swanned off to drink and dance with celebrities.

'Bring them both! The more the merrier. Now, I think my car's outside, I heard it tooting. This way, poppets.' Jessica made *go on* movements with her hands, and Cat knew she was being included with the Westies, but she didn't mind being shooed outside. Jessica's party would be an evening of endless possibilities. And if Jessica was with Mark, then surely she'd want to show him off. Cat knew that, in her position, she wouldn't hide him away from the world for any longer than was strictly necessary.

Fairview Park was bursting into life, but Cat could hardly see it against the grit and hair being blown into her eyes. The wind was picking up, the sun disguising how cold and blustery it still was, and after half an hour even Dior, Valentino and Coco were looking as if they'd had enough. There were only so many leaves you could chase.

Cat headed towards the Pavilion café. It was a circular building with floor-to-ceiling windows so that, if you sat in the right seat, you could see most of the way round the park. It was perfect for people-watching. There was also alfresco seating under a wide awning that provided shelter from sun, rain and wind, and the Greek owner, George Ambrosia, left bowls of water outside for the dogs. Cat tied the leads to her table leg so the Westies could reach the water, and sat down, rubbing her hands.

George was out in a moment, his white apron gleaming, his glasses on the edge of his nose. His beard and moustache gave the impression of great wisdom or wholehearted scruffiness. Cat hadn't yet decided which.

'Hi, George,' she said. 'Lovely day for a kite.'

'Kites wouldn't stand for this,' George said. 'All end up in the trees.' His voice was low and gruff, the words getting lost in his beard. 'What can I get you?' He had his pen poised, his thumb pressed against the pages of his notebook to stop them from flying away.

'A large tea, please.'

'Milk, no sugar.'

'Right.' Cat grinned.

'A nice cake? Muffin, or Bakewell? Slice of lemon sponge?'

'No thanks.'

George nodded and reread his notebook, as if Cat had ordered an eight-piece breakfast rather than a cup of tea, then disappeared inside. Cat checked on the dogs – who were taking turns at the water bowl, their white tails wagging, pink tongues lapping quickly – and scanned the park.

It was busy, despite the bluster, and Cat could see why. It had just the right amount of open space and shelter, the tall trees providing a barrier against the outside world. She hadn't yet been here during the summer, though she'd come walking with Polly occasionally when she'd visited her from Brighton. She knew that the park would be as popular as the beach for picnics, ball games and sunbathing.

But now, on the edge of spring, people were hunched into their coats, hands deep in pockets. A young family raced with a small spaniel, the mother pushing a pram behind the elder children. Cat peered, thought she might recognize them from the nursery, but was distracted by a tall, striding figure walking ahead of a collie, tennis ball in hand.

Cat inhaled, then jumped when she saw that George was standing silently next to her table, holding her mug of tea. He put it in front of her, followed her sight line and nodded slowly. 'The man, the one with the dog. Saved you from the squirrel.'

'Y-yes. Although you make it sound like I was being attacked, like the squirrel was enormous, with big teeth and claws.' She started to laugh, but George was still looking at Mark.

'You need to watch that one.'

'Sorry? I need to watch who?'

'The man.' George nodded his head towards Mark.

'Why?' Cat's mouth went dry, sure George was about to impart a piece of the jigsaw puzzle.

'Watches people, writes it all down. Sits in here with coffee, black, no sugar, and a macaroon.'

He said it as if that, in itself, was suspicious. *Those treacherous macaroons.* 'And . . .?' Cat prompted.

'He watches people, writes it in his book. Big, leather, silver fountain pen. Spying maybe, taking notes, reporting back. Too quiet, brooding. Just like that programme *Spookies*. Maybe he is one, a Spooky?' George turned to Cat, a bushy eyebrow raised.

Cat bit back her laughter, wondered if she should point out that George was doing just what he was accusing Mark of: spying on people, reporting his observations to others. 'I'll make sure to be wary of him. Thanks, George.'

'No more squirrels, young lady.' He said it with sudden fervour. 'The squirrels lead you to the man, and to all sorts of trouble.'

'The squirrel wasn't my decision.'

'Take more care, avoid the squirrels.' He wagged his finger at Cat, then each of the dogs in turn, before going back inside.

'Wow,' Cat murmured. 'That was intense, wasn't it?' Dior looked up and gave a single, affirming bark. 'What do we think? Do we think George has a point? What is Mark up to? Is he spooky, or just sexy?' Cat bit her lip, refused to acknowledge that she'd said it out loud and then realized that, only an hour before, Mark had been walking Chips close to the cliffs. She knew collies were energetic, but did she really need another walk quite so soon? Had he been lying to her? Maybe George was right; maybe she needed to take a step back, leave Jessica and Mark to their own lives and concentrate on her own. After all, she had enough to think about with Pooch Promenade, skirting around Joe, and the upcoming party. Jessica's party. Cat sighed, stroked Coco's wonky ear and blew on her tea. Spooky Mark had disappeared amongst the trees.

She found Polly sitting on the wall at the side of the Fairview vet's surgery, eating a cheese sandwich and trying to keep her long hair out of her face.

'Can't you eat inside?' Cat asked, making Polly jump.

'They're redecorating the kitchen, so it's full of burly builders and smells of paint. I don't mind being out here, apart from when small dogs try and eat my lunch.' She snatched the other half of her sandwich away from Dior, and then gave him an affectionate stroke to make up for it. 'So these are Jessica's dogs? They're very pristine.'

'Just like she is.'

'And well behaved?'

'Mostly. Listen, she's invited us to a party.'

Polly stopped mid-chew. 'Seriously?' she mumbled. 'Why?'

'Because I walk her dogs, because we live on the same road? I don't know, but it's exciting, isn't it? Her house is *amazing*. And think of all the potential clients that could be waiting for us. It's a networking goldmine. You'll come, won't you?'

'I don't know . . . a party's not really my thing.'

'How can you say that all parties aren't your thing?'

'This one will be posh, and I don't know Jessica.'

'So come, and then you will. Joe's invited too.'

Polly gave her a sceptical look.

'Oh, come on, I can't go on my own! We can get glammed-up together – we've not done that since I moved in – and go and see how the rich and famous live. These opportunities don't come along very often.'

'And especially not involving tall, dark-haired strangers.' Polly grinned, her freckled nose crinkling, and nudged Cat with her shoulder. Cat had told Polly all about Mark, about his sarcasm and his trips to London and his smug chin, but now she wished she hadn't.

'That's not important.' She wrestled an empty chip box out of Valentino's mouth. 'Don't eat rubbish.'

'Why not? I thought he was your new Miss Marple project.'

'I need to leave him and Jessica alone. I need to focus on what's going on in *my* life.'

Cat's words were met with stunned silence.

68

'Okaaaaay,' Polly said eventually. 'What's happened? Did you find something out?'

Cat shook her head. 'I made a decision.'

'You realized that curiosity could kill the Cat?' Polly grinned, and Cat rolled her eyes.

'It felt all wrong. If they're together, I should let them get on with it. Jessica's a grown woman. She doesn't need my help and I was in danger of—' She stopped, turned away from her friend and lifted Valentino onto her lap.

'Danger of what?'

'Danger of messing it all up. As usual.'

'Oh, Cat, come on, I wasn't being serious.' Polly rubbed Cat's back. 'I'm eighty per cent sure you wouldn't have done anything too calamitous, but you're right, you need to leave them to it. If it turns out Mark isn't involved with her, you can re-evaluate.'

'Exactly. So this party, then.'

'Let me check my work schedule.'

'You can't be working on a Friday night, can you?'

'Late-night surgeries. We do them three times a week now, and Friday is always busy because people panic that they won't be able to see a vet over the weekend without paying a huge call-out fee, so we get all sorts. Cats eating coal, "Why is my puppy running in circles?", parrots that have stopped talking.'

'Sounds like a riot. Never mind my messed-up life, how are you supposed to have one when you spend *all* your time here or studying?'

'It's fun! And if we can reassure a few scared owners, and fix the genuinely unwell pets too, then we all go home happy. What would you do if Valentino got sick, or Disco – if Disco hurt herself on a Friday night – and the vet's was shut?'

'I'm not against what you're doing – how could I be? But I wish that . . .' Cat sighed, buried her face in Valentino's neck. 'I wish we could have our own dog. How can Joe be fine about cats, but not dogs?'

Polly stared at her trousers, following the crease line with her finger. 'He's just not. I know it's tough but . . . give it a few more months, maybe his mood will pick up and he'll agree to it. Shed's not that bad.'

'Shed's a grump.'

'You're a grump. I thought you'd be sick of dogs by now.'

'Never going to happen.' Cat lifted Dior onto her knee alongside Valentino, and he stepped neatly onto Polly's lap to give himself more room.

'Hey,' Polly laughed, 'what are you—'

'Excuse me – excuse me?'

A young man hurried towards them, holding a dog in his arms. It was white and grey – it looked like some kind of terrier, but Cat couldn't see it clearly enough to be sure.

'Sorry, but are you vets?' he rushed. 'My dog, Rummy, he's sick and I don't know why.'

'Oh God, hang on.' Polly nudged Dior onto the ground and hurried over to him. The man was taller than Polly, his black hair in tight, thick curls, and his face was fixed in concentration, as if he was willing himself to hold back his emotions. 'Let's get him inside,' Polly said. 'Rummy, is it?'

'Yes, yes. I found him like this in his basket. He's usually so full of energy and I just . . . I'm so worried.'

'We'll take care of him, Mr . . .'

'Capello. Owen Capello.'

'OK, Mr Capello, we'll see if the vet can see him right away.' She led the way inside, flashing Cat an apologetic glance, Owen and his stricken dog following closely behind.

'Oh, sad,' Cat murmured. 'That poor dog didn't look very well, did he?'

Coco looked up at her, Polly's discarded sandwich sticking out of his mouth.

'I knew you'd care. Come on, let's get back to Jessica, see how many hundreds of books she's signed while we've been gallivanting in the park.' She untangled the brightly coloured leads and made her way back towards Primrose Terrace, the three Westies trotting alongside her.

Cat was, for once, dogless. Dogless and bootless, her muddy wellies by the back door at home. She was scouring Fairhaven's clothes shops for something to wear to Jessica's party. It wasn't that she didn't have anything to wear, but she'd never been invited to a celebrity party before, and with the possibility of new business for Pooch Promenade, she needed something special.

The centre of Fairhaven had most of the main chain stores and a few boutiques, but it wasn't anywhere near as large as Brighton. She felt as if she'd been up and down the quaint, pedestrianized shopping streets several times, and had so far found a pale-blue dress that was far too tight, and a black dress that was nice, but didn't fit her 'special' criteria. However, she was determined to embrace her new town, and the centre of Fairhaven was as far as she was prepared to travel today.

She rifled through the racks inside a small, vintage clothes boutique, moving past pinks and yellows that, despite being springlike, were not entirely her.

'Can I help at all?' the woman behind the counter asked. She was older than Cat, wearing a cream jumper and jeans, friendly and not in the least intimidating.

'Uhm, I'm looking for something for a party. Something stylish, classic.'

As if the woman would be prepared to admit that any of her stock was unstylish. Cat resisted the urge to bolt out of the door.

She gave Cat an amused look. 'Any particular colours, anything you want to avoid?'

'Just . . . not too bright. And not too fussy. Or . . .' Cat shrugged hopelessly. 'It's been a long time since I picked out a dress.'

'Then you've come to the right place. Let's start over here. I think some of these could really suit your taller frame. I'm Carol, by the way.'

Half an hour later, Cat was strolling back to Primrose Terrace, holding tightly onto the cord handles of the thick cardboard bag containing her party dress. It was a black flapper dress with gold beading and a low V neckline, the tassels finishing at the knee. It was stylish and stand-out, but not too obvious. Cat felt unusually elated at the thought of getting dressed up instead of being ankle-deep in wagging tails. As she walked, she took a peek into the bag, at the pale-blue tissue paper Carol had wrapped carefully round the thin fabric, and marvelled again at how lucky she had been to find the dress. Her reverie was sharply interrupted when she found herself being pushed backwards, firm hands on her upper arms.

Cat gasped and looked straight into the dark, amused eyes of Mark. 'Steady.'

'S-sorry,' she stuttered. 'I wasn't watching where I was going.'

'Clearly. It's a good thing it was me you bumped into and not a woman.'

'Why?'

'Your forehead was aiming for here.' He pointed at his chest, which was covered by a grey T-shirt, his leather jacket open. 'Quite a good impression of a charging bull – a dainty one, of course.'

'A bull?' She felt her cheeks burn, realizing how obvious she was, skipping back from town with a posh boutique bag. She felt like a teenager.

'I did say dainty.'

'How's Chips?'

'Pining. She's livid that I've come into town without her. I've been thinking about your offer.' He raised an eyebrow.

'My offer?' Cat scanned her memory, her heartbeat quickening. She hadn't said any of those things out loud – had she?

He held her gaze, his eyes fixed so firmly on hers that she started to fidget. 'To walk Chips.'

'Oh, *that* offer. Of course, but I thought you didn't need me – my services, my . . .' She shook her head, her cheeks flaming at the thoughts that had been running through her head. 'Pooch Promenade.'

He looked away. 'It seems I might have to go back to London for a couple of days. Unexpectedly.'

He didn't sound thrilled and Cat thought of George. Maybe Mark was a spooky after all. 'I can take care of her.'

'I know. Thank you.' He squeezed her hand quickly, and Cat shuddered as his touch sent a thrill through her, all the way to her toes. 'It could turn out to be exactly what I need.'

'Sure,' she said quietly. She could see flecks of green in his brown eyes, the direction of the hairs in his stubble, and it seemed that, for that moment, he was scrutinizing her as much as she was him. She felt breathless.

'Anyway,' he said, breaking the spell, 'I'd better . . .'

'Of course, right.'

'We should take things off the pavement next time. Go for a coffee.'

73

'I'd like that. It was nice to . . . bump into you.'

He grinned, walked past her and then turned back. 'For Friday night?' He pointed at her bag. 'Looking forward to seeing you there. I've heard Jessica's parties can be on the wild side.' He widened his eyes in mock horror, turned away and strode up the road, leaving Cat flummoxed. She wouldn't be surprised if Carol was in his spook network, and he was on his way to find out exactly what dress she'd bought.

He'd confirmed that he knew Jessica well enough to be invited to her party, but how well? And was he flirting with Cat just so she'd look after Chips, or was there more to it? Did he have to go back to London unexpectedly on official spy business? Cat shook her head – she couldn't let George's madness infect her.

She had new information, but she also had more questions, and, more importantly, she wasn't meant to be interested in any of it. 'Curiosity killed the Cat. Curiosity killed that Cat.' She said it over and over, like a mantra. She wished Polly was at home, or she at least had a dog to talk it over with. She was sure Disco would tell her exactly what to do.

5

It was two days until the party and Cat had spent hours rehearsing what she would say, how she would introduce herself and Pooch Promenade, imagining the photos people would show her of their under-walked Labradoodles, Pomeranians and Dalmatians. Since she'd been spending so much time in the fresh air, with no emails to respond to and only dogs for company, Cat had become a perpetual daydreamer. Which meant that all of her party scenarios ended with her in Mark's arms, in a beautiful fairy-lit pagoda in Jessica's garden.

She'd been to visit Elsie, and turned to say goodbye, but she'd been daydreaming so hard that she hadn't noticed the older woman putting her coat on at first. 'Where are you going?'

'I've not been out today, and the doctor says I need to keep the knee moving if it's going to recover properly.'

'Doesn't it hurt?'

'There's no gain without pain, Cat. Coming, Disco?' Disco was at her feet like a shot, and Elsie deftly clipped the lead onto her collar. 'Chalky?' Chalky lifted his head, then placed it back on his front paws, his lack of interest clear. 'He's getting old.'

'You only notice that because you've got Disco. Hey –' she put her arm round Elsie – 'what's wrong?'

'Oh, nothing,' Elsie muttered into her collar and gave a loud sniff. 'He just reminds me that I'm getting old too.'

'You are not. You're the most sprightly fifty-year-old I know,' she teased, even though Elsie was well into her seventies.

Elsie smiled at her. 'Flatterer. If I knocked twenty years off *your* age you'd be eleven, and you wouldn't be invited to the party at all. Come on, I'll walk you to your door, then go to the end of the road and back.'

Twilight had cloaked everything in shadow, the Victorian streetlamps flickering on one by one, masking the stars that had begun to wink in the night sky. The air was crisp and clean and Cat breathed it in, feeling a twist of excitement low down in her stomach. 'Have you got your outfit sorted for Friday?'

'Oh, shush. People my age don't spend time worrying about what they're going to wear.'

'I don't believe you. I'll come round tomorrow and you can show me.'

'Isn't that something you want to do with Polly?' They stopped outside number nine, and Cat ferreted in her bag for her keys.

'Polly's not coming. She's got to work on Friday night. It'll just be you and me, kid.' She punched Elsie lightly on the shoulder. Disco yapped, her bark louder and fuller than it had been a few weeks ago, and gazed up at Cat. 'Sorry, Disco,' she said, 'I don't think dogs are invited. Apart from the Westies, of course.'

'What about Joe, isn't he coming?'

'Coming to what?' Joe stood in the doorway, blocking out the light from the hall. His hoody of the day was a faded terracotta, his sleeves rolled up to reveal long, slender forearms that reminded Cat just how toned the rest of his body was.

'Jessica's party,' Cat blurted. 'I've asked—'

'Roughly seventeen times,' added Joe.

'And so far, the answer has been no.'

'The answer will continue to be no until Saturday morning, when I might consider it.' Joe looked down as Disco licked his bare feet. His face was devoid of expression, as if the dog's touch had turned him to stone, but he didn't step back. Cat realized she was holding her breath. She saw his jaw clench, then he sighed and shook his head. 'Are you coming in? You're letting all the heat out.'

'You opened the door!'

'And I can close it again.' He moved backwards and Cat put her hand on the wood.

'Hang on.' She gave Elsie a quick hug, Disco a longer one and then waved them back down the steps, wincing at Elsie's pronounced limp. 'I'll come round tomorrow!' she called after her.

'Winc?' Joe asked.

She followed him into the kitchen. 'Thanks. How's work going?'

'Fine. Busy, so I can't complain.'

'Any exciting projects?' She leaned against the counter, watching him as he got out glasses, took a half-open bottle of white wine from the fridge.

'I'm still working on the designs for the local magazine and I've . . . had a request from Alison at the nursery to help her redesign their website.' His blue gaze was directed at her, and she struggled to keep her face neutral. She was happier than

77

she'd been for a long time, but she still felt stung that he was working with the woman who'd fired her without hesitation.

'Oh. That's good, I'm sure you'll do a great job.' Cat found to her horror that her voice was wavering. She remembered Alison's final words: *I can't imagine you being successful anywhere else.* She swallowed.

'It's a good project,' Joe said slowly, still watching her carefully. 'I can just about fit it in, but I wondered if . . . if you'd mind.' He poured the wine, handed her a glass. It was cool against her fingers.

'Why would I mind?' Cat asked. It came out in a high scratch.

Joe ran a hand through his hair. 'You know why.'

'You mean because I acted like a fool and she sacked me? It was my fault, Joe, and I'm much happier now. I wasn't suited to that place. Don't turn down work on my account.' She'd recovered, had maybe even sounded convincing.

'If you're sure?'

'Sure I'm sure. But thank you – for asking me. You didn't need to. But I . . .' She sighed, sipped her wine.

'What?'

'Nothing. Forget I said anything.'

'You haven't said anything. Come on, Cat, spit it out.'

They were leaning against opposite counters in the galley kitchen. She was still cold from being outside, but she could feel the heat from his body. 'My business,' she said. 'I'm putting together ideas for a website – all good businesses have a website these days and dogs, cartoon dogs are so . . . The cartoon you did on that Post-it, when you suggested "Bitchin' Walks", was incredible. But I know you disapprove, so—'

'I don't disapprove.'

'But the dogs—'

'I admire what you're doing. How you've not allowed what happened to dent your confidence, which is what I did after – after Rosalin.' He winced, his eyes not meeting hers, and Cat bit her lip. 'We're not always going to agree, but I don't disapprove, Cat. Far from it.'

'Thank you,' she murmured.

'So you want me to design you a cartoon dog?'

'Only if you've got time, and I can —'

'Sure.'

'Really?' Cat's heart skipped a beat.

'I'd love to. Anything to help.'

'Wow. Thank you. I'll pay you, of course.'

Joe waved her away. 'Not a chance. If I decided Shed needed daily walks you'd do it for free.' He gave her a sideways smile and rubbed his eyes with his thumb and forefinger. Cat couldn't help it. She flung her arms round his neck and felt his hand press lightly against the small of her back. 'Thanks, Joe, that means so much.'

'It's fine,' he said into her shoulder. 'It's nothing.'

Cat breathed in his sandalwood shaving cream and for a brief second she wasn't quite ready to let go, but the moment passed and she pulled away from him, grinning from ear to ear. She clinked her glass against his. They sipped in silence and then, because she was feeling buoyed by his good mood, and because he had agreed to help her so readily, she decided to be bold. 'Are you sure you don't want to come on Friday night? I know you've said it's not your thing, but the movers and shakers of Fairview will be there. I bet loads of people could use a local illustrator and designer, especially one as good as you.'

They moved into the living room and Joe flopped down on the sofa. 'It's a party, for people to have fun at. It's not a networking event.'

'Why can't it be both? And anyway, don't you want to have some fun? You're always so busy. You go from your office to the kitchen to the deli down the road. You can't possibly describe running as *fun,* and these opportunities don't come along very often. You never know what could happen.'

And maybe it was the wine, or his prevailing good mood, or something else that Cat was unaware of, but her daring paid off. Joe gave her a hesitant, lopsided smile and said, 'All right. Mainly just so you'll shut up about it – but I'll come with you.'

Cat could only grin at him, until that grin turned into surprised laughter, which in turn infected Joe, until they were both laughing at nothing, loudly enough to wake Shed up. The cat yawned expansively, gave them a disgusted glare and padded off in search of Whiskas.

'I can't find my heels! I've been in this house four months and it's already eaten my best shoes.'

'If they're your best shoes, how come you haven't needed them for the last four months?'

'This is not the time to be smart, Joe, this is the time to be helpful. Have you seen them?'

'I haven't,' Joe said. 'But I'll check the last of your boxes that are still out by the back door.' She heard him move past her, ignoring the pointedness in his voice, and delved further into the cupboard under the stairs. It was dusty and dark, and Cat didn't want to think about the soft fronds stroking her face, or what might be trying to live in them. She was glad she'd waited to have her shower.

'If I had a dog,' she said, 'then he'd find them in seconds. He might chew them, but at least he'd find them.'

'What was that?' Joe called.

'Nothing!'

Despite his recent good mood, Cat still felt that she was treading on eggshells with Joe, that he was like a plastic windmill that could change direction with a single puff. One word out of place and he'd take off his shirt – not that she'd particularly mind that bit – put on his grey hoody with the holes in the sleeves, and slump down on the sofa. She didn't want to turn up to the party on her own, and now she had it in her head, she couldn't imagine going without him.

She found a box of old CDs and a pair of battered orange trainers that looked like Polly's size, then her hand closed around something familiar but completely out of place. She pulled it into the light and sat on the carpet, examining the collar. It was for a large-sized dog, navy blue, no tags or studs – or Swarovski crystals – but definitely a dog's collar. Was it Polly's, brought home from a shift at the vet's? She burrowed back in, her hands going to the same place, and this time she pulled out a tennis ball, its fuzz worn away to nothing.

She jumped as something nudged her thigh, and suddenly Shed's front paws were on her leg, trying to launch his hefty weight over her and into the depths of the cupboard, claws digging into her flesh. 'No, Shed – yeouch!' She nudged him back down. 'I will never be able to get you out if you go in there. And *don't* pincushion me.' Shed closed his eyes.

'But what are these?' she whispered. 'Are they Polly's? Would you like to play fetch?' She waggled the ball at him and he turned abruptly and sat on the carpet with his back to her. Cat checked her watch and shoved the items back in the cupboard just as Joe appeared in the doorway with her black patent peep-toe heels.

'Are these what you're looking for?'

Joe had outdone himself. He was wearing a navy suit with a crisp white shirt, the dark blue of the jacket making his eyes look almost unnaturally bright. He'd shaved his designer stubble, and tamed his short hair with a product that smelled of tropical beaches. Cat nodded her approval. 'That's, uhm – you look great, Joe.'

'Likewise. Is your dress new? I didn't hear you ferreting around for it like the shoes.'

Cat smiled. 'I wanted to make a good impression.' She'd smoothed her fringe to the side, and found a pair of beaded dangly earrings to match her dress.

Joe cleared his throat. 'Oh, you'll definitely—'

The door flew open and Polly hurried in, her blonde hair flying, her cheeks pink. 'Am I too late? Can I still make it?'

'You're coming?'

'Layla said she'd cover – she was meant to be flat-viewing tonight but it's fallen through.'

'Awesome!' Cat fist-bumped with her friend. 'We can be fashionably late.'

Joe rolled his eyes. 'Even *more*, you mean?'

'Give me ten minutes. Promise.' Polly raced up the stairs and slammed the bathroom door.

Half an hour later they were ascending the steps to number one Primrose Terrace. There were gold fairy lights framing the front door, highlighting the yellow paintwork, and the house seemed to buzz with anticipation, lights on, silhouettes visible behind the blinds. Polly was wearing a short fuchsia dress, her long hair loose around her shoulders, and they had made the decision to come without coats, Cat's arms goose-pimpling in protest.

Cat raised her hand to knock and the door swung inwards. 'Oh, Cat!' Jessica squealed. 'And Cat's friends! So glad you could make it. Please come in.' Cat heard Polly gasp, and silently agreed that Jessica was a gasp-worthy sight. She was wearing a short black Stella McCartney cutout halterneck dress, with nude side panels that accentuated her curves. She had thick silver bangles on both arms, sky-high black heels and enough smoky eye make-up to reproduce a Lowry painting. Cat thought Jessica was probably in her mid-thirties, a woman whose life was dedicated to food, and yet she looked as though she was about to steal the show at a red-carpet event. 'Cat,' Jessica said, 'you don't know how much I appreciate you coming – all of you. Come and join in the fun!'

'This is Polly, and this is Joe.' Jessica greeted them enthusiastically, drawing them into perfumed hugs, kissing Joe's cheeks three times. They stepped over the threshold into the wide hallway and were approached by a waiter with a tray of full champagne flutes.

Cat took one, looked at the figures moving, chatting and laughing, and felt fear close around her. What did she think she was doing? Nobody would care that she was a dog walker – nobody would care what her name was. She was not a high-flyer in Fairhaven, or even Fairview. She'd only been here a few months, spending her days getting muddy and walking round the park. She took a sip of champagne, then another, as she, Polly and Joe stepped amongst the throngs of people. She reached out to take Joe's elbow, but Jessica swooped in, a long, bare arm around his shoulder, and dragged him off in the opposite direction.

'Ohmygosh,' Polly said, 'this is incredible. I knew she was famous, and sociable, but this is crazy-glamorous. I'm not sure my Oasis number cuts it.'

'You look beautiful,' Cat assured her. 'But it's pretty frightening, isn't it?' She did a full, slow turn, and her eyes came to rest on a sofa, just visible through a doorway. 'Elsie!' She waved, took Polly's hand and strode across the room. Her friend was already holding court, soaking up the local gossip from those around her.

'Hello, ladies,' Elsie said, raising her glass to them. 'I've been getting acquainted with your chums.'

Cat dropped to her knees. Valentino was sitting next to Elsie, Coco and Dior taking up the other cushions, their front paws on the arms of the sofa, their curiosity clear. Cat stroked them. Dior nuzzled his nose into Cat's neck and Coco, his ear folded down like a jaunty fedora, let out a delighted bark.

'They clearly love you,' Elsie said.

'They're so beautiful.' Polly lifted Dior up, cuddling the Westie against her.

'For once, Cat,' Elsie chided, 'be careful of your dress. It's exquisite, and wouldn't be enhanced by dog hairs, or fewer beautiful beads.'

'No,' Cat sighed. She kissed the top of Valentino's head and stood up. 'I'm going to get another drink. Does anyone want one?' Elsie and Polly nodded and Cat sought out one of the waistcoat-clad waiters. She spotted Joe across the room, talking to a woman wearing a leopard-print dress. She was touching him constantly, his arm, his shoulder, but Joe looked relaxed, laughing at what she was saying, one hand in his pocket. Cat felt a shiver of surprise and resisted the urge to interrupt them. How had he managed to do that? He was a hermit, a wallower by his own admission, though it was true that, this evening, he looked every inch the eligible bachelor.

Cat turned to the waiter. 'Could I take three of these for my friends, please?'

'Of course.'

Cat carefully lifted the glasses, balancing them in her fingers. 'Not that bad a party, is it?'

'What, I – no, they're – oh, hello.' She grinned, because it was the only thing that her brain could manage when faced with Mark, stylish and dangerous-looking in a Tom Ford black suit and black shirt, his dark hair impossibly shiny.

'Great dress.'

'Th-thank you,' she managed. 'I'll just take these . . .' Suddenly Polly was alongside her, prising two of the glasses out of her hands. Cat gave Polly a look and tried to tilt her head imperceptibly towards Mark. Polly returned her look, knowingly, and turned to introduce herself.

'Hello, I'm Polly. You must be Mark.'

'Why must I?'

Polly did a goldfish impression. 'S-sorry?'

'How do you know I'm Mark? I haven't met you before, have I?'

Polly turned her goldfish from Mark to Cat and back again.

Cat closed her eyes. 'I may have mentioned the squirrel incident to Polly. Polly, meet Mark. Mark, this is Polly – friend and housemate, and the other half of Pooch Promenade.'

'Though I haven't really done anything yet,' Polly added.

'Lovely to meet you,' he said. 'I'm flattered that Cat described me well enough for you to recognize me.'

'I told her you were tall, dark and overconfident.'

Mark tipped his head on one side, considering, then nodded his approval. 'Sounds about right. Good party so far?'

'Seems so. Jessica doesn't do things by halves, does she?' Cat couldn't help it. Every time she was faced with Mark, her resolve went out of the window. Her subconscious seemed intent on discovering his relationship status.

'Seems not.' He perused the room, then gave them a quick smile. 'There's someone I need to talk to – I'll catch up with you later.'

'Oooh,' Polly said as soon as he was out of earshot, 'he's a bit of all right.'

'Did you see how smug his chin was?'

Polly laughed. 'He's not unsure of himself. But I can see why you were intrigued – it can't be every day that you're approached by a man who's quite so . . . arresting. Why don't you just ask him? Ask him if he's with Jessica, or someone else, or if he's single?'

'But you've seen what he's like – he wouldn't let me live it down if I asked him out and he turned out to be with Jessica, or married, or gay.'

'Not over something like that, surely. He must have emotions just like everyone else. And if he's going to be that cruel, then he's not worth it anyway.'

'I just . . .' Cat sighed. 'I can't do anything unless I know that he's not with Jessica. She's already a client, he lives five doors away – it would be too awkward. Like you said, Pol, I have to put my business first.'

'If I were you I'd try and make room for him as well.'

It was so unlike Polly that it shocked Cat into laughter. 'You're mad!'

'I'm coming round to your way of thinking,' she said. 'Find out if he's with Jessica and then, if not, go for it. Honestly, Cat, I can't remember the last time I saw someone that good-looking in real life.'

'He's got a smug chin and razor-sharp observation. I don't stand a chance.'

'You're underestimating yourself, Cat Palmer. I say throw caution to the wind – it's a party after all.'

Polly clinked her glass, and Cat felt as though she'd been given approval from the person whose opinion she cared about most. Sadly, she wasn't sure she had the guts to go through with it. Maybe more champagne would help . . .

The champagne kept coming, and the waiters circled with trays of tiny, exotic canapés: smoked salmon and horse-radish, mushroom and halloumi, strawberry and balsamic vinegar. They were tasty, but not filling, and Cat had begun to feel light-headed. Polly was having an in-depth conversation with an older woman about horses, and as Cat knew nothing beyond *Black Beauty* and *My Friend Flicka*, she'd slipped away. She had only spoken to one person she didn't already know, and that was to ask where the toilet was.

She downed her drink and, sighing, returned to Elsie's permanent spot on the sofa. Her knee meant that she was having drinks, canapés and conversations brought to her, and Cat knew she was revelling in the attention. As she sidestepped through the crowd she saw that Elsie's current companion was Joe. He was grinning, his jacket folded over the arm of the sofa, white shirtsleeves rolled up. She had never seen him so animated, and thought that he should find a party to go to at least once a month. Maybe she should hide his hoody collection.

'Hey!' She waved.

'Cat! Come and sit down.' Joe patted the seat beside him, and Cat sat gratefully between them. 'Having a good time?'

'Not as good as you are,' she said, smiling. 'How do you do it?'

'Do what?'

'Talk to people you don't know. Approach them, launch into a conversation. I saw you with that woman earlier – I've seen you with lots of people.'

Joe shrugged and put his arm along the back of the sofa. 'You have to treat it like your one opportunity, and not give a shit what people think. Say what you want to say, and if they like it, they'll keep talking to you. If they don't, they'll walk away and you never have to see them again.'

'But how do I know?'

'You don't. You could get a Jessica Heybourne or a Mr Jasper.'

'Ugh,' she shivered. 'Don't remind me about Mr Jasper.'

'Or you could get someone in between,' Joe said, his voice softer. 'Like me. I'm not always that hard to live with, am I?' He raised his eyebrows in what Cat thought – but would never tell him – was an excellent impression of a lost puppy. A Labrador.

'No,' she laughed. 'Not *always*.'

'Good advice from your housemate, don't you think?' Elsie patted her knee. 'If it's meant to be, it'll work out. If not, then you've only lost a sliver of self-confidence which will come back anyway.'

'Right, yes.' Cat examined her knees. 'Brilliant advice. Thanks, Joe, thanks, Elsie. I just . . . it's hard, launching in. How do you bring up the subject of dogs at a party like this? I know the Westies are here somewhere, but . . .'

'So host your own event,' Joe said. 'Organize a dog get-together, invite owners to come and find out about Pooch Promenade. But not at ours,' he added quickly. 'Somewhere large and dog-friendly. Maybe the café in the park. George likes dogs, doesn't he?'

Cat stared at him.

'What?' he shrugged. 'Look, if it's a crap idea—'

'It's an amazing idea,' Cat said, her eyes shining at the thought. 'It's perfect.'

'There you go, then. Tell people that you're having a great time and that you're hosting an event soon, and the dog bit will follow naturally.'

'You're a genius, Joe!' Cat squeezed his arm.

'Knock them dead.' Joe gave her his steady, blue-eyed stare. 'You already do in that dress, so . . . go for it.'

Cat nodded, stood, and walked purposefully amongst the warm bodies. Joe was right – they all were. She was proud of her dog-walking business, and she was attracted to Mark. *If it's meant to be, it'll work out.*

She was going to talk to people about Pooch Promenade, and she was going to find Mark.

Half an hour later she'd spoken to six people she didn't know, had mentioned Pooch Promenade to a couple who lived nearby and had two retrievers, and discovered that nobody had seen Jessica or Mark for the last hour.

'Try Jessica's study,' Boris said, skewering an olive with a cocktail stick. He was tall and willowy, dressed in a green three-piece suit, his hair a shock of vibrant but (according to his eyebrows) natural orange. He ran the boutique bed and breakfast at number three Primrose Terrace with his partner Charles and two French bulldogs. He'd promised to follow Cat on Twitter and introduce her to Dylan and Bossy, and was now imparting invaluable advice about what she should do next.

'Won't she mind?'

'Just knock. Jessica knows how to put on a party – if it's not locked then it's not out of bounds. First floor, end of the corridor.' He pointed his glass towards the staircase.

Cat climbed it slowly, her sweaty palm slipping on the bannister. She shouldn't be doing this; she should wait until they reappeared. But if she could get one glance, one sign that they were definitely together, then she could stop thinking about Mark and avoid the embarrassment of being rejected. The staircase curved and the hallway below disappeared from sight as Cat found herself at the end of a corridor. There were black-and-white photographs on the wall, mostly of Jessica herself, and the thick carpet was the same pale green as the rugs downstairs.

The door at the end was ajar, a glow of light coming from inside. Cat took a step towards it, then another. Voices and laughter drifted up from downstairs. She took another step, heard a familiar shuffling sound and looked down to see Valentino, his tail wagging like a metronome, black nose angled up towards her.

Panic flared in her chest. She crouched and stroked the dog behind the ears. 'Shhhhh,' she whispered. Valentino was panting slightly, dancing backwards and forwards, happy to have found his friend. 'Stay here,' Cat said, pointing her finger at the carpet. Valentino sat down. 'Good dog.'

Slowly, so slowly, she stood and took another step towards the study. Something bumped against her leg. It was Coco, trotting beside her, and as soon as Valentino saw his brother he disobeyed Cat's instructions and came to join them. Cat repeated the process, stroking, praising, and telling them both to sit. She scrutinized the corridor, but there was no sign of Dior. 'Stay here, puppies,' she whispered. The dogs looked up at her, clearly thinking it was part of a game. Cat would have to find a treat for them; she wondered if they liked horseradish.

She took the last two steps towards the door, silently thanking Jessica for her thick, sound-absorbing carpets. She peered through the gap.

Jessica and Mark were sitting side by side on a low cream sofa, bending forwards, looking at a folder that was open on the table. Mark's elbows were on his knees, his face a mask of concentration.

Cat couldn't hear what Jessica was saying, but they weren't snuggled together, shoulders and knees not pressed close. Their body language didn't scream Secret Tryst. And if they were a couple, if they spent their days locked in each other's embrace, why pick the middle of a party to look over documents? It wasn't conclusive, but Cat felt her anxiety lift, her shoulders unknot. She wasn't stepping on Jessica's toes. She could allow herself to be attracted to Mark and maybe, *maybe* pluck up the courage to do something about it. But not now. Now she was going to . . .

'Valentino!' Jessica said. 'What are you doing in here, darling? Do you need to go outside?'

Cat inhaled and stepped back just as the door swung open. Coco raced into the study to greet his owner, and Mark and Jessica looked up at the same time. Cat was frozen in the doorway, unable to move even when Dior, following in the footsteps of the other two Westies, sat on her feet and started yelping.

Look who I've found, he seemed to say. *Aren't I a clever dog?*

'Darling Cat,' Jessica said, 'what are you doing? Is anything wrong?' She half stood, but it was Mark who was up and in front of her in a second.

'Are you all right?' he asked. 'You look terrified.' He put his hand softly on her bare arm and a shiver snaked up it, her attraction towards him winning over the terror of the situation.

'I-I'm fine,' Cat stammered. 'Dior was whining, he seemed upset so I – I was looking for you, Jessica. I'm so sorry to intrude.' Dior chose that moment to be an unreliable side-kick by rolling onto his back, legs in the air, waiting for his tummy to be tickled.

'Oh, they get like that, don't you, poppets?' Jessica rubbed noses with Valentino, holding his front paws in her hands. 'I don't think there's anything to worry about, he was probably just after attention.'

Cat nodded, aware that Mark was still looking at her, still touching her. 'Oh, th-that's fine then,' she said. 'I'll be off.' She turned to go, but he squeezed her arm.

'Why don't you come in? Jessica was helping me out with a few contacts.'

'Really?' Cat hoped she sounded interested – all she could hear was the hammering of her heart.

'An author friend's having his book adapted for the small screen,' Jessica said, sliding back onto the sofa and crossing one leg over the other. 'It's still very hush-hush, but it's quite exciting. Mark's looking for a producer for his latest screenplay, so I was passing on some contacts.'

'You're a television writer?'

'Film,' Mark said. 'One indie success under my belt – critical acclaim but cult viewing figures – and one complete flop. I'm hoping for a resurrection with number three, and while my agent's on the case, it's always good to be on the lookout for other avenues.'

'Wow!' Cat said. 'That's exciting. Amazing, really. I didn't know you were a writer.' She thought of George's fears, Mark spying on people and making notes in the café.

He laughed. 'Why would you? I haven't mentioned it before.'

'What kind of films?'

'Horror.'

'Ah,' Cat said. '*Dawn of the Dead*. Chips the dog. You love horror films.'

'Exactly.' Mark looked surprised, as if he hadn't expected her to remember. Maybe she should have pretended to forget. 'George Romero is one of my heroes.' He smiled down at her, and for the first time Cat couldn't see amusement or challenge in his eyes, just warmth and genuine interest. Should she ask now?

'We shouldn't be up here.' Jessica stood and shooed her dogs out of the study. 'I got carried away. It's unthinkable of a hostess not to be present at her own party.' She indicated the door, and Cat followed the Westies into the corridor. 'Are you having fun, Cat? You really shouldn't worry about the dogs tonight – they're utter divas. They've had me to learn from, after all.' She wrapped her arm around Cat's shoulder. 'I meant to ask you about your housemate, Joe?'

'What about him?'

'Is he single?'

Cat gawped, momentarily unable to respond. Mark was descending the stairs, looking back at her. 'He, uhm, he's had a bad break-up recently.' The moment she said it, she felt as if she was betraying Joe. Would he want Jessica to know?

'The poor darling. He's seriously sizzling,' Jessica said. 'And an excellent kisser.' And with that bombshell Jessica followed Mark down the stairs, leaving Cat next to a black-and-white photo of the hostess with her three dogs. They were captured in a rare moment of calm, their furry bodies placed elegantly round Jessica's seated form, looking up at her as though she was a goddess. Maybe she was, thought Cat. After everything she'd seen, it wasn't entirely implausible.

It was after three in the morning when they made it back home. Cat flopped onto the sofa next to Polly, kicking off the shoes that had, earlier, caused so much panic. Joe put the kettle on.

'Urgh,' Polly moaned, 'I have to be up early for lectures. Why didn't I leave earlier?'

'Because it was an amazing party,' Cat said, 'and it was impossible to leave.'

'Elsie managed it.'

'Yes, but she *is* older. And I think she was all talked out.'

'Did you find Mark again?'

'What, after my lucky escape?' Cat hid her head in her hands. 'What was I thinking?'

'Maybe,' Joe called from the kitchen, 'like usual, you weren't. You could have lost them both as clients – and friends – if they'd realized what you were up to.'

'I know,' Cat murmured. 'I was being ridiculous.'

'Did you ask him out?' Polly asked, her eyelids fluttering.

'No, because Jessica was there, and I only saw him briefly as he was leaving.'

'But you will?'

'I will,' Cat said, but she wasn't entirely convinced. She felt out of her depth now she knew he was another writer. Jessica was much more suited to him than she was. They had similar interests, they moved in the same circles of producers and agents and glamorous dinners, they were both attractive and dynamic. How could she compete with that?

But then, when he'd said goodbye, he'd put his hand on the small of her back, brushed his lips against her cheek and handed her his iPhone. When she looked, he'd already added her name into his contacts, the cursor blinking next to the mobile entry. Grinning, she'd typed her number and held the phone out to him, her heart racing when he'd purposefully brushed his fingers against hers and kissed her for a second time.

Joe put three cups of tea on the table and sat on the arm of the sofa. A couple of his shirt buttons had popped open, and Cat thought he looked happily dishevelled.

'You had a good time, Joey?' Polly asked.

He nodded. 'I did. Better than I expected – thanks for asking me, Cat.'

'Sure.' She gave him a quick smile, and then because she couldn't bear not to know, added, 'Jessica was very taken with you.' Was it her imagination, or did his cheeks flush slightly?

'She's a formidable woman,' he said.

'Good kisser?' Cat risked.

'Cat!' Polly screeched, now fully awake. 'Joey?'

He shrugged his jacket off and moved to the opposite sofa. 'She cornered me in a corridor and I . . .' He ran his hand through his hair, his brows knitting in confusion. 'It was a party, she's very attractive, I kind of . . . got caught up in the moment.' He shrugged, not quite smiling, his eyes finding Cat's.

'Joseph Sinclair,' Polly said, 'you utter hussy!'

'It doesn't mean anything,' he said. 'It was a quick kiss, not a full-on . . . look, I don't even know why I'm discussing this with you. It's not going to happen again.'

'Jessica might have other ideas.'

'Really?' He sipped his tea, his gaze suddenly anywhere but on her.

'I was piggy in the middle. "I really like your friend Joe, will you ask him to come and meet me behind the bike shed?"'

Polly screeched. It wasn't something she did very often, and it shocked them all, especially Shed, who'd been fast asleep in front of the fireplace. 'Oh my God, Joey, you've got a celebrity author after you! Who'd have thought it?'

'Shush,' Joe said. 'It was a party. Party . . . *things* happen. And at least I didn't spy on the hostess.'

'I think,' Cat said, leaning forward, 'we should make a rule. What happened at number one can only – *only* – be discussed within these walls. Like *What Happens in Vegas*. Deal?' She held out her arm, fingers clenched into a fist.

'Deal.' Polly bumped it, and they both looked expectantly at Joe.

He stared at them. 'Oh, for God's sake.' He leaned forward and bumped their fists. 'Now we're definitely back in the playground. I'm going to bed.' He stood and lifted his jacket, swinging it over his shoulder with a finger. 'Thanks for a great party, Cat. I'm glad I came, and not for the reason you think.

96

I just . . .' He shrugged. 'I had fun. Maybe I should listen to you more often.'

'Wow,' Polly murmured, 'this is a big moment.'

'Oh, shut up, Sis.' He turned towards the door, but not before Cat caught his grin. 'Night all.'

Polly put her head on Cat's shoulder. 'Looks like the King of Grump can be cheered up after all.'

'I think Jessica has magical powers. She's bewitched him.'

'He didn't look that bewitched.'

'No,' Cat agreed. 'Happy, though.'

'That could be all the champagne.'

'True.' Cat stretched her toes out and yawned. 'Maybe we'd better do a temperature check tomorrow, see how long it lasts.'

She felt Polly nod against her shoulder. 'So you didn't get to speak to Mark, not properly. Did you get any new clients?'

'I did,' Cat said, feeling the flap of excited butterflies below her ribcage. 'The Barkers at number six. They've got two retrievers, and they need someone to walk them three days a week, when Juliette has to go into the office. I'm going to see them on Sunday to firm up the arrangements.'

'So you managed to have fun *and* network?'

'I managed it. I didn't think I would, but I did. I was given some very good advice,' she added.

'Fab, good for you!' Polly put her arm around Cat, and Cat returned the hug. Contentment washed over her with the knowledge that, nearly two months in, her new business wasn't failing. It was still slow, but she hadn't messed it up the way Alison had told her she would, and – thanks to Joe – she had a plan. She was surrounded by friends, she got to spend her days out in the fresh air with the friendliest creatures on the planet, and Mark wasn't going out with Jessica. It felt as if everything was slowly coming together.

97

'Come on,' she murmured, when Polly started snoring gently into her ear, 'let's get to bed, or we'll still be here when the sun comes up.'

Cat switched off the lights, leaving the living room in darkness and her black patent heels where she'd kicked them off, no longer needed now the party was over.

In the early May evening, Fairview beach looked like something out of a daydream. Small waves crested the sand and the sun was beginning to descend, a glowing, amber orb on the horizon, giving the sea a golden shimmer. The elegant houses on the seafront looked steadily on, and it gave Cat a glow of satisfaction knowing that her cosy home on Primrose Terrace was just beyond.

She strolled near the waves, her hands in the pockets of her military-style jacket, Valentino and Dior at her feet, Coco splashing in the water, yapping at the foam as it sprayed around him. She breathed in the strong, salty air, felt it sting her dry lips. It was a week after the party, Jessica was at a fellow author's launch, and Cat could almost taste summer around the corner.

The beach was beginning to empty out. The sun's heat was not yet strong enough to linger into the evenings, and the pull of warm houses and family dinners drew people away. Cat walked past the ice cream parlour, closing up for the evening, the lighthouse silhouetted ahead of her on its rocky outcrop. It was picture-postcard perfect, quieter than Brighton and much more peaceful, much more room to think. Cat could see herself staying in Fairview for a long time, whatever happened with Pooch Promenade.

There were several dog owners on the beach, and she watched as an Airedale raced into the sea, chasing nothing but the waves. Valentino and Dior were happy to keep their feet dry, and Coco kept edging up the beach, intrigued but scared by the encroaching water. They were definitely divas, but Cat wouldn't have it any other way.

A tennis ball landed in the breakers ahead of them, and a glossy Border collie raced in and retrieved it before running back to its owner. Cat knew who it was before she'd laid eyes on him. She hid her nerves behind a smile and tugged gently at the leads, praying that, for once, the Westies would behave. Spotting her, Mark changed course, throwing the ball further along the beach so that Chips ran after it.

He was eating fish and chips from a cone of paper, the smell of vinegar wafting towards Cat, making her stomach rumble.

'Lovely evening for it,' he said, coming to a stop in front of her. 'Chip?'

'Thanks.' She took one. It was hot and greasy and delicious and, glancing up at him, she took a second.

'Nothing better than fish and chips on the beach.'

'Agreed.' The Westies settled at Cat's feet, as if aware that this was an important conversation. It made her more nervous. 'It was a good party, the other night.'

'It was. Jessica has some great party throwing skills, and it was good to meet more people from Fairview. You can't meet everyone walking in the park.'

Cat nodded. 'I've only been here since the beginning of the year, and Jessica's been a good friend.' It felt strange to think of her that way, but Cat saw her as more than just a client.

'She's very generous, very willing to help,' Mark agreed. 'I've been in touch with the producer she was telling me about, and we're meeting in London next week.'

'That's great! Congratulations.'

'And Dior's looking better, after his scare that night.'

Cat examined her wellies, aware that Mark was scrutinizing her. 'He is,' she mumbled.

'Not that there was ever anything wrong with him.' He took a chip and chewed it thoughtfully.

'No,' Cat tried a laugh. 'Just being a diva, like Jessica said.'

'Or a helpful accessory.'

'For what?' Cat looked up, squinting against the setting sun.

'For some spying. So you could come and find Jessica, or me, or both of us, and have a good excuse if you were found out. Which you were.'

'I-I don't know what you mean.' It sounded lame even to Cat. How could she have imagined, for a second, that Mark hadn't seen through her?

'I think you do,' he said. He took another chip and held it in front of her. Without thinking, Cat opened her mouth and he popped it in. 'I think you came looking for us, and I think – though this could be due to my overconfidence – that you were pleased to discover our friendship was – is – platonic.' He smiled at her, and Cat felt her cheeks redden, knowing she'd been beaten.

'Maybe.'

'Maybe?' He laughed. 'OK, I'll have to go with maybe then.'

'What do you mean?'

He turned towards the horizon, his dark eyes creased against the sun. Cat decided that, though his jawline was still very definitely smug, it was also incredibly attractive. Like the rest of him.

'I mentioned that I have to go to London next week. I'll hopefully only be away for one night, but in lots of meetings, and so . . .' He turned back to Cat. 'I was wondering, would you be able to look after Chips for me? I'll leave a key. You could feed her, walk her, spend some time with her. Give her some of the endless love you have for everything with four legs and a wagging tail.'

Cat bit her bottom lip to stop herself from grinning. 'Sure. I think I could fit Chips in.'

Mark scrunched the empty chip paper into a ball and stuffed it in his pocket. 'Thanks, I'd appreciate it.'

'Always happy to help a fellow Primrose Terrace resident.'

'I thought you'd find my offer hard to resist.' He started walking and Cat fell into step alongside him, the dogs happy to get going again, bounding along at her feet.

'You did, did you?'

'We've already established that I'm irresistible.'

Cat turned away, hiding her smile. '*You* established that a long time ago. I'm in it for the dogs. But I'd love to hear more about your films, if you can talk about them.'

'They're not secret projects, though the less said about the second one, the better.'

'The flop?'

'Exactly. Quite a spectacular flop. It took me to a bit of a dark place, made me reconsider . . . certain things. I'm not used to having my confidence dented. Anyway, I met Jessica at some lunch event, she told me about this place, about how much better it was living outside London, having space, fresh air, time to think. I made one visit here and the decision was easy. And of course Chips loves it, the freedom of the beach as well as the park. It's better all round.'

'So Jessica's just a friend?'

She sensed rather than saw him look at her. 'Just a friend. She's helped me out, as I've said, and she's fun to be around, but there's nothing more between us. What made you so sure there was?'

'You both called it Primrose Park. I guessed that you must know each other, because I don't know anyone else who's made that mistake.'

'It's not called Primrose Park?'

Cat shook her head. 'It's Fairview Park. It's not even on Primrose Terrace.'

'Well, I know that,' Mark said. 'I just took Jessica's word for it. I wonder what other lies she's told me. Maybe her friend's not really a producer at all. Her whole life could be a fabrication. She could have earned all her money through drug trafficking or money laundering. She could be sending me off to London to be murdered.'

Cat laughed. 'She got the name of the park wrong. It's not exactly a crime.'

'But look what it led to. At the very least, it's delayed things between us. You thought I was unavailable.'

Cat stopped walking, her breath faltering. Valentino, sensing the change in atmosphere, started barking, and Cat automatically dropped to her knees to soothe the dog. She took her time, stroking each Westie in turn, then pushed herself back to standing. 'You're available?'

Mark grinned. 'That depends.'

'On what?'

'On whether you are.'

Cat narrowed her eyes. 'I'd like to get to know you,' she said. 'And not just looking after Chips, though of course I'll do that. But more than that. If you'd like to?'

He held her gaze, smiled down at her in a way that made his features seem softer, the side of his face bathed orange by the sun. 'So you *are* available. Good. When I'm back from London, let's do things properly. Lunch, or dinner.'

'OK,' she said, her breath rushing back in a whoosh of elation. 'That sounds great.' She started walking again, unable to stay still a moment longer, her fingers dancing inside her pockets. The sun was nearly at the horizon, turning a fiery, coral red, the remaining people fading to silhouettes as they strolled, or jogged, or stood watching the sea.

Cat, Mark and the four dogs walked in contented silence, Coco trotting through the waves, Chips chasing new sights and smells, then running back to her master. Cat wanted to take a snapshot, to preserve it and play it over and over on a loop. She wondered how long the perfection could last, then pushed the thought to the back of her mind.

They moved away from the sea, to where the sand was replaced by uneven shingle. Mark offered Cat his elbow, and she put her arm through his, wrapping her hand round the soft leather of his jacket. They reached the edge of the beach, but he didn't pull his arm loose. Instead he slowed his step, prolonging the short journey back to Primrose Terrace. Perhaps, thought Cat, realizing how dangerous it was to hope, he wanted the moment go on for ever too . . .

Sunshine and Spaniels

PART 2

7

Cat had never seen Fairview Park looking so beautiful. The late-May breeze that drifted in off the ocean made her think of days spent building sand castles as a child. The sky was a brilliant blue with gauze-like clouds drifting slowly past. The wide expanse of green grass was humming and buzzing with families and couples and friends, all of whom had one thing in common: they were with their dogs.

There was almost every breed imaginable here today, from Great Danes to chihuahuas, dachshunds to Dalmatians. Cat was determined to see if the age-old belief stood firm, that there was a resemblance between every dog and its owner. She thought of all the doggy friends she'd made since arriving at Primrose Terrace. Elsie, with her two miniature schnauzers. All three had grey hair, but beyond that Cat couldn't see any likeness. Jessica. Cat thought of her expensively highlighted blonde hair and her three silky Westies – a diva with her diva dogs. Yes, there were more similarities there. She wondered what she should get if she was choosing a pet to match her own looks. A red setter maybe, or a pointer? Though neither would be the breed of dog she'd choose, and she'd spent a lot of time thinking about the day she could have her own.

Her newest clients, Will and Juliette Barker the professional couple at number six, had asked her to walk their two golden retrievers, Alfie and Effie, while they were at work. She didn't think either of them looked remotely like their pets.

And then there was Chips, sitting perfectly at her feet, her sleek head brushing against Cat's knee, just beneath the hem of her spring-green sundress. Cat had always thought of her as humble, elegant and well behaved. Mark could be seen as elegant in a dashing, roguish kind of way, but humble and well behaved he was not. Still, Cat found herself grinning at the thought of him, and the promised dinner on his return from London.

She approached a couple with two Labradoodles. Cat always thought of them as the hippies of the dog world: laid-back and loping, their eyes hidden behind elaborate fringes. 'Welcome to the Pooches' and Puppies' Picnic,' she said. 'I'm Cat. I run Pooch Promenade with my friend Polly, so please feel free to ask any questions. There's tea, coffee and cold drinks inside the café, along with water and treats for the dogs.'

'Thanks,' the man said. He was quite short, with a bright-blue T-shirt and a friendly face. The woman he was with smiled at Cat, her amber eyes wide. 'We're not sure we need a walker for these two, but we couldn't resist popping down when we heard about it.'

'We love dogs,' the woman added. 'It's so lovely to see so many here all at once.'

'I know!' Cat said, unable to hide her enthusiasm. 'It's such a good turnout – I had no idea it would be so popular.'

And not just for family pets and companions, but for people whose dogs were furkids – as important as children to their owners. She'd seen a young woman with spiky pink hair and porcelain skin leading two shih-tzus dressed in little tartan jackets and sunglasses, and an older woman pushing her Pekinese in a bright-blue pet pushchair. Cat remembered seeing pushchairs on a dog-accessory website, but she hadn't imagined people actually bought them. Didn't dogs *want* to walk? She hoped so, otherwise her business would be short-lived.

'If you don't mind me asking,' she said to the couple, 'where did you hear about it?'

'On Twitter,' the man said. 'I work for the local paper – though "paper" seems a bit anomalous these days so I'm always on social media, trying to keep up with the times. I think your event was mentioned by Magic Mouse – have you heard of them?'

Cat smiled and did a quick visual search of the park. She couldn't see Joe, but she knew he was here somewhere. He hadn't told her he'd tweeted the picnic to his followers. 'I have,' Cat said. 'Amazing illustrations. Have you checked them out?'

The man nodded. 'Yup. I've been following him for a while now, looking at his work. He – Joe, is it? – seems very talented.'

Cat glanced behind her, but she still couldn't see him. 'He is. He's got a real skill for cartoons as well as graphic design – his work's really versatile.'

'We're thinking of having a regular cartoon strip in the paper. It's still just an idea at the moment, but . . . you know him well, then?'

'He's a friend,' Cat said. Was that true? She hoped they were more than just housemates. 'And – sorry, I didn't catch your name.'

'Phil.'

'Do you think, Phil, if you get a chance, that you could mention today, maybe say a little bit about—'

109

'Pooch Promenade?' He gave her an easy, open smile. Was he really a journalist? 'I think that can be arranged. Good-news stories are always great for the paper. Give me your number and I'll look at it on Monday, ring for a quote.'

Cat's heart leapt. 'That's fantastic!' She handed him a Pooch Promenade card with her number on. 'Thank you.'

'And thanks for the info about Magic Mouse. I'll be in touch.'

Cat directed them towards the Pavilion Café, and waved at a family with an Alsatian puppy straining on its lead, a young boy laughing as he was dragged along behind, his father with a protective hand on his shoulder.

'Twenty names,' a familiar voice said close to Cat's ear. She spun round to see Polly waggling a clipboard. 'Twenty people have registered to receive the Pooch Promenade newsletter, and it's only eleven o'clock.' Polly was wearing a pink T-shirt and white shorts, her hair tied up in a ponytail, her freckles just starting to emerge in the sunshine. Her pale-blue eyes were alive with excitement.

'That's incredible,' Cat said. 'And the local paper said they'd put something in about today. At this rate I'll need to hire more people.'

'I'm going to try and spend a bit of time walking the dogs,' Polly said. 'I don't have much spare, but I'm being swallowed by revision and I need to make sure I get some fresh air or I'll be a gibbering wreck when the exams start. Can I help out?'

'You're serious?' Cat flung her arms round her friend. 'Oh, Polly, that would be *amazing*. I feel like I've barely seen you since I moved in!'

'I know, it's been rubbish. But my exams are three months away and then I'm free!'

'Except you have to start doing the thing you've been training to do for so long.'

'Sean, the vet, says he's really pleased with what I've done, that there's money and demand for another nurse.'

'So you can keep working there?'

Polly nodded, her lips pressed together, trying to hide what Cat could only assume was a huge grin.

'Oh God, Polly, that's brilliant! Why haven't you told me already? We need to celebrate! You'll be a fully qualified veterinary nurse.'

'And maybe I'll actually have a life!'

They hugged again, Cat feeling a swell of pride that her friend had worked hard and got to exactly where she wanted. It was impressive, and something Cat couldn't imagine doing, now that she'd turned her back on her nursery career.

But Pooch Promenade felt right. She had always loved dogs, and couldn't remember a time when she was so happy, walking people's pets round Fairview Park and the sandy beach, getting to know the locals at the same time. Now that Polly was nearly qualified, all they had to do was drag her brother out of the post-break-up dumps, and their household would be the happiest on Primrose Terrace.

'Where's Joe?' Cat asked. She stroked Chips's ears, checking that the collie hadn't turned to a statue at her side. The dog nuzzled her nose into Cat's hand.

'He's on the veranda, giving out the cards with your rates and contact details on. I think I saw Jessica prowling around there too.'

'Ah.' The friends exchanged a knowing smile 'Do you think he needs rescuing?'

'It wouldn't hurt to see how he's getting on. I'll take Chips for a bit.' Polly approached a tall, burly man with a boxer, who had what looked like a piece of bread sticking out of her mouth. Maybe she was a Street Sweeper, picking up any

111

snack she could find on her route around the park. 'Hello,' Polly said, 'welcome to the Pooches' and Puppies' Picnic. If you've got any questions I'd be happy to answer them.'

Cat gave her Chips's lead and snaked through people and dogs towards the café. It was cooler under the awning, but only just, and Cat spotted Joe at a table with a glass of iced water. There was no sign of Jessica. He was wearing a grey T-shirt and dark cargo shorts and, despite being blond and blue-eyed, he had tanned arms. Cat had imagined that, with all the time he spent hidden up in his office creating illustrations, he'd be as pale as a ghost. He didn't look like a ghost.

'How's it going?' she asked. 'Not regretting giving up your Saturday to spend it with your least-favourite animals?'

He leaned back in his chair. 'There are worse ways I could be spending my weekend.' He grinned, and Cat was surprised how relaxed he seemed.

'That's very magnanimous of you. Is all this contact starting to turn you, Joe? I mean, look how cute this one is!'

Joe sat up and peered over the table at where Cat was pointing.

'Hello, what's your name?' She crouched down and the tiny dog trotted up to her. It was white and tan, with eyes too big for its pointy face, and huge ears that had their own furry tassels. 'You look like a princess, don't you? Your ears look like those hats.' The dog looked up at her, as if expecting her to clarify. 'Oh, you know. Joe?'

Joe frowned, thinking. 'A hennin. That cone-shaped princess hat, that's what it's called.'

'Exactly. See? You're a princess. Who do you belong to?' The dog sat in front of her and put her paw over her nose, just as a man with white hair and half-moon glasses bustled through the crowd. 'Is this little dog yours?'

112

The old man nodded and sat down opposite Joe. 'Hot, isn't it? Phew. Shouldn't have layered up like I have. Hard to break a habit and go without a vest, though.'

'It is quite warm,' Cat said, suppressing a smile. 'What's your dog called?'

Joe disappeared inside the café, and Cat turned her attention to her new visitor.

'Paris,' he said. 'She's a papillon. Marie Antoinette's favourite breed. There's a Papillon House in Paris, still. Seemed appropriate.'

'She's very well behaved.'

'She's a perfect little butterfly. But sadly, a miserable one.'

'A miserable butterfly?'

'*Papillon*. It means butterfly in French. Don't you young people go to school any more?'

'That one must have passed me by.'

'But you've been to Paris?'

'Once. A long time ago.' Cat had been with her parents when she was small. She didn't remember much beyond the endless rain and straining her neck to look up at the Eiffel Tower, bearing down on her like a giant steel monster.

He smiled, a hazy look on his face. 'Most romantic city in the world. You should take your chap with you, visit all the sites – Papillon House included.'

'My chap?'

'Your young gentlemen there,' the man said.

Joe returned and put a glass of water in front of him.

'Thank you, son, very kind. Seems very well behaved too,' he said to Cat with a wink. 'A trip to Paris would be just the thing.'

'Oh, no, no, I—' She glanced at Joe, saw him silently ask a question, and turned back to the gentleman. 'I'm Cat,' she said. 'I run Pooch Promenade.' She held out her hand, and he took it.

113

'Oh, yes, I know all about you. I'm Arthur, but people call me Captain.'

'OK,' Cat said quietly. 'Can I ask—'

'Why I'm called Captain?'

'How you know about me?'

'Elsie told me. We're back-garden buddies, we chat over the wall. She said anyone and everyone with a dog would be here today, that I'd better hotfoot it down with my Paris. Don't know why, though, she doesn't need more walks, doesn't seem to want to do anything at the moment except hide under the sofa. Butterflies don't do that, generally.'

'I wonder why?' Cat crouched and stroked the little dog, who was still trying to hide her nose under an inadequate paw. She started shaking. 'She's not unwell?' Paris had a thin red collar, a tiny Eiffel Tower charm hanging off it in place of a name tag. Cat smiled at the old man's romanticism.

'Doesn't seem so. I took her to the vet's a couple of weeks ago, and they weren't sure. She's eating OK, she's affectionate with me, but it seems she's got that – arachnophobia thing.'

'She's scared of spiders?' Joe peered down at Paris. 'I guess she is quite sma—'

'No no, not that. Going outside. When you don't like going outside.'

'Oh,' Cat laughed, 'agoraphobia.'

Joe shrugged and crossed his arms. '*Arachnophobia* is spiders.'

'I am seventy-eight, boy,' Captain scolded. 'I can be forgiven for getting a word wrong here and there.'

'Of course, I didn't mean to—'

'You young studs don't like to be embarrassed, do you?' He wagged a finger at Joe and Cat turned her attention back to the sad dog, hiding her smile.

'Maybe I could ask my friend Polly to take a look at her? She's a vet's nurse, so—' Cat was cut off by a loud squeal from somewhere beyond the periphery of the veranda. 'Excuse me,' she said, getting up.

Joe was already ahead of her, and Cat followed him to where she'd left Polly and Chips. She stopped in her tracks when she saw that her friend was completely drenched, her mouth open, aghast, water running off her and onto the hot grass. Chips was trotting backwards and forwards, her fur glistening. Cat thought she'd probably enjoyed the soaking more than Polly.

'What the hell?' Joe whispered. 'Pol, are you OK? What happened?'

Cat took a step forward and then stopped. Mr Jasper was standing at the edge of the crowd that was beginning to form, holding an empty bucket.

'Oh my God,' Cat said quietly, and then, much louder, 'Mr Jasper, can I ask what that was in aid of? Because the last time I checked it was cats that didn't like water and not dogs.'

Mr Jasper fidgeted, dancing backwards and forwards like one of Jessica's Westies. She could see he was wavering, desperate to run away but knowing he couldn't. 'We don't want this many dogs here!' he shouted.

'Who's we?' Cat asked.

'Lots of us. *Lots* of people. They're a menace. Pooing and biting and making a mess.'

'It's a park! It's not like we're traipsing them through the local museum! Where else should dogs go, except the park?'

Mr Jasper gave a smug little smile. 'They should be in your homes, in your gardens. Leave the public spaces for the people.'

'Even if that is your opinion – and it's a pretty unrealistic and narrow-minded one – did you really think the best

115

way to express that opinion was coming here and throwing a bucket of water over my friend? What *possible purpose* could that serve, except making a scene? It's an unprovoked attack, it's got nothing to do with dogs, and you don't even have a banner!'

'Yes, we do,' said a familiar voice, and Cat shivered as she realized who it was.

Alison Knappett, her ex-boss – otherwise known as Knickers-too-tight. Short and prim, her dark fringe low over her serious eyes, she stepped out from behind Mr Jasper and raised a cardboard placard. She was wearing a blue dress and flat, sensible shoes, as usual looking far older than her mid-thirties. The placard was white cardboard on a wood support, and the writing was bold but neat. It said, *Say NO to dog walkers in Fairview*.

Cat faltered. Mr Jasper she could face, but not Alison. Cat knew she didn't like dogs – she'd found out to her cost just how much she hated them. But to go this far? To fire her and then try to sabotage her new business felt very personal. 'O-one banner?' she stammered. 'It's not a very big protest, is it?'

'But we've got everyone's attention.' Alison gestured around her, and Cat realized they were in the centre of a large circle of people and dogs, all waiting to see what would happen next. Polly was standing at the edge of the space and someone had got her a towel.

'Go on then,' Cat said. 'Now you've got everyone's attention, now you've ruined what was a perfectly good-tempered event, say what you wanted to say. Go on.'

Alison stepped forward but Mr Jasper put a hand on her arm.

'We believe,' he said, 'that the recent trend for dog walkers is a growing menace to our society. Dogs are a part of life, I accept that, and so does my friend. We may not like it, but we accept it.'

'No, you don't,' someone called, but Mr Jasper ignored them.

'What we can't accept, in our public spaces, where children and vulnerable people come to enjoy themselves, to get fresh air and a sense of calm, is the walking of multiple dogs in large and unruly packs. It's a recipe for disaster. If you can't control your dogs – and I defy anyone with more than four to be fully in control – then they will get loose, they will bite people, they will foul the grass and the paths where toddlers play, and they will ruin the serenity of this place.'

'Nonsense,' someone muttered.

'I have already witnessed this woman struggling to keep control of a pack of dogs, in this very park! I have *seen* the damage that can be caused, and we will not stand for it!'

'Dogs are dirty,' Alison shouted, her prim voice straining to be heard. A few people had started to make low noises of dissent. 'They're dirty and they're messy and they're pests.'

'Of course they're not! What on *earth* are you talking about?' A tall woman stepped forward, her black hair in corkscrews around her striking face, and Cat recognized her as Juliette Barker, her new client. She was half Jamaican and not, in Cat's limited experience, a shrinking violet. 'This is ridiculous,' Juliette added.

'You're imbeciles,' the man with the boxer said. 'My Molly's clean and smart and much better company than you.' Cat noticed that Molly now had a Magnum wrapper sticking out of her mouth.

Mr Jasper and Alison exchanged an uneasy glance, and tried to step back into the crowd.

'We will petition this,' Mr Jasper said. 'You just watch.'

117

'Watch the signatures *not* roll in, you mean?' boxer man said.

Captain appeared, holding Paris in his arms, her head nestled into his chest as if she couldn't bear to watch. 'You did set yourselves a hard task,' he said in a friendly tone, 'coming as a twosome to a dog lovers' event.' Alison blushed. Cat knew she hated to be wrong, and Captain's words set a new fire under her.

'Well, you can't trust her,' Alison screamed, pointing at Cat. 'She is disorganized, and a danger to young children, and completely incompetent.' She spat the last word and Cat gasped. 'Don't trust this woman to walk your dogs. Don't trust her for *anything*.'

Cat opened her mouth, but nothing came out.

She felt a warm hand on her bare shoulder and suddenly Joe was in front of her, between her and Alison. 'You've taken it too far,' he said calmly. 'You know as well as I do that what you've said about Cat is a lie. Nobody incompetent could have organized this event. She's received nothing but praise for her dog walking – you guys aside – and if you want to talk about disorganized, then take a look in the mirror.'

The park was hushed, everyone straining to hear these quieter remarks. Cat took a step forward but Joe grabbed her hand.

Alison glared at Joe, and Joe looked steadily back at her. Cat knew that Joe would win any staring match.

'You haven't heard the end of this,' Alison screeched. 'And if you think you're getting my business after this, Joseph Sinclair, then think again.' She turned abruptly, her placard bashing Mr Jasper in the knees, and tried to push her way through the crowd. 'Let me *through*!'

'Are you OK?' Joe turned to Cat and released her hand. 'Sorry I stopped you. I was trying to defuse the situation.

After what she said, I wouldn't have blamed you for punching her in the face.'

'No, you did the right thing. I didn't realize she—'

'NO!' Alison squealed. 'Get away!' They turned to see Chips standing in front of the two protesters, looking up at Alison, a tennis ball at her feet. Alison moved back into the crowd and Chips trotted forward, putting the ball down in front of her again.

'She loves you,' someone laughed. 'Though God knows why.'

'This dog is harassing me!' Alison moved further back and Chips followed, her tongue lolling out. She lifted her paw and looked up at Alison expectantly. Alison, her cheeks red, turned and pushed through the laughing crowd. Mr Jasper followed her, their placard discarded. Chips lay on the grass and rested her nose on her paws.

'What was that all about?' Polly was drying off quickly in the sun, her blonde hair forming wispy tendrils around her face. 'I didn't know Alison could be so cruel.'

'I took Elsie's puppy into her nursery,' Cat shrugged. 'She obviously holds grudges. But I'm so sorry, Joe, about your—' She turned but he was no longer next to her. 'Joe?'

Polly pointed to where Joe was crouched in front of Chips, laughing and rubbing her ears. 'Good dog,' he said. 'What a clever dog.'

'Oh my God,' Cat whispered, 'why is he doing that?'

Polly shrugged.

'He's not a dog person.'

'I never said he wasn't—'

'He won't let me have them in the house. Joe?'

Joe's shoulders tensed and he stood up quickly, flashed them a quick smile and disappeared into the café.

Cat shook her head, feeling a mixture of confusion and relief. Maybe she was right, that by coming into contact with so many dogs, he was slowly realizing how lovable they were. But he'd seemed so easy, so comfortable with Chips. 'I don't understand your brother, Polly. Either there's something I'm not getting or that kiss with Jessica turned him into some kind of dog-loving wonder boy, like a modern-day princess kissing a toad.'

Polly put her hand on Cat's shoulder. 'Joe's not a toad. It's summer, and he loves summer. The whole Rosalin-and-Alex thing is further in the past, and I think his business is doing OK, despite losing Alison's custom just now.'

'But Chips is a dog.'

'Yes, I know. Look, Cat, there's something I haven't—'

'Joe hates dogs.'

Polly was looking in the direction of the café, chewing her lip. 'It's not that simple,' she said. 'Joe's had a hard time of it, and maybe he's realized he was an arse when you first moved in. He's trying to make it up to you.'

Cat nodded. 'He's helped me with Twitter, he's given me great advice, thought of the whole Pooches' Picnic idea. He's been really helpful, actually.'

Polly laughed. 'No need to sound so surprised. He's trying hard, and whatever impression he's given you, he doesn't *hate* dogs. He's giving credit where credit's due.' She pointed at Chips.

Cat waggled her fingers and the Border collie raced up to her. She pulled a few treats out of her bag. 'That, Chips, was brilliant. Maybe some of Mark's cheekiness has rubbed off on you after all?' Chips gave a single, cheery bark. 'Do you miss him?' she asked. Chips pressed her damp nose against Cat's leg. 'Yeah, I do too. Come on, let's see if anyone still wants to talk about dog walking, or if they're all convinced I'm completely incompetent. Coming, Pol?'

They made their way across the grass, saying hello to the few people who remained. Most had drifted off after Mr Jasper's intervention, whether embarrassed to stay, or just seeing it as the perfect time for lunch. The sun was high in the sky, baking down on them all. Cat thought the dogs could do with going inside and cooling off. Maybe they'd all be happy to have a bucket of water thrown over them.

She could see Captain and his perky-eared papillon, Paris, on the veranda of the Pavilion café, talking to the owner George. And she could see Joe through the glass, helping to clear up. Cat really had to thank him for all he'd done. She'd found herself doing that quite a bit lately, and was starting to think she would have to change her opinion of him as a grumpy sod. She let Chips go ahead of her, but a dog started barking behind them and, intrigued, Chips changed course.

'Chips,' Cat called, 'come on, let's go inside.' But the Border collie was intent on her new pursuit.

A small sandy-haired dog was haring across the grass towards Chips, running as fast as its tiny legs could carry it. At the last minute it jumped, its floppy ears flying, and came to an untidy halt next to the collie.

It continued to make a high, squeaking noise like a broken bicycle horn, and started running backwards and forwards. A classic Zoomie dog, Cat thought.

She approached the puppy, cautiously at first, and then, when it seemed intent on tiring itself out, she pulled it into her arms, lifted it up and stroked its head, calming it. It was a cocker spaniel, and Cat thought it could only be about six months old. She turned its collar around and found a heart-shaped name tag. *Olaf,* it said, followed by a phone number.

Cat scanned the park. It was still busy, the grass dotted with groups kicking footballs and having picnics, but Cat could see no one who looked frantic, as if they'd lost someone important. Olaf. That name was familiar, and not just because it belonged to a snowman she'd heard about non-stop at the nursery. The nursery – that was it! She remembered Alison telling Emma to say goodbye to her dog; the little girl fighting back tears.

'Where's Emma?' she asked Olaf, who was shivering, depleted of exertion and confidence. 'Where's your family?'

'I think you might be looking for these two?' It was Joe, ushering a couple of young girls towards her.

'Olaf!' the older one squealed. They were both crying loudly, and looked ragged despite their bright sundresses and sandals.

'Is he yours?' Cat held the puppy out to the older girl. She recognized four-year-old Emma, and there was something familiar about her sister too, despite her being too old to attend nursery. 'Hey,' she said gently, 'there's no need to cry. He's had an adventure and now he's tired, but he's fine.'

'And you did well to keep up with him,' Joe added. 'I saw how fast he was going. Maybe you two need to think about careers in athletics.'

The older girl started to sniff, restraining her tears, and reached out to take her pet. She cuddled him against her, and Olaf nuzzled her cheek. Cat thought she was probably about ten or eleven, skinny, with long, flyaway mousy hair and freckles. Emma was still sobbing, one hand gripping onto her sister's dress.

'You're Emma, aren't you?' Cat asked.

The little girl nodded through her tears.

'I'm Cat, from the nursery. Do you remember me?'

Again she nodded, then gulped and wiped her eyes with her hands. 'Alison made you leave because you were too funny.'

Cat tried to hide her grin, which wasn't easy when Joe was rolling his eyes.

'Alison and I weren't always best friends, Emma, but I loved all of you, and I miss you.'

'We miss you too,' Emma said. 'And your puppy.'

'But you've got one of your own. Olaf. Is this your sister?'

The older girl gave her a small smile. 'I'm Lizzie. I'm ten.'

'Nice to meet you, Lizzie. I'm Cat, and this is Joe. Were you bringing Olaf to the park?'

They both nodded, Lizzie's eyes cast down to the ground. 'Mum said could we take him out, because she's busy with Henry. That's our brother.'

'He's only ten months,' Emma added, 'and a handful.'

'Shhh,' hissed Lizzie. 'Mum said not to say.'

'Your mum told you not to say anything?'

'About how stressed she is,' Lizzie blurted, then gasped, her eyes filling up with tears again.

'That's OK,' Cat said reassuringly. 'I won't say anything. Do you want me to come with you and explain about Olaf to your mum?'

Lizzie shook her head. 'No, it's OK. We can take him back. Mum doesn't need to know he got off the lead.'

'You *took* him off!' Emma squealed.

'I really don't mind,' Cat said, trying to head off a squabble between the girls. 'Our event's done now, and I'd like to say hello to your mum again. Do you live close by?'

'Number twelve Primrose Terrace,' Emma said proudly.

'Of course!' Cat said. That's where she remembered the older girl from – she'd passed them in the street on more than one occasion.

'What?' Lizzie asked, her slender brows lowering.

'I live on Primrose Terrace too. Oh, this is perfect. I'll just go and get Chips, and we'll all walk back together.'

'Of course,' Joe said brightly. 'We can't get away with not knowing about one of our neighbours, can we?'

Cat shot him a sideways glance and went in search of Polly and Chips.

The primroses that characterized Primrose Terrace had lasted all the way through the spring, filling the wide grass verges opposite the houses with whites and pinks and blues, as well as the more common yellow. It looked like an intricately weaved carpet, and Cat wondered who tended to them, making sure they bloomed so spectacularly every year. She wondered whether the primroses had given the terrace its name or if it was the other way around.

Opposite the houses running along one side of the road, and beyond the colourful verges, was a high red-brick wall shielding the back gardens of the seafront houses from view. Cat loved knowing that, just beyond those houses, was the endless expanse of glittering blue or churning grey water.

Their party of three grown-ups, two children and two dogs passed Jessica's extravagant house, reminding Cat that she hadn't seen the author at the picnic, either superglued to Joe or anywhere else; then the bed and breakfast, where a couple were unloading suitcases from a VW Beetle outside; then Mark's slightly shabbier house. Chips climbed the stairs and Cat thought she probably shouldn't take a strange – albeit passive – dog to someone else's house, especially when they had a baby.

'Could you get Chips settled, Polly? I'll come and check on her later.'

'Of course.'

Cat handed Polly Mark's key and Chips's lead.

She lost Joe as they passed number nine.

'I've got some work to catch up on,' he said. 'Nice to meet you, Emma and Lizzie.' He bounded up the steps, leaving Cat, the girls and Olaf standing on the pavement.

'Right then, it's just us chickens.' They made their way down the road, to number twelve.

'We didn't paint it,' Lizzie said, 'but we think we've got the prettiest house on the street.'

'I can't argue with that,' Cat said.

Number twelve was pale pink, with the same white window frames as the other houses, and a white front door. Someone had, presumably a long time ago, painted a design of pink daisies round the edges of the door, but it was so faint now Cat could only just see what it was. There were cuddly toys lining one of the upstairs windows, looking out at the street, and the downstairs curtains were shut, despite it being the middle of the day. It was a very pretty house that, with a few extra touches, Cat thought, could really stand out.

'I'll check with Mum,' Lizzie said. Emma followed closely behind, almost bumping into her sister. The door was ajar, and Lizzie pushed it open and slipped inside, followed by her sister. Cat waited, drumming her fingers on her arms. She thought she could hear someone shouting, but then the door swung open and a woman about Cat's age appeared.

'Hello?' Her voice was breathless and clipped, her irritation clear. 'Can I help?' She had reddish-brown hair tied back from her face in a scrappy ponytail, green eyes and no make-up, a silver stud glinting just above her lip. Her cheeks were pink and her eyes red-rimmed. 'Now's not a good time.'

Cat wiped her hand down her dress and held it out. 'I'm sorry to bother you, but I'm Cat. I used to work at Emma's nursery, and I met her and Lizzie in the park today.'

'They weren't meant to go to the park,' she rushed. 'They were meant to walk up to the end of the road and back, that's all. And then – I couldn't leave, because of Henry, or what if they came back and I—' She stopped and took a deep breath, shook her head. 'What's the problem?'

'There isn't a problem,' Cat said. 'I found Emma and Lizzie in the park with Olaf, and I thought . . .'

The other woman folded her arms. 'You thought what? That they shouldn't have been out without their mum? I told them not to leave the terrace, but there was some bloody dogs event in the park. I don't need you – or anyone else – telling me how to do things.'

'I'm not, I promise.' Cat glanced up the street, hoping to see Polly's instantly likeable face, but for the moment Primrose Terrace was quiet. 'I wanted to say hello. I moved into the street at the beginning of the year, and I can't believe we've not met properly yet. Also, it sounds like it's partly my fault. I put on the event in the park, for dogs and their owners.'

'Great, brilliant. Thanks for that. I don't have time for a neighbourly chat, I need to see to Henry.' She stepped back and moved to close the door, but Cat put her hand out.

'Look – can I ask your name?'

'I have to go.'

'Please. They were so worried they'd upset you. I think they were trying to help.'

'What would you know? Girls!' she called, turning away. 'Wash your hands. *Now*. No complaints.' She faced Cat again. 'Look, Cat, is it?'

Cat nodded.

'Thanks for bringing them back, but I need to get on.'

'It's just that—' Cat stopped, wondering how to broach the subject.

The girls' mother eyed her suspiciously. 'What?'

'Lizzie and Emma might have mentioned that . . . that you could do with some help.'

The young woman's eyes widened. 'They *what*?'

'The thing is,' Cat hurried, 'I run a dog-walking business now, and this event that Lizzie noticed – well, she mentioned that sometimes, with the baby, it's hard for you to get out. With Olaf. Hard for you to all have time together.' She swallowed and crossed her fingers behind her back. This had potentially been another of her Worst Ideas Ever, and she didn't want to patronize the woman or make her feel that she was a bad mother. She didn't want to get the girls in trouble either.

The young woman looked at her for so long that Cat thought she might have somehow become invisible, but then she pushed the door open wider, and Cat could see the hallway beyond. 'They said that, did they? About spending time together?'

Cat nodded.

The girls' mother rubbed her eyes and gave a tiny shake of her head. 'I'm Frankie,' she said quietly. 'They shouldn't have done that, gone to the park. They know the rules.' She gestured for Cat to come in.

'They're back, though,' Cat said, 'and they're fine.'

'It's bloody hard at the moment, with Henry and my shifts at the restaurant. My two girls are basically sorting themselves out, and I know it's not fair – they're still so young.'

She led the way into the living room, which was similar to the one at number nine, except that everything was bright, a myriad of colours. The sofas were red, the distressed wooden coffee tables dark purple, and the white walls were barely visible, covered in kids' drawings, chains of seashells, a living scrap-book of Frankie and her family. Toys, magazines and clothes in various sizes covered every surface, a pale-pink gauze hung across the doorway into the kitchen, and the threadbare carpet was hidden beneath a round, rainbow-swirl rug. It wasn't tidy, but it was vibrant and full of life.

'It's not conventional,' Frankie said, 'but so what? The kids love it.'

'I love it.' Cat took a step towards the wall and ran her finger gently across a snail made out of pasta. She felt a lump form in her throat as she realized how long it had been since she had rolled her sleeves up and covered things in paint, or glue, or Play-Doh. 'I miss working at the nursery.'

Frankie sat on the arm of the sofa and glanced at Lizzie, who was holding her baby brother. He was gurgling quietly, podgy hands reaching up towards the ceiling. Emma was in a dog basket in the corner of the room, Olaf climbing all over her. Both girls had fresh tear stains marking their cheeks.

'Emma said you were the only one who ever bothered with those kids. She's gutted you've gone. Right, Emma?' Frankie got up and ruffled her daughter's hair, then kissed her forehead.

'I loved your puppy,' Emma whispered. She squeezed Olaf against her, and the cocker spaniel started barking.

'Quiet, Olaf,' Frankie hissed. 'You'll make Henry cry.' The dog kept barking and Frankie looked despairingly at Cat, her hands scrunched into fists against her cheeks. 'Give him to me, love,' she said to Lizzie, but Lizzie shook her head.

'I'll take him upstairs,' she whispered, and hurried from the room cradling Henry.

Frankie sank back against the sofa. 'She's a good girl. Too good, in lots of ways. She shouldn't be taking on so much responsibility, and she shouldn't be asking strangers for help, but she sees I can't do it all on my own. It should be easier than this, shouldn't it? Do you want a cuppa?'

'No, I'm fine, thanks,' Cat said, clearing a space on the corner of one sofa. 'You know, I can help, with my dog-walking business.'

'As in, you take dogs for walks? How is that a business?'

Cat laughed and leant forward. 'Lots of people don't have time to walk their dogs as regularly as they want to, or things just get in the way. My friend Elsie, she's had a knee operation so she can't take her dogs for long distances. Mark up the road has to go to London at quite short notice, and some people work a lot. If you don't always want to leave it to Lizzie and Emma, then I could take Olaf out.'

'But you charge, right? You don't get sponsorship? It's your job?'

Cat nodded. She was sure that Frankie wouldn't want charity. 'But my rates are competitive and I – I just think I can help. You say you've got to work too?'

'Yeah, at Spatz. This little restaurant, supposed to be all ethical and Fairtrade. And I'm coping. Well, as best I can –' she indicated the colourful but haphazard living room – 'but they won't let me drop my hours, and when the summer holidays come round . . . It's not turning out to be the peachy job I thought it would be. I could get a zero-hours contract at the supermarket, but how would that be better?

130

I don't need the stress or uncertainty, and I could end up with no work at all.'

'I hope you don't mind me asking, but are you on your own?' Cat said it quietly, and watched as Frankie tensed and turned away from her.

'Yeah, and believe me, it's better. It may not seem it, but I promise you, things would be even more difficult. He – Rick, Emma and Henry's dad – did his best, I know that. Olaf was a present from one of his band mates, and the girls adore him, but Rick had no idea about how expensive having a dog would be, how much trouble, how he'd have to be trained, and walked, and neutered.

'And that was Rick all over. Great, creative ideas, but didn't really think things through. He was more bothered about his band and his friends and his next road trip. In the end he chose that over us. Said he'd come back and see them –' Frankie glanced at Emma and lowered her voice – 'but that was in February. Brought home the puppy and then took off. He's not even that far away – went to stay with some friends in Brighton, last I heard.'

'I'm sorry,' Cat whispered. 'And Lizzie's dad?'

Frankie smiled and dipped her eyes. 'Lizzie's dad was the greatest guy I've ever met, gorgeous and funny, and he'd probably be a great dad too, but I met him at a festival and after that night, well . . .' She shrugged. 'If I could find him again – but I never thought . . .' She tightened her ponytail. 'Not very straightforward, is it? But it doesn't mean I don't care about my family. It doesn't mean I don't want the best for them.' Frankie stood and started picking up toys and clothes, cups and banana skins, sweeping them into boxes or the bin.

Cat stood, unsure what to do. 'Of course it doesn't,' she said. 'I'm sorry to hear about your partner, and I know it's only a small thing, but let me walk Olaf. We'll do a couple of trial runs free of charge, and then, if it works out, if it makes things even a little easier, we can do something more permanent. And Frankie, I . . .' She waited for the young mother to look at her. 'I know we don't know each other, not really, but we're on the same street, and if there's anything else I can do . . . Neighbours help each other out, don't they?' She risked a smile, conscious of how she'd waltzed in and offered to make everything better, offered what could potentially be a lot of empty promises.

Frankie picked up a large cuddly seal. She clasped it against her chest, and sank her chin into the top of its soft head. 'You help out all your neighbours? Not just me?'

Cat nodded. 'I tried to do a lot for Elsie when she had her knee operation. I walk Jessica's dogs, and I'm looking after Mark's. Some of it's part of my job now, but not all of it.'

'Let's start with Olaf,' Frankie said. 'I appreciate that you took the trouble to come and see me, and having Olaf for a couple of hours, maybe Monday when the girls are back at school and nursery, would be a help. But let me do something for you. I don't know what yet. I'll think about it.'

'OK,' Cat said, unable to hide her grin. 'That sounds great. And Olaf is adorable. I'm sure he'd get on with Disco.'

'The puppy?' Emma asked. She was lying on her back, Olaf standing on top of her, licking her forehead and ears.

'She's grown up a bit now, like Olaf, but she's still very bouncy.'

'I'd like to come,' Emma said matter-of-factly. 'With all the dogs.'

'No, Emma,' Frankie said. 'It's Cat's job. She's got to be very serious about it, like you are with your colouring in, remember?'

132

'I remember,' Emma said, 'but I'd be serious about the dogs. I'd try hard.'

Frankie exhaled loudly. 'Let me think about it, and if, after a while –' she looked at Cat and Cat nodded – 'it's going well, maybe you could tag along. At the weekends, mind.'

'That's *all* I'm asking for,' Emma said haughtily, and Cat had to turn her laughter into a cough.

'Yeah, for now,' Frankie whispered so only Cat could hear, but she was smiling. 'Come on, Emma, get out of that basket and let's give Olaf his lunch. Then I might think about making you some. Salad sandwiches all right?'

'Eeewwww.' Emma screwed up her nose.

'How about some of Henry's purée?'

'No, Mum!'

'Come and help me make it, then, and I'll see if we can find something a bit more exciting.' She walked Cat to the door. 'Thanks for coming.'

'It was my pleasure,' Cat said, 'and I'll see you on Monday.'

Once Frankie had shut the door, Cat strolled home, hoping that, while she'd gained a new client for Pooch Promenade, she'd also, more importantly, made a new friend.

'I couldn't find Chips's dog food,' Polly called from the front room.

Cat stuck her head round the door. 'I thought I left it out?'

Polly looked up, her cheeks red. 'I didn't look very hard. It felt . . . weird, being in there. Amongst all Mark's things.'

'Why?' Cat asked. She found it nothing short of delightful, being given the key and trusted with his whole house. She had resisted her curiosity and limited her forays to the hall and kitchen, but just the idea of being there, looking after his dog, was enough.

She liked Mark, she hoped things might happen between them, and she didn't want to risk that for a peek in his bedroom. Besides, how could she build her reputation as a professional dog walker, picking up pets when the owners were out, if she became known as a snooper? Alison was wrong about her not being trustworthy.

'I was so tempted to look around,' Polly said, clearly shocked at her own human instincts. Cat's best friend was not the most rebellious person. 'I had to leave.'

Cat grinned. 'I'm proud of you, Polly. Embrace your curiosity.'

'No, I'm not going to! Can you go and feed Chips, please? She looked heartbroken when I left.'

'Probably because she's starving.' Polly handed her the key, and Cat made the short, sunny walk to number four.

She stepped into his hallway, which was empty apart from a winter coat hanging on a hook, leaving the door on the latch. This house had a semicircular panel of stained glass above the front door, and it made a pattern of light on the carpet, like the boiled-sweet biscuits Cat remembered making as a child. Chips came padding down the corridor and nuzzled her nose against Cat's knees, whimpering softly.

'Come on, then, let's get you some lunch.'

Chips led the way to the sparse kitchen. It had black granite countertops and plain white cupboards, lots of sharp lines and monochrome. Cat didn't know who Mark had rented the house from, but it screamed Bachelor Pad. She refilled Chips's water bowl and gave her some dried food. There was a spread of papers over one of the worktops. Cat walked past them, averting her eyes, to the back door.

The gardens along Primrose Terrace – except perhaps Jessica's – were tiny, brick-walled courtyards, and Mark's looked as though it hadn't seen any love in years. Weeds crept up through the cracks in the paving slabs, and unruly ivy trailed down from next door. There was a wooden table that had been left out for too many winters, and a broken bird table.

'This isn't great, is it?'

Chips looked up, then went back to her food.

'Still, when you've got the park and the beach, what does it matter? And he's not been here very long yet, has he? We'll give him time. Do you want to go out there?' She unlocked the back door and Chips followed her into the courtyard. It had been absorbing heat all day, and was a stark contrast to the cool kitchen. Chips trotted round the edge of the square, showing little interest in the dirt and scrubby plants that remained, and went back inside. Cat was about to follow when she saw a large ginger lump trotting round the top of the wall. Shed.

'Hey,' she called, but Shed shot her a blazing look and continued on his journey. Cat couldn't believe that Shed would voluntarily go out in the sun – he was the laziest cat she'd ever met, but perhaps that didn't mean much. Cats could be quite secretive, so maybe Shed's lazy persona was disguising other activities. She would have to watch him closely.

She rinsed Chips's empty bowl, her gaze falling on the fridge. A scrap of paper beneath a black magnet said, *Leave D. food out for Cat* and she smiled, seeing her name pinned to Mark's fridge. Next to it, a photo was half hidden beneath a magnet shaped like a clapperboard. Cat moved the magnet.

The photo was of a woman sitting on a wall in front of a Mediterranean-blue sea, long dark hair flying, a smile on her glossy lips. She was wearing sunglasses, and Cat was frustrated that she couldn't get a sense of the woman's personality, but she looked glamorous. It could be anyone – a sister, friend, an ex. Cat hoped she wasn't more than an ex.

She put the magnet back and was drying Chips's bowl when she heard the front door bang. She smiled and called to her friend. 'Decided to come in after all, did you?'

Chips barked and raced down the hall.

'I thought it was probably better than staying in the car.'

Cat dropped the bowl onto the draining board and spun round. Mark stood just inside the kitchen in a navy T-shirt and jeans, sunglasses perched on his head. His cheeks were flushed, his dark eyes alive with their usual amusement.

'I was giving Chips her lunch,' Cat said quickly, running her hand through her hair. She dropped the tea towel on the floor, bent and picked it up.

'I can see that. You are allowed to say hello, you know.' He grinned, calm in the face of her awkwardness.

'Hello.'

'Hi. I didn't mean to surprise you, but things finished early. This weather's only nice in London if you're sitting outside with a cold pint, and the thought of Fairview, with its fresh air and its various attractions, not to mention Chips . . .' Chips was superglued to Mark's side, looking up at him with adoration. 'It was too hard to resist.'

'It's lovely to see you,' Cat said. Mark's grin got wider, and Cat felt her cheeks flush. 'Did things go well in London?'

Mark tipped his head, considering. 'Not too bad. Better than expected, in fact. I was meant to have another meeting this afternoon but it got cancelled. Saturday meetings are never that productive, so I'm not too disappointed.'

'But you've found someone to make your film?'

'Could be. It's not confirmed yet, but . . .'

'You don't have to tell me. It must be nerve-racking, waiting.'

'You just have to distract yourself with other things.' He gave Cat a slow, gentle smile that was hotter than the weather, and her mouth went dry. 'Chips been OK? I've never left her overnight before, but she seems perky enough.'

'Oh, she's been fine. I spent lots of time with her last night, and she settled well. We had our Pooches' and Puppies' Picnic this morning, and it . . . it was eventful – and very popular.'

'You've got some more dogs to walk?'

'A couple, and lots more people want to be on the mailing list. It was worth doing.'

'You're on your way to Fairview domination. I'm pleased it went so well. Listen, I'm parched. How about a cold beer in the sunshine?'

Cat licked her lips. A cold beer. Mark. 'That sounds lovely, but . . .' She glanced behind her at the unappealing courtyard.

'OK, so maybe not there. Come on.' He took two bottles out of the fridge, opened them and led the way to the front of the house. He opened the door to the street, disappeared into the living room and returned with a blanket, which he spread on the top step with a flourish.

Cat laughed. 'A picnic blanket? You think of everything.'

'Of course.'

They sat beside each other and Mark handed her a bottle. They clinked, and Cat took a swig. It was cold and bubbly and refreshing, and seemed to heighten the excitement already fizzing inside her. Chips nudged her way between them and lay on the bottom step, her chin on Mark's foot.

The front steps were wide, but Cat could feel Mark pressed against her, shoulders and hips touching. The sun was baking down on them, its light showing off every colour to its full – the carpet of primroses, the pastel of the houses, glossy paints on front doors, the shine of metallic cars. Cat closed her eyes and listened to the seagulls, the sound of children screaming and laughing.

137

'Long morning?' Mark asked.

Cat opened her eyes. 'A bit. The event was full-on, but Joe and Polly were a huge help – and George in the café. It wasn't a solo effort.'

'He's a strange one, George. Always seems a bit reluctant to serve me.'

Cat smiled around the mouth of her bottle.

'What? What do you know?' Mark nudged her arm. He smelled of aftershave, something spicy, a hint of coconut.

'George thinks you are a spy.'

'A spy?'

'Yup. A spooky, he called you. Sitting in the café making notes, watching people. He told me to stay away from you.'

'He did, did he? And what did you say?'

He turned towards her and Cat shifted, facing him. 'I said I'd be extra careful around you. I don't want to get into any trouble.'

'What makes you think that spending time with me will get you in trouble?' His gaze had caught hold of hers and wouldn't let go. She thought that telling him he radiated trouble would just encourage him, so she turned away and took a swig of her beer.

'We had protesters at our event.'

'Protesting against what?' Mark laughed. 'The sea of wagging tails? Too much barking?'

'Dog walkers in the park. They said it's a recipe for disaster.'

'I hope you set them straight.'

'Ish. It felt quite personal, some of it. An attack against my new business, rather than dog walkers in general.'

'Don't listen to them,' Mark said, his voice suddenly serious. He put his hand on Cat's knee, where her dress ended, his fingertips on her skin. 'You'll always find people who are jealous of success. It doesn't matter what – jobs, relationships, dreams being fulfilled. If you're doing well, then amongst all the people who are pleased for you, there'll be a couple who hate it.'

'Always haters,' Cat nodded.

'So ignore them,' he said. And then, so close to her ear that the hairs prickled on her neck, 'Focus on the ones who are happy for you. Who want to spend time with you, and help you celebrate.'

'Mark?' She swallowed, turned her head and found that her lips were inches from his.

'Yes?' His hand cupped her face. His palm was hot, his thumb stroking her cheek.

She gave a tiny shake of her head and leaned in to kiss him. His lips were soft, his stubble grazing her skin, and it felt every bit as good as she'd imagined. It wasn't a long kiss, but it was enough. He sat back and frowned, as if she wasn't who he'd expected, but then obliterated his uncertainty with a grin.

'That was a surprise,' she said.

'No it wasn't.'

'You seduced me with your beer and your picnic blanket.'

'I think you were ready to be seduced.'

Cat shrugged, smiled at him and picked up her beer. 'Maybe I was,' she said. Chips was panting softly, her eyes closed but her ears alert, waiting to protect her master at a moment's notice. She clearly didn't think Cat was a threat.

'Maybe that wasn't enough.' He put his hand back on her knee, his fingers tracing her skin, slipping under the hem of her dress. 'We don't have to stop there.' He brushed his lips against Cat's neck.

She closed her eyes as a shiver ran the length of her spine. 'Maybe we should remember we're on the front steps,' she murmured.

'I have a perfectly good front room, bedroom even . . .'

'I don't know much about you.'

'Again,' Mark said, 'something we could easily put right.' His hand moved further up her leg and Cat pushed it off, moving sideways on the step.

'Your personality,' she clarified, determined to marshal her thoughts despite the obvious distraction. 'You, Mark. The person. The writer. What were your meetings about in London? What did you do?'

'I thought about you.'

Cat rolled her eyes. 'When you were alone in your hotel room, you mean?'

'No, I still have a place there.'

'Oh? You haven't completely committed to Fairview, then? Still testing the water?'

'I've committed. I like it more every day. I've found lots of things I want to explore.' He gave her a knowing smile. 'But when I first came here, I hadn't entirely packed up my London life. I'm slowly getting there.'

'Does that mean you're going to do something with the courtyard?' Cat thumbed behind her. 'Because it's pretty shocking.'

'Cheeky.'

'Just being honest.'

'Maybe I'll do something,' he said. 'It would be good to have somewhere to go and sit in the sun that wasn't . . .'

'Right out on the street?'

'Exactly.'

'Though I don't think anyone saw us.'

'Would it matter if they did?' Mark moved a strand of Cat's short hair off her forehead. He could make the smallest gesture seem sexy, and she felt her resolve slipping.

'No, I – no, of course not.' Not this bit, anyway, she wanted to add. She had somehow imagined that he'd want to hide what happened between them away from everyone. She was relieved – and surprised – at how much he was prepared to show his affection for her in public.

'That's good,' Mark said, 'because Boris from next door is giving us a *very* cheery wave.' He raised a hand in greeting and Boris waved back, his smile filling his narrow face. He was walking the two French bulldogs, their compact bodies jostling next to each other and hurrying to keep up with his long strides.

Cat waved back, praying that Boris hadn't seen Mark nuzzling her neck.

'I meant it when I said I'd been thinking about you.'

Cat kept her eyes on Boris's retreating form. 'And I meant it when I said I'd like to get to know you. But not in that way, not yet.'

'Another beer, then?'

'Sounds like a good start.'

Mark took Cat's empty bottle and headed back inside. Cat slipped her sandal off and stroked Chips's soft fur with her toes. The dog turned languidly to face her, then went back to sleep. Cat closed her eyes and concentrated on the feel of the sun warming her face, and not how good that kiss had been or how much she wanted to ignore the sensible part of her brain and follow Mark inside.

9

When Cat had picked Olaf up on Monday morning after Frankie returned from the school run, the young mum's eyes had been red, and Cat had heard Henry crying in the background. Frankie had hurried her out of the door, barely exchanging two words with her, and Cat had taken Chalky, Disco and Olaf to Fairview Park.

The cocker spaniel had been skittish, as if the park was the most glorious thing he'd ever seen, and Cat deduced that the little dog probably wasn't getting much time to let off steam. Olaf seemed to have even more energy than Disco, and that was saying something. Cat was reluctant to let the dogs off the lead – especially after the manner in which she'd found Olaf at the weekend – but she threw caution to the wind, ignored her lack of sports bra and jogged round the perimeter of the park. Even Chalky seemed energized by the run, barking loudly as they slowed, and rushing up to Cat for a treat with an enthusiasm he didn't usually show.

Cat knew that by walking Olaf regularly she could give Frankie one less thing to worry about, but she thought there must be more she could do. She explained all this to Polly after dinner, curled up on the sofa in front of a dark and bleak-seeming film that Cat hadn't quite caught the name of, but Joe was entirely focused on.

'He's a very sweet dog, and I'm sure he's getting lots of attention, but I'm not sure if he's walked enough. I don't mind doing that for less, or even free if it would help Frankie out.'

'She won't want that though, will she? She'll see it as charity.' Polly took a long swig of water. The front room was warm and they had all the windows open, the thin curtains reaching out towards them courtesy of a breeze that had appeared out of nowhere. If Cat stood close to the windows, she could hear the waves. It made her shudder every time – it was a magical, hypnotic sound, especially in the dark.

'But if she's desperate . . .' Cat said. 'I'm lucky enough not to know what it's like to be in that situation, but if she's struggling with two young girls and a new baby, and she can't reduce her hours because she needs the money, then a favour, however small, must be a relief? As long as we don't make a big deal of it.'

'I don't know why she got the dog in the first place,' Joe said, 'if it's already hard enough with three kids.'

'Oh, I don't know, Joey,' Polly said, 'maybe she was just being a good mum? The girls wanted a dog, and so she got them one.'

'Olaf was a present from Frankie's partner Rick,' Cat said, 'before they went their separate ways. She's definitely struggling, but Emma and Lizzie love the dog so much she can't take it away from them. And I want to do the friendly neighbour thing and help them out.'

'Did you arrange another walk with Olaf?'

Cat shook her head. 'No, Frankie was too flustered. She thanked me and closed the door. I'm going to go and see her tomorrow.'

'And what will you say?'

'I'll ask her to let me walk Olaf, and I'll . . . well, I could offer to look after Lizzie and Emma.'

'Really?' Polly frowned. 'Wouldn't you have to take Henry too?'

'I'm qualified, DBS checked. I could take them off Frankie's hands when she's getting ready for work, or when the school holidays come round.'

'Aren't you meant to be a *dog-walking* business?' Joe asked. He turned the volume up on the TV, jabbing the remote at the screen in case Cat hadn't got the point. She rolled her eyes.

'I don't like seeing someone distressed, not when they're so close by.'

'But she hasn't asked for help,' Polly said quietly. 'Why not just be a friend, walk Olaf, and see if she comes to you.'

It was sound advice, as always, and Cat sat back and tried to concentrate on the film, on someone in dark clothes ducking and diving through a shadowy, dilapidated building while sinister music played. She thought that, whatever the film was, Mark would probably love it. Mark who was going to take her out to dinner – though they didn't have a firm arrangement yet – who had kissed her in plain view of the whole of Primrose Terrace. Or maybe she had kissed him, but he had definitely started it. She tucked her feet up under her and grinned into her cup of tea.

Pooch Promenade had given her a lot to be thankful for in the last couple of months. She was happy, and she wanted to help other people be happy too – what was so wrong with that?

'Why don't I—' she started.

'Oh, for God's sake!' Joe paused the television and faced her. Polly chewed her long blonde hair, and Cat could see she was trying not to laugh. 'Why don't you what?' he asked.

'Uh, I – I hadn't quite thought,' Cat admitted. 'I just started the sentence, but wasn't sure where the end was going to go. I want to help Frankie. There must be *something* we can do?'

'Well, decide quickly, and then I can watch the rest of *Blade Runner* in peace.'

'Oh, is *that* what this film is? I've always wanted to see *Blade Runner*.'

Joe's mouth dropped open, and Cat could feel the irritation pulsing off him. He folded his arms, levelled Cat with his blue-eyed stare – slightly sinister in the film-watching gloom of the front room – and waited. Cat focused on his tanned forearms, the way his white T-shirt clung to his torso. Since the weather had warmed up, Cat was seeing less of Joe's hoodies and more reminders of how athletic he was. Occasionally, she found it quite distracting.

'So what are you going to do? How will you interfere with this woman's life in a way that makes it look like you're doing it all for her?'

'Joey,' Polly said, 'don't be such a grump. You know Cat's only trying to help.'

'If she wants to be that helpful, then why doesn't she move in with Frankie and let me watch my bloody film in peace?' He pressed play and shifted on the sofa, angling his shoulder towards Cat in a gesture of finality.

Cat and Polly exchanged a look. Cat tried to concentrate on the film and then Joe's words replayed in her head.

'Oh my God!'

'For fu—'

'Joe, you're a total genius. Thank you!' Cat leaned over and kissed him on the cheek. He recoiled in shock, then stared at her as she got up.

'Where are you going?'

145

'I'm just taking a trip down the road.'

'You're wearing your pyjamas.'

Cat glanced down. She had thin tartan pyjama trousers on and a strappy black vest top.

She shrugged. 'It's hot, nobody will mind.'

'You're not going to see Frankie now, are you?' Polly asked slowly.

Cat shook her head. 'I won't knock on the door. I just want to have a look at something, then I'll tell you my – Joe's – genius idea. Joe, you really have to stop helping me out like this, or I'll have to employ you full time and you'll have no time for Magic Mouse designs.'

'Oh, wow,' Joe said drily, 'all my dreams come true.'

Cat laughed and burst out of the front door into the warm summer's evening.

'You want me to rent my attic out?' Frankie asked, handing Polly and Cat cups of milky tea, pushing a pile of magazines onto the floor and gesturing for them to sit down.

'It's not being used now, is it?'

Frankie shook her head. 'It's a dump. It turned into the junk room as soon as Rick and I moved in, and it's been collecting all our crap ever since.'

'But it – it's boarded out?' Cat asked.

'Oh, yeah, it's a proper room. I had grand hopes of turning it into a music room once upon a time – Lizzie's learning the guitar and I play too, but like so many things, it's never happened.'

'So with a bit of sorting, it could be a room again? In our house it's Joe's room, and though it's not somewhere I've spent a lot of time, I've seen how big it is. This is such a lovely street to live on, I'm sure you'd have no problem getting a tenant.'

146

'What, with three young kids and a dog?'

'Lots of people love children and animals,' Polly said. 'Cat's right, it could bring in a good income, allow you to drop your hours at the restaurant, or find another job altogether.'

Frankie sat back and fiddled with her hair. Cat noticed that she didn't often look directly at them, her green eyes always on the move. Perhaps that came from having three children, always on the lookout for where they were or whether something was wrong. 'It would be a lot of work, and I don't have much time to myself as it is.'

'We'd help you clear it out, if you wanted?' Cat said.

'Why?'

'Why what?'

'Why would you help me? Why are you both doing this?'

Cat put her mug on the floor and Olaf padded over, sniffed it and looked up at her. She lifted the dog onto her lap. 'We want to help. Isn't that enough?'

Frankie chewed her lip. 'Seems suspicious. Seems like no one really goes out of their way like this unless there's something in it for them. You don't seem like that sort of person, but I don't get it. And if I don't get it, I'm reluctant to do it – as generous as your offer seems.'

Cat ran her hands down Olaf's long ears. It was a good question. Why did she feel compelled to help Frankie? She took a deep breath, and tried to explain. 'I moved here a few months ago, and things were great for a while, and then I lost my job.'

'At the nursery,' Frankie said.

'Right. Exactly.' Her gaze flicked to Polly, then back to Frankie. 'And lots of people were kind to me. Elsie – she's next door to us – wouldn't let me drown in self-pity. She helped me come up with the idea of dog walking. Joe and Polly helped me market it. Jessica – the author – let me walk her dogs, made me feel like I could actually do it. Everyone on Primrose Terrace has been so supportive, and I – I feel lucky. I want to pay it forward, I want to help other people. Maybe it's ridiculous but, well, there it is.' She gave Frankie a tentative smile.

Frankie nodded, stood and checked on Henry, who was asleep in his pram in the corner of the room. 'Let me have a think,' she said. 'I'm not saying no, but I don't want to say yes just like that. And I still want to do something for you.'

'OK,' Cat said, also standing. 'Take as long as you need.'

The next Saturday afternoon, Cat and Polly collected Chalky and Disco from Elsie's house, and then walked down the road to number twelve. Lizzie answered the door, her long hair in pigtails. 'Mum's going to work now, she's racing around looking for her shoes.'

'I know what that's like,' Cat said, grinning.

'We've come to get Olaf,' Polly added.

'Oh.' Lizzie looked downcast. 'OK.'

'What are you doing?'

Lizzie shrugged. 'Can I stroke them?' She pointed at the mini schnauzers.

'Of course you can.'

Lizzie dropped to her knees and gave one hand to each dog. Disco padded forward affectionately and Chalky stood still, pretending to be resigned but, Cat knew, really loving the attention.

'Our babysitter's coming,' Lizzie said. Cat thought she looked like a smaller version of Polly, all pale skin and freckles, slender limbs in denim shorts.

'Except she's not,' Frankie said, racing down the stairs. She was brushing her hair, her mobile pressed to her ear with the other hand. 'She's sick, so I'm trying to find someone else. You like Pippa, don't you?'

Lizzie screwed up her face. 'She wears too much perfume, and she spends the *whole* time snapchatting on her phone. Emma and I could be dancing on the table and she wouldn't care.' Lizzie hugged Disco, and the younger dog, while held in a vice-like grip, still managed to lick Lizzie's chin. She giggled.

'Well, there's nobody else. She'll have to do. Hello, Pippa?' Frankie turned away from them.

'We'll look after them,' Cat said. 'Won't we, Pol?'

Polly widened her eyes at Cat. 'Uhm, yes, yeah, of course.'

'Hang on, Pippa.' Frankie pressed the phone against her shoulder and turned round. 'You will?'

Cat nodded. 'We can take them with us round the park.'

'Henry too?'

Cat swallowed and glanced at her friend. She had no experience with babies. 'Of course,' she said. 'Polly's a nurse, so—'

'You are?'

'A veterinary nurse. Not maternity.' Her eyes widened even further, and Cat thought they might pop out, but she chose to ignore the silent message Polly was giving her.

Frankie looked at them for a moment, then picked up the phone. 'Pippa, I'll call you back.' She hung up. 'I don't finish until eleven.'

'That's fine,' Cat said. 'As long as you can tell us what to do for dinner, and what time it is. We can think of things to do, can't we?'

Lizzie nodded, looking warily between Cat and her mum, as if not quite believing she was about to get away with such an exciting change of plan. 'But we can't stay up late. We always promise Mum we'll go to bed on time, and be well behaved, and help look after Henry.'

'That's all right,' Cat said. 'Your mum can tell us everything we need to do, if we help you find your shoes?'

Frankie nodded slowly. She still looked sceptical, but Cat gave her what she hoped was a winning smile, and Lizzie pressed her hands in front of her in a praying motion, Disco still within the circle of her arms.

'All right then,' Frankie said. 'Henry's day bag is over here, and should have everything you need. I can talk you through it. If you're sure you don't mind?'

'We'd love to,' Cat said. Glancing at her friend, she was pretty sure Polly didn't share the sentiment.

Fairview beach was busy late on a Saturday afternoon, and even walking in the quieter Fairview cove, which allowed dogs throughout the year, Cat felt conspicuous with six dogs, two young girls and a pram. Polly, too, seemed in a state of shock. She was pushing Henry and kept peering forward, cooing at him even though he was fast asleep under the hood. Cat thought she was probably checking he was still alive.

'Stay close to us, girls,' Cat said.

Lizzie had Disco, Emma had Olaf, and Cat was in charge of Chalky and Jessica's three Westies. The girls ran ahead, crossing paths, getting the leads tangled up, but it was clear they were excited about spending time with new people and lots of dogs.

Emma raced back to Cat and Polly, Olaf sprinting alongside, his ears mirroring his young owner's flyaway hair. 'Can we go in the water?' she panted.

'What, *swim*?' Polly screeched.

'No, paddle. We'll stay close.'

'And keep the dogs on their leads?' Cat asked. 'I don't want to have to go in after them. I know it's warm, but the water's cold.'

Emma nodded. 'Promise.'

'And stay with your sister. Hold hands at all times, OK? Lizzie?'

The older girl walked up with Disco, took her sister's hand and they both headed towards the sea. The breakers were small, the sand sliding gently into a calm surf, and Cat didn't think they had anything to worry about, but she still steered their party closer to the water.

'How can you be so relaxed?' Polly asked. 'How can this be happening? We've got a baby and two girls to look after, and that's if you disregard all the dogs. Imagine if we managed to piss Jessica *and* Frankie off? They're both formidable in their own ways. I am *terrified*.'

'I'm calm because I'm with you,' Cat said, grinning.

'Oh, well, brilliant. That makes me feel so much better! God, Cat, what do you think I'll be able to do if they all disappear under the waves or the baby starts choking?'

'You're a nurse. OK, an animal nurse, but the principles are the same. Hearts and lungs and eyes and feet. And come on, it's not like we're alone. We've got Frankie's number, and the restaurant's, and there's Elsie and Joe—'

'Joe would either be killing himself laughing or running away in terror if he could see us right now.'

'Joe's a bit safe, that's all.'

'Joe thinks my best friend is a bona fide lunatic,' Polly confirmed. 'And I'm starting to agree with him. *Don't do that!*' she squealed, as Emma bent down, dangling her hair in the waves. She emerged, smiling, holding a long black tendril of slimy seaweed. Olaf yapped at it, then danced away when Emma waggled it in his direction. Cat saw the glint of triumph in the young girl's eyes, remembered that exact look from when Disco had escaped at the nursery, and knew that

Emma would grow up mischievous. She confirmed it when, still holding onto Olaf's lead, she raced towards Polly.

Polly screamed and, letting go of the pram, ran up the beach. Laughing, Cat took the pram, checked the dog leads weren't tangled under the wheels, and started pushing. Chalky looked up at her and sniffed.

'Don't look at me like that,' she said. 'I'm not a lunatic. I'm helping out.' The mini schnauzer dropped his head and carried on walking, and Cat felt a squeeze of sadness at the thought that she hadn't got the old dog's approval. Polly, Emma and Olaf fell into a heap, Lizzie and Disco not far behind, and Cat pushed Henry up the sand, wishing the wheels were a bit wider, and joined them.

'Come on,' she said, 'that's enough exertion. Time for ice cream.' Emma and Lizzie cheered and helped Polly to her feet.

'This,' Polly panted, 'is madness. Why did I let you talk me into it?'

'You're having fun, admit it. I'll buy you a ninety-nine to say sorry.'

'Oh, well then,' Polly said, rubbing her sandy hands against her shorts, 'all is forgiven.'

'Capello's Ice Cream Parlour,' Lizzie read. '*Not Just for Sundaes.*'

'But you can have one if you want,' Cat added. 'Whatever you want.'

'A waffle?' Emma asked. 'With chocolate sauce?'

Cat nodded. 'Sounds perfect.' She dug into her purse, pulled out some money and handed it to Lizzie. 'You go inside and order, and I'll find a table out here.'

'What do you want?' Polly asked.

'Share a banana split?'

Polly grinned and opened the door for the girls.

Cat pushed the pram to the side of the low building and found a large table set apart from the others. She tied the dogs up and Disco and Olaf went straight to a silver bowl of water, lapping quickly. The parlour was set back from the sand, between the main beach and the dog-friendly cove, and was clearly owned by a dog lover. Cat rocked the pram backwards and forwards and, while she was alone, quickly checked the baby was still breathing. He gurgled slightly and opened his eyes.

Lizzie and Emma raced up to the table with a large bottle of water, Polly carrying four glasses behind them.

'Ice cream on the way?'

'Sundaes,' Emma said, her green eyes wide. 'They're amazing!'

'Excellent. And d'you think Henry needs feeding?'

Lizzie nodded and went to the day bag. 'I'll do it,' she said. 'I can ask them to warm the milk up.' She took the bottle back to the ice cream parlour.

'She's very grown-up, isn't she?' Cat said.

Polly nodded. She was staring at the table, running her finger along the rough grain of the wood.

'She's ten,' Emma said. 'Six years older than me.'

'Do you think that's a lot?' Cat asked.

Emma nodded. 'It's whole worlds older,' she said seriously.

While Lizzie was cradling Henry, expertly feeding him the bottle, and Emma was giving treats to the dogs, Cat moved closer to Polly.

'Are you OK? I know this is a lot to deal with, and perhaps not how you anticipated spending your Saturday afternoon, but is something wrong? You look—'

'I'm fine,' Polly said. 'Just hot and tired. Looking forward to our ice cream.' She gave a weak smile, which didn't fool Cat for a moment.

153

When their ice creams were brought to the table, Cat thought she knew the answer.

'One waffle with Belgian chocolate sauce and sprinkles.' Emma held her hand up. 'One knickerbocker glory – for you?' Lizzie nodded. 'And one banana split, two spoons, extra cream and I took the liberty of adding some pistachio ice cream, as you said it was your favourite.'

'Thanks,' Polly said quickly, looking up at the man who had brought their ice creams out. He had thick, almost black hair in tight curls, and large blue eyes. He also, if Cat wasn't mistaken, had a dog that, about a month before, hadn't been very well at all.

'Thank you.' Cat beamed up at him. 'How's your fox terrier? Rummy, isn't it?'

'Oh.' He glanced at Polly, then back at Cat, and ran his hands down his apron. 'Rummy is back to normal, one hundred per cent, and all thanks to Polly. Honestly, I don't know what I would have done if—' He shook his head. 'All of this is on the house,' he added. 'As a very small thank-you.'

'It was the vet, really,' Polly said.

'I don't believe that. I mean, the vet, of course, but you took him in, got him through to surgery so quickly. I owe you everything.'

Cat bit her lip to stop herself grinning. 'I'm Cat,' she said, standing. 'Polly's best friend and resident Fairview dog walker.'

'Owen.' He shook her hand. 'Ice cream maker and very, very grateful dog owner. That's quite a pack you've got there,' he said. 'Careful.'

Cat glanced behind her and saw that Dior had his front paws on the bench, his bottom waggling in pre-jump mode. 'No, Dior,' she said. 'Not ice cream. Jessica would kill me.'

When she turned back, Owen was gazing down at Polly and Polly was dipping her spoon into the cream on top of the banana split. Cat felt a rush of triumph.

'If you're ever in need of a dog walker . . .' she said.

Owen shook his head. 'Rummy and I are pretty inseparable. He gets lots of walks.'

'Oh well,' Cat shrugged. 'Take my number anyway, just in case . . .'

Polly frowned as Cat pulled a scrap of paper and a pen out of her bag, scribbled on it and handed it to Owen.

'Thanks,' he said. He waggled it and walked backwards a few steps. 'Nice to meet you, and lovely to see you again, Polly.' He looked at her, his smile creasing his eyes as he put the piece of paper in the top pocket of his shirt.

Rummy, a pretty fox terrier, with brown ears and spots of grey on his wiry coat, trotted up to meet his owner, almost tripping him.

'Thanks for the ice cream!' Cat called, as Owen bent to stroke his dog and then disappeared inside.

Lizzie gave Cat her money back. 'Didn't need it,' she said. 'The nice man paid for everything.'

Emma was nose-deep in her waffle, chocolate sauce on her cheek and fingers.

'Wasn't that nice of him?' Cat kept her eyes on Polly. 'Why do you think that was, Lizzie?'

'Because he likes Polly,' she said, 'and he wants to impress her.'

Cat grinned. 'Ever thought of being a detective?'

Lizzie shook her head, giggling.

'He was just grateful for Rummy,' Polly said, 'that's all.'

'He had big gooey eyes all over you,' Emma said, looking up from her dessert. 'Just like his ice cream.'

Cat laughed, full and loud. '"Big gooey eyes",' she repeated. 'I think I know exactly what you mean. How's your pistachio ice cream, Pol?'

Polly gave Cat her *Midwich Cuckoo* stare and stuck her spoon in the banana split; she picked up a huge dollop of ice cream and, still looking at Cat, shoved it in her mouth.

Cat chuckled and picked up her own spoon. She knew Polly well enough to see that Owen Capello, with his ice creams and his dog, had definitely had an effect on her. Cat hoped her friend wouldn't be too cross when she discovered that it was Polly's number she'd scrawled on the piece of paper, and not her own.

On their way back from the beach, Cat saw Captain strolling along ahead of them, a rolled-up newspaper tucked under his arm. Their party of dogs and children was subdued, Cat and Polly – and the beach – having tired them out. She thought she could leave them in Polly's capable hands for a couple of minutes.

'I won't be a second,' Cat said, handing over the Westies' leads to Polly. She raced up and tapped Captain on the shoulder.

'Hi, Captain. It's Cat – remember me, from the Pooches' and Puppies' Picnic?'

'Oh, yes, I remember you and your chap,' he nodded, squinting against the sun. 'Elsie's friend.'

'That's right. I was just wondering, how's Paris doing? Is she any better?'

Captain's friendly gaze dropped to the ground, and Cat felt his whole demeanour change. 'She's worse, if anything. I had a battle to try and get her out today – just to the shop for the paper, I said to her, but she wasn't having any of it. She hid in the washing machine until I left. I don't know what to do.'

'Let me have a think,' Cat said, putting her hand on his arm. 'I can ask around, visit a couple of online forums.'

Captain sighed and put his hand on top of hers. 'You'd do that?'

'Of course. I know I'm just a dog walker, but I hate seeing any animals – especially of the canine variety – upset. If there's anything I can do to make Paris better, then I will.'

'Bless you,' Captain said.

'I'll be in touch as soon as I can.' Cat gave his hand a squeeze and ran back to join the others.

'What was that about?' Polly asked.

'Just trying to help out,' Cat shrugged.

'Oh.' Polly tried to hide her smile. 'That's unusual for you.'

Cat rolled her eyes and halted their party at the zebra crossing.

10

Polly had been stunned, and Cat triumphant, that they had survived their first babysitting duties. Henry had only had one bout of uncontrollable screaming, and that was once they'd gone back to Frankie's house and Cat had made some food for them all. No children or dogs had fallen in the sea, and Emma and Lizzie had gone to sleep happy, Emma prolonging her bedtime by insisting on walking two steps up, one step down, all the way to her bedroom. But when Frankie had returned, close to midnight and almost too exhausted to speak, Cat knew that walking Olaf and occasionally looking after her children wasn't going to be enough.

Summer in Fairview was proving to be glorious. A hazy May turned into a hot, fresh June, and with the summer holidays on the horizon, Pooch Promenade was picking up. Cat had had a couple of requests to look after dogs while families went on holiday, and, as much as she didn't want to turn down business, she had to remind herself that she was only one and a half people strong, and being the sole carer for dogs for more than a few days at a time wasn't yet practical.

Polly's exams were only a couple of months away now, and while her friend was hidden inside revising, Cat was spending most of her time outdoors, often doing three walks a day. She'd never considered that she'd have a job where sunburn was an occupational hazard.

'Owowowwwwwww.'

'Hold still, because it won't work if you won't let me put it on.' Polly was kneeling on the sofa, applying cold aloe vera cream to Cat's neck and shoulders. 'This stuff is meant to be soothing. You're not acting very soothed.'

'It is soothing, but it burns too.'

'It's very pink.'

'How pink?' She knew she should have worn a T-shirt rather than a strappy top, but it was such a warm day, no clouds in the sky, and she liked the breeze against her skin. Of course, that combination was what had done it.

'Ummmm,' Polly said, obviously trying to think of something nice to say.

'A giant lobster,' said another voice.

'Thanks, Joe,' Cat winced. 'I will never fail to be amazed at your ability to make a girl feel special.'

'It's one of my many talents.' He went into the kitchen and Cat heard the fridge door open. 'That does look sore.'

'Says the man who just has to look at the sun to go brown. How come that happens when you're so blond?'

'Another of my many talents,' he called. 'I'm a talented guy.'

'We thought we might go to the pub,' Polly said.

'I'm not sure the Lobster Cat should sit in the beer garden.'

'We weren't going to sit outside. And if you think, for even one moment, that I'm going to be happy with that nickname, then you can think again.'

Joe popped his head around the door and grinned. 'It has a certain ring to it.'

Cat pointed at him. 'No.'

'Coming, Joey? We're going to have an evening of de-stress. Exams, dogs, struggling neighbours.'

Joe narrowed his eyes. 'You're still trying to save that mum?'

'I'm not trying to *save* her, I just want to help.'

'You can't help everyone, Cat.' He had his irritated tone back, and Cat felt as though she was being told off by her old maths teacher, even if Joe was *much* easier on the eye. 'Eventually,' he continued, 'your brain will run out of space, and you'll be so busy helping other people that you'll start to neglect yourself. You'll stop washing, stop eating. You'll slowly lose your dress sense and have this one cow-print onesie that you run up and down the street in, looking for new crusades.'

Cat and Polly looked at him. Polly had stopped mid-squirt, and Cat could feel the cold lotion running down her back.

'It sounds like you've been thinking about that for far too long,' Cat said.

'It's an observation. You'll morph into the town busybody and people will turn in the opposite direction when they see you.'

'You think I should stop trying to help?'

'I think you need to stop interfering.'

Cat glared at him, but she felt a coldness that was nothing to do with after-sun. Was that really how she was seen by everyone? It was true that dog walking was allowing her to meet lots of new people, and, due to the nature of looking after their pets, find out about them. But interfering? She knew she'd done that to a certain extent when she'd thought Jessica and Mark were together, but she hadn't gone too far, and things had turned out all right in the end.

More than all right. She gave a little shudder when she thought of the kiss.

'Are you OK?' Polly asked. 'I'm nearly done.'

Mark hadn't been in touch much since then, and their few text conversations had been fleeting. He was busy working on amendments to his script, popping backwards and forwards to London, but on the last couple of occasions he'd taken Chips with him, so she couldn't even spend time with his dog.

Joe sat on the sofa and started demolishing a cheese toastie. 'I thought we could eat at the pub.'

Joe shook his head. 'I can't come. I'm behind on a commission, got to spend the evening doodling away.'

'Something fun?' Cat asked. She wasn't going to make a thing of what Joe had said. If that's what he thought, then she'd just have to let him think it and move on.

'A new logo for a shoe shop in Fairhaven. It's a good job, but not the most creatively challenging.'

'Nothing . . . more cartoony?' Cat thought back to her conversation with Phil at the Pooches' Picnic. She wondered if he'd contacted Joe.

'Nope,' Joe mumbled through a mouthful of sandwich. 'No such luck.'

Cat shrugged, then winced as her tight skin cracked. The doorbell chose that moment to trill through the living room, and Polly went to answer it.

Joe kept his gaze on Cat, and she looked at her knee, picking a bit of hair off it. Ginger hair. She wondered how Shed was coping with the hot weather, thought of him trotting along

Mark's wall, looking very unlike the solid, immovable lump she knew, but then Polly led Frankie into the living room and all thoughts of the cat disappeared.

'Frankie, what's wrong?' Cat stood and put her hand on Frankie's arm. She was wearing black trousers and a black T-shirt with *Spatz* written in red, but her face was pink and puffy, her long hair loose, some strands sticking to her mascara-streaked cheeks. 'Sit down. Do you want a drink?'

Frankie shook her head, sniffed loudly and perched on the edge of the sofa Joe was sitting on. She glanced at him and Joe raised a hand in greeting. 'I-I can't stay long,' she said, 'I've left Lizzie with the others, and I need to get back. But I—' She inhaled, closed her eyes, then seemed to give her whole body a shake. She opened her eyes and sat up straight. 'I got fired today,' she said. 'They wanted me to give the top back, but I told them I wasn't walking home in my bra.'

'Oh God,' Polly said. 'I'm so sorry, Frankie.'

'What happened?' Cat asked. 'What did they do?'

'Henry wasn't well this morning, so I took him to the doctor's. I called work, told them I'd be late and why, and they said if I was late then I shouldn't bother turning up. I thought they were joking.'

'How can they fire you because your son was ill? Is he OK now?'

Frankie nodded. 'He's got a virus. It should clear up in a couple of days. But I'm not going to ignore my kids when they're ill or they need something. The reason I'm doing this job is so that I can look after them. It's just bullshit.'

Polly seemed taken aback by the expletive, but Cat was pleased Frankie was angry – angry was productive, misery was not.

'Right then,' she said, 'so what are you going to do? Get a new job? Ask for your old one back?'

'I'm never going back there, not for a million quid. I'll get a new job, but . . . but I was thinking about what you said. A few weeks ago.'

Polly and Cat exchanged a glance. Polly drummed her fingers against her lips. 'About the attic?'

Frankie nodded. 'It's not doing anything, sitting up there full of junk. I think we could cope with a lodger, as long as – as long as they could cope with us.'

'You're a lovely family,' Polly said softly. 'If they understand your life's always going to be a bit hectic, then I'm sure you'll find someone.'

'And who wouldn't want to live on Primrose Terrace?' Cat raised her hands up to the ceiling. 'In this house alone you can have all your dog walking, pet rescuing and scribbling needs sorted.'

Frankie frowned, but there was a hint of a smile on her lips. She brushed hair out of her eyes. 'Scribbling?'

'I'm an illustrator,' Joe said, finishing his sandwich.

'Do you do kids' books?'

He shook his head. 'Branding, websites, logos. That sort of thing.'

'He was going to do me a dog cartoon for the Pooch Promenade logo,' Cat explained to Frankie.

'I've started it,' Joe sighed. 'I'm just tied up with paid work at the moment.'

'You know I'll pay you – you said you didn't want me to.'

'I don't. I'll do your cartoon next, and for free, but I need to get this commission finished. When have I said no to you before, Cat?'

'I can think of one or two occasions.'

Frankie looked between them and raised an eyebrow. 'God, how long have you two been married?' She sniffed loudly, then smiled.

Polly laughed. 'See what I have to put up with?'

'So this room then,' Cat said quickly. 'When shall we get started?'

It was a bright, sunny day, Cat was sure, somewhere beyond this landing, with its full washing basket containing a pile of colourful clothes and a small cocker spaniel. The room behind them, door ajar, was a pink palace: pink bedding, candy-floss walls, pink curtains that were still closed and turning the light a deep fuchsia colour.

Henry was asleep in the pram downstairs; Frankie hadn't wanted to wake him after dropping Emma off at nursery. She was standing with Polly and Cat, looking up at the narrow flight of stairs that led to the closed attic door. At least whoever had done the conversion had fitted a proper staircase – Cat had had visions of lugging a load of boxes down, and then furniture up, a wooden stepladder.

'So this is it,' Polly said.

'This,' Frankie said, sighing, 'is it. Sure you want to help with this?'

Cat folded her arms and nodded. 'Of course.' It wasn't only dark on the landing, it was stuffy, and she could feel beads of sweat pooling at the waistband of her shorts. Her sunburn had begun to fade, and peel, and start to itch. 'We came up with the idea, and we're going to see it through.'

'All right,' Frankie said. 'But don't say I didn't warn you.' She gave them a grim smile and climbed the stairs. Olaf hopped out of the washing basket and followed her up, his claws ticking on the wooden steps.

Frankie opened the door and dust escaped, dancing below the ceiling light. 'Oh my God!' She closed the door.

Olaf barked.

'What?' Polly asked, panic at the edge of her voice. 'What is it?'

'Dead body?' Cat asked. 'Family of rats, mice, sparrows?'

Frankie stared at them, her mouth open.

'Have you realized you've already got a lodger, just one you didn't know about?' Cat climbed the stairs and slid past Frankie, opening the door. Olaf stood just inside, his tail wagging.

'Oh,' Cat said, when she saw the challenge they were faced with. 'OK. I see what you mean.'

'What is it?' Polly asked. 'I'm about to die of suspense here.'

'It's . . . a treasure trove.'

'It's a crap hole,' Frankie corrected.

'Everyone has a different perspective, don't they?'

From where Cat was standing, she could see boxes and boxes, some open, some closed, stacked almost up to the angled ceiling. There were crates with books in, an old standard lamp with the wiring spilling out, a clutch of broken umbrellas and what looked like a miniature totem pole. The air was thick with dust. It crept into Cat's nose and mouth and eyes, making her blink. Olaf barked, skittered a bit and then sneezed. Cat picked him up and he buried his warm nose under her chin.

Polly joined them on the tiny landing and gasped.

'So,' Frankie said. 'What happens now?'

'Now,' Cat said, 'we start searching for treasure. Can Olaf help?'

Frankie grinned. 'I think Olaf would be pretty upset if we didn't let him.'

'Right then, what's in box number one?'

They worked until it was time for Frankie to pick Lizzie and Emma up. The girls were chatty and excited after their days at school and nursery, and their excitement grew at the boxes piled up in the living room. There were newborn baby clothes and toys, knick-knacks from Frankie's mum's house, candle-sticks and tea-light holders of all shapes and sizes. Frankie, Polly and Cat had been putting things into piles – things to sell, things to keep, things for the charity shop and the tip.

'If there's enough,' Polly said, 'you could do a car boot sale. Some of these art deco holders would be snapped up.'

'And even broken things,' Cat added, hefting a box of spare towels down the stairs. 'People at car boots are vultures. If they see something they think they can fix and sell on for a pound more than they bought it for, they'll go for it.'

'Or sell it on eBay. That's a huge business now.'

'I considered being an eBay seller,' Cat said, 'very briefly, when I lost my job.'

'What were you going to sell?' asked Lizzie. She was rifling through a box of Christmas decorations.

Cat shrugged. 'I hadn't got that far. Thought I might slowly go round our house and take things I thought Polly and Joe wouldn't miss.'

'Hey,' Polly said, laughing. 'Our house is pretty minimalist.'

'Yes, apart from the foxes.'

'Foxes?' Lizzie asked.

'I have a thing about foxes,' Polly admitted. 'I've collected them since my mum bought me a cuddly one.' She smiled and looked away. Cat knew that Polly found it hard to talk about her mum, who had walked out when she and Joe were still small. 'Now I have ornaments and pictures, a hot-water bottle . . .'

'Curtains?' Emma asked. 'I have pretty curtains.'

'You have Disney everything,' Lizzie said.

'I don't have curtains,' Polly said, 'but that *is* a good idea.'

'Where would you get fox curtains from?' Cat wiped her forearm across her grubby forehead. 'And more importantly, why would you want to?'

Polly ignored her. 'Have you seen the fox that lives round here? I mean, there must be a few, but there's a really glossy one that's often about.'

Lizzie and Emma shook their heads, Emma's eyes wide.

Frankie brought in a jug of iced squash and five glasses. 'I've seen it on my way back from the restaurant, trotting down the street after dark, sniffing in bins. It doesn't look hungry.'

'I-is it big?' Emma whispered.

'Quite big,' Frankie admitted, running her hand over Emma's long hair, 'but there's nothing to be scared of. If anything, Mr Fox is a scaredy-cat. He wouldn't come near us.'

'W-what about Olaf? Will he eat him?'

Frankie crouched in front of her daughter. 'No, my poppet, Olaf is safe with us, and with Cat and Polly. Mr Fox wouldn't be interested in him, and even if he was, we'd look after him, wouldn't we?'

'Of course!' Lizzie said brightly. 'And Olaf wouldn't go near him. He's more interested in shoes. Look.' She pointed, and they all turned to see Olaf sitting in a box of old wellies and walking boots, chewing happily.

'Oh God, Olaf.' Frankie lifted him out, and a red-and-white spotty wellie came with him. Frankie set him on the ground and he stuck his head inside the boot, his tail wagging madly.

Cat laughed, took out her iPhone and snapped a photo. 'That is one cute spaniel you've got there. And entirely safe from foxes.'

167

'Foxes are just like dogs, anyway,' Polly said. 'They're from the same family. The main difference is they're wild, whereas all the dogs we know are tame.'

'Olaf doesn't look like a fox,' Emma said.

'Which dog is most like a fox?' Lizzie asked.

Cat sat cross-legged on the floor, and thought of all the dog breeds she'd come across.

'There's a dog called a spitz,' Polly said. 'They have thick fur because they come from where it's really cold, and mostly they're white, like Arctic foxes, but some are like a red fox.'

'It sounds like Mum's job,' Emma said, 'and we hate them now.'

'Oh, yeah,' Frankie said, 'Spatz. Well done, Ems.'

'There's a papillon,' Cat said. 'I met one at our picnic, the same day I met you. They're really small, smaller than Olaf, with a much pointier face, and big ears. The one I saw was called Paris. I'll see if I can introduce you to her.' She had asked Elsie about Captain after their picnic, and Elsie had shrugged him off as just a friend, but Cat had noticed the way the older woman became suddenly fidgety, pouring more tea and rearranging the sofa cushions.

'Should we get back to it?' Polly asked. She downed her squash and stood up, brushing dust off her shorts. 'That room's not going to clear itself.'

'Can we help?' Emma asked.

'As long as you're careful,' Frankie said. 'No carrying *anything* down the stairs, and if you don't know what something is, *ask me* before you pick it up. Understood?'

'Yes!' both girls squealed. Cat drained her drink and followed Olaf back up the stairs. She'd surprised herself by enjoying the clear-out so far, despite the heat and the dust, but she was still holding out for a secret stash of gold or a valuable antique vase. That way Frankie wouldn't even have to rent the room out, but could refurbish the whole house exactly as she pleased, give up the idea of having to find a new job, and spend all her time with her kids, watching them grow up.

'What I need now,' Polly said, as they dawdled up Primrose Terrace towards their own house, 'is a long hot shower and a huge glass of cold white wine.'

'Or pink wine.'

'Or pink fizzy wine.'

'Mmmmmm.'

'It makes a change from revision, though,' Polly added. 'I needed a break.'

It was still warm outside, the sky slowly turning the colour of peach juice, but compared to the stuffiness of Frankie's attic room it felt cool and delicious. Primrose Terrace was basking in its summer glory. The primroses had faded now, but the grass was a lush green, the windows of the elegantly curved houses reflecting the glowing, lowering sun.

'Would you have a spitz?' Cat asked. 'If you could have any dog?'

'I don't know, I haven't thought about it. I'd like a large dog, an Alsatian or a Weimaraner. God, I'd love a husky or a Saint Bernard, but I think you need to live on a farm to do them justice. They need so much space and I don't think our place quite cuts it. What about you?'

'I'd love any dog,' Cat said, 'except maybe a chihuahua.'

'You don't want a handbag dog?'

'I'm worried I'd lose it, under the bed or in the dishwasher. Also, I think I've had enough of dogs in handbags for the time being.'

169

Polly laughed. 'Fair point.' She unlocked the door to the sound of swearing, and Shed shot out between her legs, faster than Cat had ever seen him run, and then assumed a casual stroll as he made his way up the terrace.

'Joe?' Polly called. 'What's wrong?'

Joe was standing at the dining table, pressing his palm over his left forearm. A Budweiser bottle lay on its side, bubbly liquid seeping into pieces of paper that were fanned out on the table. 'Sodding bloody cat. He jumped up here and scratched the fuck out of me.'

'Let me see,' Polly said. At first he shrugged away, but Polly took hold of his arm and prised his hand away from the wound.

Cat peered over her shoulder. 'Ouch, that looks nasty.'

'It's quite deep, Joey. Have you washed it?'

Joe shook his head. Polly had assumed her authoritative tone, and Joe looked so crestfallen, his head cast down, that Cat wanted to reach out and ruffle his mess of blond hair.

'Come on then,' Polly said. 'It's going to sting, but you need to clean it out or it could get infected. You might even need a tetanus shot.'

'I don't think it's *that* bad.'

'You don't know what that cat's been scratching. Trees or carpets or—'

'Expensive leather handbags,' Cat chimed in.

'Don't start,' Joe said.

'Right. Rinse it under the hot tap – as hot as you can stand – and I'll go and get my kit.'

'You're going to clean it with animal medicine? Isn't that a bit twisted?'

'I have some straightforward antiseptic, Joey. Stop being so stubborn.' Polly disappeared upstairs and Cat started tidying the sodden papers on the table, seeing if any could be rescued. They were cartoons, rough pen sketches without colour or shading. Cat turned one round to see what it was.

The title *Curiosity Kitten* was scrawled across the top, a drawing beneath it of a cat with huge, Disney-esque eyes, peering round a door. There was no order to the sketches and they looked as though Joe was trying things out: the kitten peering in through a window, its back legs scrabbling to stay on a precarious pile of boxes; the kitten lifting the lid on a large pan, the inside of the pan visible for the reader's benefit, a piranha waiting to jump up; the kitten tiptoeing to a door, behind which was a pair of cats on a sofa, their tails entwined, a heart pulsing between them.

Had Joe already been contacted by the local newspaper? It looked more like a cartoon strip than any kind of logo. Was he working on this in secret, not wanting to tell anyone until it was confirmed? And what would happen to the kitten each time? Did he have a happy outcome, or, as the sketches suggested, was he destined for death or heartbreak? Maybe if Shed had scratched Joe earlier, Cat could imagine that the cartoons were a form of revenge, but there was no way Curiosity Kitten was modelled on the fat ginger cat. This kitten was undoubtedly cute.

The sketches were brilliant, and Cat could see that the idea had endless potential. From simple situations like pressing a large red button marked *Don't push*, to recreating film scenes – the kitten pulling back a bed-sheet, a horse's ear just visible. It was funny and adorable, it could be sad, or enchanting, or—

'What are you doing?' Joe asked close to her ear, and Cat jumped.

'I-I was tidying up. You've got beer—'

'Never mind.' He scooped the papers up. He had washed the scratches and they glistened, deep red, along his arm. 'I'll sort these out.'

'Joe, these are—'

'They're dumb,' he said, not looking at her.

'No! God, no, Joe, they're—'

'Going in the bin.' He stormed out of the room, taking the sketches with him. Cat slumped against the table. Maybe he wasn't as over Rosalin as Cat had believed. If he thought those cartoons were rubbish then he was either seriously deluded, or stuck so far in self-doubt it was unlikely he could ever be pulled out.

'Joe . . .' She hurried after him, determined not to let him sink into misery, and felt something crack under her shoe. She bent down and picked up a tiny silver Eiffel Tower. It was on a ring, as if meant to go on a bracelet or necklace, and it rang a familiar, tinkling bell in Cat's mind. She thought of Captain's small, terrified dog, and the little Eiffel Tower charm she had been wearing on her collar. How on earth had it got into their house?

11

Cat lay in bed that night, twisting beneath the covers, too hot to be under them, not prepared to relinquish them entirely, wondering how the papillon's collar charm could have found its way into her house. She hadn't seen Paris since the Pooches' and Puppies' Picnic, and Captain only briefly on her way back from the beach, and while she'd been to Elsie's house, she hadn't gone into the back garden. How could it have got there? Unless . . . she turned her pillow over and sank her forehead into it. She wouldn't be able to say anything until she was sure – it would be bad enough telling Joe if she had proof, let alone if it was just a theory.

In the morning, Polly appeared at the dining table with a huge stack of textbooks and gave Cat an apologetic smile.

'Studying?' Cat asked the obvious.

'I have to, Cat, I'm sorry. I want to help, but I've got tons of revision.'

'OK. Joe?'

Joe was almost non-existent in his quietness, and Cat

wondered if something had happened, beyond his cat attacking him and her discovering his sketches.

'What?' he asked.

'It's Saturday. We made a good start on Frankie's attic yesterday but there's still an Everest of boxes left, and that's only part of it. We have to sort through them, and chuck things out, and then we have to clean it and turn it into a new place. It needs to be the most desirable rental room in the whole of Fairview, and I thought, with your artistic eye, you might want to help?'

He shook his head. 'Not today, Cat.'

'You're not using your injury as an excuse, are you?' She smiled, but Joe didn't look up from his toast to see it. His arm had been expertly wrapped in a thin bandage by Polly, and Cat wondered if he'd wear it long enough to get a weird tan line on his arm.

'No, just trying to finish this commission.'

'Curiosity Kitten?'

'*No*, Cat, I told you that's rubbish, I—'

'OK, OK.' Cat held her hands up. 'I get it. Sorry. Right, it'll be me, Frankie and the girls then. See you later.' She was going to visit Frankie, but there was somewhere else she needed to go first.

Silver Street ran parallel to Primrose Terrace, but instead of counting the houses and trying to work out which one backed onto Elsie's, she had asked her neighbour for Captain's address. Silver Street was on a slightly smaller scale, and without the elegant curve the terrace had. But what they lacked in size, these houses made up for in postage-stamp front gardens. Captain's was a small square of neatly mown grass, framed by a border of busy Lizzies in pinks, purples and whites.

'Captain,' she said, when the old man opened the door dressed in a navy T-shirt and shorts that showed off thin, brown legs. 'How are you? Could I come in for a moment?'

He peered at her over his half-moon glasses, then nodded and stepped back, inviting her in. His house was full of light, with white walls and colourful paintings, as if it was a mini art gallery. Cat was drawn in by the numerous seascapes, calm waters with sunsets and moored yachts, tumultuous oceans, one that showed Fairview beach, with the lighthouse standing proudly on its cliff.

'Fancy a drink? Not got much in, but I can offer you instant coffee, or a glass of wine?'

It was half past ten. 'No thanks, Captain. I came to see how Paris was getting on. Is she still under the weather?'

He stopped in the kitchen. His eyes were wide with sadness, and he shook his head slightly. 'I'm not sure she's got long left. She's just gone into herself, like she can't bear to be around anyone – not even me. When she's not in the washing machine, she's hiding under the cushions.'

'Oh, no, oh, I'm so sorry. Are you sure?'

'I don't know what to do. The vet's had another look at her – with your pretty friend, I think – and he's assured me she's not ill.'

'Where is she? Can I see her?' Cat didn't want to say anything yet, not until she was sure.

Captain nodded and led the way to the front room.

At first Cat couldn't see the little dog anywhere, but then she found her, curled into a tiny ball in one corner of the sofa, half buried under a cushion. Cat crouched, reached forward and gently stroked Paris's head. She expected her to jump up in shock or run away, but she burrowed deeper into her corner, her whole body shaking.

'Oh.' Cat felt a lump form in her throat, but she lifted Paris up and held her small, warm body against her chest. 'Come on, Paris,' she said, 'come on, little one.' She kissed the silky fur. The dog snuggled into her, hiding her head against Cat's collarbone. Cat couldn't bear the thought of such a beautiful, gentle thing being so afraid. She ran her hand down Paris's back. 'Wasn't she wearing a collar?'

Captain nodded. 'It's broken. She's only been going out in the garden to do her . . . business, then running straight back in. But yesterday she came in without her collar.' He brought it over and Cat looked at the thin red fabric. It looked as though it had been torn in half, and the little loop where the tiny Eiffel Tower had hung was ripped. 'I think she must have caught it on a bit of branch, but since then she won't go out at all, not even to . . . I've had to set up a litter tray and –' he took a deep breath – 'I'm at my wits' end.'

'Captain,' Cat said, standing and gently placing Paris back on the sofa, 'I've got a theory, but I need to do a bit more work on it.'

'You think you might know what's wrong?'

'I might. I have to be sure, but – I'll hopefully know more in a few days. Can I come back?'

'You're welcome any time, lovely girl. You and your fella.'

Cat thought she'd leave it until their next meeting to set Captain right about that. After all, Joe might not be speaking to her next time, let alone be treating her kindly enough to be mistaken for her fella.

Over the next few days, the mood at number nine Primrose Terrace continued to be too morose for Cat's liking. It was a hot, beautiful summer and, while Cat knew Polly had exams to study for, and Joe was under pressure with work, neither of those things seemed to be good enough excuses to stay holed-up inside. Studying could be done in the park or on the table in their courtyard, and surely illustrations were better created in real, beautiful sunlight? But for once Cat could sense that this was not the moment to push either of them, and so she spent her time at number twelve, working systematically through the boxes, sometimes just with Frankie and Olaf, sometimes with Emma and Lizzie's upbeat, energizing help.

In between these forays into the darkness, Cat was busy with Pooch Promenade, getting as much time out in the sunshine as she spent hidden away. And Elsie's knee was almost fully healed, so while it meant losing her as a paying client, she often gained a walking friend.

Today, she and Elsie were taking Disco and Chalky, and the Barkers' two retrievers Alfie and Effie, on a long route up to the seafront. It was the first time Elsie had walked this far since her operation, and they were taking it slowly, enjoying the sea breeze whispering through the July afternoon's heat. Cat was wearing a floaty, burnt-orange dress that flickered around her knees, and had found a pair of gold gladiator sandals comfy enough to wear when she was dog walking.

Alfie and Effie were some of the strongest dogs Cat had met. They were gentle and friendly, but liked to make the most of being outside and use up their energy, and Cat was trying to slow them down, at least until they got into the park. Besides, she needed to look at something.

There was a tiny vintage boutique in a row of shops facing the sea. Cat had always thought it was a strange location, next to the fish-and-chip shop and the seaside-staples store (selling castle-shaped buckets and jelly shoes) but it occasionally had nice pieces of weatherworn furniture, and, as they had a tight budget to refurbish Frankie's attic room, she was keeping her eye out.

'What do you think of this?' Cat asked, pointing to a cabinet in the boutique's window. It was distressed wood, and painted a very pale yellow. Cat wouldn't mind having it in her bedroom back in the House of Doom. No, doom was a bit strong. House of Woe? House of . . . Misery? That conjured up all kinds of horror-film thoughts, and things definitely weren't *that* bad. Yet.

'Cat?' Elsie asked. 'Are you even listening to me?'

'Yes – of course.' She hadn't heard a word her friend had said.

'It's a lovely cabinet, but it's a hundred pounds. I thought Frankie needed to get the best deals possible? Argos would have one for a third of the price.'

'But Argos is so . . . unromantic.'

'This is a room for a lodger, yes?'

Cat nodded.

'Then you need it to be simple and smart. Let *them* stamp their own personality on the place. But most of all, let Frankie decide.'

'Are you coming, on Saturday?'

'To your refurbishing party?' Elsie leaned on the low wall at the edge of the beach, and Cat sat down, bringing the dogs to heel next to her. Disco stood on her hind legs, asking to be let up. She was almost as big as Chalky, and still bouncy, and not suited to flimsy dresses and bare knees, but Cat could never resist. She hauled her up and hugged her.

'I think I'll make an appearance,' Elsie said, 'though I might not be up for traipsing up and down those stairs all day. Who's coming?'

'Frankie and the girls, obviously, and Charles and Boris from the B&B want to cast their expert eye over it, which I hope means they'll help make the room really appealing, and maybe Mark.' Cat kept her voice light, but Elsie pounced on the name anyway.

'And how is Smug Mark?'

'He's . . . fine. A bit absent, if I'm honest, but he's coming back from London at the weekend, according to his latest text, so I hope he can help for a bit.'

'Absent?' Elsie asked, frowning. She was wearing a long, navy dress with a turquoise flower pattern, and her dangly green earrings sounded like miniature wind chimes in the breeze.

'He's quite elusive. I mean, when he's here and he's with me, it's –' Cat gave a little shudder – 'lovely. But that's not very often. And if things kick off with his film, it's likely to be even less.'

'You don't know that,' Elsie said. 'But why not ask him?' She put a hand on Cat's arm. 'Don't buy into his elusiveness, don't let him be vague. Ask him direct questions and make him tell you the answers. I haven't been in a relationship for a long time, but I do know that mystery is only attractive for so long.'

'I'm finding that out,' Cat said grimly. 'But you're right, I should just talk to him. Why is everyone so difficult to talk to at the moment? Apart from you, Elsie.' She covered the older woman's hand with her own, and Disco licked her arm.

'You mean Joe and Polly?'

Cat fed each of the dogs a treat and looked out at the sea. The tide was turning, the dark sand drying quickly as the waves receded and the sun continued to beat down. 'They're both so busy with studying and work. But I want them to come on Saturday. I'm treating this as a Primrose Terrace social event, and they're part of that, so . . .' She shrugged. 'Jessica's gone to sunnier climes for the next few weeks, though God knows why when we've got so much sun here, and the Westies are in luxury kennels somewhere outside Fairview, but other than that it should be a full house. *If* my housemates decide to crawl out from their respective holes.'

'Don't be too hard on them, Cat. Not everyone can get paid for strolling round in the sunshine.'

'I know, I just . . . It's *summer*. We should be lying on the grass staring up at the clouds, sunbathing on the beach, in beer gardens. Fairview is a holiday destination, and we're lucky enough to live here.'

'Have you said all that to them?'

'If I say more than three words in a row, they make angry shushing noises.'

'Well, then, make them come on Saturday.'

Cat laughed. 'As if it's that simple.'

'Come on, Cat, if anyone can find a way, then it's you.'

Disco scrabbled to get down, and Cat took Elsie's hand and pulled her to her feet. They made their way slowly back towards Fairview Park, Alfie and Effie eager to get to the large expanse of grass where they could run and play.

When she reached home, exhausted and hot, Cat sat on the front step and took out her mobile. Ignoring the slight shake of her hands, she scrolled through to Mark's number and hit the call button. She waited for his voicemail to kick in, and was caught off guard when he answered on the fifth ring.

'Hello?'

'Hi, Mark, it's me. Cat.'

'I know.' She could hear the amusement in his voice. 'Your name came up on the screen. Remind me to take a photo of you so I can see you next time. Better still, ring off and FaceTime me.'

'What? No, I – I was wondering if you wanted to come to a kind of clear-out refurbishment party that I'm organizing

180

at number twelve on Saturday? I mean, you don't have to, and you'll only just have got back, so—'

'I'd love to.'

'You would?' Cat leaned her head against the door frame.

'Well, I'm not sure I'd *love* to spend the day clearing out someone else's house, but there's nobody else I'd rather get sweaty with.'

How did he do it? How did he come up with these lines so quickly? Cat glanced behind her to check that nobody could have overheard. 'Right. OK, that's great. We're starting at eleven but come whenever you can.'

'It's in the diary.' He rang off and Cat stared at her phone, wondering once again how he could make her feel so wanted and so irrelevant at the same time.

Cat gathered together a boxful of wood and floor cleaners, window spray and dusters, cleaning cloths and a dustpan. She was sure Frankie would have all this, but too much was better than too little. She tied her hair back from her face with a blue spotty scarf, and tripped over Shed on her way to the front door.

'Move, Shed.' The cat wound himself around her legs. She wasn't sure she could prove her theory, but she was convinced Shed had something to do with Paris's unhappiness. Was he bullying her? She was such a tiny dog and Shed was so large. She knew he stalked through the back gardens, so was he waging a war of terror, like a pets' protection racket? How else would the charm have found its way into their house?

'Need some help with that?' Joe hurried down the stairs and took the box from her. He was wearing grey cargo shorts and a black T-shirt, and a look Cat hadn't seen for a while: he looked relaxed.

'I thought you weren't coming today.'

'I changed my mind. You've spent weeks helping Frankie, and I decided it was time I pitched in. If you'll still have me?'

Cat smiled. 'As long as you're sure you can cope with pure daylight? I don't want to have to clean up your vampire ash with my dustpan.'

'Ha ha. Need anything else?'

'Just my box of chemicals. Polly's doing a shift at the vet's this morning and said she'd try to come later on.'

Joe led the way down Primrose Terrace, and they found Emma standing at the doorway like a tiny soldier on sentry duty.

'Who are you?' she asked.

'I'm Joe. I met you a while back, in the park.'

'Are you coming to help with the money-spinner?'

Joe and Cat both laughed. 'Is that what Frankie's calling it?'

Emma nodded. 'She says it's going to solve all our problems, and that we'll have a new friend too, to play with us and with Olaf.'

'OK.' Cat felt her stomach constrict. What if, after all this work, nobody wanted to rent the room out? Or they did, but they didn't get along with the family, brought strange people back or turned out to be a domestic nightmare? She'd told Frankie she'd help her, but what if this caused more problems instead? She hadn't realized quite how high their expectations were.

'Hey,' Joe said quietly. 'What's up?' He put the box down and turned Cat round by the shoulders so she was facing him.

'Nothing.'

'I don't believe you. I know your worried face.'

Cat met his gaze and saw genuine concern in his eyes. She felt a sudden, unexpected urge to fold herself against him, to let him wrap his arms tightly around her. It came from nowhere, and she brushed it quickly away. 'I just – I hope this works. For Frankie and the girls.'

'Of course it will,' he said. 'You've worked too hard for it not to.'

'*I* haven't done much, it's been them.' She gestured to the kitchen, where Lizzie and Frankie were making tall glasses of cold squash and putting biscuits onto a plate.

'They wouldn't be doing it if it wasn't for you.' He reached up and ran his finger gently down the side of her face, from her forehead to her chin, as if he was drawing her outline. Cat froze, her breath stalling somewhere above her lungs.

They stared at each other for a moment, then Joe dropped his hand and patted the pocket of his shorts. 'Drink?' he asked and, before Cat could respond, went to greet Frankie. Cat pressed her palm against her cheek. It was hot in Frankie's living room, the sun streaming in great swathes through the window.

'Hello?' a familiar voice called. 'Anyone in here?' Boris stepped into the living room, ducking his head as if he expected to be too tall for every doorway.

'Hi, Boris!' Cat gave him a quick hug.

His partner Charles followed him in. He was shorter and darker than Boris, with skittish eyes that didn't rest anywhere for very long, and seemed to Cat incredibly shy. They were both dressed in outfits Cat thought were too fashionable to go to the pub in, let alone for lugging furniture about. Olaf barked, jumped out of his basket and raced up to Charles and the two French bulldogs on leads at his feet.

'We brought Bossy and Dylan, I hope you don't mind?'

'Course not,' Frankie called. 'The more the merrier.'

The dogs greeted each other enthusiastically, and Cat crouched, saying hello to the two Frenchies. One was black and one fawn, and both seemed mildly interested by her, but were in no way as exuberant as Olaf or the Westies. Maybe Boris and Charles had trained them to be aloof: fashion-show Frenchies. She made them both feel welcome, then stood.

Joe was leaning against the wall, his hand in his pocket, looking at her.

'Sorry, Joe, I didn't think. Are you—'

He waved her away. 'It's fine. I've pretty much come to accept that wherever you are, dogs won't be too far away.'

She squeezed his arm. 'I think that—'

'Right, guys,' Frankie said. 'Thank you all so much for coming, and thanks to Cat for organizing this weird room-sorting fun day. I really appreciate it.' Cat grinned.

Frankie was looking more alive than Cat had ever seen her. Dressed in a 100% Organic T-shirt and cut-off jeans, her long auburn hair tied back from her face, her freckles making her look even younger than she was, she was exuding energy and – Cat thought – hope. Cat crossed her fingers behind her back.

Frankie took Boris and Charles out to the tiny utility area, where she'd been storing the bits of furniture they'd accumulated. Rather than listen to Elsie and abandon the vintage cabinet for a soulless Argos model, Cat had done a deal with the shop owner and got it for a reduced price and a part-exchange with some of Frankie's old, but surprisingly valuable, candle holders. There was also a bedside table, a pretty upright lamp and an oval mirror that they'd discovered in the attic and decided could be rescued with a little bit of care and attention. The bed and canvas wardrobe – from a discount furniture store – were due to be delivered at some point during the morning.

'What are we doing?' Joe asked.

Cat pointed at the box. 'Cleaning. Any other takers?'

Emma put her hand up. Cat held out a duster, but Emma shook her head and, taking the handheld hoover, led the way up to the attic.

It didn't take long for Cat and Olaf to fall in love with Frankie's dust-buster. The spaniel chased the hoover, barking constantly, sneezing when the dust whirled in spirals around him. Emma, Cat and even Joe spent the first half an hour laughing at the dog's antics and not getting much done at all. But once the wooden floor was dust free they started on the floor polish, opening the window as the synthetic pine scent filled the room.

'Emma, do you want to take Olaf downstairs for a bit? You could help the others with the furniture.'

'Why?' Emma asked. 'Do you want to do kissy things in private?'

Cat felt her cheeks flush and Joe turned away, coughing into the wall. 'No, not at all. Joe and I, we're not— I'm just worried the chemicals are a bit overpowering.'

Emma shrugged, gave each of them a look that was far too perceptive for a four-year-old, called to Olaf and went traipsing down the stairs.

The silence she left them with was as stifling as the air, and Cat started polishing, working in small circles, focusing all her energy on getting out the marks left by furniture and boxes, stains that had built up over the years.

'How's your work going?' she asked eventually. Joe was in the opposite corner and didn't look up.

'Good, thanks. Busy, which I should be grateful for, but it can get wearing when it's full-on for so long.'

'Do you give yourself holidays?'

'Not really. When Alex— When there were two of us, one of us would go and the other would stay. Now it's just me, I haven't thought about it.'

'You need some proper time off.'

'I bet you haven't had any since you started your dog thing.'

'My *dog thing*?'

'You know.'

'Pooch Promenade.'

'That's the one.' He gave her one of his rare grins. It dimpled his cheeks and made him look carefree, as if he didn't have work pressures or the remains of a broken heart. It was hot in the room and his cheeks were pink, sweat darkening the hair at his temples. Cat found herself unable to reply and felt suddenly ridiculous, kneeling and scrubbing away at the floor. She stood up, intending to go and get another drink – anything – but footsteps on the stairs stopped her and Polly appeared in the doorway.

'I'm here,' she said, panting. 'And look who I've found.'

She stepped into the room and Mark followed her, dressed casually in a dark-green T-shirt and faded navy shorts, his sunglasses on his head. He raised a hand in greeting and Cat wondered whether she should hug him or shake his hand, but he leaned forward and kissed her on the cheek.

'I hope I've not missed too much,' he said.

'Oh, no,' Joe replied. 'There's plenty of cleaning left to do.'

'Do you two know each other?' Cat asked.

'I don't think so.'

Joe stood up, wiped his hands on his shorts and shook Mark's hand. The room felt tiny with the four of them in it. 'I'm Joe, Cat's housemate, Polly's brother. You're Mark?'

'I am. Heard lots about me?' Mark grinned.

'A few bits and pieces,' Joe admitted. 'Nice to finally put a face to the name. What was it you called him, Cat?'

'Tell us what we can do,' Polly said quickly, clapping her hands. 'Come on, before we all succumb to the heat.'

'Right, OK.' Cat flashed her friend her best grateful grin and put them all to work.

The tension slowly disintegrated and, while there was a bit of one-upmanship between Joe and Mark that had Cat and Polly rolling their eyes at each other, Cat started to have fun. The floor began to gleam, the walls were wiped clean of years'-old grime, and the window was soon glistening, proudly displaying a view of perfect blue sky.

Frankie called them down for sandwiches, and they found Elsie in the kitchen making cups of tea and coffee. Cat and the others flopped gratefully onto sofas and cushions that Frankie had laid out on the floor, and Boris and Charles gave them a furniture fashion show.

The vintage cabinet and the bedside table were now a beautiful dusky blue, their handles and knobs silver, and looked as though they had been made to go together. The lamp stand and mirror frame were also matt silver, and all had baked dry in the tiny courtyard, so they could go straight into the room when it was ready.

'And the finishing touch.' Frankie pulled a rug out of a giant carrier bag. It was the same dusky blue as the furniture, with swirls of white and purple. It was bold, but Cat knew it would work perfectly with the wooden floor, white walls and simple furniture. 'Ta-da!'

'Wow. Where did you get that?'

'We found it,' Charles said. 'We went shopping for a few bits for the guest house, we saw this and then found some paint to match. Frankie's given us carte blanche.'

'As if I wouldn't,' Frankie said. 'This room's going to look the tops. I might set you to work on the rest of the house after this.'

'Oh, no, it was nothing.' Boris waved her away, but Cat could see that he was pleased. She suddenly realized that, despite all the people in the room, it seemed far too quiet.

'Where are the dogs?' She sat up, panicked.

Frankie grinned and pointed to Olaf's basket.

Cat clapped her hand over her mouth. Olaf and Disco were in the basket, snuffling gently, using each other as pillows. Chalky and the Frenchies were lying in a row next to the basket, all snoozing, an ear twitching occasionally.

'What did you do?'

Charles shrugged. 'They overexcited themselves. It's fairly adorable.'

'It's the loveliest thing ever.' Cat knelt in front of them and took a photo on her iPhone. She imagined her own dog snuggled alongside the rest. A Cairn terrier or a Jack Russell, something small and affectionate. One day, she thought, sighing to herself as she watched them sleep.

'Should we get back to work?' Joe said, finishing his tea. 'There's a lot left to do.'

Frankie nodded. 'But let me do some of the cleaning this afternoon. I feel like I haven't got my hands dirty.'

'How about you and I put the bed together,' Elsie said to her, peering out of the window.

'Is it here?' Lizzie squealed.

'I think so, my love, unless someone else on Primrose Terrace has ordered the whole of the furniture store.' Elsie shook her head. 'Do they really need a lorry that big for one flat-packed bed and a canvas wardrobe?'

They watched from the window as a huge articulated lorry tried to reverse down the terrace, lights flashing, beeping, manoeuvring jerkily past the parked cars.

'Oh my God,' Boris said, 'it's going to be a catastrophe.'

'Maybe he needs someone to talk him in?' Mark hurried outside, careful to shut the front door so that no dogs ended up near the wheels, and tried to gesture and shout the lorry into a good position. It made Cat feel hot just watching it. She flapped her purple vest top, trying to get air to circulate around her body, and rearranged her spotty bandana. Sweat was running in rivulets between her shoulder blades, and she could feel the grime beneath her fingernails. She caught Joe's eye and he looked quickly away. Cat frowned, realized she was too tired to think about anything other than floor polish and furniture, and went upstairs to give the window a final clean.

'Mum says it's time for ice cream!' Lizzie shouted, running down the stairs. Cat looked up from where she was sitting on the living-room floor, surrounded by dogs, typing an advert they could put on websites and in the local paper. Once the room was finished, she would take some photos to go with it. Boris and Charles, their interior designing well received, had gone back to see to their guests, and Polly was making tea for the reduced party.

Elsie, Frankie, Joe and Mark were putting the furniture together, and Cat felt grateful that she could be elsewhere. It was half past five, they had worked all day, and if they didn't find someone to take Frankie's spare room after all their effort then Cat would eat her bandana.

'Ice cream's a great idea,' Polly said.

'And the dogs could do with a run-around,' Cat added.

'We're going to the ice cream parlour,' Lizzie said, 'because they do the best ice creams. Elsie said so.'

Cat glanced at Polly, but her expression was blank. 'Do you know what, lovely Lizzie, why don't you take Polly with you? I've got to finish off the advert, or all our hard work will be for nothing.'

'OK,' Lizzie said brightly.

'Oh no, it's fine,' Polly said, 'I'm happy to stay.' But Lizzie grabbed her by the arm and started putting the leads on the dogs. Cat smiled into the laptop and kept quiet, waving them goodbye as they left.

Without the dogs or the girls, and with Henry asleep in his cot upstairs, the living room was unusually quiet, save for the sound of Cat tapping on the laptop keys, and voices, laughter and banging drifting down from the top floor. Cat reworked the advert, more to keep her mind off other things than because it needed it, and didn't notice Mark until he was crouching in front of her, lifting her chin to kiss her.

'I missed you,' he said. 'I thought about you all the time.'

'Me too,' she said, but she didn't sound convincing, mainly because she wasn't sure she believed him. If he'd really missed her, wouldn't they have been on the phone to each other every night instead of one quick call and a few flirty texts? She was attracted to him, but she still knew hardly anything about him. As Elsie had said, his mysteriousness was becoming less attractive.

He kissed her again, more passionately this time, as if he'd read her thoughts and wanted to prove her wrong.

She kissed him back, and told herself it didn't matter, that whatever was destined to happen, would happen. Mark broke away and kissed her below the ear. 'We need to do something about this,' he murmured.

'What?' Cat asked, running her fingers up his neck and into his thick hair.

'This, between us.'

'I thought you were going to take me out to dinner?'

He sat back and looked at her, his easy grin firmly in place. 'I was, wasn't I?'

She nodded.

'Let's do it then. Next week.'

'Next week as in next week, or as in three months' time?'

'Cat—' Mark frowned, but the front door banged open and the girls spilled inside, empty-handed.

'No ice cream?' Cat called.

'Look who we found!' Emma shouted, and Cat watched as Polly followed them in, and then Rummy, his ears and tail alert, and then Owen, carrying a large cool box. He closed the door with his bum, gave Cat a wide grin and nodded a greeting.

'It's Gooey-eyes!' Lizzie added, clapping her hands together. 'We've got *so much* ice cream.'

The room was finished and Cat wondered if Polly and Joe would be cross if, after all this, *she* moved into number twelve – then at least Joe could watch *Blade Runner* in peace next time. It looked spectacular, and not just because she was experiencing a huge sugar rush from Owen's ice cream.

'That,' Owen said, peering in over Polly's shoulder, 'is one groovy bedroom. You really expect me to believe it was full of boxes a few weeks ago? It's better than the Meridian Hotel on the seafront.'

'Can I quote you in my advert?' Cat asked. 'Local business owner says . . . Maybe you could come round to ours on your way home and we could finish writing it. What do you think, Pol?'

'I think, I . . .' She gave Cat a sideways glance, a sideways *Don't*. 'I need to study.'

Cat bit her lip.

'Not tonight, though, Sis,' Joe said, 'not after all this hard work. We should all celebrate with a night off.'

'Ice creams were our celebration,' Frankie said, one arm around each of her daughters. 'I need to get these guys bathed and to bed.' Emma's eyes were struggling to stay open, and Lizzie had a dreamy smile on her face, along with smudges of dirt and, possibly, ice cream. 'And now I've got Henry down, I don't want to risk waking him.'

Cat took a final look at the beautiful bedroom, with its clean lines and thick, swirly rug – so different from the box-cave they'd started with a few weeks ago – and pulled the door closed.

As they spilled out into a perfect summer evening, Cat hovered on the doorstep. 'It seems a shame not to come to your own celebration.'

Frankie shook her head. 'Don't be silly – you've worked harder than anyone. Thanks so much, Cat. I don't know what I would have done without this. I know it's not done yet, I know I need a lodger and a new job and . . .' She ran her hands over her hair, shrugging slightly. 'It would be so much worse if I didn't have this. It's like a beacon of hope at the top of our pink house – like the light on the lighthouse.'

Cat rubbed her arm. 'I didn't do a lot. I shoved an idea at you and you didn't close the door in my face.'

'And I've thought of what I can do for you in return.'

'Oh?'

'Do you play guitar?'

Cat shook her head. 'Nope. I don't think I have a musical bone in my body. I did drama at uni and they wouldn't give me a part in any of the musical productions.'

'Let me prove you wrong.'

'I don't know,' Cat said. 'I might be a lost cause.'

'I'm sorry,' Owen said, bouncing up to the top step. 'Did you say you were looking for a job?'

Frankie nodded slowly, narrowing her eyes. 'Yeah, but—'

'What kind of thing?'

'I worked at Spatz, but I didn't really fit in there. With Henry and the girls, I need to be able to drop everything at a moment's notice, and they weren't flexible. I know it's not ideal, but I can't compromise for my kids.'

Owen waved her words away. 'Spatz in town, the restaurant?'

'Yeah. Why are you being so cryptic?'

'I'm not, I'm not,' Owen said, holding his hands up. 'It's just we're short-staffed at the ice cream parlour, and I don't know if you fancy—'

'Yes,' Frankie rushed, and Cat had to stifle her laugh. 'Sorry to be blunt, but yeah, that would be great. Even a few hours a week would make a huge difference.'

'Wow, that was easy.' Owen grinned and shook Frankie's hand.

Cat looked at Frankie's beaming face, then Owen's endlessly cheerful one, and resisted the urge to jump up and down and cheer. Instead she skipped down the steps and flung her arms around Polly. 'Owen's given Frankie a job,' she whispered.

'What?'

'Don't be jealous, you're going to be an animal nurse. But it must be hard knowing that Frankie will be working with Owen *and* ice cream.'

They watched as Frankie gave them a final wave. 'Let's sort out a date for your first lesson,' she called, before she closed the door.

'Lesson?' Polly frowned. Cat shrugged her question away, and Owen joined them on the road, his cool box now empty, Rummy and Disco chasing each other's tails on the pavement.

'So where's this celebration? If I'm welcome, of course. I have hijacked this party a bit.' He rubbed the back of his neck, his black curls bouncing.

Cat asked Polly a silent question and her friend gave an almost imperceptible smile. 'It's at ours,' Cat said.

'And can Rummy come? I mean, you're a dog walker so I assume so, but—'

'Oh. No, actually, maybe we need to—'

'It's OK,' Joe said.

'Seriously?' Cat hadn't meant to squeal quite so loudly.

Joe rolled his eyes. 'Don't make a big deal of it. Let me see if Shed's at home, and then . . .' He pointed up the road and started walking.

Elsie looped her arm through Cat's, and Mark fell into step on her other side. 'I have to head off,' Mark said. 'Chips is at home, and I promised Jessica I'd update her on my screenplay and all the trials and tribulations of London.'

'Is she back?' Cat asked lightly, trying to ignore the churning in her stomach. He was choosing Jessica over an evening with her and her friends.

'She got back last night,' Mark said. 'But she's not getting the Westies from the dog hotel until tomorrow, so . . .'

So they'd have a dog-free night. Just the two of them, in Jessica's beautiful back garden, on a sultry summer evening . . .

'Sure. But if you don't book somewhere for us to go for dinner then I'm going to have to do it myself.' She grinned, hoping her insecurity wasn't showing.

'I'll do it,' he said, and then whispered in her ear, 'but I do like it when a woman takes charge.'

'Is that why you've been so hopeless at organizing it?'

He laughed and kissed her on the lips, causing her to trip over a loose paving stone and pull Elsie off balance.

'Good grief,' the older woman said. 'This is not something I need to be a part of.' They'd reached number ten, and while Elsie said goodbye to Owen and Polly, Mark moved Cat aside, kissing her again, his hands tight round her waist.

'I'm sorry I can't come back,' he murmured. 'Next time.'

'Jessica's not the only one who wants to hear about your film, you know. I *am* interested, even if I'm not a part of the celebrity inner circle.' As soon as she said it she realized she sounded petty, but Mark grabbed her hand, squeezed it and kissed the side of her mouth.

'I'll book somewhere *really* special, and I'll tell you all about it.'

'I'll go grey waiting!' she called after him, and heard him laugh as he strolled up Primrose Terrace.

'I'm pooped too,' Elsie said, 'so we're going in.'

Cat bent to say goodbye to Disco and Chalky, pressing her nose against their sun-warmed fur.

'Are you OK?' Elsie asked.

Cat heard the weight in her friend's tone, and wasn't sure she could look at her. She nodded.

'Don't let him string you along, Cat. I know he's tempting, with his good looks, his glamorous job and his charm, but remember when you first met him, you were worried he'd break Jessica's heart. Give yourself that same level of care and attention. I'll always be here, and you've got Polly and Joe too, if anything goes wrong. But best not to let your heart get broken in the first place. That sounds terribly risk-averse, but . . . some people are worth it, and some are just passing ships.'

'I know,' Cat said, 'and I'm not taking it too seriously. We're just seeing where things go at the moment.'

'Well, make sure that place *isn't* down the garden path.'

'I'd pretty much be happy with anywhere beyond our front doorsteps, to be honest.'

'Tush. Now – go and celebrate. You've earned it after all that hard work.'

Cat leaned against the door frame and peered into the living room. She could hear Polly and Owen chatting in the kitchen, and Joe was pouring crisps into a bowl on the coffee table. Rummy was at his feet, his square face angled up expectantly.

'These aren't for you,' Joe said, sitting down and rubbing the dog's ears. 'And don't get any ideas about laps, because if my cat catches you, you'll be done for. Not *Cat* Cat, short brown hair, great smile – not her. She's not mine, and she'd take you to her room if she could – no, that sounds wrong.' He frowned and rubbed his eyes.

Cat was transfixed, watching him talk to the dog as if he owned him. She didn't want to interrupt, and she wanted him to say again that she had a great smile, simply so she could believe he'd actually spoken the words.

'I'm talking about my cat Shed,' Joe continued. 'Ginger, grumpy, not the most affable pet, not cute like the *other* Cat. I only got Shed because—'

'Is white OK? It's been in the fridge.' Owen and Polly brought the bottle and four glasses into the room, and Joe sat back, his hand dangling over the edge of the sofa. Rummy settled at his feet, and Polly gave her brother a quick smile and ruffled his hair. 'All right?' she asked.

Joe nodded, and Cat's confusion grew. She remembered Polly's words at the picnic, that it wasn't as simple as Joe just disliking dogs.

'Where's Cat?' Owen asked.

'Probably gone to shower and change,' Polly said. 'She was particularly grubby.'

Cat glanced down, saw that her vest top and shorts were smeared with grime, and that her fingers were black, and thought she should probably meet her friend's expectations. She tiptoed silently up the stairs and spent too long in the shower.

In a blue fifties-style dress with black polka dots, and with her short hair still damp, Cat felt like a new person. She was also famished. The living room was empty and the windows were wide open, letting in fresh air and the smell of grilling meat.

'Oh God,' she said, 'do we need to track down that barbecue?'

'That's a good idea,' Joe called from the kitchen. 'Why don't you start with our back garden?'

Cat gawped. 'We have a barbecue? How has it taken this long for us to use it? It's not been a wet summer.' Cat slipped past Joe and stood on the back doorstep. A silver gas barbecue was open, sausages and chicken kebabs smouldering on top. Rummy lay close by, raising his head roughly every five seconds to sniff the air, much as Cat was doing.

'Because I've been too busy revising and Joe's essentially lazy and couldn't be bothered to dig it out of the shed.' Polly and Owen were sitting at the patio table, their heads close together.

'I have now, though, haven't I?' Joe handed Cat a glass of wine. He was wielding a pair of tongs and Cat thought he looked incredibly sexy, but probably only because she was so hungry.

Cat turned to admire the barbecue instead of Joe, and took a long swig of wine. 'This is better than all the treasure in Frankie's loft. It's perfect, thank you.' Contentment washed over her like a wave. She felt she belonged here, in this tiny courtyard with her best friend, and with Joe, and Owen – who she was confident she'd have the opportunity to get to know better.

She'd helped Frankie out – she was sure they would find someone for the room – and she had enough dogs to walk to

198

keep her afloat, but with room for more. Mark *was* going to take her out to dinner, and if he didn't then she'd take him. At that moment, she felt as though there wasn't much she'd want to change.

'Earth to Cat,' Joe said. 'You OK? You're miles away.'

'I'm OK,' she nodded. 'I'm more than OK. I'm . . .' She tried to think of a way to put all her thoughts into a single sentence, and found she couldn't. She stepped forward and wrapped her arms around him, resting her head on his shoulder. She felt him go still. Maybe her earlier, irrational thought hadn't been so irrational after all. 'I've been wanting to do that all day,' she said before she could stop herself.

'Why?' he asked quietly.

She looked up at him. 'Because you've helped me so much. Renting out the attic was your idea really? So was the Pooches' Picnic, and you've put up with me. With my ideas and my interruptions and my . . . my dogs. You've been a good friend, Joe.'

He inhaled and smiled down at her. 'Yeah, well, you're not so bad most of the time. You've certainly made things less boring.'

Cat laughed. 'I'll take that as a compliment.'

'It's the only one you're going to get. The sausages are about to burn.' He tapped her on the shoulder and she released him, thinking that he'd been much more complimentary when he thought she wasn't listening.

'Is Rummy allowed sausages?' Joe asked.

Owen frowned and looked at Rummy. The dog came to stand in front of his owner. 'Go on then,' he said. 'Just one, though. I don't want to spoil his diet.'

'Says the man who runs an ice cream parlour,' Polly laughed.

'Ice cream brings sunshine into everyone's life.' Owen raised his hands up to the sky.

'I agree,' Cat said, lifting her glass. A loud screech broke through the evening quiet and Shed raced along the back wall, jumped into the courtyard and, without even stopping to smell the grilling meat, disappeared inside the house.

'What was that about?' Owen asked.

'Oh, he's just doing catty things,' Joe said, waving his hand.

Cat closed her eyes. She couldn't keep putting it off. 'About that,' she said. 'I think Shed might have been terrorizing one of the local dogs.' She held her breath, waiting for his earlier warmth to drain out of him. She wasn't sure she could cope with his disapproval right now, not on such a perfect evening.

'What are you talking about?' His expression was more curious than annoyed, and Cat ran inside and returned with her one bit of evidence – the Eiffel Tower charm.

It was after midnight when they finally peeled their bums off the plastic seats and went inside. The dusk and the temperature had fallen so gradually that they'd barely noticed until the outdoor light had dimmed and finally sparked out, swallowing them in darkness.

'Bedtime, then?' Polly stood and stretched.

'If the night wills it, then it must be so,' Owen intoned, his voice low and dramatic. 'Besides, it's way past Rummy's bedtime.'

'Not yours, though?' Polly asked.

Cat fumbled for the glasses on the table, and Joe put his hand on her arm. 'Leave them out here until tomorrow. They won't come to any harm overnight.'

'What about Shed?'

'He can see better than we can in the dark. He'll avoid them.'

'You sure you don't mind, about Paris?'

200

'Of course I mind,' he said, pausing at the back door to let her in first. 'I mind that my cat's been beating up some poor little dog. But do I mind that you told me? No. I'm glad you did.'

'I know there are things we can do to stop him going in Captain's garden.'

'Tiger poo or something,' Owen said. 'My mum used to hate the cats doing their business in her veggie plot, so to stop the small cat poo she got large cat poo from the garden centre. They're scared of it, I think.'

'I'll check it out. Thanks, Owen. It's been lovely to meet you properly. I'm glad you could come tonight.'

'Me too, and I'll – uh . . .' He turned to Polly and held his arms out in a comical but, Cat thought, nervous gesture. 'I'll see you soon?'

Polly grinned and kissed him on the cheek. They were about the same height, only Owen's curls making him seem taller, and Cat thought that their babies would have blindingly blue eyes, like something out of a sci-fi film.

'Yes, you will.' Polly walked him to the door.

Cat put her hand on Joe's chest, stopping him. 'Give them a moment.'

Joe rolled his eyes. 'Isn't it bedtime?'

'Let them say goodnight.'

He nodded. He looked tired, his eyes crinkled at the edges. 'Cat?'

'Yes?' She swallowed.

'When you go and see Captain, will you let me come too? I'd like to apologize.'

Cat exhaled and smiled up at him. 'Of course. That would be great.' The front door closed and Polly leaned against it, her eyes closed. 'Night, Joe,' Cat said.

'Goodnight.'

'Is Captain even going to let us in with these?' Joe held up the boxes of Silent Roar and waggled them at Cat. They had a photo of a male lion on the front and looked, Cat had to admit, like some kind of practical joke.

'The guy in the shop said it works, and he's a huge nature lover, has the whole of Fairview's blue tit population in his garden regularly. Captain doesn't want Paris to be upset, so I'm sure he'll try anything.'

'All right then, but you lead the way.'

Captain welcomed them, gave Joe a cheery handshake and ushered them into the living room, then disappeared into the kitchen to make them all a cup of tea. Cat ran her sweaty palms down her skirt, hoping he would forgive them when he found out they owned the cat that was frightening his dog.

She sat on the sofa next to the curled-up furry bundle. She reached her hand out, but Paris lifted her head and barked, then jumped up and sat on Cat's knee, yelping excitedly.

Joe fixed her with his blue stare. '*This* is your depressed dog? Cat, seriously, what's going on?'

Cat gawped at Joe. 'I have no idea,' she said, just as Captain came in with three full cups, slopping tea over the side as he put them on the table.

'This is a turn-up, isn't it?' he chuckled, pointing at Paris.

'It's amazing. She seems like a different dog. We came to help, but . . .' Cat was lost for words.

Captain leaned forward, his elbows on his knees, his expression conspiratorial. 'I caught the blighter. In the act, as it were.'

'The blighter?' Cat moved the boxes of Silent Roar behind her on the sofa. Out of the corner of her eye, she saw Joe trying to keep a straight face.

'A *cat*! A giant, ferocious cat has been terrorizing my Paris, and lots of other pets too, I wouldn't wonder.'

Cat closed her eyes. 'Captain, we're really sorry but—'

'He was more like a panther than a cat. Nearly as big, black silky fur, yellow eyes.'

'A *black* cat?'

'Yes. Why, love? You look put out by something. Is the tea not nice? I checked that the milk wasn't lumpy.'

'No, it's not that, it's – we thought that – I mean . . .'

'What Cat's trying to say, Captain, is that we thought it was my cat upsetting your dog. I have a cat, you see, he's large and ginger and not always the best tempered, and . . .'

'We found this in our house.' Cat took the charm out of her bag and held it out to Captain. She'd also bought Paris a new collar, this time in a beautiful royal blue.

He put them on the table. 'Thank you for finding it, and for the lovely new collar. Very generous. It's a wonderful city, Paris.' He was lost in thought, and Joe frowned at Cat. She shrugged. 'Ginger cat, you say?' Captain asked eventually.

'Yes,' Joe said. 'He's quite a bruiser.'

'He's a pussy, in both senses of the word.'

'Excuse me?'

'I've seen him trotting round the walls, perfectly happily,' Captain said. 'And I've seen the two of them, him and the panther. Your cat, I'm sorry to say, doesn't stand a chance. He runs away caterwauling, ears flat back, the whole nine yards.'

Joe leaned back and folded his arms. 'Hang on a moment . . .'

'How did the charm end up in our house?' Cat asked.

Captain shrugged. 'I reckon it was the panther pulled off my Paris's collar. Your cat could have got it stuck on his claw, or the panther could have had a fight with him. Beats me, but it's not your cat caused my Paris to suffer, that's for sure.'

'And she's so much better,' Cat said. The little dog was trotting backwards and forwards on the sofa, sniffing the air.

Captain chuckled and rubbed his hands together.

'We brought you lion poo –' Cat held out the boxes – 'to stop the cats coming into your garden.'

'Lion poo's all very well, and thank you for your kindness, but I can guarantee that panther won't be coming back. I shot it.'

'You *killed* him?' Joe said, aghast.

Captain's chuckle turned to laughter. 'Good God, girl, your fella may be well behaved, but he's not got much grip on reality, has he? First thinking my Paris was scared of spiders, and now this. No, of course I didn't kill him. I've got something much better.' He pushed himself up and left the room.

Joe rolled his eyes, exasperated, and Cat resisted the urge to laugh.

'No,' Captain said. 'No need for lion poo or killing the blighter when you've got this.' He brandished a huge, luminous green water gun with a pink trigger. Cat remembered having one when she was little, and, after everything else, the thought of Captain standing at his back door in his half-moon glasses with the Super Soaker, picking cats off the back wall, was too much for her to bear. She collapsed into heaps of laughter on the sofa and Paris started barking, her long ears pricked up, ready for anything.

Cat and Polly took Jessica's Westies and Olaf to the park that evening. The sun was descending towards the trees and a blackbird was singing in the still air. Valentino, Coco and Dior seemed delighted to see Cat, and the feeling was mutual. She'd missed them, and as nice a kennel as they'd stayed in, she was sure they preferred being back at home with Jessica and having the park to run around in.

Cat recounted her and Joe's visit to Captain's, and Polly laughed nearly as much as Cat had done at the image of the old man with a Super Soaker.

'You figured it out together,' Polly said, 'and another Fairview resident and his dog are happy.'

Cat grinned and bent to let the Westies off their leads. Olaf barked and danced in circles, and Cat also released him, watching with relief as he stayed close to the others, running along the treeline. 'It's turned into a lovely summer,' Cat said, keeping a close eye on the dogs. 'And I can't imagine anywhere I'd rather spend it. How's Owen?'

Polly shrugged. 'I've not spoken to him since our barbecue.'

'But you will?'

'Once the exams are out of the way.'

'Pol—'

'Don't, Cat. I need to focus on them. I can't let anything distract me, especially not now they're so close.'

'But you got on so well with him.'

Polly gave her a quick smile. 'I did. But he knows I'm studying, and . . . I'll see what happens when I'm free. Free!' She lifted her hands up and raised her face to the sky. 'I can't wait.'

'Me neither.' She grabbed Polly's hand. 'We can celebrate for at least a month.'

'Oh.' Polly spun to face her. 'Did I tell you that Leyla at work is interested in Frankie's room? I mentioned it and she said she's been looking for somewhere for ages. I've passed on Frankie's details.'

'That's amazing news, Frankie will be thrilled!' Cat and Polly fist-bumped, and Cat skipped up the path after the dogs. She'd not met Leyla, but Polly had mentioned her before, and Cat couldn't imagine that someone who dedicated her life to looking after animals could be anything but wonderful – she just had to look at her best friend to see that. She called the dogs back and waggled her bag of treats, handing the leads to Polly when her phone rang.

'Hello?'

'Next Wednesday, seven o'clock, I'll pick you up.'

Cat grinned. 'Where are you taking me?'

'You'll just have to wait and see,' Mark said. 'But I hope it'll make up for taking so long to get my arse in gear. Although –' Cat could hear the smile in his voice – 'the best things are always worth waiting for.'

'Are you trying to convince me that *you're* the best thing?'

'You'll have to wait and see about that, too.'

Cat put her hand against her cheek. 'So much to look forward to,' she cooed.

'You'd better believe it.' She heard the click as he hung up, and put her phone in her pocket.

'Who was that?' Polly had the dogs back on their leads, and they were looking up at Cat's bag of treats. 'Oh, don't tell me, I can see from your grin. Has he finally decided to take you out, then?'

'He has.' Cat bent to stroke the pets and give them all a treat. 'Aren't you good? Especially you, Olaf. Lizzie and Emma will be very proud of you for coming back when we called.'

'Details? Oh, no, don't tell me,' Polly said again, 'there aren't any. Well, I'm sure wherever he's taking you will be glorious. I'm happy for you, Cat. Despite his dawdling he seems nice, and he's pretty stunning to boot.'

'He's both,' Cat said, smiling. Though along with the happiness of finally having a date in the diary, she felt a sense of unease. He *was* stunning, and had never been anything but nice to her, and he was clearly capable of charming the socks off a centipede. But he still felt out of her reach, as if he was behind glass, or floating underwater. He wasn't immediately warm the way Owen seemed to be, or straightforward like Joe. She wondered if, after their date, she'd feel closer to him.

But with her life in Fairview, her dog-walking business and her new friendships all going so perfectly, was finding the man of her dreams on top of all that too much to expect? As they turned in the direction of Primrose Terrace and the dogs sensed they were on their way home, Cat tried to put Mark out of her mind. Hopefully he would prove to her that he really was worth waiting for.

Raincoats and Retrievers

PART 3

Cat was about to go on her first date in a very long time, and her nerves were making her indecisive. She rearranged her elfin-cut hair, ruffled it, smoothed it and ruffled it again, turning her head in the mirror.

It was partly the long gap – she'd been single for nearly two years now – and she'd settled a bit too well into single life. Daniel and she been happy together at the beginning, but Cat had never been able to summon up the adoration for him that he undoubtedly felt for her. Cat sometimes wondered whether she was looking for something that didn't exist, whether she should have stayed with Daniel and waited for her affection to grow into love, but the dominant, more romantic part of her brain told her that there was more out there for her, someone she could truly fall for. Was tonight the start of that?

There was no denying that her nerves were mostly to do with Mark – it wasn't just that it was a date. Cat shuddered just thinking about him. Tonight was the culmination of months of fancying and sidestepping, flirting and innuendo, one kiss on the front steps in early summer.

She had chosen her best dress for the occasion: deep red with a cinched-in waist, full skirt and scooped neckline. Her sandals were pale gold with a low heel, her toenails as red as her dress. Fairview was under the spell of a shimmering August sun, and it had been the kind of day when winter seemed impossible, something that never visited the south coast. Cat couldn't imagine a setting, or a scenario, more perfect – and yet along with the anticipation, she was also apprehensive.

Cat had never met anyone as good at flirting as Mark was. He had the ability to make her feel like the only woman in the world, and could turn on the charm like a Bunsen burner. And despite his promising her dinner almost as soon as they met, it had taken months to pin him down. Their earlier dinner date had been put off because he'd been called away to London, his latest script in the early stages of production. Cat had had enough of him being mysterious and elusive. She wanted to get to know him.

'Cat,' Joe called from the bottom of the stairs. 'It's seven fifteen. Isn't he coming at half past? Are you still in the shower?'

Cat grinned. 'I'm nearly done!' she shouted. 'Thanks, though!'

Joe wasn't mysterious. He was dependable, honest (sometimes a bit too honest), and straightforward, qualities Cat was beginning to find as attractive as the man himself. They were slipping into an easy friendship, which apparently now included timekeeping duties.

She spritzed perfume behind her ears, checked the contents of her red evening bag and went downstairs, treating the others to a full twirl.

'Wow.' Polly looked up from her revision notes, her chewed pen-lid falling onto the table. She had her final exams over the next few weeks, an anxious wait until the end of September and then – Cat was confident – would be a fully qualified veterinary nurse. At the end of the month Cat would have her best friend back, and she couldn't wait.

'Cat Palmer,' Polly said, 'you look amazing.'

Cat gave a nervous smile. 'Thanks. Thought I'd make an effort.'

'You'll knock his socks off,' Polly assured her.

'He probably doesn't wear socks in the summer,' Joe said. 'He's probably the kind of guy who wears brogues without socks. I bet he's that guy.'

'Joe!' Polly hit her brother's arm and Shed looked up with one open eye from where he was lying, splayed out along Joe's lap.

'Sorry,' Joe said. 'You look fantastic, Cat. I just – I hope he treats you well, that's all.'

Polly laughed. 'You're not her dad.'

'No,' Joe admitted, 'but that doesn't mean I can't look out for her. I'd look out for you.'

'Awwwww.' Polly grabbed her brother round the shoulders and pulled him towards her. Joe rolled his eyes and put up with the hug for three seconds, before shrugging himself out of it.

'Thanks, Joe,' Cat managed. His comment was working its way into her brain, mixing with her own anxieties, but the doorbell rang, making her jump, and she realized she no longer had time to worry.

This was it.

Cat ran her hands down her dress and, turning away from her friends, went to open the door.

'Hello,' Mark said, giving her his full-beam grin, and Cat's nerves were swallowed by desire.

Mark was wearing a white Ralph Lauren shirt, the top two buttons open, over dark jeans and navy shoes. Cat couldn't see socks, but then she couldn't see ankles either. His dark-brown hair had been cut recently, but still had enough length to be attractively messy, and his brown eyes latched instantly onto hers.

'Hi,' Cat said.

'I've come to take you for a walk, if that's OK?' Mark raised his eyebrows.

'A walk? I thought we were going out to dinner.'

'A short promenade with the owner of Pooch Promenade, before our meal. I've been harbouring a lot of jealousy for all those dogs, so now it's my turn.'

'Ah. Well, I'm not really wearing the right shoes . . .'

'No,' Mark agreed, eyeing her appreciatively, 'you don't tend to walk them looking like that. You're stunning. It's a very short walk, I promise. Shall we?' He held out his elbow and Cat leaned back into the living room, gave Polly and Joe a final wave and then took Mark's arm and closed the door behind her. They walked the short distance from number nine to number four, and Mark unlocked his Audi.

'There,' he said. 'That's the walking part done with. Though I guess if we're both well behaved . . .'

'What?' Cat asked, sinking into the warm leather passenger seat.

'Well,' he said, 'you give your dogs treats, don't you?' He flashed her another grin and started the engine.

'Little bone-shaped chews,' Cat said. 'Though I wouldn't recommend them as an appetizer. I tried one once and it was disgusting.' Her mouth was drying out. She wasn't in Mark-mode, ready to deflect his quick comments and his innuendo.

'That's not quite what I meant,' Mark said, his voice light.

'Oh.' Cat closed her eyes as realization dawned, feeling a warm flush creep up her neck; nerves were jumbling her

214

thoughts and she felt clumsy and awkward. 'Where are we going?' she asked, hoping the change of subject would give her some breathing space.

'You'll see.' Mark pulled away from the kerb. Like everything else about him, his driving was assured. He wasn't overly fast, but once they'd left the wide streets of Fairview, then the sprawling suburbs of Fairhaven, and made it onto the A-road that rose up behind the town and gave a stunning view of the sea, he put his foot down. They were going east, and Cat had to peer past Mark to watch the sun dropping spectacularly over the water.

He was so close, his thigh just beyond the gear stick, and Cat wished she could reach over and casually put her hand on it. But her palms were sweaty, and she'd probably end up grabbing it too hard, or missing it altogether and . . . she shook the embarrassment of that thought away. 'You didn't want to stay in Fairview, then?' she asked.

'I told you I'd take you somewhere special,' Mark said. 'Not that Fairview isn't great, but – I owe you this. For taking so long to get round to it.'

'I'm intrigued,' she said. 'I don't know the area beyond Fairhaven very well.' This was much safer ground. She leaned her head against the headrest.

'Neither do I, but I had help. Someone we both know who's quite good when it comes to food.'

Cat sat up and looked out of the window, hiding her face from him. Jessica. Did he confide in her about everything?

'Jessica suggested it?' she asked, trying for lightness and not managing it. 'Then it must be good.'

'We're about to find out.' Mark, unaware of, or ignoring, her discomfort, indicated right and drove down a twisty, narrow road before turning between two trees and onto a gravel driveway. They were still high up, and the low building they parked in front of sat snugly on the side of the hill, as if it had been carved out of the rock. Mark helped Cat out of the car, and they approached the entrance, the sign above confirming they'd reached Highcroft Manor and Vineyard. Beyond the building, Cat could see neat rows of vines sloping down towards the sea, rays of golden sun picking them out in sharp relief.

'If the food is as good as the view . . .' Cat murmured.

'And you already know the company is,' Mark said cheekily. He put his hand on the small of her back and led her through the door.

They were greeted by a smartly dressed woman with a high, tight ponytail. Mark gave his name and she led them into a large square room with a bar at its centre, floor-to-ceiling windows making the most of the landscape beyond. The carpet was cream, the tables and chairs dark wood to match the bar, the lighting low but warm. The whole place exuded luxury. They could easily be in southern France rather than perched on a hill overlooking the English Channel.

Mark had reserved them a table against the window, and he held back Cat's seat for her, then sat opposite as the restaurant manager handed them the menus.

'This is spectacular,' Cat whispered, feeling awkward and underdressed, despite the effort she'd made. The restaurant was full, but the atmosphere was soft, quiet, well behaved. Cat's nerves ratcheted up a notch as she was handed a wine list as long as her arm, the offerings mostly in French. 'But I don't know anything about wine.'

'Let me pick that,' Mark said. 'Just focus on the food.'

'Oh, right.' Cat said. 'OK.' She felt a burst of anger that he was taking charge, that he'd brought her to a place where she couldn't be in control of her choices. But then, was that his fault? It was Jessica who'd suggested this place, and the reminder of that didn't make her feel any better. She glanced over the menu, her eyes widening at the descriptions: *Seared, hand-dived scallops; Beetroot with nuts, seaweed and chocolate.*

'This place is something else,' she whispered. 'I don't know where to start.'

She tried to keep the exasperation out of her voice but Mark looked up, a hint of a frown lowering his brows. 'We just need to pick what we like the look of, identify some ingredients we know. Beetroot and chocolate?'

Cat screwed her face up.

'You've never had chocolate beetroot cake?'

Cat shook her head. 'You have?'

'No,' Mark said, grinning. 'It sounds disgusting. Jessica's really outdone herself here,' he said, eyes scanning the menu again. 'One of them looks like it might be a steak, if you ignore the fancy bits. Do you like steak?'

Cat smiled, loosening up a little; Mark's cheeky good humour was starting to infiltrate her tense mood. 'Love it. And I think that starter is pâté and toast, even though it says *galantine de canard with organic olive crostini and champagne jam.*'

'What a waste of champagne.' Mark shook his head. 'But that's two courses we've deciphered. Let's leave the pudding and be spontaneous, pick the one that makes the least sense.'

'And the wine?' Cat held up the wine list.

'We could make up for the jam and have champagne.'

'But you're driving.'

'I can have one glass.'

'No, wait—' but Mark had already called the waiter over, and Cat didn't want to hiss at him to stop, so she focused on the orange glow of the sun as it sank closer to the horizon. If she lived somewhere with a view like this then she'd give up on life. She'd sit in a chair, slowly fusing with the fabric as she watched the changing sea and sky, the clouds, the sun, birds and boats passing her.

'Cat?'

'Sorry.' She turned back and smiled. The lights in the restaurant had dimmed, a candle in a tarnished silver holder flickering between them, and Mark was looking at her with his dark, smiling eyes. Cat felt the butterflies low down in her stomach.

'If I'd known this place was going to be quite so pretentious, I would have taken you somewhere else.'

'It's definitely impressive. And the view is stunning.'

'I was going for special, not incomprehensible.'

Cat shook her head. 'I'm sure the food will be delicious, even if the descriptions are a bit over the top. Mark, you've brought me to a beautiful restaurant for dinner. There's nothing to apologize for.' She felt that maybe, after her initial awkwardness and nerves, things were changing. He was apologizing – she'd never seen him anything but entirely confident up until now – so perhaps she was about to see beyond his charm and flippancy, and discover more of the real him? *This* was what she'd been waiting for, and she wasn't about to let the chance slip by. 'Tell me about your films. I want to know everything.'

'Everything?' He raised an eyebrow. 'Not about the disaster.'

'Especially the disaster.'

She listened intently, pausing only when the waiter interrupted them with the champagne, as Mark told her about writing the screenplays, about the challenge of finding someone to make them, the shooting process, artistic differences, location nightmares. His films sounded like the gritty

218

British horrors that Cat would find late at night on BBC2 and turn off, because she couldn't bear the thought of going to bed alone afterwards. Not Hollywood slashers, full of glamorous people and too much unrealistic blood, but dark corners on dingy estates, things lurking where they shouldn't, scenarios on the edge of being possible.

Since they'd met, Mark had been smooth and over-confident, but now he was self-deprecating, telling Cat about mistakes he'd made, personality clashes, upsetting one lead actress by mistaking her for the make-up assistant. He made Cat laugh, and he seemed entirely focused on her, the candle-light flickering along his handsome jawline. It was still smug, but now that smugness seemed somewhat justified.

Mark topped up her glass as their empty plates – which had contained excellent pâté and toast – were cleared away.

'It's another world,' Cat said. 'It sounds impossible, juggling all the different elements, making sure everything works and the film gets made. And everyone swallows them up in an hour and a half and then forgets about them.'

'Or not,' Mark said. 'Like everything creative, some films stay with people for a long time. That's all I'm trying to do, make a film that matters to some people.'

'You know, you don't *look* like a horror-film writer.'

'And what's a horror-film writer supposed to look like?' Mark narrowed his eyes, and Cat could see that he was intrigued, wanting to know what she thought of him.

'Grungy,' Cat said. 'You're so polished, and . . . effortless. You're not dressed in a Marilyn Manson T-shirt, sitting in a dark corner, scribbling madly and watching *Hammer Horror* reruns.'

'How do you know I don't do that? That's *exactly* what I do when I'm writing.'

'Come on, Mark.'

'Have you studied horror writers?'

Cat shook her head. 'You think I should have done some research for tonight?'

Mark laughed. 'I would have been touched, and perhaps a little disturbed, if you had. But you should google some famous horror writers. Sam Raimi, of *Evil Dead* fame, could pass as a mild-mannered businessman. And if you're after polished, take a look at a photo of Wes Craven.'

'The *Scream* films?'

'And *A Nightmare on Elm Street*. Good smile, nice suits. You don't have to look like a freak to want to write about freakish things, but I *do* get obsessed when I'm in the middle of a story, neglecting everything else. It's a good thing I have Chips to remind me when it's food time, or I'd slowly starve to death.

'And if we're talking stereotypes, what about you? You're not a typical dog walker. I think of middle-aged, fleece-wearing women with scrappy ponytails, unbranded trainers and an inability to converse with anything that has less than four legs. You're none of those things.'

'That's what I'm gearing up for,' Cat said. 'Give me a few years . . .' She grinned. 'Do you want to leave now?'

He returned her smile, shaking his head slowly.

'OK,' she continued, 'so I can get over the fact that you don't look the part –' Mark rolled his eyes – 'but what's the plot of your latest film? The one you're trying to make at the moment.'

Mark glanced at the tabletop, moved his spoon around. 'It's about a man who moves out of London to a rural town, to be close to his mother, who's dying in a care home. He's had to rent somewhere at short notice, and it's far too big for him. He's in this strange place, summoning the courage to confront his mother about this huge, unresolved secret from his childhood, and he realizes that he's not alone in the house.'

'Wow. That sounds . . . scary. And different, from your last two. Not so grizzly.'

Mark nodded. 'I thought, after the last one went so wrong – I mean, everyone's pitched a film on a dark, run-down council estate. It's not original any more, and the panning it got told me that. I wanted this setting to be much lighter, to see if I could still create that darkness, to build it around this guy who's been wrong-footed by everything, dealing with his past, family secrets, moving away from his existing life to a large house with – supposedly – only him in. It's different, but I know it can work. And I can't be the only one, because I've got this producer interested, so . . .' He shrugged, but Cat could see the fire in his eyes, pinpoints of colour high on his cheeks. She could see how much he cared.

'It sounds brilliant – definitely creepy. I've gone cold just thinking about it. Did you get your inspiration from Fairview, and your house on Primrose Terrace?'

'Not originally.' He narrowed his eyes slightly. 'I started it before I moved here, but now I'm suddenly living in a house that's too big for me, away from London . . .'

'Life imitating art.'

'Looks like it,' Mark said, taking a drink of water.

'Any dogs in it?' Cat asked.

'Is that the only way you'd be interested in seeing it?' He laughed.

'No, of course not. But I was thinking of all the different ways you could get a dog into a horror film. Maybe not the plot you've just told me, but a dog could come across the first dead body, digging in the garden, or – like the one Chips is named after – it could be a rescue dog. Or, or –' Cat began

221

to get animated, waving her arms about – 'you could have zombie dogs. Has that been done before? Zombie dogs would be fast and small, they'd get among people's ankles and bite them, turning everyone much quicker. And it would be extra terrifying, because dogs are usually so lovable. Actually –' Cat screwed her face up – 'maybe not that last one. I'm not sure I'd like it.'

'No zombie dogs then,' Mark said. 'Got it.'

'But maybe this guy could have a dog, a companion, who also senses that something's wrong with the house. It would prove to him that he's not going mad, give it more credence.'

Mark gave her an appraising look. 'You might be onto something there.'

'Oh, I don't know – ignore me. But I'd love to see your films.'

He laughed.

'What?'

'You said that like someone was holding a gun to your head.'

'I did not!' Cat protested. 'I would like to see your films, but just maybe . . . maybe not with the lights off. I'm not good at watching horror films before bed.'

'Even if you weren't on your own?' Mark asked, leaning back in his chair.

Her insides fizzing, Cat returned his gaze.

Their steaks arrived and they ate in a charged silence until Mark asked her how the dog walking was going, whether Polly had finished her exams and how Frankie was getting on with her lodger. Leyla had loved the room and was moving in sometime that week.

Cat was pleased that she'd been able to help Frankie and her children. She was fitting in to life at Primrose Terrace, and there was a niggling voice at the back of her mind asking her if it was wise to have a relationship with one of the neighbours. Mostly she told that voice to back off, because it was hard to meet people, and you couldn't base your relationship decisions on how awkward it would be if things went wrong.

Mark topped up her glass, and Cat sipped the bubbles, enjoying the taste of top-quality champagne.

'Now,' Mark said. 'Dessert?'

'Undecipherable dessert.'

They found their answer at the same time: *Lemon posset with caramel honey tuile and pomegranate espuma.* Cat watched Mark order them with a straight face and, when the waiter had gone, and she had managed not to descend into giggles, he reached over and took her hand.

The sun was just a thin line of burnished red marking the break between sea and sky, and she could see herself and Mark reflected back at her in the window.

'Cat,' he said, and there was something about his voice that made her breath catch in her throat. 'I'm sorry it's taken me so long to get to this point.'

Cat shook her head. 'You've been busy, it's OK.'

'It's not. I have been distracted, with the move, the new film. But I don't want you to think that you've been an afterthought. You haven't.'

'OK.' Cat swallowed. 'Thank you. I did wonder if we were going to sidestep around each other for ever. But this is – this is great. Getting to know you. A little bit, anyway.'

'This isn't a one-off,' Mark said. 'At least, I don't want it to be. But what do you think? It hasn't been a total disaster, has it?' His thumb stroked her hand.

'Not at all,' she said. 'Despite the threat of beetroot and seaweed, I think it's going well.'

The candle cast shadows of his eyelashes on his cheeks, and his skin looked dark against the crisp white of his shirt. Cat shivered and rearranged her serviette on her knee.

'Are you cold?'

'No, I'm fine. How's Chips?'

'She's good,' Mark said. 'I took her for an extra-long walk this afternoon, through the park and up along the cliffs, so hopefully she's tired out and not missing me too much. You have a cat, don't you? What's his name?'

'Shed. He's OK, though he's not actually mine, he's Joe's. I wouldn't have picked a grumpy ginger cat as a pet.'

'It's always puzzled me, why you don't have a dog of your own.'

Cat gave him a quick smile. She didn't want to say anything to turn Mark against Joe. If things kept going in the right direction, she wanted them to be friends. 'It's not practical with Shed there, he can only just tolerate human company. But I'm not short of canine companions. The Barkers' retrievers are lovely – quite different to the schnauzers or the Westies. They're strong and they like long walks, but they're very affectionate, playful. I somehow feel more confident when I'm walking them.'

'I don't think I know the Barkers.'

'They live at number six. In their forties, I think, their kids are grown-up and off being independent, and Will and Juliette both have quite high-powered jobs. Juliette works at home some days, but when she's in the office I take Alfie and Effie out. Will likes surfing. There's quite a bit of it around here, apparently.'

'Now that's something I haven't tried,' Mark said.

'Would you like to?'

'Oh, I'm up for anything once.'

Cat narrowed her eyes. 'Anything? Even eating a fugu fish or swimming with sharks?'

'Sure.' Mark shrugged. 'Why are your fears so marine-based?'

'They're not – those things just popped into my head. I love the sea. I suppose if your passion is horror, you don't scare particularly easily.'

'Other things scare me,' Mark said. 'Unpredictable things.'

'Like what?' Cat asked, and then, because it was going so well and she wanted to try and match Mark for playfulness while also doing a bit of digging, added, 'Because saying you're afraid of commitment isn't unpredictable.'

Mark grinned. 'I know *that*. You're doing me a disservice, that's not what I was going to say. And I'm not afraid of commitment. I was in a long relationship, before this.' His grin faded, but he held Cat's gaze.

'How long have you been single?' she asked quietly.

Now he did look away. 'Nearly a year.'

'And how long were you together?'

'Six years,' Mark said. 'Moving down here was – is – part of the fallout. Getting some space, starting again.'

'Six years is a long time,' Cat said, thinking of the photo of the woman on Mark's fridge door. But if they'd broken up . . . 'She must have meant a lot to you.'

'She did,' Mark said. 'You can't be with someone for that long and not feel it when it ends. But it did, and you get past it. It's how life works. And tonight, this – with you – it's the most fun I've had in a long time.'

He took her hand again, and Cat opened her mouth to reply, but the moment was broken by the waiter delivering their desserts to the table. Cat looked down at the pale-yellow blancmange, the blob of vivid pink foam and golden sugar decoration. She dipped her spoon in and brought it to her

225

lips, her eyes widening as the flavours hit her tongue. 'Wow,' she mumbled, 'indecipherable food is delicious.'

After Mark had refused to let her go Dutch and had paid the bill, and they'd finally pushed their chairs back from the table, the restaurant was nearly deserted. The three courses and coffee had gone some way to counteracting the most-of a bottle of champagne that Cat had drunk, but she was still feeling a warm, hazy glow.

They stepped out into the night-time breeze and Mark wrapped his arm around her waist. He opened the car door for her, but before she'd had time to get in, he cupped her face, pulled her towards him and kissed her. It felt delicious, her whole body tingling in response to his lips on hers, and the whisper of the hilltop breeze. She wrapped her arms around him, his warmth contrasting with the goosebumps on her arms.

They were quiet on the drive home, Cat breathless from the kiss and the anticipation of what could happen when they got back to Primrose Terrace. The lights of the town winked in the darkness as the Audi purred down the hill into Fairhaven and then the more familiar streets of Fairview, finally stopping outside Mark's house. He leaned over and kissed her again, his fingers caressing her neck.

'Do you want to come inside?' he asked.

'Yes.' Cat waited for Mark's smirk, his wide, charming grin, but he just nodded and climbed out, opening the door for her.

They made it up his front steps before he kissed her again, enclosing her in his arms under the soft glow of the hanging lantern over the front door. Cat let herself be drawn in. She had almost lost herself to him completely when a familiar voice called up to them.

'Cat, is that you?' She broke away and turned, blinking quickly, and saw Juliette Barker, her black corkscrew curls pulled away from her face, hands clasped in front of her. She was wearing a cream business suit that looked almost peach under the street light. Cat thought for an awful moment she was about to be told off for kissing in public.

'Juliette. Hi. How are you?'

Juliette nodded and gave a quick smile. 'Fine, fine. Sorry to disturb, but could you walk Effie and Alfie tomorrow? Only Will had told me he was going to be at home all day, and I've arranged a series of important meetings in the office, but now he's got some surfing meet-up that he apparently has to attend. Anyway, he can't take the dogs and nor can I. Are you around? I was coming to your place but I looked in this direction and . . .' She indicated the pair of them standing, post-snog, on the doorstep.

'O-of course I can fit them in,' Cat said. Mark ran his fingers up Cat's back and she tried to shimmy away from him. 'What time?'

'Eleven? They'll be running rings round the furniture by then, and I—' She sighed and pinched the bridge of her nose. 'Sorry, this is incredibly rude of me. I can see you're in the middle of . . .'

'It's no problem,' Cat said, not wanting to get into a discussion with her neighbour about what she was or wasn't in the middle of. 'They're such lovely dogs, and sometimes things don't fit easily into working hours.' She smiled, and Juliette seemed to relax a little.

'Great, thank you.' She glanced between them. 'You're Mark, aren't you?'

'Guilty as charged,' Mark said, holding his hand up in a static wave. 'Nice to meet you.'

'Do you like surfing?'

'Never tried it,' Mark admitted. 'Your husband, Will, he enjoys it?'

227

'Far too much,' Juliette said. 'Well, maybe that's unfair. He enjoys it at the expense of almost everything else. I know it's a good hobby, it keeps him fit, he gets lots of fresh air – but he seems so obsessed with it. He spends his life down at that cove. Why do men get so obsessed with things? It doesn't seem healthy.'

'I get obsessive,' Mark said. 'Not about surfing, but my work – my writing.'

'And Joe, my housemate,' Cat joined in, 'is anal when it comes to so many things. Feet on the coffee table, talking during films. Dogs in the house . . .' she added quietly. 'I think it's just a man thing.'

'He used to be obsessed about work,' Juliette said ruefully. 'But not any more. Now it's new wetsuits, streamlining his board, catching the waves as if they don't happen every hour of every day. He's started talking in a new language – it's all "hang fire", or, no, what is it? I'm sure it's "hang" something. I can't remember.' She sighed and shook her head, a curl escaping and falling over her face.

Mark and Cat exchanged a glance.

'Sorry,' Juliette said, shaking her head. 'I don't mean to – I'm still interrupting. I'll leave you to it.'

'No, Juliette,' Cat said, 'we don't mean for you to go, it's just . . .'

'Thank you so much for walking the dogs tomorrow, Cat. Have a good evening.' She gave them a brusque smile and turned, her court shoes echoing as she walked the few yards back to number six.

Cat watched her go, her embarrassment at being interrupted fading as Mark snaked his arm around her waist. But as she spun to face him she noticed a car parked further up the road, and her stomach swooped for an entirely new reason.

'Now,' Mark murmured, his lips brushing her neck. 'Are you coming inside? I don't think there's anything you can do to prepare for walking Juliette's dogs, is there?'

Cat closed her eyes. His touch and his taste, his confidence, his dark eyes, they were all so enticing. 'I – I can't,' she said. She put her palms flat on his chest. He flinched slightly and tried to pull her closer, but Cat resisted. 'There is nothing I would like more than to come in with you right now. But I can't.'

'Why?' He smiled at her, only a hint of confusion on his face. 'Because of Juliette?'

'No, not that. Because the red Renault with a *World's Greatest Inventor* bumper sticker that's parked outside number nine belongs to my parents.' She sighed and rested her head against his chest, which was a mistake, because it felt good and it made her even more reluctant to leave. 'They must have come for an impromptu visit and – depending on how long they've been there – Polly and Joe might be beyond rescuing.'

'Then there's no need to go back,' Mark said, 'if it's too late to save them.'

'I'm so sorry,' she murmured, leaning in for a final, delicious kiss. 'If I thought I could get away with it, I'd stay.' Reluctantly, she left Mark standing on the top step, watching her. His face gave nothing away, no frustration, no flicker of disappointment. She reached number nine, searched through her bag for her keys and then, pushing open the front door, went in to face the carnage.

14

Cat's mum and dad were wedged on the smaller of the two sofas, Shed stretched out with his head on her mum's lap, his back legs on her dad's. The cat was snoring. Despite the weather, her dad Peter was wearing his usual fishing waistcoat over a short-sleeved shirt, and Delia, her mum, had her sunglasses perched on her head, sending her short brown hair into disarray. Polly was sitting opposite them, hands clasped together, and Joe was on the arm of the sofa, as if trying to make it obvious that he wasn't staying. He'd probably been there, his bum going numb, for hours. That's what happened in the presence of Cat's parents – you couldn't escape.

'Cat,' Joe said, standing as she walked in. She could hear the relief in his voice, and she flashed him an apologetic look. 'How was it?'

'Catherine, dear.' Her mum reached her arms up towards her as if she was a toddler asking to be picked up. Obviously, Shed couldn't be disturbed. 'It's so lovely to see you.' Cat reached down and hugged her mum, taking in her overly floral perfume, and then her dad with the musty workshop smell that hung around him like a fog.

'You too,' she said, 'though you could have called ahead, told me you were coming. I kind of had plans tonight.' She gave them a tight smile, and folded her arms.

Her mum and dad exchanged a cheeky look. 'We wanted to surprise you,' her mum said.

'We had no idea you'd be out on a *date*,' her dad added. 'Couldn't fathom it at all! Joe and Polly have been the perfect hosts in your absence. How much detail do we get?'

'Hardly any,' Cat said, not adding that the potential for juicy gossip would have been much greater had they not turned up and cut short her evening.

'Oh, come on, Cat,' Polly said, standing up and embracing her friend, 'we're all dying to hear how it went.'

'And I'm sure they've heard enough about my handheld seed sower,' her dad chipped in.

Glancing at Joe and Polly, Cat thought that a truer word had probably never been spoken. She could see Mark again whenever she wanted – she hoped all was not lost there – but her friends would never get their evening back.

'All right then,' she said, rolling her eyes and flopping down onto the sofa, 'but is there any tea left in the pot?'

Cat gave them the edited highlights of her evening, focusing on the grand venue and food, the view from the top of the hill, and skirting around the conversation and her complicated feelings for Mark. Her parents seemed placated, mainly because her dad was a keen gardener and was appalled that he'd never visited one of the vineyards along the south coast, and her mum wanted to hear about every flavour and ingredient Cat had eaten.

'Well,' Delia said, when Cat's words had dried up and Shed had disappeared out through the cat flap. 'We don't want to keep you all. We're in the bed and breakfast up the road. Lovely couple, both men, two dogs. Perfect little alternative family. The room is English cottage luxury, silver wallpaper – sounds awful, but it works.'

'You're staying?' Cat said, only just managing to keep the squeak out of her voice.

'Only for a couple of days, love,' her dad confirmed. 'Thought it would be easier than driving back. We'll take you out to dinner tomorrow. Have a proper catch-up, hear all about the dogs and this Mark chap.'

'And we want to meet some of your new doggy friends.'

Cat led them to the door, let them take their turn to smother her in their hugs which, she had to admit, couldn't be beaten by anyone, then waved them down the terrace until they climbed the steps to Boris and Charles's.

It was close to one in the morning, and while Cat was tired, Polly and Joe looked as though they'd had the life sucked out of them.

'I am so, so sorry,' Cat said, sinking onto the sofa. 'What time did they arrive?'

'About half an hour after you left,' Polly said, grinning. Polly had met them on several occasions over the years, and so had prior warning of Cat's overenthusiastic, eccentric parents, and the way they doted on their only child. Cat knew Polly liked them, though she wasn't sure how welcome their surprise visit was mid-revision. It was Joe who looked shell-shocked.

'So you've had them here all evening?' Cat's voice had dropped to a whisper.

Joe nodded and ran a hand over his face. 'To be fair they brought lemon drizzle cake. And home-made sausage rolls and cheese-and-onion pies. We didn't have to cook, but I'm going to have to run a marathon to use up all the carbohydrate.'

'My mum's a great cook.'

'Why don't we get home-made sausage rolls?'

'Because I'm a dabbler,' Cat said. 'I'm nowhere near as good as Mum is. I'll have a go if you like, but not now. Now, I'm going to bed.'

They all traipsed up to the first floor, and Joe headed on to his attic bedroom.

'Why are they staying?' Polly asked, pausing at the bathroom door. 'Brighton's not far.'

'Because it is inconceivable that my parents could go out to dinner without consuming at least two bottles of wine. If they were going back to Brighton, then one of them would have to drive.'

'So I shouldn't expect you to be sober tomorrow night, then?'

Cat closed her eyes. She felt utterly exhausted, and the thought of dinner with her parents which, while fun, would again be late and boozy, wasn't an entirely happy one, especially after they'd waltzed in and interrupted her evening with Mark. If she hadn't noticed their car, done the right thing and rescued her housemates, where would she be now? After a shaky start, the date had gone well. Cat felt she knew Mark a lot better, could start to see him as a real person instead of the glossy, overly confident persona he projected, and she wanted that to continue. With the image of his dark eyes, and his lips so close to hers, dancing in her mind, she said goodnight to Polly and, gratefully, climbed into bed.

'So this is Alfie, and this is Effie.' Delia pointed at the dogs in turn. 'Alfie's curlier, Effie straighter,' she said, as she eyed the two boisterous retrievers.

'That's right,' Cat said, sidestepping a pair of greyhounds coming the other way. She hadn't banked on her parents wanting to actually join her on one of her walks – nobody else had to deal with 'take your parents to work' day, and her mum's sandals were not ideal, especially with the two retrievers who, Cat knew by now, wouldn't slow down for anything.

Her mum and dad bustled along behind her as she did a wide circuit of the park, warming the dogs up before she let them off the lead. As her Pooch Promenade client list had grown, she had tried out different ways of walking the dogs, and knew that Alfie and Effie were best walked on their own, as their larger size and energy meant that she'd struggle if she had Jessica's Westies or Elsie's mini schnauzers at the same time. And this was an impromptu walk, the one Juliette had asked for while Cat had been trying to kiss Mark on the doorstep.

'So it's going well, then?' her dad huffed, almost jogging to keep up. 'You seem very adept at it, I must say.'

Cat laughed. 'At walking? I've had lots of practice.'

'You're in charge of the dogs,' Peter clarified. 'I can see that they like and respect you.'

'They're gorgeous, friendly dogs,' Cat said, bending to stroke Effie. There was something so sturdy and dependable about the retrievers; with their large brown eyes and loping movements, they were completely different from the bounding, cheeky Westies.

'And they belong to your neighbour?' Delia asked, jumping as a football came sailing towards them. A small, blond-haired boy raced up to collect it, apologizing noisily.

'Will and Juliette Barker, they live at number six, a few doors down. They've been clients for a while now, but . . .' Cat thought of Juliette's exasperation as she'd mentioned Will's surfing. 'But I might be walking them a bit more. Not that I'm complaining, of course. I just . . . I'm not sure things are that rosy between them, and I don't like seeing people unsettled.'

'No, love, you never could.' Peter gave Cat a quick hug and held his hand out for the leads. 'Let me have a go, eh?' Cat handed them over and watched as he stood up straighter, his arm rigid at his side, his feet moving like one of those speed walkers. Alfie looked up at his new, unfamiliar walker, barked once and picked up his pace.

Cat laughed, and Delia slipped her arm through her daughter's. 'You don't mind us coming unannounced, do you?'

'It's lovely to see you,' Cat said, 'but if you'd called ahead I could have been in, rather than leaving you with Polly and Joe.'

'But they're lovely!'

'I know that,' Cat said pointedly.

'Ah.' Delia gave her a sideways look. 'You mean we imposed on them?'

Cat shrugged. 'I'm sure they loved you, it's just – it was their whole evening.'

'I know. But your dad and I, we just get carried away. They were so friendly – that Joe's a real dish, too, have you never thought about maybe . . .'

'Mum!'

'Sorry, sorry, of course. You've got this new man, Mark. I'm dying to know more about him.'

Cat felt herself mentally closing in, like a flower folding its petals up in the dark. 'He's nice, but – it's early days. Last night was our first proper date. He's charming and gorgeous, and he knows how to say just the right thing. I'm attracted to him, no doubt about that.'

'But? Come on, Catherine. I know when there's a "but" hovering behind those big brown eyes of yours.'

Cat sighed and followed the progress of a Weimaraner as it raced effortlessly across the grass, silver coat shimmering in the sun. 'He's a bit *too* smooth. Even after dinner with him, and we really talked, he still seems a bit beyond my reach – not physically, but the real Mark.'

'Worth a few more dates to find out?'

Cat replayed the kiss in her mind, the way her whole body responded to his touch. When she was with him she was absolutely certain, as if he had a hold over her. It was when she was apart from him that the doubts resurfaced. 'I think so. Just to see what happens.'

'And if he's gorgeous and charming, why not bed him and then move on? Everyone we meet plays a different role in our lives. Maybe his is a "harmless fun" sort of role?'

'Mother! I cannot believe you just said that.'

'Oh, I think you can.' Delia patted her hand, her arm tinkling with the bracelets that ran from her wrist almost to her elbow. 'What's this coffee shop like?' She pointed at the Pavilion café.

'It's nice, but the cake's not as good as yours.'

'Let's get a coffee and a sample, shall we?'

'What are these dogs up to?' her dad called. Alfie and Effie had stopped in front of Peter and were looking expectantly up at him, pressing their noses worryingly close to his crotch area.

'They know it's run time – they want to be let off the lead.' Cat unclipped their leads and the two dogs raced off towards the trees. Unlike her first, unsuccessful walk all those months ago, Cat didn't feel nervous. She knew Alfie and Effie would come back to her when she called. She was now a confident dog walker, learning more about the temperaments of the different breeds – and of the individual dogs she walked – every day.

The park was full of picnicking and playing families – the whole of Fairview was bustling with holidaymakers enjoying the sun and sea – and Cat felt completely at home. As she led her mum and dad over to the Pavilion café, she felt that she had something in her life that they could be really proud of her for. Neither of her parents was conventional – her mum made greeting cards to sell, and her dad was forever inventing new tools and entering the vegetables and flowers that he grew into competitions and shows – but both had had long, more traditional careers before turning towards their passions.

Her dad had worked in insurance, but had given it all up to focus on his inventions and his allotment. Cat still remembered the arguments when he'd told Delia what he was doing, but Cat's mum had seen how happy the change made him, how their relationship had somehow been gifted back to them. Delia had been a legal secretary and, if her stories were to be believed, had been basically running the firm before she decided to give it up a few years ago to follow her own creative instincts.

As far as Cat knew they were both blissfully happy, living in their small semi-detached home on the outskirts of Brighton, and she hoped they saw her change of direction as something similar, even if she was choosing to do it earlier in her working life than they had.

They settled down at a table on the veranda, and Delia and Peter scanned the menu. 'Blueberry muffin,' Delia said. 'That's just what I'm after.'

'And I'm going for the triple-chocolate cake,' added Peter. 'What do you want, love?'

Cat thought back to the fancy, delicious posset she'd had at the restaurant the previous evening, and wondered if it had spoiled her for sweet things for ever. 'A toasted teacake for me, please.'

'Is that all?' her dad asked. 'I suppose you're saving your appetite for dinner this evening. Good thinking, Catherine.

We don't get to spoil you as much now you're not within touching distance. Better keep a good amount of space for that.'

Cat rolled her eyes and grinned as Peter went inside to order, and Alfie and Effie, right on cue, ran across the grass towards them.

After her second walk of the day, Cat dropped the Westies off at Jessica's grand house at the end of Primrose Terrace and made her way slowly up the street, glancing instinctively at the bed and breakfast as she went past. Her parents had gone to visit the lighthouse that afternoon, but with another walk scheduled Cat had declined to join them. Now she had a couple of hours' rest before walking into Fairhaven town centre with her parents. The clouds had drifted over and the glorious, August sun was hiding, taking its warmth with it.

Cat climbed the steps of number ten and knocked on the door. Elsie opened it and ushered her friend in. 'Tea? I've got Earl Grey or Lapsang Souchong.'

'Lapsang, please.'

'Biscuits?'

Cat shook her head. 'I've got dinner with Mum and Dad this evening, so I'm saving space.'

'Go and say hello, I'll be there in a second.' Elsie left her to make the tea and Cat went into the living room, dropping to her knees as Disco and Chalky came to greet her. Disco was close to being full-sized now, but was still, in all other regards, a puppy, and couldn't wait to put her paws on Cat's shoulders and lick her face in an over-exuberant welcome. Chalky waited patiently behind, his eyes hidden by his bushy eyebrows, and then gently nuzzled into Cat's open arms.

'Come here, you lovely thing.' Cat hugged the older dog. Chalky was the old guard out of all the dogs she knew. She wouldn't admit it to anyone, but she looked up to him. She saw him as the voice of reason – even though that voice was limited to barks and whines – somehow always knowing whether she was making the right decision or not, giving her a look or pressing his wet nose against her hand. She wished she could formally introduce him to Mark and watch what he did.

Chalky gave a loud sniff, turned and snuggled down in the basket under the window. Disco stood on the sofa and barked happily into Cat's face.

'Disco, tush.' Elsie put the tea tray on the table and sat next to Disco. The young dog bounded onto Elsie's lap, rucking up her long grey skirt. 'If you don't behave you'll have to get down.' Disco looked sorrowfully up, and then settled onto the sofa next to her, head on her paws.

Cat accepted a cup of tea and sat opposite her friend.

'So,' Elsie said, 'it seems a lot has happened since the last time I saw you. Your date with Mark, and then your parents coming. Are they just up for the day?'

Cat shook her head. 'They turned up unexpectedly while I was out with Mark. I'm not sure Joe will ever forgive me.'

Elsie chuckled. 'That boy will forgive you anything, I'm sure.'

'What, because he's had to live with me all this time? Surely that would make him less patient, not more.'

'He's fond of you. That much is obvious.'

Cat let her shoulders relax. Elsie's house was a haven, full of human and canine warmth, and she always felt calmer when she was here. 'I think he might almost be over Rosalin.'

'I think you might be right,' Elsie said, giving her a wide smile. 'Now, tell me all about your date with Mark. Was it worth the wait?'

'I think so,' Cat said cautiously.

'Don't hold back your enthusiasm,' Elsie said. 'Really, I can't cope.'

Cat rolled her eyes and then told her, in more detail than she had her parents or Joe and Polly, but without the smouldering end to the evening that was curtailed first by Juliette and then her mum and dad.

'Will you see him again?'

'I'd like to. And I think he'd like to see me. Once my parents have gone – and they're only here until tomorrow – we might pick up where we left off.'

'Oh? Oh, I see. I think it went better than you're letting on then.'

'It was . . . going well, and then Juliette came to ask if I'd walk Alfie and Effie this morning.'

'She knocked on Mark's door?'

'We hadn't quite made it inside.'

'Ah.' Elsie pressed her lips together, and Cat could see she was trying not to laugh. 'Trust Juliette. She's certainly not backwards about coming forwards.'

'The same could be said about Mark,' Cat said, reliving the happy shiver of his kiss. 'But Juliette was on a mission. She apologized for interrupting us, but it didn't seem to embarrass her unduly. I don't think I would have gone near anyone who was . . . occupied like that, not even if it was Polly or Joe!' She shrugged away the unsettling idea of Joe being locked in an embrace with someone.

Elsie leaned forward and poured more tea. Disco looked up from where she was snoozing and raised a single ear. 'It's not dinner time yet,' Elsie said softly. 'Juliette's been a bit distracted recently, and I've walked past a couple of less-than-amicable conversations between her and Will on the front steps. It seems those steps can be a location for all manner of encounters.' She gave Cat a look. 'Some people seem to forget they can actually go *inside* their houses.'

'Mark and I got a bit carried away,' Cat said defensively. 'That's all. Did you hear what their arguments were about? Juliette seemed pretty unhappy that Will was going off to see his surfing friends and leaving the dogs at home. That's why I got the extra walk.'

'I don't often see him without a surfboard these days,' Elsie admitted.

'Doesn't he work? When they first became my clients, the main reason was that they both worked full time. Juliette did a couple of days at home, but the dogs were alone the other three. They've not mentioned that things have changed but, come to think of it, I can't remember the last time I saw Will in a suit.'

'You didn't know?' Elsie looked surprised.

'Know what?'

'He's given up his job. I don't know all the details, but Juliette's given me the bare bones. He's fed up of the long hours, the late nights, the stress and the weight piling on him. She didn't say it outright, but I can see it wasn't a decision she approved of.'

'Wow.' Cat sat back on the sofa. 'I suppose if she's the only one bringing in money now, then I can understand her being angry.'

'From the blasts of cold air whenever I see them together, it's more than just angry. Making that kind of decision's a big change,' Elsie said. 'Especially when it's not been made as a couple.'

Cat nodded, thinking back to the rough patch her parents had been through when her dad did something similar. 'Maybe Juliette doesn't fully understand why Will did it, or he's reluctant to tell her? Maybe she's angry about him making the decision to leave his job, but rather than face up to it, she's turning all her anger towards the surfing.'

'There could be all kinds of reasons behind what's happening, but what I would say, Cat, is that it's best if you don't get in the middle. Your . . . curiosity wouldn't be appreciated there, and while I think it's worth you knowing so you don't put your foot in it, try to be as distant as possible. Walk Alfie and Effie, stay polite and friendly, but if either of them starts trying to get you on their side, back gently off. Let them get on with whatever they have to do.'

It was good advice, as always, from her friend. And Cat did have a tendency to try and solve problems that weren't hers to fix. Not this time, though. A relationship break-up was definitely not something she wanted to get involved in, and besides, she was hardly an expert. She was having enough trouble trying to sort out her own love life.

For the second evening in a row, Cat found herself getting ready for a meal out. She was sure the venue would be less exclusive luxury and champagne, and more hearty, good food and friendly service – they were the kinds of places her parents went for and seemed to have a knack of being able to find. The weather felt as though it was turning, despite still being August, and Cat selected a black maxi dress with a fuchsia pattern along the hemline and a wide fuchsia belt.

Closing the wardrobe, she stepped backwards into her second-hand guitar, and jumped as it reverberated. She'd bought it the previous week, and was due to have her first lesson from Frankie in the next few days. She wasn't sure she was cut out to be a musician, but Frankie had insisted, wanting to pay her back for all her help, and Cat was looking forward to trying something new. She thought, maybe, she'd try and learn something festive in time for Christmas. Even she must be able to perfect one tune by then. But she didn't even have time to pick it up and strum it now; she had fifteen minutes before her parents were due to arrive, and someone had sneaked into the bathroom without her realizing.

She waited until she heard the shower turn off, and then the bathroom door open. She rushed onto the landing and almost straight into Joe, naked apart from a towel wrapped round his waist.

He put his hands on her shoulders. 'Where's the fire?'

His blond hair was wet and tufty, his cheeks pink.

'S-sorry, I need to finish getting ready. I didn't mean to barge into you.'

'No harm done, and sorry if I jumped in front of you.'

'Running?'

He nodded. 'I thought I'd make the most of the cooler weather. Are you heading out? Not going to leave us at the mercy of your parents again, are you?' He smiled.

She gave him a playful punch on the arm. 'No, they're taking me out to dinner. I'm sure if I asked, you'd be more than welcome to come.'

'No thanks. I've got my eye set on a Thai takeaway and a *Grey's Anatomy* box set.'

'*Grey's Anatomy*?' Cat murmured, wondering if it was too late to cancel on her parents. 'You like *Grey's*?'

'Who doesn't like Meredith and McDreamy?'

'Is Polly watching it with you?'

Joe shook his head. He looked like a Diet Coke advert, standing there in his towel with his blond, dripping hair. She thought he probably had no idea how attractive he was – the total opposite of Mark's over-confidence – which in some

243

ways made him even more attractive. 'Polly's helping Leyla move into Frankie's house.'

'That's happening this evening?' Cat asked.

'It is. I've met Leyla once or twice – I think she's been a bit of a mentor for Polly during her training, she's been a nurse at the vet's for a while – and she seems lovely. Friendly, maybe a bit shy. I don't know what her domestic habits are like, but from all outward appearances she's an ideal tenant. It's a success story that's all down to you.'

Cat felt a glow inside at the knowledge that her plan had actually worked, and Frankie now had a lovely lodger in her attic room, helping out with the bills and giving Frankie the chance to spend more time with her young family. 'Oh my God,' she said, clutching her hands together in front of her, 'that's fantastic news! But I should be helping them. I should do that, and then come and celebrate with you and McDreamy.'

'No, you shouldn't,' Joe said. 'Polly's got things under control at Frankie's. Go out and have a great time with your folks. They don't seem like typical parents – they're definitely more fun than our dad.'

Cat nodded. 'They're good parents, and I'm lucky to have them. Tonight won't be torture, but passing up *Grey's Anatomy* for anything just seems wrong.'

'I'll probably still be watching it when you get back. You can come and join me. Anyway, won't they be here soon? I should let you get on.' He slid past her and hurried up the second flight of stairs. Cat watched his retreating back and felt a new wave of attraction towards her best friend's brother at the fact that he loved her favourite medical drama series, and that he was prepared to own up to it.

15

As Cat and her parents left the restaurant – an Italian bistro in Fairhaven town centre that Cat hadn't ever noticed before, but was just the right blend of good food and cheerfulness – the wind cut into them like a knife. It was still August, supposedly the best part of summer, but there was a cold bite in the air. During dinner, she'd overheard snippets of conversation from holidaying families preparing for days at the beach, and wondered if they'd change their plans, or be stoic and end up shivering behind windbreakers, getting sand in their eyes; British holidaymakers tended towards the latter. The summer had started early and been glorious, so they were probably going to make up for that with an early slide into autumn.

'All right, love?' Her dad squeezed Cat closer to him, and she stumbled, wishing she'd worn flat shoes. It was a twenty-minute walk back to Fairview and Primrose Terrace, and the copious amounts of Chianti, followed by the obligatory shot of limoncello, wasn't going to make it easy.

'Yes, thanks, lovely evening.' Cat leaned into him as they walked.

'I meant about what we told you, about our decision. I know it's a bit of a shock.'

It was, and Cat was trying not to think about it. Her dad had other ideas.

'I think it's a brilliant plan,' she said, 'so exciting. But – what about your plot? Your plants? If you're off travelling around Canada for a year – minimum – what will happen to them?'

'Aha,' Peter said, clearly prepared for this question. 'Jimmy from the next plot along is going to take it over. There'll be less to do during winter and, depending on what happens, he'll have full rights to all plants and produce while he's looking after them. I couldn't be leaving it in better hands.'

'And your house?' Cat asked.

'We'll rent it out, my love,' her mum chipped in. 'We're not selling it. I know it seems hypocritical, bemoaning the fact that you've moved an hour down the road, and we're about to swap continents, but we'll stay in touch – there's email and Skype, and we'll share all the photos with you. You could even come out and join us for a few weeks, though you might not want to when things are going so well for you here. Your new, flourishing business, all those gorgeous pooches, your new man and your friends. We're so proud of you, Catherine, for striking out on your own. Being self-employed gives you so much freedom, and you've taken it upon yourself to go after what you want.'

'And now you're not with your dear old dad,' he added, thumbing his chest, 'there's no problem with dogs.'

Cat nodded. She'd never had a dog growing up, as her dad was allergic to them. Fine with wood dust and soil and all kinds of other irritants, but not dog hair. 'I love dogs,' she sighed, and realized she sounded like a typical drunk. She had hoped that the chill would help to clear her head, help her understand that her cheery, stay-at-home parents were going to fly to Canada, buy a huge, North American-style camper van and drive through the Rockies, but she was feeling hazier than when they'd left the restaurant.

'I know, love,' Peter said. 'Heart of gold, that's your problem.'

'When's that ever been a problem?' Delia scolded, shaking her head.

'Gold's fragile. Easy to get that gold broken.'

Cat looked up at her dad, at his over-serious tone, and his lowered brows, and burst out laughing. 'Gold's not fragile,' she said. 'Not like glass or paper or spun sugar.'

'I'll have you know the tensile strength of paper is '

'Peter,' Delia warned. 'None of this now. No need to spoil a good evening with physics.' She nodded decisively and picked up her pace.

Cat and her dad shared a conspiratorial eye-roll and Cat tried to stop giggling. She had really enjoyed the evening, even if her parents were a bad influence on her. At least her first walk the following day wasn't until after lunch. She could sleep off the inevitable red-wine hangover.

After what seemed like hours, they turned into Primrose Terrace. They were late enough that the sun had gone completely, and Cat stared up at the houses as they passed, starting with the high numbers and working their way down towards Jessica at number one. There was a light on in the attic window of number twelve, and Cat imagined Leyla settling in, making the beautiful room her own with some trinkets, make-up, perhaps a cuddly toy – she loved animals, after all.

They reached number nine and cat looked up at the facade. 'I'll walk you to the B and B,' she said. The living-room light was on at home and she knew Joe would be in there, watching *Grey's Anatomy*. She was torn between wanting to join him and slipping straight up to her room. She didn't want him to see her so drunk. Maybe a few more steps would help with her sobriety, even if it was harder on her feet. Ahead of them, a car door slammed and Juliette and Will got out of their silver Passat.

'I can't believe this, Will,' Juliette said loudly. 'I told you about the dinner party weeks ago. It's with a really important partner.'

'It's Keith's birthday. I'm not letting him down, and you shouldn't either. Someone else can do the client dinner, it shouldn't have to be you every time.' Will was in his mid-forties, with short, light-brown hair and the beginnings of a paunch that, Cat now knew, he was trying to ward off with surfing. He had a friendly face and warm green eyes that always seemed to be smiling. Except now.

'But *this time* it does, for reasons you won't understand.' Juliette took carrier bags out of the boot and shut it. 'So you'll have to say sorry to Keith for me, and I'll do the dinner on my own. Again.' Juliette rifled in her bag for her keys.

'Come on, Jules,' Will said. 'Say no to them, just this once.'

She shook her head, lips pressed together. 'I can't, I have to—' She noticed Cat, who, not wanting to walk straight through their argument, had slowed her pace, her parents falling into step behind her.

'Hi, Juliette,' Cat said. 'Will.'

'Oh, Cat,' Juliette said, 'thank you for walking Alfie and Effie today. When I got home they were happily exhausted, so you must have given them a good run.'

'I did. This is my mum and dad. Mum and Dad – Will and Juliette.' There was a round of hand-shaking, then they stood awkwardly on the pavement, the evening chill making them shiver, nobody wanting to seem rude by ending the impromptu chat.

248

'Mum and Dad helped walk Alfie and Effie today,' Cat said.

'Fairview's so lovely,' Delia said, nodding enthusiastically. 'So bright and cheerful, but not as . . . hectic as Brighton. The beaches are glorious. We were down by the lighthouse today, and some of the sand was completely empty – in August!' She laughed, and Juliette joined in.

'The water's too dangerous,' Will said, 'especially round those cliffs. The currents and rip tides mean it's not safe even for paddling, so families steer clear. And where the cliffs have eroded, it's much harder to get down to the beaches.'

'You know lots about the coast,' Peter said. 'I like a man who knows his terrain. We're planning a trip out to Canada, and I've been glued to our computer, researching where we can go during the winter, where's too treacherous in the ice, where we have to be on extra-vigilant bear-watch!'

'That sounds like an amazing trip,' Juliette said, putting her bags on the ground and pulling her coat close around her.

'Holiday of a lifetime,' Delia said, 'and it's never too late for one of those.'

'Never too late to follow your heart,' Peter added, and Cat winced.

Juliette gave Cat a quick, sharp glance, and Cat tried to make a face that conveyed it was just coincidence, and that she hadn't been talking about them with her mum and dad, but in her drunken state she had no idea how that face had come out.

'I think our next trip will be Australia,' Will said, his eyes lighting up. 'Our son's out there on his gap year at the moment, and it would be great to fly out, catch up with him—'

'Catch some waves,' Juliette added with a tight smile.

'Love, that's not what I was thinking—'

'That'll be a change, then,' Juliette snapped, and then straightened her shoulders and smiled. 'Sorry, it's been a long day. And it's hard to think about dropping everything and flying off around the world when there are so many responsibilities here. I don't mean to be a killjoy.'

'Good to meet you,' Will cut in, his smile suddenly gone. 'See you soon, Cat.' He took the keys out of Juliette's hand and, without looking at her, unlocked the door and went inside.

Cat bit her lip and was just about to say goodnight, eager that they remove themselves from the tense atmosphere, when her father spoke.

'You know,' Peter said, 'what I've learned over the years is that it's easy to build up our responsibilities so much that they become overwhelming, and then our judgement gets clouded. Sometimes it makes sense to take a step back, to step out of the cloud.'

Juliette stared at Peter for a moment, her expression unreadable. 'Well,' she said, 'my cloud's a pretty stormy one, and I'm not sure I can outrun it just now. It was nice to meet you, but I should check on the dogs.' She shook Delia and Peter's hands again, and nodded at Cat. 'Next week, normal time?'

'Sure. See you soon.'

Cat walked her mum and dad up to the B and B in silence, accepting a hug from each of them at the bottom of the steps.

'Trouble in paradise,' Peter said, gesturing up the terrace.

Cat nodded. 'But it's not our business.'

'You were butting in there a bit,' Delia said to her husband. 'We don't know them, and Juliette seemed . . . on edge even before you imparted your wisdom.'

Cat could hear her own thoughts in her parents' words, but she wasn't going to get involved. Not this time. 'I want to talk about you,' she blurted. 'I think what you're doing is incredible. It's just not – not what I expected. But I want you to be happy.'

'I know, love,' her dad said. 'And we'll see you lots between now and then, I hope? And Christmas. We can have a great Christmas before we head off.'

'A festive send-off,' Cat added.

'Exactly. Oh, goodbye, Catherine,' Delia said, giving her another squeeze. 'Take care of yourself, and let us know how it goes with Mark, eh?'

'Sure,' Cat said. She waited until they were inside, then turned towards home.

Without her dad to lean on, Cat felt unsteady on her feet and, concentrating on putting one foot in front of the other, she didn't notice Mark until he was inches in front of her. He had Chips on a lead, his other hand clamping his phone to his ear.

Cat gasped and he looked round, and Cat saw something – irritation, anger – flash across his face. The collar of his leather jacket was turned up against the sudden cold, and his whole body seemed stiff and uptight. He turned his face away from her, said something into the phone and hung up.

'Hi,' Cat said. 'How are you?'

'Fine. You?'

Cat nodded, her mouth drying out at the lack of warmth in his eyes. 'G-good, thanks. I've been out to dinner with my mum and dad.' Chips nuzzled her nose into Cat's hand in greeting, and Cat stroked the collie's silky ears.

'Ah, the infamous parents.' He gave her a quick, tight smile. 'Looks like you've had a good night. Sorry, but I need to take Chips in.'

'Sure,' Cat said. She leaned towards him, hoping for – at the very least – a kiss on the cheek, but he moved away from her and climbed the steps to his front door, Chips bounding up alongside him.

Cat stared at his front door for a few seconds after it had closed. She couldn't have imagined a scenario so different from the previous evening's, on that very doorstep. Was there something in the air? Had the sudden arctic blast brought with it a wave of bad temper? First Juliette and Will, and now Mark. She'd never seen him so cold, so inattentive, and it seemed especially out of character after the previous evening, when she had thought they were finally getting closer.

With a growing sense of disquiet, she stumbled back up Primrose Terrace. As she passed Will and Juliette's house she heard a door slamming and the dogs barking, wound up. She sighed, imagining how the bickering had elevated once they'd got inside. Not waiting to hear raised voices, she hurried past and gratefully put her key in the lock of number nine.

'Is that my sister or my Catmate?' Joe called as Cat pushed the door closed behind her. She hung her coat up, kicked her shoes off and went into the living room, flopping down on the sofa opposite him.

'Very funny. As you can see, it's me.' She threw her arms wide.

The room was full of the lingering, aromatic scents of Thai food, and the only light came from the TV in the corner of the room. When Joe was watching TV or a film, he did it seriously. He was wearing a pale T-shirt with an indiscernible logo on it, and faded grey shorts. He paused the television and turned his blue eyes to her. 'Good night with your folks?'

She nodded. 'Yeah, lovely, thanks. We went to this Italian in the town centre. Trattoria Rustica.' She tripped slightly over the name, and bit her lip.

Joe nodded, scrutinizing her. 'I've been once or twice. They do a good seafood linguine.'

'I had meatballs. How's *Grey's*?' She glanced at the screen. 'Which episode are you watching?'

'The end of Season Four.'

Cat's eyes widened. 'With the candles on the hilltop?'

Joe smiled. 'I've not got to that bit yet, but yeah.'

'That's the most romantic ever.' Cat got up and moved to the other sofa, next to Joe. 'Start it up again, I promise I'll be quiet.'

Joe laughed. 'Do you want a drink first?'

'No more wine. I've had way too much.'

'Coffee?'

She leaned her head back against the sofa. 'Coffee would be lovely. Thanks, Joe.'

She closed her eyes and listened to him move about in the kitchen, boiling the kettle, the quiet chink of mugs. Joe liked *Grey's Anatomy*. He made her coffee. He was straightforward. OK, so he wasn't always in a good mood, but then everyone was allowed their ups and downs, and if he wasn't happy with her, he told her. He wouldn't try to get her into bed one night, then act like she was a stranger the next. Well, Joe had never tried to—

'White. Two sugars.'

Joe cleared a space on the table, shoving a copy of the local newspaper down the side of the sofa cushion, and put the drinks down. He sat next to her, his weight causing Cat to roll slightly towards him.

'Sorry,' she said, moving away.

'You're quite drunk,' Joe said.

'Yes, thanks, Sherlock. I had realized.'

Joe was grinning at her, and Cat suddenly felt ridiculous. 'Maybe I should go to bed.'

'I've made you coffee, and we're almost at the good bit. Four seasons of backwards and forwards, and this is when Meredith and McDreamy finally get it together. You can't go now, come on.' He reached across her and pressed Play on the remote. Cat focused on the screen and the scenes she knew almost off by heart. She was acutely aware of Joe beside her, his shoulder brushing hers, and felt as though his eyes were on her the whole time, which was ridiculous because it was *this episode*, and there was no way he wasn't watching the screen.

At the end, after the American, overly romantic conclusion, Cat realized she had a lump in her throat.

'Well,' Joe said, switching the DVD off and plunging the room into near-darkness. 'There you go. Meredith and McDreamy happy ever after.'

'Except we both know they're not,' Cat said. 'Because it all goes wrong again, and then . . .' She couldn't even say what happened in the end, because it was too upsetting.

'But in this moment, right now, if I don't put another DVD in, they're happy.'

'You can't freeze a moment in time.' Cat sipped her coffee. It was lukewarm, but it was sweet against the wine taste hovering at the back of her throat.

'Isn't that what memories are?' Joe turned towards her, and Cat could feel his breath on her face.

'Yes, but – you can't live your whole life inside a memory. You have to move forward. I think you're doing that adbi – admirably. Whoops.'

Joe reached behind him and switched on the lamp. Cat blinked and rubbed her eyes.

'What am I doing *admirably?*' he asked.

'Moving on from Rosalin. You seem much happier recently.' She hadn't meant to be so blunt about it, but it was too late now.

He narrowed his eyes. 'I do? Have you been watching me closely?'

Cat shrugged. 'I live with you, I'm your *Catmate*. It's kind of unavoidable. You're only moderately grumpy now.' Cat's phone gave a short, merry jingle and she cleared the screen and silenced it, turning her attention back to Joe.

'I love how tactful you are when you're drunk.'

'Isn't honesty best?'

Joe looked away, looked back at her. 'Sure. Even if you're going to regret baring your heart in the morning. So if we're being honest, and your defences are down, how's it going with Mark?'

Cat sighed dramatically and closed her eyes. 'Fuck knows. Yesterday, after our date, he asked me back inside. He was attentive and charming and lovely. But when I bumped into him on the way home tonight, he couldn't get away from me quickly enough. I don't get him.' She shook her head. 'I fancy him, but I don't *get* him. Do you get him?'

'I barely know him,' Joe said. 'But he seems . . .' He scratched his cheek, searching for an answer. 'Slick.'

'Like an oil slick?'

Joe laughed. 'You said it, not me.'

'Tell me what to do,' Cat sighed again. 'Come on, Joe, you always know what's best. Tell me what I should do.'

'That's a lot of responsibility you're putting in my hands.'

Cat reached forward and grabbed his hands. Joe flinched, surprised, but then let her take them. 'They're such good hands,' she said. 'Your hands are your talent. They're steady and warm and they hold onto things well. They *have* to know what I should do about Mark.'

'I think you're giving them powers they don't have,' Joe said. 'And I don't think I'm the best person to ask. Rosalin was a car crash.'

'Why?'

Joe laughed humourlessly. 'Because she ran off with my best friend. I thought Polly told you? And she took something really important to me.'

'Your heart?'

'Oh God, Cat,' Joe rolled his eyes. 'Don't be such a soppy drunk. No, not my heart, though she bruised that quite a bit. No.' He looked at her. 'She took something else. Something that maybe I should have told you about before. Look, Cat . . .' He sighed and his gaze drifted down to their hands, which were still locked together. 'This thing about me and dogs . . .'

Cat held her breath. She knew he was about to tell her something important. 'You and dogs,' she murmured, and then, unable to stifle it with her hand, turned away to yawn.

Joe dropped her hands. 'Another time. Not now.'

'Why not now?' She leaned forward and tried to take his hand again, but missed and ended up pawing at his thigh.

'Because it's time you went to bed. Come on. Coffee's not working, sleep will.'

'I want you to tell me about you and dogs. I *love* dogs.'

'I know that.'

'So what is it?'

'It's nothing, really. Come on.'

He stood up and held out his hands. Cat took them and she let him pull her to her feet. His gaze met hers, and she was struck by how much warmth there was in his eyes; warmth that went all the way to his core. She inhaled.

'You OK, Cat?' he asked softly.

She swallowed and nodded, not trusting her mouth to say anything sensible. She wasn't sure it would be tactless again, but it might go too far in the opposite direction.

'My parents are moving to Canada,' she blurted instead.

'*What?*'

'Well, not moving. Taking a camper van, travelling around for a year. Maybe more.'

'Wow.' Joe shook his head slowly. 'That's huge. How do you feel about it?'

Cat shrugged. 'Don't really know. Weird. They're happy, which is good, but I've always taken it for granted that they'd be close by. Even moving here, they're still so close.'

'Able to turn up on your doorstep when you least expect it?' Joe said, smiling.

'Exactly.' She returned his smile, instantly feeling better. How could Joe make her feel better by just being there?

'You'll be fine,' he said quietly. 'They'll stay in touch, and you've got us now. I'll ply you with wine and limoncello whenever you're feeling bereft.'

'That's a very kind offer,' she whispered.

'Upstairs?'

'I'll wash this up and get some water. Maybe some toast.'

'Do you want me to do it?'

'I'm not that drunk,' she said. 'I don't think, anyway. Fuzzy round the edges.'

'You're cute when you're fuzzy.' Joe grinned.

'But not when I'm not fuzzy?' She folded her arms.

'I didn't say that. Don't get all indignant because I gave you a compliment.' He took her coffee cup from her and went into the kitchen.

'I was going to wash up!'

'You were too slow.'

'How would you like it if I said you were really sexy when you were angry?' She leaned against the kitchen door frame. 'That's not a compliment.'

'You've never seen me really angry.'

'I've seen you a bit angry.'

'And you thought I was sexy?' Joe ran the cold tap and filled a pint glass with water.

'It was an example. I'm not saying it's true.'

'But is it?' He put the water down and turned to face her.

'Joe, that's not the point.'

'Is it?' He took a step closer.

'I'm going to bed.' Cat turned too quickly and stumbled. She put her hands out, and the dining table saved her fall, her wrist twisting as her body weight landed on it. 'Yeouch!'

'Cat?' The main light flicked on and then Joe's hands were on her waist. He pulled her upright and turned her to face him. 'Are you all right?'

'Fine,' she murmured. 'It's nothing.'

He gently took her hand. 'Your wrist?' He slid his fingers up her palm and then along her arm. His touch was light, it made her feel peculiar, a feeling that her drunken brain couldn't quite pin down, but which was overriding the burning in her wrist.

'I've just jarred it. I'll be fine, honestly.'

'If you're sure.'

'I'm sure.' She drew her arm back, away from him. She needed time on her own, to let her brain slow down, otherwise she'd never get to sleep. 'Thanks for the coffee, though, and for the romance.'

Joe's eyebrows knitted together and Cat pointed at the TV.

'Ah,' he said. 'Meredith and McDreamy.'

'Happy ever after. Night, Joe.'

She waited until she heard him reach the first landing, then start the ascent up to his room, and then, clutching her wrist, she went back to the sofa and pulled out the copy of the *Fairhaven Press* that Joe had moved earlier. He'd done it so casually, but before he'd moved it she'd noticed, in the harsh light from the television, the piece of paper sticking out of it; the one with Joe's telltale pencil lines on it.

She sat down and looked at it, her stomach flipping as she realized what it was. It was another Curiosity Kitten cartoon, drawn on a scrappy piece of paper, like the sketches that Joe had ripped away from her grasp when he'd seen her looking at them. He'd shoved it inside a copy of the paper, so did this mean he was working for them, seeing where his drawing might fit in amongst the other content? Why hadn't he told anyone?

Here the cute, undoubtedly female Curiosity Kitten was at the bottom of a flight of stairs, looking determinedly up at a shut door at the top of it. Behind the door, visible only to the viewer, the room was bulging with stuff ready to burst out on the poor kitten as soon as she opened it. Cat could see boxes, a lamp, a guitar and, in the corner, a small and beautifully drawn dog. A cocker spaniel.

The butterflies in Cat's stomach beat their wings faster. Curiosity Kitten was wearing a spotty bandana around her head, a box of cleaning products at her feet. There was a guitar, and Frankie was teaching her the guitar. There was a cocker spaniel, just like Frankie's dog, Olaf. There was a curious cat wearing a spotty bandana, who wanted to open the door. Cat had convinced Frankie to open her attic door – she had wanted to help her, and Joe had initially said she was interfering.

Cat sat back and rubbed her head. Could Joe really be drawing a cartoon about her? Using her nosiness for his own artistic purposes? This had to be her, opening Frankie's attic door, preparing to go through the boxes and turn it into a usable room. It had been a success – Joe had said that himself only earlier that evening – but here, Joe was depicting it as a disaster scenario. The kitten would be sent tumbling down the stairs by the piles of stuff, including Olaf, who she and Joe had found running in the park, the event that had led her to Frankie in the first place.

Her curiosity was getting the better of her again – is that how Joe saw her?

She tried to think back to the other cartoons she'd seen. What had the kitten been doing in those? Could any of them be directly attributable to her? She couldn't remember, her fuzzy brain not letting her into those recent memories as clearly as she would like. Frustrated, she threw the newspaper across the room, half expecting more cartoons to come flying out. She retrieved it and leafed through every page, but that was the only Curiosity Kitten she could find. She put it back inside, and returned the newspaper to the side of the sofa.

So much for Joe being straightforward.

Feeling extra weary, and with a headache starting up behind her eyes, Cat had forgotten about her wrist. Pain shot through it as she went to push herself to standing, and she cried out. Flopping back on the sofa, Cat covered her eyes with her hands and forced down a sob.

How had things gone from feeling so right earlier that day, in the park with her mum and dad, to feeling so wrong tonight? The wine obviously wasn't helping, but she hadn't imagined her parents' impending move to the other side of the world, Mark's sudden coldness, or the cartoon she'd discovered. Mark was not as into her as she thought, and Joe was hiding things from her. How could she have misjudged them both?

The sound of the front door startled her and she looked up to see Polly, standing in the doorway wearing jeans and a T-shirt with an owl on it. Her calm blue eyes looked concerned.

'Cat?' she said. 'Whatever's wrong?'

And the familiar sight, the kindness in her eyes, was Cat's undoing. Her sob was loud and ugly, and in a moment Polly's arms were around her. Cat hugged her back, her arms circling her best friend's slender frame, her tears damping her long blonde hair.

In the morning, Cat couldn't decide whether it was her head or her wrist that was more painful. If only she'd drunk that pint of water before she'd gone to bed. If only she'd put some frozen peas on her wrist to stop the swelling. If only she hadn't bumped into Mark on her way home, or let her curiosity get the better of her when Joe moved his copy of the newspaper. She smiled to herself; her curiosity had led to her discovering that Joe was creating a cartoon about her curiosity. She knew he would laugh at that if she told him she'd found out about it, but she wasn't going to. She hadn't even told Polly.

Her friend had comforted her after her drunken outburst, and Cat had told her what had happened with Mark, and about her mum and dad's plans. Polly, knowing Cat so well, had assumed that she was most upset about her parents moving away, and that the blip with Mark was just that, and would be easily explainable. Cat didn't want to admit to herself – or to her best friend – that she was more bothered by Joe's secret.

Keeping things from Polly made her wonder about their friendship. She'd been living in the house since January, and she had realized that, despite being happier with this living arrangement than any other, and relishing her physical closeness to Polly, she didn't know her best friend inside out.

She had never felt she couldn't talk to her about something until now, and that was only because it was about Joe. But was Polly always so open with her? Had her friend been in touch with Owen since the barbecue? They'd got on so well, but Polly hadn't confided in Cat at all. How was she really feeling about her exams? What did her friend think about Rosalin? What *was it* with Joe and dogs? Both he and Polly had hinted that it wasn't just pure dislike that was stopping Cat from having one of her own – after all, Joe had been friendly enough with Rummy, Owen's fox terrier, when he thought Cat couldn't see him. There was something they were both reluctant to tell her, and that made her feel uneasy.

Cat was hungover and confused. She *was* a curious person – she couldn't really have a go at Joe for thinking that – but she'd felt closer to him last night than she'd ever felt before: watching *Grey's Anatomy*, opening up about Mark and Rosalin. But then she'd been knocked for six by the discovery of his new project. If he was using her as a model, why did it have to be her curiosity that he focused on? Was that at the forefront of his mind when he thought of her?

And she had no idea what was happening with Mark.

Cat didn't feel up to confronting either of them, and, as she turned over, inviting sleep to call her back, she thought of Juliette and Will, and their encounter the previous night.

They had seemed so unhappy, so at odds with each other, as if they were two strangers who both happened to be talking to Cat and her parents at the same time. She knew Elsie had warned her off getting involved, but if she could just make them talk to each other, make Will open up to his wife about why he'd quit his job and was spending so much time surfing, then wouldn't that be helpful rather than harmful? They could always say no.

The thought made Cat feel slightly easier, and she soon fell back into a deep, dreamless sleep, oblivious to the sound of the wind battering against the windowpane.

16

Cat's good intentions turned to nothing, because while Cat wanted to help Will and Juliette, a part of her brain was telling her to leave them to it. She didn't know them very well, and things were never as simple as they seemed. Besides, what would she say? *I can see that your marriage is in trouble, and I want to help? I'm sure there must be more to your husband's sudden lack of responsibility than meets the eye? My parents are happier than they've ever been and you need to give Will a chance?*

Juliette was always kind to her, and Cat didn't want to risk upsetting her, so she continued to walk Alfie and Effie and say nothing. Just as she tried to act normally around Joe, while not mentioning that she knew he was drawing a cartoon about how calamitous she was. She'd also pushed all thoughts of Mark to the back of her mind. It had been a few days since he'd all but ignored her on the doorstep, and there hadn't been a single text, or call, or sighting of the man who had until recently been so attentive.

She found herself looking wistfully up at his house just as Jessica sashayed past, jacket wound tightly around her against the unseasonably cold weather, her knee-length boots soft brown leather.

Cat herself had exchanged her summer dresses for cropped trousers, a striped boatneck jumper, and a cotton scarf to keep the wind from her neck.

'He's gone to London,' Jessica said. 'Didn't he tell you?'

Cat shook her head, feeling a cold sting of distrust. 'No, he didn't. Did he take Chips?'

Jessica nodded. 'He wasn't sure how long he'd be, so he took her with him. He didn't seem very happy about going, though. I wonder if things with his film have fallen apart? Just when it was going so well, too.'

Cat chewed her lip. 'Oh, I hope that's not it – he seemed so positive about this one.' But if that was true, it could explain his distance that night, though she would still have appreciated a text to tell her that he was going. And then a memory flashed into her mind. Talking to Joe on the sofa; her phone distracting her and her clearing the message without reading it. She hadn't gone back to look at it, had felt so despondent about Mark that she'd refused to even consider sending him a message. With dread crawling into her stomach, she resisted the urge to get her phone out immediately.

'He may need a shoulder to cry on when he gets back,' Jessica said, rubbing a manicured hand up Cat's arm. 'And I think that your shoulder would fit perfectly. Cute jumper, by the way. Trying to coax back the sunshine? I've pretty much given up.' She flicked her blonde hair behind her shoulder and gave Cat a warm, polished smile.

'It might not be gone for good,' Cat said. 'If we all believe enough, keep our fingers crossed.'

'I wish I had your optimism.'

Cat laughed. 'I don't feel very optimistic at the moment. Thanks for telling me about Mark.'

Jessica frowned. 'Of course. I would have thought he'd have told you first. Must get on – are you picking up my darlings tomorrow?'

Cat nodded and watched her walk away, then pulled her phone out of her pocket and went into Messages. There was one from Mark, which read:

Sorry about before. I have to go to London, a few weeks maybe. Shit happens. Will be in touch. M.

Cat closed her eyes. It was an apology, of sorts, but it didn't fully explain his behaviour. And he hadn't been in touch again, no follow-up text or phone call to explain why he'd had to go. She tapped out a reply:

I've only just found this! Hope all is OK, call when you can. Cat. Xx

She walked back towards number nine. Mark had had to go to London at short notice. His film was in trouble, which was awful, so perhaps there was nothing more to his coldness towards her. Had she been too quick to jump to conclusions? Everyone was allowed a bad day, weren't they? Mark would be away for a few weeks, and when he got back, Cat was going to be bold, take the bull by the horns, stop asking everyone what they thought of him and find out what she thought of him – every bit of him – for herself.

Despite the miserable August, the biting winds and the squally rain, Fairhaven – and picturesque, seaside Fairview in particular – was a popular holiday destination. Families braved the weather to make the most of their time off work and school. The beach was busy, kids untroubled by a few showers because they would get wet swimming anyway, parents sheltering under colourful parasols doubling as brollies. The Pavilion café was constantly busy, the picnics and games of cricket continued (if a little less enthusiastically), and Fairhaven town centre was chock-a-block with people shopping and café-hopping. The local mood was as buoyant as ever, and Cat wanted to applaud everyone for their resilience.

Polly see-sawed between revision and exams, and on the last day of August she left the house early to sit her final one. Cat hugged her goodbye, trying to dispel the nerves in her own stomach, and – with a day off, unusually – thought she might join the holidaymakers, walk into the town centre and browse round the clothes shops.

But as she left home, she found herself turning towards the Barkers' house instead of the shops, and before she'd had a chance to properly examine what she was doing, she'd walked up the steps of number six and knocked on the door. She expected Juliette to answer, only because she was the one Cat usually talked to, so was taken aback when Will opened the door, his green eyes smiling at her.

'Hi, Cat, how are you?' He was dressed in a bright-yellow T-shirt and shorts that ended in frayed hems, but there was a shiny black wetsuit underneath, skintight to his wrists and ankles. It looked weird. 'I didn't think you were taking Alfie and Effie today.'

'I'm not,' Cat said. 'I'm, uhm . . .' She glanced around her, looking for inspiration, and saw the retrievers' leads hanging on a hook by the front door. 'I was wondering if they were OK?'

'OK how?' Will folded his arms, his feet wide apart. Was he practising? She couldn't help it – everything she thought about him was now connected to a surfboard. Did he sleep in his wetsuit?

267

'They seemed a bit . . . snappy with each other last time I took them out. Like they needed to – to sort a few things out.' Where was she going with this? She couldn't help Will and Juliette by using their dogs as a metaphor.

'Really? They seem fine now.' Will pointed to the front room, and Cat took a step forward and peered through the doorway. The two retrievers were curled up in a single basket, a twist of sleeping paws and tails.

'Oh,' Cat said. 'My mistake, then. Sorry to have bothered you.'

'You didn't bother me,' Will said, 'though I am wondering if that's what you really came here for. Because "snappy" sounds a bit more like me and Jules, not our dogs.'

Cat considered laughing his comment away, trying to take it as a lucky escape, but she couldn't. Her shoulders sagged. 'I'm sorry. I noticed that things seemed a bit . . . rocky between you the other night. And it's really none of my business, but I—' What could she say? That she was a professional interferer?

'I heard about what you did for Frankie and those lovely girls,' Will said.

'You did?'

Will nodded. 'News travels fast round here. Have people been talking about us? On Primrose Terrace?'

Cat shook her head. 'No. Not really. I mean, Elsie and I may have mentioned that . . .'

'That we've not kept things as quiet as we could have?' Will gave her a rueful smile.

'It was silly of me to come,' Cat said. 'It's none of my business.'

'Listen, I'm about to head down to the cove, do a bit of practice. Fancy coming?'

'To surf? I've never surfed.'

'You could look after Alfie and Effie. They're allowed on that part of the beach, and I was going to leave them sleeping and walk them later, but this could kill two birds with one stone.' He grabbed his keys from a table, whistled to the dogs, who deftly untangled themselves and came running, and joined Cat on the top step. 'And then you can tell me why you really came to see me. Deal?'

Cat didn't have anything she desperately wanted in town, anyway. 'Deal,' she said.

She and Will sat on the soft sand of the cove, watching Alfie and Effie play close to the water. It was still early, and with this area of the beach mostly deserted, they had taken the opportunity to let the dogs off the lead for a bit. Cat had skinny jeans and a red cable-knit jumper on under her navy parka. It would be September tomorrow, still technically summer, but she felt as though she needed all the layers she could get.

She hadn't seen the waves as large as this before, had often brought the smaller dogs to this area and let them play in the shallows.

'I didn't realize it got like this,' Cat said, pointing.

'It's not the most consistent beach for surfing round here, but when it's good, it's one of the best.'

'And the dogs don't get in the way?'

Will shrugged, dug his toes deeper into the sand. 'Not really. And mostly people are pretty considerate. The surfers here are like their own little community, backing each other up, looking out for one another. I guess that's partly to do with how dangerous it can be, but mainly it's just because everyone's so laid-back, so friendly. The moment other surfers turn up, we'll put Alfie and Effie on their leads.'

'I'm holding you up,' Cat said. Will's surfboard was still strapped to the roof bars of the Passat in the car park. 'Don't you want to make the most of it?'

'Of course, but . . .' He scrutinized Cat, appearing to weigh something up in his mind. 'I think you have something to say. About Juliette and me. About the fact that we've not been getting on as well as we could. It wouldn't take an Einstein to work it out, would it?'

Cat looked out to sea and squinted. 'Oh, no, I don't really. I mean . . . every relationship has its ups and downs, doesn't it?' It was Joe, rather than Mark, who came to mind, and she pushed the thought away. 'It's none of my business.'

'It is when we're keeping the whole street awake with our arguing,' Will said, sighing. 'We've clashed, recently, over my decision to give up work.'

'I'd heard,' Cat said softly. 'My dad did a similar thing. He used to work in insurance, and one day he just packed it in, started spending his time at the allotment and inventing these weird gardening contraptions. Some of the stuff he comes up with . . .' She shook her head. 'A watering-can hat thing so you can keep your hands free while you're watering, and he's been working on this handheld rotating seed sower.'

'An innovative Monty Don?' Will laughed.

'Something like that. He's never going to set the horticultural world on fire, but he loves it. He's happy and . . . after some initial misgivings, my mum is too. And now – you heard the other night – they're packing up to go travelling round Canada, in a bloody camper van!' She laughed. 'They both had such straightforward jobs, but now . . . They're proof it doesn't have to be nine to five. I guess I don't need to tell *you* this, though.'

'I'm touched that you've taken the trouble to come and talk to us – well, me. It sounds like your parents have been through it, too. The thing is, I've not given up work, I'm just taking a break until the end of the year. My job in London was long hours sandwiched between a long commute. Sometimes I stayed in London and didn't see Jules for days. It was stressful, it was a world of pressure that I thought I was coping with.

'And then my friend, Thom, died. I'd worked alongside him for years and he was always cheerful. *Always.* Even when a deal went wrong or he'd spent his birthday staring at a computer screen. Nothing ever got to him.'

'What happened?' Cat whispered.

Will shrugged, looking out at the waves. 'He had a heart attack. He was forty-seven years old. I'm a year away from that, and I – I thought, fuck it. Get away from the pressure. And surfing is my release. It's the most freeing thing I've ever done, it's made me alive to so many things I've been ignorant of for years. God knows, I've tried to get Jules to come with me.'

'She's not keen?'

'It's almost as if she sees surfing as the evil that's lured me away from her. But I'm at home every evening, I'm cooking more, making the effort, and her reaction is to spend more time at *her* office. I've done this because I love her so much, and I miss her. But I don't know how to get through to her.'

'Is she worried about . . . the financial impact?'

Will sighed and rested his head on his folded arms. 'I don't think so. We've got enough saved, we've been careful, and I've told her this is only until the end of the year. I'm already putting feelers out for something closer to home. Our kids are grown up, Alex is off in Australia and Corrine's at university. I thought it was time for Juliette and me to spend time together, but she thinks it's the ideal opportunity to focus on her career.'

271

'It sounds tough.' Now that Cat knew more of the truth, she thought Elsie was right. She didn't have the experience or understanding to help them. 'Have you spoken to Juliette, *really* spoken to her about it?'

Will shook his head and whistled to his dogs as a large, bright-blue van pulled up in the car park and a man and woman emerged, already dressed in wetsuits. Will waved at them and the couple began walking over.

'That's Harvey and Zara,' Will said. 'They pretty much live in the van, chasing the waves around the coast. And the van's a surfer's treasure chest. If you need to borrow it, they've got it. Harvey, Zara!' Will stood and shook their hands. Cat pushed herself up and greeted them.

'Good to meet you, Cat,' Harvey said. He had a fuzzy ginger beard, some of the hairs close to blond, and his face was weather-worn and freckled. Zara was petite, with jet-black hair and porcelain skin that seemed unaffected by the sun. Her large eyes were dark grey.

'You should try the waves some day,' Harvey added when Will explained that she was a dog walker and had never been surfing.

'What dog do you have?' Zara asked, her eyes lighting up.

'Oh, none of my own yet. It's a bit complicated.'

'Well then, you need to meet Paddlepuss.' She turned and called back to the van. 'Paddlepuss?'

Cat watched as a small fawn pug jumped down from the back of the van and ran, as fast as his short legs could carry him, over to their group. His tiny, curled tail was wagging, and Cat dropped to her knees, let him lick her arms and rubbed the short fur between his ears.

'Oh my God,' she whispered, 'he's adorable. Why Paddlepuss?'

'He's only good with small waves,' Harvey said, grinning. 'Not a full surfer, yet.'

'It's a surfing term,' Zara said, when Cat frowned. 'For someone who stays in the shallows. Paddlepuss loves the waves, but he's never going to be able to go too deep with those tiny legs.' She looked down at him, and Cat could see the adoration in her eyes. She felt a sting of envy.

'It's a great name.' Cat laughed as the pug danced in small circles and then went to sniff Alfie and Effie, who were standing close by, panting after their run.

'If you ever want to have a go,' Harvey said, pointing to the water, 'we can kit you out. Just say the word.'

'Thank you,' Cat said, clipping the leads onto the retrievers. 'I will.'

'They seem nice,' she said to Will as Harvey and Zara went to get their surfboards, Paddlepuss trotting along behind them. 'And what a lovely dog.'

'They're good guys. And as I said, everyone helps each other out – you can pretty much tell that just from saying hi.'

'I can,' Cat admitted. 'So why don't you let me try and help you?'

'I'm sorry?' Will asked.

'Let me look after Alfie and Effie for a night. I'm three doors away – I could pop in regularly to check they were OK, walk them. Take Juliette away, somewhere without surfing and work phone calls and your dogs. Just the two of you. Talk to her properly. If she understands it better, if you tell her how much all this means to you, maybe she'll be more accepting.'

'You're happy to do that?'

'More than happy. It's easy for me, and it could make all the difference to you.'

'God, Cat –' Will ran his hand back through his hair – 'that would be wonderful. Thank you. Now all I need to do is convince Juliette to leave her work iPhone at home and come away with me.'

Cat left Will unstrapping his board from his car and took Alfie and Effie up along the cove, stopping at Capello's Ice Cream Parlour. Despite the colder weather, they were still working to their longer opening hours, and Cat could see Frankie through the window. Not wanting to leave the dogs on their own she waved, and her friend came out to greet her.

'Cat,' she said, 'it's lovely to see you. And these guys!' She gave each of the retrievers a hug. 'How are things?'

'I can't complain,' Cat said. 'How are the girls, and how's Leyla settling in?'

'Oh, Cat, Leyla's a dream!' Frankie shook her head. Even in her Neapolitan-coloured apron, Frankie still managed to retain her individuality, with a black T-shirt underneath and several thin braids running through her ponytail. 'She's friendly and polite, so clean, great with the kids. She's already done babysitting duties, though one of Lizzie's friend's mums has got all four of them – Olaf included – for me today. Owen's been so flexible about my hours, and the girls still can't get over me working at an ice cream parlour.'

'You're beaming,' Cat laughed.

'There's a lot to beam about. Most of it down to you.'

Cat waved her away. 'I planted a seed, that's all.'

'You got my arse into gear, and I met Owen – and Leyla – through you and Polly. You don't get how much you've helped out.'

'I'm happy to,' Cat said. 'Truly. But I've come to ask you something else. I'm having a few drinks for Polly tonight at ours – she's sitting her last exam right now – and I wondered if you wanted to come?'

'I'd love to, but being away from the kids all day I want to spend the evening with them. Can I take a rain check?'

'Of course.'

'What about Owen?' Frankie waggled her eyebrows. 'I'm sure he'd like to come and congratulate Polly.'

'Does he talk much about her? I have no idea if they've spent any time together since he came to yours that day.'

'He did,' Frankie said, 'right afterwards. It was Polly this, Polly that, Polly loves pistachio ice cream, and have you seen the colour of her hair, and isn't Polly one of the nicest people you've ever met? He literally bounced around the ice cream parlour. But recently, not so much. Her name's dropped out of the conversation, and Owen's sunny demeanour has gone with it.'

'He was keen, then?'

'Understatement of for ever.'

'I *know* she was too,' Cat said, folding her arms. 'I know it. And I know Polly's oversensible when it comes to things like studying, but if she's planning on keeping the man of her dreams waiting in the wings until everything feels just right, then she'll lose him.'

'Maybe she'll get in touch now her exams are out of the way?'

'If he comes tonight, then she won't have to.'

Frankie grinned. 'Are you sure that's wise? If you don't think they've seen each other, I mean.'

Cat shrugged, wondering if this was a step too far. But then life was short – the story about Will's friend proved that – and if you couldn't grasp your dreams by the hand, the way her mum and dad were doing, well then, what were best friends for?

'Is Owen in?'

Frankie shook her head. 'He and Rummy are visiting a supplier.'

'Can I give you the details of this evening and ask you to pass them on to him?'

Frankie shook Cat's hand. 'Consider me your co-conspirator. And let me get you a coffee and a scoop of ice cream. Which flavour?'

'Do you have vanilla?'

'Cat, we're an ice cream parlour. What do you think?'

Polly was upstairs in the bath, and Cat was rearranging bowls of snacks and the mini sausage rolls she'd spent the afternoon making. Her earlier bravado at inviting Owen had faded to a gentle nausea, especially when Owen had texted her, responding enthusiastically to her invitation. She should really have asked Polly.

'Why are you so nervous?' Joe asked. 'It's a few friends, and unless you've accidentally sprinkled cayenne pepper in the snacks, they'll be delicious.'

'I'm not nervous, I just – I want Polly to be pleased. She looked pretty exhausted when she got home.'

'She'll appreciate this,' Joe said. 'It's not a rave.'

No, but I have invited Owen, Cat thought. She could already picture the disappointment in Joe's eyes when he found out she'd interfered again. She swallowed and swapped round the olives and the Monster Munch, went to get glasses and ducked just in time to avoid bashing her head against the cupboard door she'd left open.

'Cat, Cat.' Joe put his hands on her shoulders. 'Slow down. Everything's fine.'

She turned to face him, smoothed down the front of the blue wool dress she'd changed into. 'I don't know.'

'It'll be great,' Joe said, fixing her with his stare. 'Would I lie to you?'

No, Cat thought, but you've been keeping things from me. But she didn't say that. 'You can't predict the future,' she said instead, and as if to prove her point, Shed shot through the cat flap, into the living room and jumped on the coffee table. Wotsits and Wotsit dust spread themselves liberally over the carpet.

'Shit!' Cat squealed. 'Look.'

Joe calmly went to the cupboard under the stairs and got the hoover out. Cat watched him clean up, then refill the bowl from the multipack Cat had bought, and put it back on the table.

'Ta-da!' He grinned and spread his arms wide.

'I've invited Owen,' Cat rushed. 'Polly doesn't know.'

Joe dropped his arms, his smile disappearing. 'What?'

'I thought she'd want to see him.'

'And you didn't think it would be best to ask Polly first? Do you even know whether they've been spending time together? They could have had a couple of dates and decided it was over.'

'If that was the case she would have told me before now. And he wouldn't have agreed to come so readily.' She folded her arms.

'But Polly might not want him here,' Joe said.

'Do you know that? Has she confided in you?'

Tight-lipped, Joe shook his head and they stared at each other, anger fizzing between them – Joe's new and bright, Cat's old and worn; Curiosity Kitten-shaped resentment that she was too afraid to confront him over. They were saved by the doorbell.

Cat went to answer it.

'Look who I've found!' Elsie gestured for Owen to go in ahead of her. He was carrying a bottle of champagne, and looked fresh and handsome in a red-and-white checked shirt and jeans. He greeted Cat and went into the living room, and Elsie reached forward and gave her friend a hug. 'What is it?' she asked. 'You're stiff as a board.'

'Polly doesn't know Owen's coming,' she whispered into her friend's ear.

'Oh, Cat.' Elsie sighed wearily, and Cat's heart beat faster.

At least Joe was hiding his anger, laughing with Owen and organizing drinks.

'It'll be fine,' Cat murmured to Elsie.

Elsie didn't look convinced, but she went into the living room all the same, leaving Cat in the hallway with her head in her hands. Shed was sitting under the coat rack, next to the radiator, looking up at her. Cat crouched down.

'Shed,' she said, rubbing his ears, 'what the fuck have I done?' Shed purred and shut his eyes in contented bliss. 'At least you appreciate what I'm trying to do here.'

'Cat?' Polly said. 'What's going on? I heard voices.'

Cat shot up and faced her friend. Polly's hair was wet from her bath, and she was wearing jogging bottoms and a pink Fat Face hoody.

'A-are you wearing that?' Cat asked.

Polly laughed. 'What's wrong with it? I'm so relieved the exams are over. I'm going to spend the next few days loafing, and not feeling guilty that I'm not revising every spare second of the day.'

'I-it's just I might have organized a mini celebration for you.'

'What, now?'

Cat nodded, swallowing down the lump in her throat.

'Well, that's OK,' Polly said, descending the stairs. 'Who's here?'

'Elsie,' Cat admitted, glancing towards the living room.

'That's great,' Polly grinned. 'We can crack open a bottle of wine.'

On cue, Owen popped his head round the door, gave Polly his best smile and held up the bottle of champagne. 'I think it deserves more than just wine. It's so good to see you, Polly, it's been far too long.'

For the second time in ten minutes, Cat watched as a pair of blue Sinclair eyes lost their smile and their warmth and hardened into anger. Anger aimed entirely at her. 'O-Owen,' Polly stuttered, 'I didn't know you were coming.'

'You didn't?' Owen's mouth dropped open, and Cat was sure it was her imagination, but his shiny curls seemed to wilt a little. 'I thought Cat said—'

'Cat didn't say anything to me.' Polly's smile was wide, but entirely humourless.

'I'm so sorry,' Owen murmured. 'Maybe I should go.'

'Oh, no, don't go.' Polly pushed past Cat and took Owen's arm, ushering him back into the front room. 'You're here now, and it would be good to catch up. I can talk to Cat about this later.'

Cat stayed in the hall, focusing on the shrivelling feeling that was taking over her insides, and saw Joe watching her. She couldn't work out if it was anger or disappointment that was shadowing his expression, but she didn't feel like finding out.

She turned towards the front door, wondering if her friends would forgive her for planning this disaster and then leaving them to it. Another perfect scenario for Joe's Curiosity Kitten cartoon, she thought bitterly. And, as if aware she needed rescuing, a loud banging reverberated through the walls. Cat didn't care who it was – at least it was a distraction. She flung open the door, relief coursing through her, and was met with the very beautiful, very angry face of Juliette.

'Cat,' she said. 'A word, if I may?'

'S-sure, except we've got some friends—'

'Fine. This won't take long. I just came to tell you to butt out. I can't afford to lose you for Alfie and Effie, otherwise I'd be cancelling our dog-walking arrangement too, but my marriage is *none* of your business. I know I spoke to you about the surfing, I know you may have . . . seen some things, but that doesn't give you the right to try and *fix* us. Whatever you said to Will earlier, you can forget about it. Understood?'

Cat opened her mouth, but nothing came out. She could sense the change in atmosphere, knew that everyone in the front room was listening intently, and thought that at least it would take the attention off her faux pas with Owen.

'O-of course, Juliette. I'm so sorry. It wasn't my place.'

'No, it wasn't. Remember that in future.' Juliette turned on her navy, patent court shoes and strode down the steps and back to her own house.

Cat closed the door and pressed her forehead against it.

'Wow,' Joe whispered, coming up behind her. 'What's your next party trick?'

Cat laughed humourlessly and turned to face him. She knew tears were threatening to spill out of her eyes, but there was nothing she could do about it. This was all of her own making. 'Wait until you try the sausage rolls,' she said. 'They should complete the circle of disaster.'

'Great,' Joe said softly, squeezing her arm and giving her a smile that was so reassuring. The first tear escaped and began to make its way down her cheek. 'Can't wait.'

17

After Juliette's interruption, the small celebratory gathering soon relaxed. Cat's sausage rolls were met with appreciative noises, and Owen's champagne added some much-needed fizz to the evening. Cat was, in part, vindicated, as Owen and Polly were soon sitting next to each other on the sofa, and stayed that way for most of the night. While they were chatting with Joe and Polly's colleague Leyla about the ice cream parlour, and whether Owen should expand his menu to get more business when it was quiet, Elsie cornered Cat.

She had been trying to stay elusive, keeping an eye on empty glasses and crumbs on the carpet, acting as a silent hostess rather than risking upsetting anyone else, but she had known that she wouldn't be able to avoid Elsie for the whole evening.

'Cat, what were you thinking?'

'About what?' Cat asked, putting a fresh bowl of olives on the dining table. 'Inviting Owen, trying to solve Juliette and Will's problems, or just in general, at this very moment?'

Elsie exhaled and shook her head. 'Some people don't want help sorting things out. They want to be left to get on with it. And you hardly know them. I'm surprised he welcomed your offer of help.'

'Will was lovely,' Cat said. 'I hadn't really spoken to him since we organized the walks, but he was kind, and receptive, and told me why he'd decided to leave his job. What he's doing makes so much sense – he lost someone close to him, and he wants to make more of his life, of his time with Juliette. She can't see it. She thinks he's being weak, or irresponsible.'

'But you haven't heard her side,' Elsie said, dropping into one of the dining-table chairs. 'You don't have enough information to understand it, and you shouldn't try. It has to be between the two of them.'

'But that's what I was trying to help with. I told Will to take Juliette away for a night, that I'd look after Alfie and Effie. I thought they could get away from work, from their routines, and talk it through.'

Elsie looked up at Cat, her lips curving into a knowing smile. 'It's an excellent idea, and if Will had been clever enough to suggest that without mentioning you, then he might have got away with it.'

Cat leaned against the table. 'What do you mean?'

'Imagine if Mark came to see you tomorrow, and said, "Jessica has suggested I take you away for a romantic weekend." Would you be delighted, or confused and upset that he'd been discussing your relationship with Jessica?'

Cat tried not to bristle at the thought. 'That's a very good point.' She sighed. 'Well, no use crying over spilled milk. I messed up, and I'm lucky I haven't lost them as a client, though Juliette might still change her mind about that.'

'I can see both sides,' Elsie said. 'I can see where she's coming from, but she's also asked you to walk the dogs at short notice, and hasn't been that subtle about the reasons. If you knew them a little bit better, she might have been touched at your kindness.'

'Except Polly knows me better than anyone, and she's not touched.'

They looked at Polly and Owen, taking up one seat of a three-seater sofa, squished together like peas in a pod. Owen kept looking at Polly in a way that made Cat a bit weak at the knees, and Polly's initial scowl had transformed into a constant, beaming smile. Joe was opposite them, talking animatedly, and Leyla was stroking Shed, who had returned to the gathering and was pretending to be the friendliest pet on the planet. Cat felt a strange twist of loneliness.

'She'll forgive you. You were clearly right, after all.'

'But it wasn't up to me, was it? I do too many things without thinking, without asking, and tonight is a prime example.'

Elsie rubbed her arm. 'Don't be so hard on yourself. Your intentions are always good. You just need to pick your battles a bit more carefully.'

Cat managed a smile. 'You're a wise old bird, Elsie Willows.'

'Less of the bird, thank you very much.'

'Sorry. Make it up to you with another sausage roll?'

'I'm completely stuffed, but these are delicious. You should cook more often, have peace offerings on hand to give to everyone you've annoyed. They'd have no option but to forgive you then.'

'You think so?'

Elsie nodded. 'Everyone's heart is connected to their stomach, so good food is always a winner.'

Cat wondered who she should try to make it up to first.

After Elsie and Leyla had left, Cat felt like a spare wheel. She cleared up what she could and tiptoed to the doorway, hoping she'd escape without anyone noticing.

'Cat?' It was Joe. 'Where are you off to?'

'I'm bushed,' she said. 'Thought I'd head up to bed.' She pointed towards the stairs, in case he'd forgotten where her bedroom was.

Joe glanced behind him. Polly and Owen were deep in conversation. He followed Cat out and ushered her up to the landing, stopping outside her bedroom door.

'You did good,' Joe said.

Cat laughed. 'Hardly. Unless my aim was to piss off everyone within a hundred-metre radius.'

'You've not pissed me off. And your instincts about Polly and Owen were spot on. Maybe she needed that push.'

'I wasn't trying to replace myself with Owen in Polly's affections.'

'Come on, it won't come to that,' Joe whispered. 'You put a lot of thought into this evening, and Polly will see that.'

'And now I need to go to bed.' He was being so kind, so supportive of her, his usual irritation a distant memory. She wondered why that was, but all she could come up with was that he felt guilty about the cartoon. Cat the calamitous, curious kitten. She shook her head.

'Hey,' Joe said, 'don't worry about it.' He reached out and put his arm round her shoulders, pulling her to him. Cat resisted at first, but his touch was comforting. If she was truly honest, it was more than comforting. She leaned her head on his chest and closed her eyes, breathing in his faint, spicy aftershave. She could hear his breaths, slow and even, perhaps a slight hitch of tension or emotion. His hand was pressed against her shoulder, his fingers light on her skin. She wanted him to move them, to slide them up her neck and into her hair.

Their stolen hugs were becoming more frequent and, maybe it was her imagination, but now there was a silent charge between them, a current of electricity she was finding it harder to ignore. But he was Joe, housemate and best friend's brother, creator of a secret cartoon about her tendency to interfere – not about her dog walking, something that put her in a good light, that she was proud of. Joe was a serial Cat Palmer disapprover; enough that he wanted to immortalize that side of her in his work.

And he wasn't Mark.

She pushed back and gave him a quick smile. 'Thanks.' She hadn't meant it to, but it sounded sarcastic.

'No worries,' Joe said, slightly stiffly. 'Goodnight.'

She watched him disappear up the second flight of stairs, and then went into her own room, desperate to wipe the evening's events from her mind and start fresh in the morning.

Cat left the house early the next day, glad that she was walking Valentino, Coco and Dior, Jessica's Westies. When Jessica opened the door, Cat launched into a hug, catching the glamorous author off guard.

'What was that for?' Jessica laughed, pushing Cat back to arm's length and looking at her.

'I'm not sure,' Cat admitted. 'For not being annoyed with me.'

'Why would I be?'

'I'm making quite a good job of infuriating everyone recently. I'm looking forward to taking your dogs out, getting some fresh air and some time to think.'

285

'Come round for coffee next week,' Jessica said. 'I've got deadlines to meet, but once I've sent my book off to my editor and have my head above water, we should spend the morning putting the world to rights.'

'I would love that,' Cat said. 'Thank you.' She bent to clip the Westies' leads onto their collars, opening her arms as they spilled towards her, licking and nuzzling and wagging. Cat embraced them, their non-judgemental, loyal little bodies showering her with affection. She wasn't sure it was possible to piss off a dog (except maybe Chalky, who was far too wise for his own good). Perhaps that was one of the reasons she loved them so much.

Wrapped up against the cold in a hound's-tooth jacket with a wide belt, Cat strode into Fairview Park, the Westies bounding at her feet. She tried to clear her mind of her worries, but kept circling back to them: Polly's anger, Joe's cartoon, Juliette's fury at her interference, and Mark's absence. Everything felt in a muddle. She spent as long as she could with the three Westies, letting them off the leads, giving them treats, indulging in their needs for cuddles and conversation. She talked to all her dogs, and she was sure they understood her.

As she began to make her way back to Primrose Terrace, she saw Mr Jasper. He was shuffling along the path around the park's perimeter, handing out leaflets, a satisfied smile on his face. Cat changed direction, intent on avoiding him, but a moment later there was a tap on her shoulder.

'Good to see you've only got three dogs today,' he said. 'You're being responsible for once.'

Cat turned round, gritting her teeth. 'Glad that you approve,' she said. 'Not that it's up to you.'

'No,' he said, rocking backwards and forwards on his heels. 'No, not up to me at all. But I do have *some* sway.'

'With what?' Cat asked. 'Your protest was weeks and weeks ago, and nothing's come of it. I haven't seen any signs, nothing in the paper.'

'Oh, you just wait,' Mr Jasper said, his eyes flashing. 'You'll see.'

Cat felt a jolt of worry. She couldn't face the thought of this man threatening her business, not on top of everything else. 'Look, Mr Jasper, can't we talk about it, hear each other out and come to some kind of truce? If you got to know the dogs, then—'

'Sorry, young lady, I have to go. Things to do, people to see.' He gave her a saccharine smile, glared at the Westies and hurried down the path towards the Pavilion café. Cat watched him go, her eyes narrowed, and resolved to find out if he was being serious, or if it was just another scare tactic.

As darker clouds rolled in overhead, Cat dropped the Westies off, using her key so as not to disturb Jessica, and gave them each a brush. The dogs raced to their baskets, snuggling down by the French doors that overlooked Jessica's beautiful garden.

Cat shoved her hands in her pockets as she made her way up Primrose Terrace. The grass verges were still green and lush, but Cat knew that, really, summer was over. It was another thing to add to her misery.

This wasn't like her. She usually made the best out of a bad situation, but things were getting to her. She'd made mistakes, she felt out of sorts. She went past the bed and breakfast, saw Bossy sitting in one of the windows, his exaggerated Frenchie frown giving her a moment of amusement. She waved at the dog, but he stayed stock-still, as if he was an expensive statue.

287

Next to them was Mark's house. Cat looked up at the windows, her heart rate increasing as she saw the living-room light was on. A quick glance confirmed that the Audi was parked outside. Mark was back? She checked her messages, determined not to jump to any conclusions, but there was nothing.

Brilliant – he was back and he hadn't told her. She started walking again, the wind getting into her eyes, making them sting.

She'd almost made it to the Barkers' house when she heard footsteps behind her, but she kept walking until a hand landed firmly on her shoulder.

'Cat Palmer, will you please stop for one second?'

She turned and looked up at Mark. Mark with his soft brown wool jumper, his dishevelled hair and those dark, amused eyes. He looked tired, maybe, a slight pallor to his skin, but that could be due to the absence of the sun.

'You're back,' she said.

'I've been back thirty minutes. I'm back and I'm staying.'

'For good?'

'For the foreseeable future.'

'What about your film? Jessica told me things had gone wrong, that—'

'Let's not talk about my film.'

'But that night, when you left, you were so off.'

'Off?' He frowned.

'With me. You barely said hello, acted as if I was a stranger. The day after our date. You'd had some bad news, I get it, but even so.'

'I wasn't thinking.' He rubbed her arm. 'I was distracted, I'd just had a shitty phone conversation. I'm sorry. Let me make it up to you now.'

288

She stared at him, wondering whether to believe him.

'Come on,' he continued. 'I want to hear how you've been. I want to immerse myself in Fairview, and all it has to offer. That's mainly you, Cat, in case you were wondering.' He grinned down at her, but Cat couldn't raise a smile.

'What's wrong? I was counting on you to fill me with enthusiasm and happiness. Are you really that mad at me?'

'Sorry,' Cat said, sighing. 'It's not just you. It's not you at all, really.'

'What is it, then?'

'Long story. Lots of them, in fact. Lots of little stories that culminate in the fact that I'm an idiot.'

'Don't hold back on the self-pity for my sake, please.'

Cat glared at him, but a smile was tugging at her lips.

Mark took her hand. 'Come in and tell me about it.'

Cat glanced at her house, where exam-free Polly could be waiting to confront her about Owen, or Joe could be waiting to be kind to her while drawing her falling head first into a pond, or getting her fingers burned. Number nine was complicated, but wasn't Mark complicated too?

'Come on, Cat,' Mark said softly. 'These last few weeks have been tough for me. I know we can make each other feel better. And Chips is dying to see you too. Come and say hello to her, at least.'

Cat narrowed her eyes. She had to give it to him – he knew how to get to her.

'OK,' she said, 'lead the way.'

Mark's front room was sparsely decorated and a little on the soulless side, with black leather sofas and a huge television on one stark white wall. But there was tea, and some fancy chocolate-covered coffee beans, and Chips had been eager to say hello to her and now, warmer and with Mark's full attention, Cat had to admit she was feeling better.

'You're too generous for your own good,' Mark said, once Cat had told him her sorry stories, including that she and Joe weren't getting on as well as they could be, but with no mention of cartoons. 'You spend too much time thinking of other people, and not enough about yourself.'

'I'm not sure that's entirely true.' Cat shuffled round to face Mark, to look into his dark eyes. 'I hate people being unhappy, I hate unrest and disquiet, and so I . . . fumble my way through things, focusing on what I want to happen but not the fallout, the unintended consequences.' Wasn't that what Alison had said about her? Had she been right all along? Cat closed her eyes. 'Ugh.'

'No "ughs",' Mark said, lifting her chin. 'You've told me what's wrong, now we have to come up with a way to forget about it.'

'What happened in London?' Cat opened her eyes. 'What's happening with your film?'

'It's on hold,' Mark said. 'Not yet the final curtain, just a longer interval than I'd planned. But let's not talk about that either. Forget about the sadness.'

'How do you propose we do that? Isn't this the last of the chocolate?' She held up the bowl with the few remaining coffee beans in it.

Mark smiled at her and shook his head. 'You, Cat Palmer.'

'Me what?' Cat returned his smile.

'That's how we'll forget – by focusing on you.'

'But I'm the cause of my sadness, so how can I use me to forget about it?'

'Don't be so difficult,' Mark said, leaning in and kissing her. Although she had known it was going to happen, the thrill of his touch went through her like lightning. She let him kiss her, let it transport her back to hotter weather and his front doorstep, his touch as gentle and as tantalizing as the summer breeze that had wrapped itself around them.

Was it really this easy? A month without speaking, then straight back to this? But as Mark's kiss intensified and she responded, she felt everything else slip away, felt all her worries disappear as his presence, and his lust, took her over. Yes, she decided, as he wrapped his arms around her and pulled her against him, it was this easy. After all, they were only carrying on from where they'd got interrupted last time.

It was starting to get dark when Cat gave Mark a final kiss in his hallway – this time just inside the front door, unseen by neighbours. The orange glow of a streetlight slipped through the decorative glass panels, casting Mark in a soft light, marking him out amongst the shadows.

'When will I see you again?' he asked.

'When do you want to see me?'

'Now. Tomorrow, and the next day, and the next.'

'I could probably do one of those,' Cat said, pretending to consider it. Mark rolled his eyes and kissed her again, pulling her towards him. Cat resisted, slipping out of his grasp and bending to stroke Chips, who had joined the small farewell party. She looked back at Mark, standing in his jeans and an open shirt, and then, smiling to herself, she stepped out into the night and closed the door gently behind her.

Her hair was still wet from the shower, the chill finding her head, and she wrapped her coat around her and dawdled back to her house, to Polly and Joe, and all the niggles she'd left behind.

She should feel elated that she'd taken the next step with Mark, and that he didn't want to forget her now they'd made their way into his bed. She should be skipping down Primrose Terrace. And she couldn't deny that sex with Mark was as incredible as she'd imagined, that it was fun but intense, with no room for awkwardness after the months of building desire. His confidence was infectious, and they just seemed to *get* each other. Even thinking about it made her breathless.

She glanced up at the Barkers' house, thought she saw the curtain twitch, and sighed to herself. Were her other worries clouding her happiness at being with Mark? Was she chronically down in the dumps? Mark was gorgeous and attentive, sexy and charming, and – despite earlier concerns – definitely into her. What was there to feel weird about?

Trying to shrug it aside, she climbed the steps of number nine and unlocked the door, stepping into a pool of light spilling out of the front room and the sound of canned laughter. Joe and Polly were laughing at something on television, Shed stretched out between them, his eyes closed. They looked up when she came in.

'Cat,' Polly said enthusiastically, 'where have you been? We're getting a takeaway.'

'You've waited for me?'

'Of course.'

'And you're not mad at me?' She glanced at Joe, who was looking at her, his blue eyes narrowed.

'No,' Polly sighed, 'no, I'm not.' She got up and gave Cat a tight squeeze. 'I was a bit cross last night, but only because I was tired, and surprised. Owen and I, we . . . we like each other, and I guess I was being a wuss about it. And you sprang it on me – if I'd had the choice, I wouldn't have been wearing my jogging bottoms. But I had a great time and so I want to thank you, and apologize.'

Cat's chest contracted with relief. 'Oh, Polly. There is nothing for you to apologize for. I've been so worried.'

'You silly Cat,' Polly murmured, standing back. 'Hey, your hair's soaked. Is it raining? I can't hear it.'

Cat glanced behind her as if, on cue, it might start raining and give her the perfect alibi.

'Noooo,' she said, drawing the word out, 'it's not raining.'

Polly and Joe both looked at her, waiting for the end of the sentence. 'I . . . uhm, Mark's back, and so I . . .'

'Cat!' Polly squealed. 'Seriously?'

'You went swimming together?' Joe asked, sarcasm heavy in his voice.

Cat tried to smile at him, but he looked defeated, his gaze not quite meeting hers. Her stomach gave an unexpected twist, and she didn't know what to say. 'Something like that,' she murmured, flopping onto the sofa opposite them.

'So you and Mark, you're serious then? After all this time.' Polly shook her head. 'I'm so happy for you, so happy!'

'Me too,' Cat said. She knew she didn't sound convincing. It was a big change, she told herself. It would take a bit of getting used to, that was all.

'That's great,' Joe said, matching Cat for enthusiasm. He ran his hand through his hair. 'And,' he sighed, 'perhaps it will soften the blow.'

'What blow?' Cat saw Polly and Joe exchange a glance, and her stomach twisted harder. 'What is it? What's wrong?'

Joe picked up a leaflet from the dining table. He came over and crouched in front of her. She resisted looking at the piece of paper and instead looked at him, at his short blond hair in thick, untidy tufts, his skin holding onto the brown glow, the smattering of freckles he'd acquired over the summer. His too-blue eyes were looking at her with undisguised sadness. Her gaze dropped to his mouth, his jawline, the sparkle of blond stubble.

She inhaled and reached out for the paper. Joe let go of it, but didn't drop his gaze.

'What is it?' she said again. She wanted him to tell her and protect her all at the same time.

He broke his hold and glanced down, and Cat read the words once, twice, three times.

Only some words stuck in her mind:

Notice from Fairhaven Council . . . in response to petitions . . . meeting to decide . . . Fairview Cove . . . dogs . . . no longer allowed . . . hours of nine a.m. and six p.m. . . . all year round.

'W-what?' Cat looked up. 'Is this a joke?'

Joe shook his head. Polly looked upset.

'Dogs might not be allowed at the cove any more? Why didn't we know about this? Why haven't we had a chance to protest?' She thought back to Mr Jasper's words in the park, and realized that *this* was what he'd been talking about. Not just an empty threat. A real, heartbreaking one.

'It seems Mr Jasper has gone about it in a pretty underhand way,' Polly said, 'though I'm not sure how he's managed to get so far with it under the radar.'

'It's awful,' Cat said. 'It's the same hours as the main beach, so there won't be anywhere we can take dogs during the day. They love the beach, they love the water. During the winter it'll be dark at the times they're proposing, and you can't take dogs on the beach in the dark.'

'I know, Cat,' Polly said. 'I'm so sorry.'

Cat felt her anger rise, her hands gripping the paper tightly. Joe reached out and put his hand over hers and, feeling a spark she didn't want to acknowledge, Cat flinched and drew back. She glanced him a silent apology, but he sat back on his haunches, wiped his hand over his face.

'Sorry, Joe,' she murmured. 'I just can't believe that he would go this far. Or that the council would even consider approving it.' She read the leaflet again, forcing herself to take it in. 'The council meeting's on the first of October,' she said. 'That's so soon. God, Disco and Chalky *love* the cove.'

'It's crap,' Joe said, 'but Cat, there's still the park, and there isn't much we can do about it.'

'Isn't there?' she said, defeat creeping into her voice. She thought of Alfie and Effie playing in the waves, Zara saying that Paddlepuss loved the water, Will telling her that all the surfers looked out for each other. Dog walkers were the same – she only had to remind herself of her Pooches' and Puppies' Picnic to know that. 'Isn't there?' she said again, waggling the leaflet, her eyes lighting up with a kernel of an idea.

'I don't think so,' Polly said. 'I mean, what could we do?'

'Hang on, Sis,' Joe said, 'I know that look on Cat's face.'

'What?' Polly said. 'What is it, Cat? Joey?'

'There is something we can do,' Cat said. 'I mean, we can't guarantee it'll work, but we've got a month to show the council that this isn't what we want, that Mr Jasper's not representing the views of the whole of Fairview.'

'What, Cat? What are you going to do?'

'I'm going to do what I do best,' Cat said, grinning. 'I'm going to interfere.'

18

Cat was on a mission, and she only had a month to achieve it. She set about it with a fervour she hadn't felt for years, and with the knowledge that what she was doing was right for Fairview.

At the beginning of the year, when she'd first moved to Primrose Terrace, would she have been as concerned? She'd always loved dogs, but they hadn't been a part of her life then the way they were now. Now she was a dog walker, she was part of the community, and she would stand up to anything that threatened them.

She started an online petition, wrote letters to the council and the *Fairhaven Press*, set up a @dogsatthecove Twitter account and a Facebook page. She had clients and friends she could call on to help spread the message throughout Fairview and, as outraged as Cat, Jessica had used her influence to talk about it on the local radio stations and promote the campaign to her thousands of followers.

In a short amount of time, Cat had built up momentum. She'd had one meeting with a local council officer who had spent an hour not meeting her eye and giving her vague, unsatisfactory answers, but after some follow-up emails she'd convinced them to send someone to attend the event she was organizing.

More than anything else, she'd been walking the dogs at the cove. She'd talked to as many people as possible, giving out flyers with petition links and the council's email address. And when she was dogless – and despite September continuing to be colder than usual, with strong winds and sporadic sunshine – she was on Fairview's main beach, convincing those without dogs that it was still important, asking them to support her, to let her show them that dogs had as much right to a beach as people did.

But she needed more of an incentive for her grand finale than just the beach and a variety of different pooches, especially if she wanted to do more than preach to the converted – so she needed to speak to Will.

She'd continued to walk Alfie and Effie, but her exchanges with Juliette had been short and businesslike, and she hadn't seen Will at all. She wondered if he'd gone away on his own, whether her offer of help had, in fact, led to them growing further apart.

She phoned Juliette and asked to speak to the two of them together. Juliette was sceptical at first, but agreed to see Cat when she promised it was nothing to do with their personal life.

She sat on their wide, cream sofa, stroking Alfie's curly coat while the retriever snoozed gently, his head on her lap, Effie at her feet. Cat noticed that husband and wife sat apart, a sofa cushion unoccupied between them. She noticed, but she knew to ignore it.

'What's this about, Cat?' Juliette asked. She was wearing jeans and a fitted red shirt. She looked calm, and immaculate as always, but there was a fire in her eyes that Cat was wary of, especially after their last encounter. 'Are you putting your rates up?'

Cat shook her head, swallowing. 'Nothing like that. Juliette, Will, I don't know if you saw the notice that dogs might be banned from the cove?'

Juliette narrowed her eyes, and Will nodded. 'Yeah,' he said. 'It'll be an absolute killer. I mean, lots of my –' he glanced at his wife – 'surfing mates have dogs. You met Paddlepuss. It's always been relaxed down there, and not the first choice for families, so it seems a little on the harsh side.'

'It's ridiculous, nothing more to it,' Juliette said. 'Has it got anything to do with those people at your event? The little podgy man and that Minnie Mouse girl?'

Cat had to stifle a laugh at the thought of Alison as Minnie Mouse, terrorizing small children at Disneyland. She nodded. 'I'm sure they're behind it, and we – that's me and my house-mates, Polly and Joe – think it's unfair that they've managed to get so close to the decision without us being given the chance to have our say. So –' she sighed – 'I'm sorry to ask a favour, but I was wondering if I could have your help?'

'What can we do?' Will spread his hands wide, the gesture matching his warm smile.

'I was wondering how you felt about being part of my grand finale? You and your surfing friends?'

'And doing what?' Juliette asked sharply. 'How could they possibly help with this?'

Cat sat forward on the sofa. Alfie opened one eye for a moment, nuzzled further into her lap and went back to sleep. 'Let me explain,' she said, unable to stem the bubble of excitement at the last stage of her plan. It would hopefully help to keep dogs at the cove, but it might also, surreptitiously, be a way of bringing Will and Juliette together without either of them suspecting a thing.

Cat woke on the last day of September to the sound of rain pelting against Mark's bedroom window. She closed her eyes and snuggled into his back, the reality of the date eluding her for several blissful moments.

Mark groaned and rolled over, wrapping his arms around Cat and burying his face into her neck.

'Let's not get out of bed today,' he said, his lips tickling her skin. 'The weather's giving us the day off.'

'Very tempting,' said Cat, 'but dog walkers are immune to the weather. And I've seen you walking Chips in the rain, looking all sexy and dishevelled like a tormented hero.' She turned to face him.

'Tormented hero?'

She nodded.

'I'm surprised you noticed. I seem to remember you had your hands full with several overexcited dogs and a terrified squirrel.'

'You rescued me, and I would have been pretty ungrateful if I hadn't taken the time to appraise my rescuer. Why did it take us so long?'

'What?' Mark asked, his brow furrowing. 'To get the dogs away from the squirrel?'

'To get to this?' she kissed him.

'Ah,' he said softly. 'The best things are the ones you have to wait for. If we'd done it sooner, it might not have been as good.'

'That's some twisted logic,' Cat murmured. 'But I'll let it go, for now.'

While she'd been launching her protest at the looming dog ban, she had also been kept busy by Mark who, true to his word, had shown no signs of leaving Fairview or even slipping back to London for a few days. He was attentive and fun to be with, and hadn't lost any of his smoulder as they spent more time together. Cat was relishing it, finding out more about him, although part of her worried that he was still holding something back; that she wasn't quite getting all of him.

She understood that he had film wrangles to sort out, and sometimes his phone would ring and he would disappear into another room, shutting the door and leaving her with Chips and her thoughts for long periods of time. But it was his life, his passion, and she couldn't begrudge him that.

Splitting her time between number four and number nine Primrose Terrace wasn't complicated. She felt bad that Polly had just got her free time back and she wasn't around much to spend it with her, but she hoped that Polly was so wrapped up in Owen that she hadn't really noticed.

'At least the dogs and surfers won't mind the rain,' Mark mumbled.

Cat's heart missed a beat and she sat bolt upright. 'Shit! It's today! How could I have forgotten? Stop being so distracting.'

'I could distract you for longer if you like. It doesn't start for a couple of hours.'

'But I have to be organized,' Cat said. 'I need to make sure everything's in place.'

Mark rolled onto his back, closed his eyes for a moment and then got out of bed. 'Come on then. I'll cook us breakfast and we'll be ready for everything today has to throw at us.'

'We?'

'I'm at your mercy for the whole day. Chips too. This is important to you – and to Chips – so it's important to me.'

Cat grinned, bounced out of bed and gave him a long kiss. 'Thank you,' she said. 'You practically perfect person.'

Mark counteracted her soppiness by lifting her up and depositing her back on the bed. Cat didn't have the inclination to protest.

By the time they reached the cove the rain had slowed to a soft drizzle, and Cat thought she could see the clouds parting in the distance. She was wearing a padded parka over a fleece and leggings, all of which was over her swimming costume. Mark was in a black North Face jacket, jumper and jeans. Cat wasn't sure if, despite telling him at least five times, he had his swimming trunks on.

Harvey and Zara were already there, their mobile surfers' 'grotto' parked in the car park, back doors open onto the beach.

'How are the waves?' Cat asked, running up to them.

Harvey shrugged, stroked his long, fuzzy beard. 'Not bad. Not epic, but not a damp squib either.'

'Probably better for first-timers,' Zara said. Her black, silky bob was slicked back off her face, and Cat wondered why someone who spent most of their time in the water felt the need to wear so much eyeliner. It must be super waterproof.

'That's perfect, then.' Cat nodded decisively.

'You think this'll work?' Harvey asked. 'This surfing dog mash-up?'

'I don't know,' Cat said, 'but I hope so. The petition's got over four thousand signatures, and Jessica Heybourne's been helping to spread the word. But I thought we needed something special, something that would appeal to everyone – not just dog walkers – and show how we can all enjoy the beach together. Surfing's a big appeal, but there's also paddling, the barbecue we're putting on, just spending time down here – it's so beautiful.'

'So you wanted to fill this place with as many people as possible?'

'As many people and as many dogs as possible. I've got a council officer coming, someone from the *Fairhaven Press*, Fairhaven FM. I want to make a big noise, show them we're not happy with what they're proposing.'

'Sounds awesome,' Harvey said, 'but then we already love surfing, and we're pretty fond of Paddlepuss too.' The pug was sniffing at their feet, skirting round Chips with either nervousness or adoration, it was hard to tell which.

Leaving the surfers to get their van organized, Cat and Mark began unravelling the banners she'd made. *Say No to the Dog Ban at the Cove. Dogs and Surfers Unite. Sea Dogs For Ever.* They staked them into the sand, then began setting up an area with disposable barbecues, cool boxes and thermos flasks.

Joe and Polly were the next to arrive, bringing food and paper plates. Joe had a rolled-up banner tucked under his arm. They joined them on the sand and Mark and Joe shook hands, eyeing each other warily. Cat watched them with an uneasy feeling in her stomach until Joe unfurled his banner, and the beauty of the design took her breath away.

A wave ran along the bottom, cresting at the end and carrying with it a dog on a surfboard, complete with sunglasses and wide surfer grin. Above, in bold, colourful writing, it said, *Let Surfing Dogs Hang Ten.*

'Joe, that's incredible!' Cat flushed. 'I hope it survives the weather, because I want to keep it for ever.'

Joe, rugged up against the cold in cargo trousers and a navy Animal hoody, shrugged and grinned. 'I've used waterproof pens, so hopefully it'll last.'

'This,' Polly said, waggling the Thermos flasks, 'is going to be amazing. A dog-and-surfer sit-in. I hope the council can see how important it is.'

'They've promised me they're coming,' Cat said, 'and so is Phil from the *Fairhaven Press*. He's bringing his Labradoodles.'

She glanced at Joe and he looked away.

'Who else is coming?' Polly asked.

'All our guys,' Harvey said, joining them. 'We never miss a party – especially when it's for a good cause.'

'And people without dogs will hopefully want to come and try surfing, to join in, to support us,' Cat said. 'Harvey and Zara have got wetsuits and boards in their van that everyone can borrow, and a few of the surfers have agreed to show them how to do it.'

'Can I try?' Elsie asked as she approached over the sand.

'If you want to,' Cat grinned. 'You too, Captain.' She hugged them both, then crouched to greet the mini schnauzers. Disco stood on her hind legs and rubbed her nose against Cat's cheek, while Chalky took the opportunity to lie on the sand, his head on his paws. 'But you don't have to, Chalky,' she said, giving the older dog an affectionate rub. 'We won't make you hang ten, I promise.'

Paris trotted up to her, and Cat felt a rush of affection for the little dog who, when she'd first met her, had been as timid as a mouse. Now the papillon with the amazing ears strutted around the small group, commanding affection from everyone in turn.

'My little Parisian lady,' Captain chuckled. He was wearing a navy hat with an anchor on it, and seemed in excellent spirits – whether because of the event or at being in Elsie's company, Cat wasn't sure.

'What's hanging ten?' Mark asked, pouring tea into plastic mugs and handing them round. 'I haven't got a clue about surfing.'

Harvey grinned a laconic, bearded grin. 'I think you've just volunteered to be our first guinea pig,' he said. 'Come on, let's get you kitted out.'

'Oh, no,' Mark said, turning his smile on Harvey, 'I'm fine. Maybe later.'

'No excuses. Come on, mate, it's awesome.'

'I think Cat needs me,' Mark said, trying to pull away.

Cat kissed him on the cheek. 'I need you to set a good example. If Mr Confident is reluctant to do it, then nobody else will have a go.'

Mark gave her a pained look and let himself be led to the van.

'Right,' Cat said, rubbing her hands together. 'Let's get this show on the road.'

By midday the cove was full of people milling about, having picnics and catching up with friends and, all the while, dogs and surfers went into the water, the four-legged chasing balls, the two-legged waves. Harvey had even tracked down a trained surfer-dog who competed in tournaments around the country. A Jack Russell, Bodhi was riding the waves on his own miniature surfboard, wearing his own doggy life jacket. Jessica, resplendent in a blue wetsuit, and with her Westies at her feet, was talking to a local television station, gesturing around her and captivating the interviewer.

Will and Juliette arrived with Alfie and Effie, and Cat's nerves increased. They seemed to be chatting amiably, and Juliette looked beautiful and relaxed in cropped trousers, flip-flops and a loose-fitting orange blouse.

Cat waved to them. The retrievers were straining to get off their leads and join in with the other dogs. Cat knew that a huge dog fight would be a disaster, but when she'd promoted the event, she'd stressed the need for owners to keep control of their pets, and she was confident that they'd all be responsible. Nobody wanted to end up calling on Polly's services.

'Goodness, Cat,' Juliette said, casting her eyes across the cove, 'you certainly know how to put on an event.'

Cat grinned. 'I think lots of people feel as strongly about this as I do. Thanks so much for coming. We've got the food starting over near the car park, Harvey and Zara are lending surfing equipment to anyone who wants to try it, and, so far, everyone seems to be having fun. The main thing is that it's busy, and Mr Council-man over there can see that we're all getting along, and that we care.' She pointed to where a beanpole of a man, wearing a white shirt and dark trousers and shoes, was taking notes on an iPad.

'Good,' Will said, nodding. 'So, where do you need me?'

'Well,' Cat said, 'Mark's being taught how to surf by Harvey.' She pointed to where Mark, looking effortlessly sexy in a black wetsuit, was standing on top of a surfboard on the sand, arms outstretched. 'And I was wondering if you could teach some of the others who are waiting? I want them to stay here, keep the place busy for as long as possible, and if they get to have a go at surfing . . .'

'Oh.' Will's eyes widened. 'I haven't ever really *taught* anyone before—'

'Not a proper lesson, just a bit of fun, how they can ride in on their tummies. You're so warm and friendly, and I think Harvey might be a little bit hardcore for some of them.'

'OK,' Will said, running his hand through his hair. 'Sure, I'll try.'

'Great!' Cat clapped her hands together. 'Let's introduce you to the new recruits.'

While Will was talking to a group of eager teenagers, Cat took the opportunity to circulate her petition and thank people

305

for coming. She approached Mr Beanpole, who was intent on his screen, his glasses slipping down his nose.

'So,' she said, 'what do you think?'

He looked at her, his greying eyebrows lowered. 'You've certainly caused a stir,' he said. 'And I've collated the letters we've had over the last month, which amount to over two hundred.'

'And over four thousand signatures,' Cat said, her heart rate increasing. 'Most online, but some more today.' She waggled her clipboard. 'It would be madness to stop dogs from coming to this beach, can't you see that?' She gestured towards the water, where dogs and children were playing happily in the shallows, Paddlepuss, Disco and Valentino among them.

'The decision is being made tomorrow.'

'And this is all our evidence. Haven't we done enough? What's our protest like, compared to the opposition?' She thought of Mr Jasper and Alison, and shuddered.

Mr Beanpole glanced at his iPad and sighed. He looked up again, his expression weary. 'I'll have to compile it all before the morning.'

Cat clasped her hands together. 'But you'll take it to them?'

'I can't ignore this,' he said, shaking his head.

She nodded, trying to keep her poise, but her excitement bubbled up and she hugged him. 'Thank you,' she said, kissing him on the cheek, 'thank you for coming. This means so much to so many people in Fairview.'

Mr Beanpole stared at her, blinking, then gave her a quick, embarrassed smile. 'I need to go and write all this up.'

'Have a hot dog first,' Cat said. 'They're delicious. And come and find me before you go – I'll have another fifty signatures for you by then!' She pointed him in the direction of the barbecue and raced off in a whirl of elation, wondering who to tell first – everyone had put so much effort in.

She spotted Phil from the *Fairhaven Press*, notebook in hand, his Labradoodles loping alongside as he spoke to a young woman with a baby strapped to her back. A hand landed on her arm and she spun round.

'Joe.'

'Hey.' He seemed on edge, his smile not quite meeting his eyes.

'What's up?' she asked.

'Nothing, I just came to see how things were going. The barbecue's busy, the beach is rammed. You've done it again.' He glanced behind him.

'*We've* done it. I just spoke to the council officer, and he's realized how many people want the dogs to stay. He's going to take the petition to the committee. He can't promise anything, but I got the impression that we've done enough to beat Mr Jasper at his own game!' She put a hand on his arm, expecting a high-five, a hug, a grin at the very least.

'That's great,' he said instead. 'Look, can I talk to you? We don't . . . you're not around so much, at home.'

'Of course.' She frowned. 'Give me ten minutes. Jessica can't stay all day, and she's been such a large part of this. I'm sure we wouldn't have done it without her, so I need to tell her the good news.' She squeezed Joe's arm, ignoring the butterflies that had started fluttering low down in her stomach, and went to find her friend.

After speaking to Jessica she was accosted by the radio station, and soon realized it wasn't easy to give an interview when your mouth had dried out. Why did Joe want to speak to her? She had been so good at ignoring her feelings over the last month, throwing herself into her relationship with Mark and the protest. Now she was faced with the prospect of having to confront them.

She veered over to Juliette, who was watching Will teach a group of people how to go from crouching to standing, their surfboards still safely on dry land.

'I had no idea,' Juliette said to Cat as she approached. 'I mean, how could I? I blocked it out, refused to acknowledge the change.'

'The change in Will?' Cat asked softly.

Juliette nodded and folded her arms. 'I was angry. Partly because Will had made this huge decision without me, and partly because it was such a courageous thing to do. I felt that, when Alex and Corrine went off to start their own lives, I was being left behind. I'm sure all parents feel that. But I thought Will and I were in it together, carrying on in this new, strange life without our kids, being there for each other. And then he quit his job, just like that. I was – it sounds silly, but I've been so scared he's going to leave me too. And that's what the surfing felt like, him leaving me.'

'So why didn't you go with him? Why didn't you let him show you all this?' Cat gestured towards the beach.

'Because I was scared. Because I wanted to show *him* that he couldn't just run off and leave me to carry on with our old life on my own, so I dug my heels in. It wasn't that it was surfing, specifically, just that he had something else to focus on – something we didn't do together. I thought if I refused to accept it, he'd eventually give it up and come back, find a job, go back to the way things were.'

'And now?'

Juliette laughed softly. 'He's never going to give it up, look at him.' Will was animated, smiling and chatting to his new students. 'And why would he?'

'Change is hard,' Cat said, 'any kind of change. But . . .' She thought of her parents and their plans, how nervous she felt about them being so far away. 'Sometimes you just have to embrace it, let people do what they need to, see it from their point of view. If you can't bring Will back, then why not follow him?'

Juliette laughed louder. 'What, try surfing?'

'Why not? Everyone else is. Give me five minutes to hand over our petition and round up the troops, and then we're going to give it a go.'

On the beach, practising the moves, Cat felt elated, as though it was almost possible that, once in the water, with the undulating, breaking waves beneath her, she would be able to stand up and ride them in. Will's group consisted of Juliette, Cat, Joe, Polly and Mark, and he soon had them laughing and attentive, and, Cat could tell from the faces of Joe and Mark especially, confident about their chances.

'I've already done this part,' Mark said, 'with Harvey.'

'So you're an expert now?' Joe shot back.

'I wouldn't say that.' Mark grinned, hopped off his board and wrapped his arm around Cat, kissing her on the cheek. 'We're all beginners, aren't we?' Joe didn't respond.

Cat gave Mark a quick kiss, now conscious of Joe so close, Joe who she still hadn't spoken to, corralling them all into surfing so she could delay the talk he wanted to have with her.

They graduated to the water which, despite the wetsuit, Cat decided must have come directly from Alaska it was so cold, and all of them were faced with reality. The reality that surfing elegance was earned by spending hours in the freezing sea, limbs and squidgy bits squeezed into skintight wetsuits, falling off at least a hundred thousand times, filling your eyes, ears and mouth with salty, seaweed-infested water.

They could just about stay on the surfboards if they came in to the beach on their stomachs. Anything more than that was impossible. Will had, tactfully, not shown off his own skills, but was coaching them in turn.

Cat, finding herself in the water for about the hundredth time, smiled as she watched Will helping Juliette stand up in the shallows. Juliette was able to show off her stunning figure in a red wetsuit, and Will was gripping her hands tightly, walking in with her. Juliette was laughing.

'What are you grinning about?' Polly gasped, wading through the sea towards Cat. She looked as cold as Cat felt, blinking water out of her eyes, her surfboard bobbing happily behind her. 'Look, Cat, just like dogs. We're tethered to our surfboards. It's going well, isn't it?'

'I think so,' Cat said. 'And look.' She nodded her head surreptitiously in the Barkers' direction, and Polly followed her gaze.

'Did you *plan* this?' Polly whispered loudly.

'Sort of. I mean, not really, but . . .' She shrugged. 'It's a happy side effect of today's event.'

'Cat, you devious little—' Polly jumped forward, grabbed Cat's arms and pulled her under the waves.

Cat had time to start squealing, and then her mouth filled with water and, as quickly as she could she shot back up and wiped her eyes. 'S-so unnecessary,' she spluttered.

Polly was grinning. 'How much fun is this?'

'What, dunking me like an apple?'

'No, silly. This. Surfing. It's such a shame Owen couldn't make it. He said he'd try and get back from the suppliers early, but I guess he's been held up.'

'He might still come,' Cat said. 'We can fit in hours of surfing practice before it gets dark. But I'm not sure any of us are going to be signing up for the national championships any time soon.' The experts were further out, bobbing on the swell, waiting for the perfect wave to ride in on. Bodhi watched from his Jack Russell-sized surfboard, outclassing them all, as Cat and her fellow paddlepusses wobbled for a few seconds before upending themselves into the water.

Except for one.

'Apart from my blasted brother,' Polly said, sighing. 'Do you think he was swapped at birth and he's a secret Australian? Or maybe our mum was half seal.'

'Can seals surf?' Cat asked.

'You know what I mean. Whatever it is, it's bloody annoying. He's going to gloat at us for ever – or rather me, because you're hardly at home any more.'

They watched as Joe went from lying on the surfboard to crouching in a single, deft little jump, his arms spread wide, wobbling slightly, his lips pressed together in a determined, exhilarated smile. It was very impressive.

'That's amazing, Joe,' Will called, still at Juliette's side, clutching her as she fell into him and off her surfboard. Joe gave a quick salute and then, as he came in towards the shore, managed to stand up.

'How does he do that?' Polly said, her voice thick with envy.

'Strong thighs,' Cat said, clarifying when her best friend shot her a curious look. 'He goes running a lot. That must help.'

'Oh. Yeah. One more go? I'm getting hungry.'

'You're on. Mark,' she called, 'we're heading in soon. Want to try once more?'

'God,' Mark said, paddling over to them astride his surfboard, 'I thought you'd never ask. I am not, it turns out, a fish out of water.' He shot Joe a quick look, then turned back to Cat with a grin. 'I think there are much better ways we can entertain ourselves.'

'It's been fun trying, though.' Cat waved as she saw Frankie walk down to the water pushing Henry in a buggy, Emma and Lizzie running down to paddle, clutching their shoes. Olaf yapped excitedly at the surfers just out of reach in the water. 'Look how many people have come.' She took in the full beach, the sun beginning shyly to show itself, making the sand gleam.

'I think we all know that's down to you,' Mark said, coming up alongside Cat and leaning down for a watery kiss. 'It's been a triumph.'

'Just one committee meeting,' she said, holding up crossed fingers. 'And over four thousand signatures.' Cat gave them her best triumphant smile, but she knew their success wasn't guaranteed. At least she could be confident they had done everything they could.

Cat peeled off her wetsuit and her sodden swimming costume in the tiny changing room in Harvey and Zara's van, grateful for the modicum of privacy. She was freezing, and glad that she'd brought several layers with her. Harvey, Frankie and Elsie were back at the barbecues, and Polly and Mark were sorting out more hot dogs, burgers, sardines and vegetable kebabs.

She could hear people chatting and laughing outside, dogs barking in different pitches, Alfie and Effie and Chips deeper and longer, Olaf and Paris, and occasionally Disco, with their higher-pitched, sharper barks. Cat couldn't imagine this beach without dogs, couldn't imagine not being able to bring them down to the water's edge apart from at sunrise and sunset. Dogs, like people, needed diversity, a change of scene, and if

312

she was left with only Fairview Park to walk them in, she didn't know what she'd do. She hoped they'd done enough.

She heard someone clear their throat just outside the van. 'Won't be a sec,' she called, wrapping a large towel around her, luxuriating in its warmth and comfort. Her limbs felt weary from the surfing, her whole head still shifting slightly up and down in time to the waves she was no longer immersed in.

'Cat?'

Cat froze. It was Joe. 'I won't be long,' she said. 'Just getting dressed.'

'Can I come in?'

Cat felt a flash of panic. 'I've got no clothes on. I'm in my towel.'

'That's fine.'

'For you, maybe—' Cat started, but the side of the van slid open and Joe hopped in and closed it behind him.

'Joe!' Cat squealed, clamping her arms round her. 'I'm half naked.'

'Then we're on an even footing.' He had his wetsuit pulled down to his waist, his honed torso, wet from the sea, on full display.

'I still think that puts me at a disadvantage,' she murmured, trying and failing to avert her gaze.

His blue eyes were bright from the exertion, and it was clear that he'd loved it. Were Polly and Cat about to lose Joe to the call of the waves? Except that Cat couldn't lose him, because she was never at home. She was always with Mark. Mark . . .

'Seriously Joe, what is it that—'

'I have to tell you something.'

'Something that couldn't have waited until I was dressed and out of this cramped van?'

313

'I tried to tell you earlier. I wanted to speak to you in private.'

'This evening, then?'

Joe shook his head. 'There's too much momentum. This will be going on all day and night, whether here or back at ours, and I'll just – you're never around any more, and I'll never get you on your own.'

'Why do you want me on my own?' He was very close to her now, within touching distance. His stare really was the most direct, gripping . . .

'I wanted to ask you something.'

'Oh, yes?' Cat held her towel tighter. It was far too small a space to be having a sensible conversation in.

'And it's quite a . . . a personal thing. It's something I should have asked earlier.'

'OK,' Cat managed, the word coming out as a croak. 'W-what is it?'

Joe looked down at his feet, looked up again, and, without warning, took Cat's hand. She gripped desperately onto her towel with the other one.

'I've been speaking to Phil at the *Fairhaven Press*, and he's asked me to do a cartoon strip. For three months initially, and then, if it goes well, on a permanent basis.'

Cat should have felt relief that he was finally going to talk to her about the cartoon, but there didn't seem room for relief amongst all the other thoughts tumbling through her head. 'That's amazing,' she said. 'Great news, Joe. I'm so happy for you.'

'It really is a dream, something I've wanted to do for as long as I can remember. It's just that, this idea I've had . . .' He ran his free hand through his damp hair, looked away for a moment. 'It's . . . well, it's not you – but it's about you. Sort of.'

'Curiosity Kitten,' Cat said.

Joe went still. 'How did you know?'

'I've seen some of your sketches.'

'I know, but . . . how—'

'There was a rather telling one of a cat about to open an attic door and have a load of crap fall on her.'

'Shit,' Joe murmured. 'You weren't meant to see that. You weren't meant to know until—'

'Until what?'

'Until it was confirmed. I'm not mocking you, Cat, I want you to know that. It's just that some of your . . . some of what you . . .' He trailed off, shook his head.

'I'm a great subject for a calamitous cartoon? I'm so ridiculous that I'm worth documenting?' Cat felt anger rise up, hot and sharp, inside her.

'No!' Joe urged. 'Not at all. I really don't think that.'

'What do you think, then? Because generally, curiosity kills the cat, and that doesn't strike me as a very positive way of thinking about someone.'

'You don't want to know how I see you,' he said, his voice dropping.

'Yes I do. Of course I do. I felt pretty hurt by what I saw, and I've been waiting . . . well, a while for you to come and talk to me about it.'

'I'm sorry,' he said. 'I never meant for that to happen. It's just, you inspire me, Cat. More than anyone I've ever met.'

'Inspire you?'

'Yeah.' He gave a quick, lopsided smile. 'Like a muse or something. You've got so much energy, and passion. And you may not always get things right, but you've got the biggest heart of anyone I know. And you make me laugh. Curiosity Kitten is all those things. She's pretty much you.'

'Oh,' Cat said, her anger dissolving, replaced by understanding, by the feelings that had been hovering at the back of her mind and which had come to the fore when they'd watched *Grey's Anatomy* together, when he'd reassured her, wrapped his arms around her. 'Oh. Right. Well.' She wanted to look away, wanted to lose eye contact with him and have a moment to compose herself, which wasn't going to be easy in the current situation.

'Cat.' Joe reached his hand up to her face and rubbed his thumb against her cheek. 'There's something else.'

Cat tried to think over the thudding of her heart. 'What?' she whispered.

'I know it's really bad timing, but I have to go—'

'Cat?' The second voice was outside the door, but it was loud and, unmistakably, Mark. 'Are you still in here?' Cat and Joe looked at each other, eyes wide, and Joe let go of her hand and began pulling up his wetsuit, just as Mark slid the van door open.

Cat and Joe both froze, Joe with his wetsuit pulled up over one arm, Cat with her towel wrapped round her. Mark's expression changed from relaxed to shocked in a single, sickening moment. At the same time, Paddlepuss, small and excited and soaked from the sea, raced up, grabbed hold of Cat's towel and pulled. She was quick, but not quick enough, and the towel fell to her ankles before she'd realized what was happening. She screamed and reclaimed it.

Wrapping her towel even more tightly around her, and trying to avoid the shocked gaze of her friends on the beach, Cat gave Joe a quick, apologetic look and, nudging him gently out onto the sand, pulled the van door closed.

Cat sat close to the water, letting the sea spray cool her face. She stroked Chalky, who was lying at her side like a small, furry bodyguard. She had ignored the entreaties of Elsie,

Polly and Juliette, and, after jumping down from the van fully dressed, had hurried to the end of the cove, pleased that, in the end, it was only Chalky who had followed her. Chalky, who was always a comfort, who she'd be lost without.

'What shall I do now, then?' she asked, rubbing the fur between his ears. 'What on earth am I meant to do now?'

Chalky sniffed loudly and let out a short bark.

'I know,' Cat whispered. 'It's crap, isn't it?'

She hadn't seen Mark or Joe when she'd left the van, but she'd been keeping her head down, wanting to clear her mind rather than face either of them. It should be straightforward. She was with Mark now, and what had happened in the van had been a misunderstanding – surely Mark would believe her when she explained it to him?

Except that Joe had made it clear that he wanted something to happen. He had called her his muse, he had touched her face, softly, tenderly.

She leaned her head on her folded arms and listened to the rhythmic sound of the waves. The protest, the surfing, and the worries of her neighbours had become distant, fleeting thoughts at the back of her mind.

She closed her eyes, trying to empty her head of everything, but she couldn't stop replaying Joe's touch, or the look in his blue eyes, the way her whole body had frozen, alive with anticipation, waiting for his next words. No, it wasn't straightforward at all, and for once Cat had no idea how to fix it.

Tinsel and Terriers

PART 4

19

Cat was cold and confused and had some explaining to do. As she walked back to Primrose Terrace from Fairview Cove, her coat pulled tightly around her, she wished she still had Chalky at her side to reassure her.

The day had gone so well. With the show of support, the strong possibility of success and the fun she'd had surfing, she'd let her worries drift away, and so of course one had come back to plant itself firmly in front of her.

The trees lining the road shook in the wind and Cat shrunk further inside her coat. Her hair was still damp from the sea, and the cold made her head sting. Autumn was well and truly underway. She loved this time of year. She loved the excitement of Halloween and fireworks, and then the influx of lights and colours as people blotted out the winter greyness with sparkling festivity.

It would be her first Christmas living on Primrose Terrace, and although she'd be in Brighton with her parents on the day, she'd been looking forward to getting into the festive spirit, planning decorations and parties with Mark, Polly and

Joe. She wanted to celebrate a year that had seen so much change for them all.

As Cat turned into Primrose Terrace, she shuddered at the thought of Joe standing so close to her, his blue eyes, bright from the exhilaration of surfing, latched firmly onto hers. She had been trying to ignore the feelings that had been bubbling inside her, that told her she was upset because she wanted Joe to care about her – *really* care about her.

And then Joe had said just that. He had confessed about the cartoon, and told her that she was his inspiration. He had stroked her cheek, and his expression had filled in all the blanks.

But Cat was with Mark now. She had finally taken the next step with him. He was occasionally still mysterious, as if he was hovering just out of reach, but she was learning to accept that was part of who he was. Since Joe had walked into the van, however, she had done more thinking than she could bear, and she still wasn't sure about her decision.

It had taken a long time to get to where she was with Mark. Could she really throw it away on one hurried conversation, one tender look? She tried to forget about the stolen hugs, the moments she'd shared with Joe over the last few months, and the way her heart rate increased when she pictured the warm smile that crinkled his blue eyes.

She was relieved and terrified when she saw Mark's Audi was parked outside his house. He'd driven to the cove to take banners and food for the barbecue, so she knew for certain that he'd returned home.

Swallowing down the lump in her throat, she climbed the steps up to number four and rang the bell. She heard it echo inside, and then fast feet running down the corridor. She bit her lip and waited for the door to open.

Chips ran straight into her, nudging her nose into her legs. She stroked the dog's silky ears, but she couldn't take her eyes off Mark. He was wearing the jeans and jumper he'd had on at the beach, his dark hair drying untidily around his face, but his expression was darker than she'd ever seen it. His lips were pressed together, and his brown eyes looked at her with a cold detachment that made her insides shrivel. She'd done nothing wrong, she told herself. She just had to make Mark believe it.

'Can I come in?' she asked, resting her hand on Chips's soft head.

Mark was silent for a moment, then gestured for her to come inside.

Cat perched on the edge of his leather sofa, wrapping her arms around her. Mark stood in the doorway.

'Are you cold?' There was an edge to his voice, but Cat could also hear disappointment in it. She'd managed to disappoint so many people recently, in one way or another, but she hadn't imagined it could happen with Mark.

'No, I'm fine, thanks. Come and sit down.' She patted the sofa next to her.

Mark hesitated, as if there was a delay between the words leaving her mouth and reaching him, but then he joined her. Cat was conscious of the gap between them: hands, knees not touching.

'I wanted to explain what happened, in the van.'

Mark nodded. 'Go on. I'm all ears.'

'Right.' She swallowed. Chips was lying on the floor under the window, and she wished she could bury her head in the collie's warm fur. 'What you saw – nothing happened. Nothing was happening, nothing was going to happen. Joe wanted to talk to me because . . . I'm not there any more. At number nine. I'm always here.'

'So he has to pick the moment you're naked to come and find you?' Mark asked sharply.

'No, of course not. That was a mistake. He just wanted to talk to me about something.'

'What?' Mark clasped his hands in front of him, his elbows on his knees. Cat was struck all over again by how handsome he was, with his dark, messy hair, his strong jawline. But without his usual charm, without the light of amusement in his eyes, he was a different person. An image of Joe, looking at her with real compassion, flashed in Cat's mind and she pushed it aside.

This was the hard part.

Cat didn't want to lie and she knew she'd done nothing wrong, but the truth about Joe's cartoon wasn't going to reassure him.

She ran her finger along her jeans. 'He's had a job offer, a new project, for the local paper. It's a cartoon strip, and he – he wanted to use an idea that sort of relates to me.'

'*Relates* to you? What does that mean?'

Cat looked at the floor. 'His idea is a character called Curiosity Kitten. It's this kitten who gets into all kinds of scrapes because she's curious.' She thought back to the sketches she'd seen. 'Like opening a box with something dangerous inside, trying to see into a window and falling off her makeshift ladder, that kind of thing.'

'And that's you because . . .?'

'Because I'm curious, Mark. I do stupid things like that. Sometimes they work, like with Frankie and her attic room, and sometimes, like seeing what would happen if I took a puppy into a nursery, they backfire spectacularly.'

'So what you're saying,' Mark said, shifting round to face her more directly, his knee brushing hers, 'Is that Joe's

324

drawing a cartoon that takes the piss out of you? And he didn't think you'd have a problem with that?' He laughed. 'Is he for real?'

Cat shrugged, sensing that he was on the verge of thawing. Of course that was what she wanted, but she had never intended to make Joe out to be the bad guy. 'He wanted to make sure I was OK with it,' she said. 'I was put out to begin with, but is it really so bad being the subject of someone's work? Don't you put people you know in your films?'

Mark shook his head, dismissing her change of subject. 'That's what he wanted to talk to you about? In the back of the van, both of you half naked?' He caught her eye and Cat felt her cheeks colour, but annoyance flashed through her – why was he making this so difficult?

'That was unintentional. I was getting changed, and he was – he'd just finished surfing.'

'Oh yes,' Mark said bitterly, 'the star surfer.'

'Mark, come on—'

'Come on?' he shot back. 'I open that door to find you and your housemate Joe, who, by the way, is clearly besotted with you, standing inches apart, skin on show, and you expect me to believe it was a chat? Why did he need to talk to you right then? Was it just inspiration he wanted from you, or more? Or maybe you'd agreed to meet him there so you could debrief each other.'

'Of course not,' Cat said, her voice rising. 'Joe wanted to talk to me, and it was just the wrong time. It was so the wrong time.' She risked reaching out and taking his hand. He didn't flinch, but he didn't slide his fingers between hers either. 'Nothing has ever happened between me and Joe. I want to be with you. Hasn't the last month proved that?'

Mark looked out of the window, his dark brows knitting together. 'It was humiliating, Cat, finding you like that. I know you've always been close to him—'

'He's my housemate.'

'And it caught me off guard. Surely you can see why it would upset me?' He turned back to her, squeezing her hand.

Cat felt a momentary resistance before squeezing back. She was relieved the confrontation was over, but it wasn't the thunderbolt she'd been hoping for, a jolt of contentment that told her she was making the right decision, that this was where she was meant to be. 'Of course I can,' she said, 'and I'm sorry. It was a misunderstanding – of course I can see how it looked – but Joe and I are just friends. I love spending time with you and Chips. We've only just started getting to know each other, and I don't want it to end now.' She risked moving closer to him, and she could see a flicker of the old Mark in his eyes.

'I don't either.' He pulled her towards him, wrapping her in his arms. 'I don't want to lose you, Cat. I've lost – I just, I don't want to lose you. Stay here tonight.' Mark pushed her back to arm's length and gave her his warmest smile. 'Don't go home.' He ran his hand down the side of her face, cupped her chin and kissed her.

Cat responded to his touch, telling herself she'd made the right decision and she was lucky that Mark had understood. He was sexy, charming, fun to be with *and* forgiving.

But her conversation with Joe was unfinished and she couldn't stop it playing on her mind. Ignoring everything else that had happened, they were good friends, and she couldn't leave things as they were. She should be mad at him – he had cornered her in the van, forced her into a position where she had to make this apology to Mark – but all she could think was that she didn't want to give up on their friendship. She needed to clear the air. She'd do it first thing tomorrow.

Cat unlocked the front door and stood at the foot of the stairs, listening. It was the day after the protest, the first of October, and Cat had no idea how late the beach barbecue had gone on the night before. She knew Polly was working today, and she hoped she'd have the chance to speak to Joe alone.

'Hello?' she called.

She was met by silence. Not even Shed came slinking out of the living room.

She climbed the stairs and went into her room, throwing her coat onto the bed. Her gaze fell on her dressing table and the 'Bitchin' Walks' cartoon Joe had drawn for her when she was trying to come up with names for Pooch Promenade all those months ago.

Walking over to it, she traced the cartoon dog with her finger, thought again of him so close to her, the way her anger had dissolved, replaced by feelings she didn't want to admit to. How she had hung onto his next words.

She closed her eyes, trying to push the thoughts away, and was jolted back to reality by a loud bang outside her door, followed by footsteps. Peering out onto the landing, she saw a large black suitcase sitting at the bottom of the stairs that led to Joe's attic bedroom. She lifted it. It was heavy.

She heard someone moving about downstairs, quiet swearing. She followed the sounds and stood in the living-room doorway, watching as Joe rifled through papers on the dining table, a red hoody flung over his shoulder, arms strong and tanned against his white T-shirt. She inhaled and Joe turned, his eyes widening as he saw her.

'Cat.' He cleared his throat.

'Hi.'

'I wasn't expecting you back.'

'I do still live here,' she said softly.

'I know,' Joe said, 'but I thought after yesterday you'd be staying with him. I'm sorry if I made things hard for you. I should have thought about how it might look.'

'I did have a bit of explaining to do,' Cat said. 'It wasn't my finest hour, or my happiest.'

Joe sighed. 'I'm so sorry. But he's OK? Mark, I mean?'

Cat nodded, her lips pressed together. She saw that Joe was holding his passport. 'You're going abroad? I saw the suitcase.'

'There's this course, in Portland. Illustration, graphic design, the whole shebang. I've wanted to do it for ages, but it's always oversubscribed. I've been on a waiting list.'

'And a space has miraculously become available right now?' She said it quietly but was shocked by the cynicism in her own voice.

'I found out a couple of weeks ago.' He left space for her to complete the sentence. *And you weren't here to tell.*

'Right, wow. Congratulations. How long's the course?'

'It's three weeks, but I might take some time . . . I've always wanted to go to that part of America, so I'll probably travel down the coast, visit San Francisco.'

'So how long?' Cat whispered.

Joe shrugged. 'I'll be back for Christmas. Your first at Primrose Terrace. I did – I was going to tell you yesterday.'

'Ah.'

'The paper are trialling my cartoon, running it up until Christmas. And then, if they're happy, it'll be a regular feature in the New Year. I wanted to get my skills fully up to date, and this course—'

'You don't have to explain to me.'

328

'But I feel like I do.' Joe put his hand on her arm, sending a spark through her. 'After what I said yesterday, and then . . . this. It was planned, Cat, I have to go and do this. I'm not running away.'

'I wouldn't blame you if you were.'

'Why? Because I made such a big fuck-up?'

'No – that's not what I meant,' Cat said hurriedly. 'I don't want it to be awkward between us.'

Joe squeezed her arm. 'I don't either. Some space between us will be good.'

'And it sounds like an amazing opportunity.'

'It'll put me at the top of my game.'

'You've always been at the top of your game, Joe. You're ridiculously good at what you do, your cartoons, your banner.' She found she was grinning, and he returned the smile, the tension between them lifting. 'And as well as all that, you've helped me so much this year, you've always been there. You're just a really great person.'

'You're not so bad yourself,' he said softly, his blue eyes locking onto hers. 'And I'm sorry I won't be here for the next few weeks. But I think now, maybe you don't need – not that you ever *needed* someone, but . . .' His words trailed off and they both looked away.

'And the whole Curiosity Kitten thing?' Cat rushed. 'I don't mind, really. I would never stop you realizing your dream, especially not for vanity's sake, for some silly misunderstanding.'

'Thank you, that means a lot. I hope you know, now, that I'm not making fun of you.'

Cat looked at the floor.

'I mean it, Cat. You've made your mark on Primrose Terrace, you've helped so many people. Your curiosity, your tenacity – this place wouldn't be the same without you.'

'Everyone would be left in peace, you mean?' She gave him a rueful smile.

'Yeah, maybe. But without you, they wouldn't have seen their potential. Frankie, the Barkers, Polly and Owen. You spread good vibes, positive thinking. Kind of like a real-life Santa.' He laughed. 'I bet you love Christmas, don't you?'

Cat sighed. 'I do love Christmas, but . . .' She didn't want to voice her sadness, the fact that this Christmas would see her parents leaving England to go to Canada, how much she would miss them. And here was Joe, doing the same thing. She'd almost got around to the idea of her parents being out of arm's reach, but she tried to imagine the house without Joe's presence, and found she had a mental block. How could she enjoy the run up to Christmas without him there?

Her phone rang and, giving Joe an apologetic glance, she answered it.

'Hello?'

'Miss Palmer? It's Mr Cawston, from the council.'

'Oh.' Cat crossed her fingers. 'Yes? H-how did it go?'

'I'm afraid today's council meeting has been cancelled. We've had some apologies, and there aren't enough people to make it quorate – to pass decisions.'

'Oh,' she said again. 'Oh, right. So what happens now?' She made a face at Joe.

'Your item's been moved to the next agenda.'

'When's that?'

'The end of the month. I assure you I will let you know the outcome.'

'OK,' Cat said warily. 'There's been nothing else, has there? Since yesterday afternoon?' She thought of how Mr Jasper would have reacted to their protest, and knew that, given the

330

opportunity, he wouldn't leave it alone. 'No more evidence from the opposition?'

'I can't say at this point,' Mr Cawston said. 'I will let you know what happens, of course.'

'But you have to give us a chance to—' Cat dropped her head, frustrated, as the line went dead.

'What's happened?' Joe asked.

'No decision on dogs at the cove until the end of the month.'

'Shit, I'm sorry. But it doesn't make a win any less likely?'

'I don't know,' Cat admitted. 'He wouldn't say if they'd heard any more from Mr Jasper. Crap. What if he's heard about our protest and gone back to the council? He's now got another month to strengthen his argument. What if he's done enough?'

'He won't have. Not after what you achieved yesterday.'

'I'm not so sure.'

'It'll be fine,' Joe said. 'An early Christmas present.'

'I'll want to celebrate – or commiserate – with everyone. You and Polly and Jessica and Elsie.' She didn't think bringing Mark's name into the conversation would be helpful. 'But you might not be here.'

'I'm coming back. And we'll have a great Christmas.'

'You don't strike me as the Christmas type,' Cat said, smiling.

Joe gave her a look of mock horror. 'How can you say that? You have no idea!'

'So, what do you love most about Christmas, then?'

'Eating and drinking too much, silly hats and pointless presents, Christmas films. Not having to do anything except hole up in the warm with the people I care about.' He held her gaze, and Cat's stomach did a small, unhelpful somersault. It sounded perfect.

'What time's your flight?' she asked.

331

'First thing in the morning. I'm travelling down to Heathrow tonight.'

'Right.' Cat nodded. 'Well, I have to—' She pointed behind her.

'Of course. Go, walk dogs, have fun. I'll see you soon.'

'Sure,' Cat said, a lump forming in her throat. 'You too, Joe. I hope it's wonderful.'

They stood facing each other, unsure what to do next, and then Cat heard Joe whisper '*fuck it*' and he closed the gap between them, pulling her into his arms. Cat closed her eyes, wrapped her arms round his waist and listened to his heart beating, letting herself indulge, for a few moments, in how good it felt to be so close to him. She was so relieved that she'd come home, that she hadn't turned up the following day to discover he'd already gone, that they'd been able to have this goodbye.

It was only temporary, Cat told herself as they broke apart, the lump still firmly in her throat. He'd be back in a few weeks, resuming his place on the sofa, ready to have a lazy, indulgent Christmas with them all.

So why did it feel like the bottom had fallen out of her world?

'I want to do something for Christmas,' Cat said later as she and Mark sat on the sofa in front of an old horror film.

'Like what?' He turned to her, pushed her hair back from her forehead. 'I thought we could get a turkey and hibernate – take Chips for a long walk, have a quiet day just the three of us.'

Cat shook her head. 'My parents are going to Canada straight after Christmas, so I have to spend it with them. But I didn't mean the actual day, I meant the build-up. Something that all of Primrose Terrace can get involved in.'

Mark leaned back and folded his arms. 'What do you mean? Not another protest?'

'No, no no. Well, unless we get bad news from the committee. I mean something fun, something Christmassy.'

'Why?'

'Why not? Don't you think this is the best place you've ever lived? Everyone here, Jessica, Frankie and her kids, the Barkers, Boris and Charles, they're all so friendly. Why can't we do something, you and me, Polly and . . . and Elsie. I'll have a think.' She took a sip of wine and stroked Chips's soft fur with her bare foot.

'Christmas is hectic enough without having something else to organize on top of presents and food and family.'

'Have you got family you want to see?' Cat asked.

Mark shook his head. 'Not really.'

'Your mum and dad?' Cat realized she knew very little about Mark's family.

'We're not close,' he said. 'They live in Spain now, they do their own thing.'

'Oh, that's sad. Why's that?'

'No real reason. They wanted to go to Spain, I was living my life here. It works fine.'

'But don't you want to see them? Spain's not that far.' Cat felt a flip of unease at the thought that that could happen with her own parents. What if they loved Canada, decided to make a permanent life for themselves out there? Or – she brushed the thought away, but it returned, stronger, and lodged itself firmly in her head. *Oh yes,* she heard herself say, *I used to know Joe Sinclair, the famous illustrator. He lives in Portland now, does his own thing.* Cat took another gulp of wine.

'I don't mind,' Mark said. 'I have enough to keep me busy here, and I saw them at the beginning of the year. I'd much rather spend this Christmas with you.' He snuck his arm round her waist, pulled her into him. 'But just you, not the whole street. I'm sure Jessica will organize some kind of party. I don't think you need to worry about doing anything else.'

'Well, I could speak to Jessica, see if we could organize something together. We could involve the dogs – almost everyone here has dogs, and they should be included.'

Mark laughed softly. 'You're pretty determined when you want to be.' He kissed her forehead.

'Isn't that why you like me?' Cat grinned.

'Partly,' Mark admitted. 'There are other reasons too.' His kisses travelled further down, to her nose, her cheek and then her lips. 'Lots of other reasons.'

'Good,' Cat said, kissing him back and then wriggling out of his reach. 'Me too. But right now I need pen and paper. I'm definitely organizing something for Primrose Terrace. This is going to be their best Christmas yet.' She jumped up and, before Mark had time to change her mind, went in search of a notepad.

20

Two days before Halloween, Cat was walking Jessica's Westies when her phone rang. It was the day of the rearranged council meeting, and she'd taken Coco, Dior and Valentino on an extra-long walk to distract herself. Mr Cawston had said he would call her as soon as the decision had been made.

Pulling her phone out of her pocket, she sat on a bench at the edge of Fairview Park, the cold immediately seeping through her tunic dress. The Westies stopped at her feet and Dior sat on them, warming her toes through her boots.

'Hello?'

'Miss Palmer? It's Mr Cawston here, from the council.'

'Hi, Mr Cawston,' Cat chirped nervously. 'How are you?'

'I'm very well, thank you. I'm calling with the outcome of today's committee meeting.'

Cat closed her eyes. 'It went ahead, then?'

'Indeed.'

'That's . . . good. Did Mr Jasper do anything else to make sure the ban was imposed, before . . .?'

'Not after your sterling efforts. It really was an effective campaign which, I'm pleased to inform you, has been successful. With the weight of public opinion, our councillors have agreed to continue to allow dogs at the cove.'

Cat opened her eyes, resisted squeaking at Mr Cawston and leant over to stroke the Westies. 'That is incredible news,' she said, 'thank you so much.'

'No need to thank me – it was all your hard work that won them over.'

'Wow,' Cat said, 'will you be letting everyone know? I can help too, but—'

'Yes, we'll get notices out, make sure Fairview residents are aware of the decision. It's been good working with you, Miss Palmer.'

'You too, Mr Cawston.'

She waited until he'd hung up, and then she knelt on the concrete and embraced Coco, Valentino and Dior, letting them lick her face and cover her bottle-green coat in their trademark white hairs. 'You've got your beach,' she said. 'It's yours. For ever. What do you think of that, eh?' She sat on her haunches and, blinking tears out of her eyes, took in the beauty of Fairview Park, the trees, almost bare for the winter, the other dog walkers and their running, playing pets. She really did love living here.

She took the dogs back to Jessica's house, eager to tell her the good news.

'It wouldn't have happened without you,' Cat said. 'We wouldn't have been able to spread the news nearly as far, or get as many signatures. The campaign might have sunk before it had even got going.'

'I don't believe that for a moment,' Jessica said. 'You're the driving force behind everything dog-related in Fairview.

336

You've come here and worked your magic. You're incredible, Cat.'

'Well, I—' Cat ran her hands down the front of her coat. 'I'm not sure about that, but I *was* wondering if I could talk to you about something. I've been thinking of doing something Christmassy that can involve everyone on Primrose Terrace, and you're always so sociable. Mark said he thought you might be organizing a party.'

'He did, did he?' Jessica smiled and flicked her long blonde hair over her shoulder.

'If you are – and there's no pressure, I promise – I was wondering if I could combine it with something? Can we have a proper chat some time?' Dior was standing with his front paws on Cat's legs, and she bent and ruffled his ears.

'Tonight,' Jessica said, clapping her hands together. 'Come round here this evening. We can have wine, a few snacks, and a brainstorm – like a Christmas committee. Who else?'

'What?'

'Who else can be on the committee? I'm not sure it's Mark's thing.'

'I can ask,' Cat said, but she thought Jessica was probably right. She couldn't imagine him getting enthusiastic about tinsel and mince pies, perhaps not even on the day itself. 'And I was going to speak to Polly.'

'Bring her, and anyone else you can rope into it. Seven o'clock. I must dash now, but I'll see you later.' She kissed Cat on the cheek. 'I think with you and me leading the way, whatever we come up with will be pretty unstoppable.'

'That's what I'm hoping,' Cat said.

Cat turned in the direction of the vet's surgery. There would be nobody at home, and Mark had spent the last few days immersed in paperwork. She didn't feel like sitting quietly and waiting for him to notice her. Besides, Polly had been a huge supporter of Pooch Promenade from the beginning, and Cat wanted to share her good news.

She pushed open the door into the clinical white reception area. They'd obviously decided that late October was too early for decorations.

'Is Polly on her lunch yet?' she asked the receptionist.

'About ten minutes, I think. Take a seat and I'll let her know you're here.'

She sat next to a woman with short, carroty hair, a Barbour jacket, and a small cream dog on a lead. A Cairn terrier, Cat thought.

'He's adorable, can I stroke him?'

'Of course,' the woman said.

Cat bent and ran her hands along the dog's shaggy back. He turned to her and sniffed her boots. 'What's his name?'

'Bisto,' she said. 'One of my kids came up with it. I like it for him – he's bold and stocky, so it suits him – but they're far too keen on food-related names. They're trying to name all our neighbour's puppies things like Popcorn and Curry.'

'Your neighbour's just had puppies?'

'Very unexpectedly, poor love. Her little mongrel has somehow managed to have her wicked way with another dog, and there's five healthy pups, just born.'

'What's she going to do with them?' Cat asked, her eyes wide.

'Well, she's eighty-nine, and she doesn't want any more dogs. I've spoken to lovely Polly here, and she's going to put a sign up, see what else she can do. They're cute pups, cream and brown, a little scruffy, but utterly loveable. I'm a firm believer that dogs aren't just for Christmas, but they'll

338

be ready to leave Mum mid-December, and I'm sure they'll be snapped up. Here.' She pulled a piece of paper out of her pocket, scribbled something on it and handed it to Cat. 'If you're interested, just get in touch with me and I can introduce you.'

'I will,' Cat said. 'Thank you.' She read the details on the piece of paper. *Five mongrel pups, three male, two female, ready 20 December.* Followed by a name and phone number.

Cat was still staring at it when Polly appeared, her long blonde hair tied back, nurse's dark-green scrubs on under her duffle coat.

'Cat,' she grinned. 'How are you?'

'I've come to take you for lunch. I have news.'

Polly glanced behind her. 'I can't. I only have half an hour, then I need to be back here. I was going to grab a sandwich.'

'OK, so how about this evening?'

'I thought you'd be at Mark's. Owen's coming over.'

'Ah.' Cat grinned. 'Well, how do you both fancy coming round to Jessica's to help us work on the plan for Christmas at Primrose Terrace?'

'Why do we need a plan?' Polly sounded wary, but Cat could see the excitement in her eyes.

'To make this the best Christmas ever. Are you in?'

'I'll have to make sure Owen doesn't mind.'

'Brilliant! Seven o'clock.'

'But, Cat, I need to ask Owen first.'

'When has Owen ever said no to anything?'

Cat left Polly rolling her eyes and, with an extra spring in her step, returned to Primrose Terrace.

'You know you're welcome to come,' Cat said, following Mark from the kitchen to the living room. 'The more heads the better.'

339

'I'm not sure my head's tuned to Christmas yet. It's not even November.' He sat down and scribbled something on a printed letter, still doing the paperwork.

'November's two days away, and the shops are bursting with Christmas stuff already.' Cat peered over his shoulder but could only make out part of the logo – something *Lawyers*.

'That's not necessarily a good thing.' He gave her a quick smile and turned back to his work.

'I can see I'm going to have to do some de-Scrooging here,' Cat said, 'Christmas is the best time of the year.' She tried to ignore the voice in her head that was reminding her how much Joe loved Christmas, the picture he had painted of hibernating from the cold with the people he cared about. She sat on the sofa beside Mark and reached her hand up, running it through his hair, but her nail caught on his scalp and he moved his head away, turning to her with an irritated expression.

'Look, Cat.' His face softened. 'Sorry, I just – I'm a bit busy. But I can't wait to hear what ideas you come up with. It's you and Jessica and Polly?'

Cat nodded. 'Owen too, I think. And Elsie, because it would be impossible to do anything worthwhile without her input.'

'It sounds like you've got everyone you need – I'm sure I'd just get in the way anyway.'

'Oh no,' Cat said weakly, shaking her head. 'Of course you wouldn't.' But it wasn't Mark's absence she was concerned about. Cat thought of the ideas that had been jumbling in her head for the last few days, and knew that Joe would have been able to organise them and better them, and come up with a final, perfect plan. She didn't know how they would cope without his creative input, and she didn't want to think too hard about the fact that he wasn't back yet, or how acutely aware she was of his absence at number nine Primrose Terrace. She was sure Shed was pining too.

'I have to go, or I'll be late.' She kissed Mark on the cheek, raced to the door and turned, but he was already engrossed in the documents again, his script or lawyer contracts. Feeling a flush of relief that he found whatever it was more worthwhile than Christmas, she headed out into the cold night.

Cat, Elsie, Polly and Owen sat around the huge table in Jessica's luxurious kitchen. The bank of windows looked out over the back garden, which was in darkness save for white fairy lights woven through the branches of an ash tree. In soft lamplight, and with bottles of spiced red wine and a cinnamon-flavoured candle, Jessica had instantly got them in the festive spirit, and was putting the Michael Bublé Christmas album on to complete the effect.

'So,' Elsie said, 'Christmas at Primrose Terrace. What are the options?'

'I'm having a party,' Jessica said. 'The spring "do" was so successful that I couldn't imagine not holding another one.'

'That was a great party,' Polly sighed. 'I had so much fun.'

'So did I,' Jessica said, smiling. 'I hope your delicious brother's going to hotfoot it back from America in time for this one. He sounds like he's having far too much fun!'

'Sounds like?' Polly asked, frowning.

Cat stifled her gasp and stared at Jessica.

Jessica gave Polly a cat-like grin. 'I'm redesigning my website, my whole brand. A fresh look for a new year, and you know me, I'd much rather support local businesses. I emailed Magic Mouse designs and Joe told me he was in Portland. Some of the photos he's been sending me – it looks gorgeous.'

'He's sent you photos?' Polly asked. 'I've only had two.'

Jessica preened. 'We're going to meet up when he's back, but for now the email exchange is working well. I think he can see what page I'm on.'

Cat doodled a picture of a Christmas tree on her notepad and tried not to think about Jessica's flirtatious emails to Joe.

'Well, I —' Polly shook her head. 'It's fantastic that you've asked him. He'll be so busy he won't know what to do with himself!'

'I'd better get some mistletoe in,' Jessica said. 'An essential element of any Christmas party. And Joe will be a great person to manoeuvre underneath it.'

'I'll tell him you said that,' Polly said, laughing. 'I'm sure he'll be flattered.'

'I hope he'll be more than just flattered,' Jessica said, running her polished nails up the stem of her wine glass.

Cat felt her cheeks burning, her mouth drying out.

'So,' Owen said, rubbing his hands together. 'What are your thoughts, Cat? You said you wanted something that could work with Jessica's party.'

Cat swallowed, nodded and turned to her notes. 'I was thinking of organizing some kind of game or competition that the whole of Primrose Terrace can take part in. Offices have Secret Santas and Christmas buffets, and there are always family games at Christmas – charades and quizzes. I thought about a quiz, but I'm not sure it would bring the street together in the way I want to.'

'A treasure hunt?' Owen suggested. 'Taking people all over Fairview, with a Christmas theme and the prizes given out at Jessica's party.'

They pondered this, Polly chewing her pen. 'But if everyone knew it was ending at the party, wouldn't that defeat the purpose?'

'And it's only going to get colder between now and Christmas,' Elsie added, 'so I'm not sure it would play to everyone's strengths.'

'True,' Owen said, his head on one side, his black curls bouncing. 'Maybe that's more a summer thing.'

'A competitive element would be good, though,' Polly said. 'That way people would make an effort.'

'So something that can be judged, with prizes awarded at the party?' Jessica went to the cupboard and took out a box of dog biscuits. She shook it, and the three Westies, followed by Owen's fox terrier Rummy, and then Disco and, finally, Chalky, pattered in from the dog den where they'd been playing. She crouched, her grey cashmere shawl brushing the floor, and gave out the treats.

'I like prizes,' Owen said. 'Pets win prizes?'

Cat nodded. 'I want to involve the dogs somehow. It's such a doggy street. Except . . .' She glanced at Polly. 'We don't have one.'

'No,' Polly said, 'but that means we could judge it. Especially as you're the resident dog walker.'

Cat thought of Joe's insistence that she couldn't have dogs in the house, the hints that he and Polly had given her since the spring that the reasons were complicated. She still hadn't got to the bottom of it, but had begun to accept it. The details that the woman at the vet's had given her were still in her coat pocket, but she had her clients' dogs, and she got to spend time with them every day. Perhaps she wasn't destined to have one of her own.

'So, one thing for the dogs,' Elsie said, 'one for the humans.'

'Something sparkly and fun and creative,' Cat added. 'There's *loads* of creativity on this road – Boris and Charles are super stylish with their bed and breakfast, there's

Frankie and the girls who are always doing crafty things, and then us.'

'Sure,' Polly said. 'Just think of the banner Joe designed for your event.'

'Exactly.' Cat could picture it perfectly when she closed her eyes. It was rolled up under her bed, within reach whenever she wanted to have another look at it. 'Something Christmassy and crafty.'

'Tree decorations?' Elsie asked.

'Good,' Cat said, 'but I think it needs to be bigger.'

'Christmas trees?' Owen suggested. 'People go to town with their trees.'

Cat nodded. 'That sounds great, but . . .' She frowned, thinking. 'Something *even* bigger. Something we could all enjoy without having to traipse through everyone else's house. Maybe . . .' She stared out of the window, seeing the glimmering fairy lights against the reflection of them sitting round the table. She turned back, mouth open, and Jessica caught her eye.

They spoke together.

'Christmas lights.'

Jessica's smile was triumphant.

'Lights?' Polly asked, 'on the trees? Isn't that the same as decorations?'

Cat shook her head, dropped to the floor and pulled Disco towards her, lifting the mini schnauzer up. Disco pawed at Cat's dress and licked her cheek.

'Not on the trees, on the houses. Primrose Terrace is one of the prettiest roads I've ever seen, let alone lived on. All the houses have their own character, so why not have a lights competition? See who can decorate theirs the best?'

Owen sat up. 'Everyone would have to decide whether they wanted to go for classy, just a couple of colours, or all-out with reindeers and Santa climbing up the side of the house. You'd have to think tactically as well as creatively.'

'You could judge it, Owen,' Elsie said. 'You don't live on Primrose Terrace.'

'Are you kidding? There's no way I'm being left out. I'll help with number nine, if –' he turned to Polly, taking her hand – 'if you'll have me?'

Polly grinned, her pale cheeks flushing. 'Of course I will.'

Cat buried her smile in Disco's fur. The young dog yelped, jumped down and went to be overfriendly to Chalky who, having had his treat, was lying on the floor next to Jessica's glass-fronted wine cabinet.

'We'll have to get someone else to judge it,' Jessica said. 'Someone unconnected with Primrose Terrace. Maybe someone at the *Fairhaven Press*?'

'To judge a Christmas lights competition?' Owen asked, incredulous.

'Why not?' Jessica said. 'I've done enough interviews with them. I'm sure if I got in touch they'd spare a reporter.' She left the room and came back with the day's paper. 'I'll see if I can find someone.'

Cat swallowed, her eyes drawn to the newspaper. 'We could ask Phil,' she said, 'who I've been in touch with about doggy events, and the protest. He might be happy to do it.'

'Oh, of course!' Jessica said. 'Of course he would, silly me.'

Jessica moved the paper aside. 'Right. Let's think about the details and the dog element.'

'Dogs and lights aren't a good mix,' Elsie said. 'There could be chewing issues.'

'No, you're right, we need something distinctly dog-related.'

Quiet settled on the room as they thought, the only sounds the soft crooning of Michael Bublé, the occasional crackle of the candle, and the snuffling of the dogs. Cat, inches away from the copy of the *Fairhaven Press,* had become distracted. Thursday was the day Curiosity Kitten was published. She didn't know if Joe had sent in a whole batch of cartoons to run while he was away, or if he was sending them from America, but they had been appearing for the last three weeks. So far they had been final versions of sketches that Cat had already seen – the kitten about to lift a lid on a pan containing a piranha, scrabbling on a box outside a window – but she'd come to look forward to them, to feel the connection to Joe while he was hundreds of miles away.

With the excitement over the result of the protest and planning a Christmas event, she hadn't yet looked at today's cartoon. She was sure Polly had. She often mentioned to Cat how proud she was of her brother, how well he was doing in the States, which meant he was keeping in touch with her. Cat had no right to expect him to contact her too, especially not since the events of the protest, but she couldn't deny that she missed him, and that Curiosity Kitten had become an important part of her week. She'd gone from feeling affronted by it to counting the days until it arrived.

'Dog secret Santa?' Polly asked. 'We could buy them all something, have a Santa give them out at the party.'

'Have a person dressed as a dog dressed as Santa?' Elsie asked, sipping her wine.

Polly sighed. 'OK, that sounds a bit weird. Maybe not.'

'Some kind of dog show or parade,' Owen said. 'A dog fashion show. Is that cruel?'

'Why would it be cruel?' Jessica asked, appraising her Westies as they tussled good-naturedly on the kitchen floor.

'Dressing them up. Making them wear outfits.'

'I don't think so,' Elsie said, 'not if it's only for a few hours.'

346

'Valentino loves his little tartan jacket,' Jessica said.

'Of course he would,' Polly said, laughing. 'He's called Valentino.'

'So let's take it a step further.' Owen leaned forward. 'How about fancy dress? A Christmas lights competition for the houses, and a fancy-dress competition for the dogs. It could be judged at the party, if you're happy to have dogs there, Jessica?'

Jessica sipped her wine, thinking. Cat remembered how beautiful and dressy everyone had been at her spring party.

'We could have the fancy dress early afternoon,' Cat said, 'then come back later for the party and the lights judging. That way the dogs could all go home and de-robe, and the adults could have fun without worrying about their pets causing havoc.'

'I like your style,' Owen said, pointing at her. 'You've got a pretty solid events head on your shoulders.'

'Why, thank you,' Cat grinned. 'We're all coming up with some good ideas.'

'Excellent Christmas committee,' Elsie said, raising her glass. They all clinked, and Jessica opened another bottle of wine as the music moved seamlessly from Michael Bublé to Christmas hits and the first bars of Wham's 'Last Christmas'. Polly hummed along, swaying in time to the music.

Jessica leaned over the table, her long blonde hair falling over her face. 'It's November in two days, so we need to let everyone know. They can't be expected to put on a good show if they don't have long enough to prepare.'

'What do you think you and Mark will do?' Elsie asked.

'I still live at number nine,' Cat said. 'And I'm not sure Mark will be up for any of this. He'll take some encouraging.'

'So encourage him.' Elsie squeezed her arm. 'If anyone can, then it's you. And if Owen's helping Polly, and presumably Joe will be back too, that leaves you free to help Mr Charming.'

'Mr Charming horror writer,' Jessica added. 'You might end up having the scariest display on the road.'

'That could be fun,' Cat laughed. 'I'll remind him that it's Christmas and not Halloween.'

'I think we should give people ideas,' Jessica said, 'encourage creativity, something grandiose. Let's have a look at some displays on the plasma screen.' She got up and, taking her wine, led the way out of the room. Cat hung back, waiting until Elsie, Polly and Owen had followed her, and turned to the copy of the *Fairhaven Press*.

It was usually on page thirty, alongside the brainteasers and opposite the letters page. She wondered how many people had admired or laughed at the cartoon and felt a strange swell of pride. Not for her involvement, but on Joe's behalf. She turned to the right page and smoothed the paper down.

There was Curiosity Kitten, large eyes, confident stance, with a surfboard under her arm, the lapping waves of the sea behind her. Cat let out an involuntary gasp, her cheeks colouring. She looked at the next frame. The kitten was walking towards a van, *Surf Shack* written on the side in Joe's bold bubble writing.

Cat's head started to pound.

The third frame showed Curiosity Kitten starting to pull back the sliding door of the van, her smile wide, and then in the fourth and final frame the door was fully open, and inside there was a huge shark, a shocked expression on its face, a wetsuit pulled halfway down its tail.

Cat laughed out loud. There was no question that this was related to Mark finding Cat and Joe inside the van, but Joe had twisted it on its head, turning it into a funny cartoon. People would enjoy the mutual shock of the kitten and the shark as they encountered each other without realizing its significance.

Only she and Joe would get it, and of course Mark. She wondered what he would think if he saw the cartoon, whether she would have to defend what had happened again, or if her explanation had been enough.

Cat ran her finger over the paper, drinking in the details of Joe's drawings, the character that he gave to his animals, the details on the van and the surfboard, the lapping waves. She didn't hear Polly come in.

'Are you coming, Cat?' She asked, her eyes bright in the low light of the kitchen. She glanced down, saw what Cat was looking at, and gave her a gentle smile.

'Remind you of something?'

Cat gave a start. She had never fully explained to Polly what had happened in the van that day, though a few people – Polly included – had seen her running away down the beach after Mark had opened the door on them. She wondered if Joe had confided in her. Polly must have noticed her confusion, because she clarified.

'The day of the protest. That cramped changing space in the back of Harvey's van.'

'Yes,' Cat said slowly. 'It, um, it has a bit more significance, I think.'

'It does?'

'Joe came to see me, when I was changing that day. It was when he told me about Curiosity Kitten, and the . . . inspiration behind it.'

'You mean his hapless housemate?' Polly grinned.

'Exactly.' Cat eyed her best friend, wondering if she had any idea. It seemed that Joe hadn't given any explanation to his sister, keeping the affairs of his heart to himself. 'And he might have . . .' she wondered what to say, wondered if she had any right to tell Polly how Joe felt.

'What?' Polly asked, drumming her fingers over the cartoon.

'Well, Mark found us in there together and he—'

'Jumped to conclusions?'

Cat winced.

Polly went very still, her fingers no longer drumming. 'He *was* jumping, wasn't he? There's nothing . . . oh my God!'

'What?'

'Joe moved his flights. His course didn't start until last week, but at the last minute he changed them to two days after the protest, said he wanted to do some exploring. I realize now, he always mentions *you* in his emails, always asks how *you're* getting on. He asks after Shed too, and Owen, but he mentions you in *every one*.' Polly rubbed her arm and looked out over Jessica's darkened garden, the fairy lights still twinkling. 'He misses you, Cat.'

Cat was gripped by a sudden fear that Polly would blame her for encouraging him, for forcing him away. She didn't think she'd encouraged him, she certainly hadn't meant to. She hadn't allowed herself to accept that she had feelings for him too. Of course, now he was gone, those feelings had been let loose, and she couldn't tell anyone how much she missed him. 'If I've hurt him—'

'No,' Polly said quickly. 'I mean, not unless you . . ?'

Cat shook her head. 'I've been with Mark.' Not *I am with Mark*. She closed her eyes.

'Oh, Joey,' Polly said to herself, and then to Cat: 'He's fallen for you. And I guess after Rosalin, after all that he went through with her, he must have thought that . . . that it would be best to get away. To give himself some space.'

'I never meant for this to happen,' Cat whispered.

Polly shook her head. 'You're with Mark now, and I'm so happy for you, Cat. I want you to be happy, and I want Joey to be happy, and sometimes things don't slot together neatly the way you want them to. He's done this, gone away, to protect himself. I just wish he'd told me. But look,' she said, forcing levity into her voice, 'he's having a great time out there, and if what Jessica said is true then he's at least got that distraction to take his mind off things.' Polly hugged her and Cat breathed in her friend's soft perfume, trying not to think about Jessica, her seductiveness and her glamour and her shimmering confidence.

She wished she could be honest with Polly about how she really felt, but she knew that, first, she had to be entirely honest with herself, and make some decisions. She had to be clear what she wanted.

Cat looked down at the cartoon again, at the shark looking shocked in his wetsuit. A smile tugged at her lips, and at first she didn't hear the phone in her pocket.

'Cat,' Polly said, 'you're vibrating.'

Cat pulled her phone out, frowned at the screen, and answered it. 'Mum? What is it, what's wrong?'

'Nothing's wrong, darling,' her mum trilled. 'The opposite, in fact. Things are moving at a pace here, a few decisions being taken out of our hands and, well, it all culminates in the fact that we're going to Canada in a fortnight now, not January.'

'In *two weeks*?' Cat screeched. 'What? Why? What about Christmas?'

'Come and see us next Saturday, Catherine, and we'll have Christmas early.'

'Right, but ' Cat rubbed her forehead.

'No buts. There's really nothing to worry about.'

'I don't have your presents yet. I'm not prepared. There was so much I wanted to do!' She heard the panic in her voice and swallowed.

'You don't need to do anything, love.' Her father had taken over the phone. 'Just bring yourself.'

'But you're really going? In a couple of weeks?'

'It's time your mum and I had our adventure. Don't fret. We'll explain everything when we see you. Lots of love to you and your fella.'

'Take care, darling,' her mum called, and the line went dead.

Polly looked at Cat, and Cat stared back, her eyes filling with tears.

'Oh gosh.' Polly said. 'I heard most of that.'

Cat nodded and forced a smile. 'Let's go and look at Christmas lights,' she said. Getting up from the table, she wrapped her arm through her friend's and, taking a final glance at Joe's cartoon, left the room.

21

Cat sat on her mum and dad's squishy sofa and clinked glasses with them. It was half past two in the afternoon, but it was their Christmas day, and that meant prosecco with lunch. Cat was so happy for them, so excited about their adventure, but she was also feeling untethered. Her parents had always been close to her, no more than an hour away, apart from when she was at university. She'd been living her own life, and since moving to Primrose Terrace had gone a few months without seeing them, but had taken it for granted that she'd always be able to return to Brighton and knock on the door.

Their original January departure date had allowed her to put off thinking about it, to focus on more immediate things like Mark and dog protests and housemates. But now the date was rushing up to meet them, and Cat had spent the last week trying to get her head around it, making sure she had their presents ready while also getting news out in Primrose Terrace about the Christmas lights and dog fancy-dress competitions. She was exhausted.

'Cheers,' her dad said. 'Here's to new adventures for us all.'

'I'll drink to that,' Delia added.

'Me too.' Cat held her glass up and took a sip.

It was early November, just after fireworks night, the air full of smoke and blowing leaves, but in her parents' living room, Christmas had well and truly arrived. Cards were strung around the wall – mostly her mother's own designs, and a few that their friends had sent early once they'd been told the new plan – and paper chains decorated the mirrors and mantelpieces. An artificial tree took up one corner of the room, its branches pulsing with fibre optic light: blue, then red, then yellow, gold, pink, green. The room smelled of pinecones and roasting turkey, and Christmas carols played low in the background. It was like Santa's grotto on a grey November day.

'So this camper van,' Cat said, 'it's definitely roadworthy? And you have to get it now?'

Peter nodded. 'It's in great nick. And the guy's moving himself, so he needs to have it gone before the end of November. I doubt we'll find another deal like this one, so we went ahead and snapped it up. We're picking it up from Vancouver, and then it's on the road we go!' He pointed his arm up to the ceiling like Superman, and Cat's mum grinned.

'You can't wait,' Cat said softly.

'It's a dream come true,' Delia said. 'We've talked about it for years, but somehow never thought it was *us*. It wasn't something we did, just pack up and go travelling. But then we thought – why not? What's there to stop us? We're biting the proverbial bullet.'

'Which is what the turkey will be like if I don't check on it.' Her dad squeezed Cat's shoulder as he left the room.

Cat gazed into her glass.

'Are you all right about all this, darling?' Delia swapped sofas, squashing up next to Cat, the soft fabric of her long,

354

red dress brushing against Cat's bare legs. Cat was wearing a short navy dress and leather boots, silver jewellery. It suddenly seemed over the top, despite the occasion. 'You seem a bit down.'

'I'm just trying to take it all in,' Cat said. 'That you're going next week.'

Cat's mum rubbed her back in small, circular motions, as if she was a baby that needed burping. 'But you've known we were going for a while now. And it's only a couple of weeks early. You've got Polly, and Mark. All your friends in Fairview.'

'I know that,' Cat said. 'But you'll be so far away.'

'Technology brings everything closer,' Delia said, holding up her iPad. 'We can do FaceTime now, send you our photos. Distance doesn't count for anything if you don't let it.'

Cat nodded, thinking how she hadn't heard directly from Joe since he'd left. Over a month ago now, with only Curiosity Kitten to remind her he still existed. That and her thoughts. This week's cartoon had been Curiosity Kitten walking to the beach – past an arrow-shaped sign saying *The Cove* – swinging a picnic hamper, then getting there to discover the sand was overrun with dogs of all different sizes and breeds. Needless to say, Curiosity Kitten had turned and run in the opposite direction, but Cat knew that word had reached him that their protest had been successful. A note under the cartoon strip reminded people of the council's decision to continue to allow dogs at the cove.

Was Joe letting her know that he was thinking about her? Or was this latest cartoon something the paper had asked him to do to reinforce the news about the council decision? She wished she could talk to him. She was sure Polly would give her his email address, but at the same time she knew he wanted some space, and she had to respect that.

'The turkey's looking delicious.' Her dad returned and topped up their glasses. 'You'll have to take lots of it back with you, there's enough to feed a small army and we can't take it with us.'

'It's a shame Mark couldn't come today,' Delia said gently. 'It would have been lovely to meet him.'

'I know,' Cat said, 'but he's got lots on in the run-up to Christmas. I think he's trying a really big push with his film. It got put on hold, and he wants to get it going again.'

'A busy man,' Peter said, nodding approvingly. 'It's good that he's ambitious.'

'Oh yes,' Cat said. 'He's really passionate about his films.'

Her parents exchanged a glance, and Cat took another sip of prosecco. She had asked Mark to come with her today, but he had insisted he couldn't spare the time. Since the first meeting of the Christmas committee, she'd barely seen him. He'd been tied up with film negotiations, and Cat hadn't pushed the issue, trying to deal with her own conflicted thoughts. She hadn't expected him to come, and had never once pictured the four of them sharing an early Christmas together. In her head, it had always been her and Mum and Dad.

Cat understood that their relationship was relatively new, and that meeting parents was a big thing, but Mark knew that if he didn't meet Peter and Delia now, it would probably be a year before he'd get another chance.

He'd also shown little enthusiasm in the Christmas lights competition, and had refused to dress Chips up in anything other than her usual lead and collar. Cat understood that not every dog owner was comfortable dressing their dogs up, and of course she respected that. But everyone else on Primrose Terrace was getting involved in the lights competition, if not the dog fancy dress.

She had gone over it again and again. Was she too demanding, expecting too much of him? After all, he had helped her with the

356

protest, had been enthusiastic about it until Joe had upstaged him on the waves and then caused problems later.

It wasn't that Mark wasn't attentive – when they were together, he could make her feel like she was the only person in the world, so much that it was sometimes dizzying. But when he was engrossed in his work, either in Fairview or in London, it was as if Cat didn't exist. She felt like she'd been put into a neat compartment in his life, not allowed to break free and spread out into all of it.

He didn't talk to her openly about his films or his family unless she badgered him. He only expected that she be there to share a meal with, watch a film together, make love. It was nice, but was it enough? Shouldn't they be interested in every part of each other's lives, challenging each other, exploring new things together?

'You all right, love?' Peter asked. 'You're awfully quiet.'

'I'm fine,' Cat said, 'I'm just tired. Shall we open presents?'

'Perfect plan.' Delia knelt on the carpet and burrowed under the tree, pulling out beautifully wrapped packages, handing them out. Cat joined her mum on the floor, pushing thoughts of Mark to the back of her mind.

Her mum and dad had got her some new perfume and a beautiful leather journal, with a small, embossed dog in the corner of the front cover.

'In case you want to write about your doggy exploits,' her dad said. 'This year's a big one for you, love. Not everyone's bold enough to start their own business, and it's not easy to make a success of it. Don't underestimate your achievements.'

'Thanks, Dad.' Cat breathed in the leather smell, ran her hand over the soft cover, the embossed dog. 'It's gorgeous.' She used to write in diaries as a child, the kind with a lock and key that made you feel like your secrets were the biggest in the world, but she hadn't written her thoughts down for years. The journal pages were too pristine, too white. She wondered what she could possibly write that would do it justice.

She leaned behind her to drag out a bag she'd stowed under the coffee table, kept separate from the other presents, the practical things she'd got for her parents' trip. A hot-water bottle, slipper socks and an eye mask for her mum, an impressive lantern torch for her dad. 'I wanted to do something for you, to have something to remind you of me – of here.'

Delia laughed. 'We're hardly going to forget our only daughter, are we?'

Cat held out the present and Delia took it, passing it to Peter so they could pull off the gold paper together.

Cat watched them unwrapping it, wondering if it was a selfish present. She hadn't had as long as she'd wanted to put it together, and it wasn't perfect, but she hoped they would like it.

'Oh, Catherine,' Delia said, staring at the front cover of the photo book. 'This is incredible.'

'It's got some family photos in, some from ages ago, and some more recent pictures.'

'You've done captions.' Peter moved closer to Delia so they could look together. 'What's this? *Peter Palmer and his world-famous watering hat.* Do I detect a hint of sarcasm?' He grinned at her.

'Not one bit.' Cat returned the smile.

'Oh, look,' Delia said, 'there are some of you at Primrose Terrace.'

'I thought you might like a few. I'm sorry I haven't been better at inviting you to visit.'

Cat watched her parents as they examined each photo: one from the Pooches' and Puppies' Picnic of her and Polly and Joe, Chips at their feet. One of Polly and Cat on the sofa at number nine, Shed lying across both their laps, legs outstretched. A couple of Cat in the park, the mini schnauzers at her feet, that Elsie had taken for her to use on her Twitter and Facebook pages. There was a photo of Cat and Mark at the cove on the morning of the protest, the waves behind them.

'Don't you two look lovely together,' Delia said. Cat thought she was talking about her and Mark, but saw that her mum was pointing at a photo of Cat and Joe the night of Jessica's spring party. It was a hasty selfie that Joe had snapped while they were waiting for Polly to get ready, Cat in her black flapper dress, Joe in his blue suit and disarming smile.

Cat thought back to the change in him that night. It was the first time since she'd moved to Primrose Terrace that he'd come out of his shell, and he'd ended up giving her the confidence to talk to people about Pooch Promenade.

'That was a good night,' Cat admitted. 'And Jessica's organizing another party for Christmas. They're very glamorous events.'

Her mum nodded. 'Joe scrubs up well, doesn't he? Generous *and* gorgeous.'

Cat sat back on her haunches and picked up her journal. She pressed her cheek against the cool leather and tried not to meet her mum's eye.

After Cat had eaten and drunk more than she thought physically possible, and with her mum bringing the chocolate log through to the living room in case any of them – laughably – felt peckish, they settled in front of *Elf* – her dad's favourite Christmas film. The curtains were still open, and Cat was distracted by the fireworks outside, the bright lights, the bangs. While Christmas in New York played out on the television,

Cat curled her legs up under her and thought about her Christmas in Primrose Terrace.

Would she be spending the day with Mark? He clearly wanted her all to himself, while she was organizing events that would involve all the residents, and what about Polly and Joe? She lived with them, Polly was her best friend, so now she wasn't seeing her parents, shouldn't she spend at least some of the day with them? She wondered what Joe was doing at that moment, what time of day it was in Portland, whether his course was still going on or if he was travelling round exploring new places.

She looked at her parents cuddled up on the sofa, chuckling at Will Ferrell and exchanging looks that, anyone could see from a mile away, were full of love. They were completely at home in each other's company. They shared everything, their deepest thoughts, their fears. They argued – her mum hadn't held back when she'd disagreed with her dad about important things – but they worked through it, they battled it out, and they were stronger because of it.

That wasn't how Cat felt about Mark. They hadn't been together that long, but she'd known him now for nearly ten months, and she felt that in some respects they were still strangers. She hadn't told him how worried she felt about her parents being so far away, because she didn't think he'd get it. She only knew that he wasn't close to his mum and dad, she had none of the details, so she'd been similarly vague with him.

No sooner had they got together, than they were pulling apart again. She knew that this was as much her fault as his, but he hadn't mentioned it or made an effort to spend more time with her. She didn't feel close to Mark the way her parents so obviously were. She was attracted to him, but she didn't feel a sense of companionship, of friendship. And desire without friendship, in her mind, wasn't a relationship.

Picking up her wine glass, turning away from *Elf* and looking out into the dark November night, the bursts of bright light adding to the festivity of the cosy living room, Cat let her mind wander where, until now, she hadn't allowed it to.

Joe didn't have a dog, so that was a moot point, but there was no doubt he'd get involved in the Christmas lights competition. She wouldn't be surprised if Polly had already emailed him and he was thinking up ideas while he honed his drawing skills. And, even as a friend, Joe would have come with her to her parents' house because he would have known how important it was to her.

He might have argued with her about what she was bringing, they might still clash over how to decorate the front of their house, but he wouldn't gloss over things and leave her to it. It would matter to him, and he'd tell her how he felt.

Cat jumped as her dad let out a loud guffaw at something on the screen and her mum slapped him on the arm, her face a mask of mock disapproval. He kissed her, his lips lingering on her cheek. Cat barely noticed the rest of the film, and only realised it was over when the credits finished and the DVD flipped back to the menu screen. Her parents had fallen asleep, her mum's head resting on her dad's shoulder, her dad snoring gently.

Leaning forward, Cat picked up the remote and switched the DVD player off. The TV flicked back to one of the Freeview channels and she was about to turn it off when she heard a familiar voice. She looked up, her breath catching in her throat as she saw McDreamy approaching Meredith, who was standing on a hilltop, surrounded by candles.

The end of *Grey's Anatomy*, Season Four. When, after endless complications, missed opportunities and misunderstandings,

Meredith shows McDreamy how much she loves him with a grand, romantic gesture.

She sank back onto the sofa, Meredith's words melting away to nothing as her mind filled with her and Joe's, from that night back in August. Words about Rosalin and Mark, and about happy every after. *You're cute when you're fuzzy.*

Cat watched the screen, cradling her wine glass, her stomach churning with a mixture of dread and excitement. She had made a decision, and she knew it was the right one. Even if she'd missed her chance with Joe, she couldn't be in this relationship when her heart was with someone else. For once, she had to listen to it.

In the morning, her head clearer than she had expected, Cat stepped out of early Christmas and into a cold, bright day.

'Well then,' her dad said, standing next to Delia at the end of the front path, 'see you in a few months.'

Cat nodded, inhaled and squeezed her dad as tightly as she could. 'Have a magical time,' she said into his shoulder, 'and stay in touch. I want to know everything.'

'That's a dangerous thing to say,' Delia said, waiting for her turn and then engulfing her daughter. 'We'll email you constantly. You won't have time for dog-walking or romance if you go around saying things like that.'

'I'll fit it all in,' Cat said.

'Look after yourself, my darling.' Her mum let the tears fall, not bothering to wipe them away. 'Keep going with everything, keep living your life. We're so proud of you.'

Her dad gave her another hug, nodding fervently. 'We are, my love. We couldn't be prouder.'

'Thanks,' Cat murmured. 'I will. And I'm proud of you too. For following your dreams, for being so brave.'

'I doubt we'll be brave if we encounter one of those grizzly bears,' Peter chuckled.

'You'll probably make friends with it.' Cat laughed and wiped her cheeks, putting her bag in the back of the battered Fiesta that Joe and Polly shared, and which she'd borrowed for the journey to Brighton.

'Merry Christmas, Catherine,' her mum said.

'Happy Christmas to you too.' She hugged them each again, then climbed into the driver's seat and pulled away, waving in the mirror, watching her parents get smaller and smaller and finally, as she turned the corner, disappear from view.

The living room of number nine Primrose Terrace looked like the lights department at John Lewis after an earthquake had hit. Polly and Owen were standing in the middle of the tangle, and Rummy was lying on the floor, his head on his paws as if he'd already been told off more than once. There was no sign of Shed.

'Is this the attack of the killer lights?' Cat asked. 'Because you look like you might be in trouble.'

'Cat, how was Christmas?'

'Lovely,' Cat said, 'but also sad. That's it. They're off, to Canada, for ages.' She felt the lump in her throat resurface and pushed it away. She had to be strong, especially for what she was about to do.

'Oh, Cat.' Polly held her arms out as if she wanted to hug her friend, but strings of fairy lights came with her and she looked like a monster covered in decorative seaweed.

Cat burst out laughing. 'Is this all for our house?'

Owen nodded. 'We weren't sure which colours to get. I thought we could try them all out and see which combination works best.'

'Wow.' Cat nodded. 'I'm impressed by your dedication.'

'I'm a competitive guy. And now you can help – you've just had Christmas, so I expect you to be fully immersed in festivity.'

Cat smiled at Owen, thinking for the millionth time how perfect he was for her best friend. 'I will, but I have to go and do something first. Keep at it, though. You might have untangled yourself in time for next Christmas if you work solidly between now and then.'

She left Owen and Polly gawping at her and then, with her stomach doing somersaults, she made her way back out into the sunshine.

Mark opened the door wearing his leather jacket, and with Chips's lead in his hand.

'Hello,' he said, leaning forward to kiss her. 'You're back early.'

'Mum and Dad have lots to do,' Cat said. 'And I needed to get back.'

'Did you have a good time? Give them a good send-off?'

Cat nodded. 'It was quiet, but it was lovely. Very Christmassy. And – don't take your coat off.'

Mark had started taking off his jacket, but he paused and gave her a questioning look.

'You're taking Chips for a walk? Let me come.'

'Sure?'

Cat nodded. 'I could do with the fresh air.'

The trees in Fairview Park were mostly bare, the ground smattered with fallen leaves, and George had roped brightly coloured strings of lights around the awning of the Pavilion café, large gold stars hanging down from the ceiling inside. Cat and Mark walked in step with each other, nodding at other dog walkers, throwing a tennis ball to Chips, who never tired of racing off and bringing it back to her master.

Cat remembered when she'd first met Mark, not too far from where they were walking. How she'd been caught off guard by his assertiveness, intrigued by the air of mystery he carried with him. She had come to realize that, despite all the things that attracted her to Mark, she didn't want someone who was charming but distant. She wanted closeness, and it wasn't fair to try and make it work, to wait for something that she wasn't convinced would ever come, when her heart wasn't in it.

She shoved her hands into the pockets of her dark-green coat and glanced up at his strong, handsome profile. She closed her eyes momentarily, swallowed and stopped walking.

'Mark,' she said.

'Cat.' He smiled at her, an eyebrow raised. 'Why have we stopped?'

They were under a row of plane trees along the edge of the park. Cat spotted a bench and sat down.

Mark stared at her for a moment, his Adam's apple bobbing, and then joined her.

'I need to talk to you,' she said quickly, her mind flashing back to a few weeks before, her apology, her attempt to rescue their relationship even though Joe was already taking up residence in her thoughts.

'Oh no,' Mark said lightly, 'those fatal words. I'm sorry, Cat, but I'm not dressing Chips up as Frankenstein. Not even my love of horror can convince me to make my Border collie look like a stuffed toy.'

Cat shook her head. 'I get that, I totally understand. It's not that.'

Mark's smile faltered a little. 'You don't want to spend Christmas with me? You've decided to go out to Canada with your parents and leave Primrose Terrace? You're taking the success of Pooch Promenade to London and—'

'No! Mark, stop. Please. This is difficult enough as it is.' She squeezed her hands into fists and watched as Mark's smile disappeared and the amusement in his eyes was replaced with a hardness that Cat had only seen once before.

'What's difficult enough?'

'I – I think we should end it,' Cat said. 'End us.'

Mark stared at her, barely noticing as Chips raced up and dropped the tennis ball at his feet. Grateful for a reason to turn away, Cat picked it up and threw the ball as far as she could.

'Can I ask why?' Mark said eventually. 'Why now?'

Cat sighed. 'Because I don't think it's working. I mean – we get on, and you're lovely, you're gorgeous and funny and smart and sexy, and—'

'So what's the problem?'

'It doesn't feel enough. For me.'

Mark turned away, squinting out over the park. Cat watched him.

'Is this because I didn't come to your parents' with you?'

'No. Partly. I mean – I just want more. More than fun, and that's what it feels like with you, Mark. It feels like it's all a bit of fun.'

Mark gave a hollow laugh. 'I've never had anyone complain that they're having fun with me.'

Cat shook her head. 'No,' she said quietly. 'Well, maybe I'm wrong. Maybe I'm going to regret this, but it's how I feel, and I don't think it would be fair of me to—'

'Oh, spare me the pity. You don't think it would be fair of you to keep it going? Is that it? Could you be any more of a cliché?'

Cat breathed in, shocked. 'Sorry. I thought I should explain.'

'You want to finish with me, that's all I need to know.' He stood up and turned away from her.

Cat stood too, wrapping her arms around herself. 'I'm sorry.'

'Don't be.' He started walking, whistling to Chips, and Cat felt her legs wobble beneath her. He hadn't tried to change her mind. He hadn't pleaded with her or told her how much he cared about her, or that it had meant anything to him. Perhaps that was anger, the only way he could deal with it, but it made her think that she was right, that his feelings for her weren't any more than surface deep. Cat watched him walk a few paces, bend to stroke Chips's ears, then throw the ball and turn back round.

He came towards her, and Cat's heart pounded. Was he coming back to apologize, or to get a better explanation? 'Mark—?' she started.

'I know what this is,' he said. 'This is about you and Joe. That's the real reason you're doing this.'

Cat was frozen, unable to speak, as if someone had poured superglue over her.

'You've been interested in him all along, and now you've decided that you've got a chance with him. You're picking him over me?'

'That's not true.'

'You've been playing us both, and now you're giving me up because he drew you a fancy banner and posed on a surfboard? He draws cartoons for a living, for fuck's sake. He doodles on pieces of paper. I make films.'

'It's really not about—'

'You think he can satisfy you as much as I do?'

'Mark—' she tried again.

'Seriously, Cat. The guy's a tool. You've been leading me on the whole time, and now you've come to this deluded conclusion.' He was standing close, staring down at her.

Cat swallowed, and then felt her anger flash.

367

'This decision is about me, Mark. Not Joe. It's about what I want from a relationship, and what makes me happy. I'm sorry it's not worked out with us, and I get that you're angry, but there's no reason to attack me, or anyone else.' She reached out and put a hand on his arm, but he flinched away. 'I'm sorry, Mark. I never meant to hurt you.'

'You haven't. Don't lose any sleep over it – I'm not going to.'

Mark turned and strode towards the exit of the park, Chips catching up and trotting alongside him, her tail wagging happily. Cat sat back down on the bench, her whole body trembling as relief and guilt washed over her.

As hard as it was, she'd done the right thing. And his anger had been justified. Nothing had happened between her and Joe, but he'd been in her thoughts, and therefore it hadn't been fair on either her or Mark.

She pushed herself up and, feeling vague and disconnected, unable to focus on any one thing, she made her way slowly back to Primrose Terrace. What she needed now was Polly and Owen: her friends and a warm living room, a cup of tea and a mindless job untangling Christmas lights. She'd made a commitment to the Primrose Terrace residents, and it was just what she needed to take her mind off her own worries. She wasn't going to let them down.

22

When Cat got home, the front of the house was alight with pink and blue fairy lights, like something out of a Disney film. Owen was dangling out of Joe's bedroom window, snaking a third trail of lights down to Polly, who was standing on the top step, arms outstretched.

'Oh my God,' Cat said. 'Are you wrapping the house in lights? Is there any kind of strategy behind this?'

'We're trying a few things out,' Owen called down. 'This isn't the final version.'

'Owen, be careful!' Polly called. 'Go back inside!'

Owen gave a quick salute and disappeared inside the window. Shed tiptoed out of the front door and wound his furry body around the two friends, and Cat scooped him up and into her arms. 'Why can't you just be a little dog?' Cat asked. 'Hmm?'

Shed purred at her and butted her chin with his forehead.

'He's having a hard time of it,' Polly said. 'Trying to get used to Rummy being here. I'm actually quite impressed with the way he's coping.'

'No fights yet?'

'One miaowing-whimpering match,' Polly confirmed, 'but no contact. Owen's going to sit them down together this evening and see if he can get them to be friends.'

The idea made Cat smile, despite everything. 'Pet mediation?'

'He's feeling confident. Did you do what you needed to?'

Cat glanced at Polly, who was giving her the Midwich Cuckoo stare. 'I did,' she said, the words drying up. She nodded decisively.

'Want to share?'

Cat put Shed on the floor and went inside, undoing her coat. Polly followed her in, and Owen hurried down the stairs. 'I've just got to plug this in, and—' He looked up, saw their faces and took a step back. 'I might have a look at some of those star-shaped lights we got. See what we can do with them.'

Polly gave him an indulgent smile and turned back to Cat. 'What's happened?'

Cat perched on the arm of the sofa. 'I've broken up with Mark.'

Polly's eyes popped open. 'What? Why?'

'Because it wasn't working. Because I wasn't feeling it, because . . .' She shrugged. 'Because he wasn't enough. I don't think we had that connection. I didn't feel like we were letting each other in. It's as much my fault as his – probably more mine, but . . . there it is. It's over.'

'Oh, Cat.' Polly knelt in front of her and put her hands on Cat's knees. 'I'm sorry. You don't think that, over time, you could have got to know each other, that he could have been enough?'

Cat turned to look out of the window. 'I don't think so,' she said softly. 'Not the way I felt. So . . .' She put her hands deep in the pockets of her coat, and pulled out the piece of

370

paper with the puppy details on that she'd picked up at the vet's. She threw it onto the coffee table.

'Oh God,' Polly sighed. 'That's so shitty, Cat. However it's happened, whoever's decision, it's not nice. I'm sorry. And especially straight after saying goodbye to your parents. Are you going to be OK?'

'I am,' she said, replaying Mark's anger in her mind and feeling another rush of guilt. 'I feel pretty crap right now, but I did it. I broke up with him, and it was the right decision.'

'So what's the course of action?' Polly said, her blue eyes wide. 'Get hideously drunk? Get some old plates and smash them in the courtyard? Hide under your duvet and have a good cry? I can help with some of those. Or . . .' She glanced behind her.

'Or?' Cat asked, narrowing her eyes.

'Or get stuck into Christmas. Owen's—'

'Yeouch!' There was a loud bang and the overhead light went off.

'Owen?' Polly squealed. 'Are you OK?'

'I'm fine, I'm fine. I tripped the circuit breaker, that's all.'

Polly pressed her hand against her chest. 'Shit.'

'I think Christmas,' Cat said. 'Owen needs all the help he can get.'

'Agreed.'

Cat stood and pulled Polly up, and the two friends looked at each other, unspoken gratitude passing between them. Cat didn't know what she would do without her.

'Right.' She held her fist out and Polly bumped it. 'Let's do this. Let's do Christmas.'

November and December continued to get colder, snow threatened on the weather forecasts but rain stayed away, and the occupants of Primrose Terrace worked hard on their Christmas light displays. Cat spent more time than usual peering out of the windows, even though she had a better excuse than most people to walk up and down the terrace. She was already delighted by the efforts people had gone to.

Frankie, Emma and Lizzie – with Leyla's help – were doing animal-themed lights. They had strings of songbird-shaped lights hanging from the roof, donkeys and sheep and cows – originally part of a nativity-themed light display – attached to the front walls. Boris and Charles had, so far, gone for elegant white and gold to match the Christmas tree that stood in the front window, and was occasionally accessorized by Bossy and Dylan.

The Barkers, recently back from a three-week holiday to see their son in Australia, were – to Cat's shock – going all out with a sled on the roof and Santa climbing the chimney. They'd only just started their display, and Cat was eager to see how far they were going to take it. Jessica's house was conspicuously bare, but she'd told Cat that she had it all planned out, and didn't want to show her hand until the last minute. Elsie, suffering with a bad cold, had employed the help of Captain, and when Cat had popped round to take her some homemade soup, had found them at the coffee table working on a diagram that they'd quickly hidden from view.

Almost everyone was taking it seriously. Cat and Polly's house was bare again, their multitude of lights stored in Joe's office, while they did some more thinking about what would be most spectacular.

The one notable absence, which didn't surprise Cat in the least, was number four. It remained steadfastly Christmas-free and, Cat had noticed, hadn't had the Audi parked outside for several days. She'd had no contact from Mark since they'd broken up, and for that she was grateful.

As the weeks had passed, she'd settled into her decision. She missed certain things about their time together – she couldn't deny that they'd had fun – but there was no deep sadness, no ache in her heart. Her pulse didn't increase when she thought about him, she just felt sad and guilty, like she'd treated him badly, like she should have made the decision sooner.

It was the second Thursday of December and Cat was dressed in stonewashed jeans and a black boatneck jumper, waiting for the *Fairhaven Press* to come through the door as if it was a card from a gentleman caller.

Every time Cat thought about Joe, about his continuing absence, her chest gave a funny little pang that, she was sure, wasn't normal. He'd been gone for over two months. A three-week course, and he'd been away over twice that long. What if he loved it so much that he decided to stay out there long term and do what her parents were doing? Nowadays, even illustration could be done remotely – he'd proved that with Curiosity Kitten.

'Whatcha up to?' Polly asked, coming into the living room in her pyjamas. The two of them had spent an enjoyable Sunday the previous weekend decorating the house, and a huge tree – far too big for the room – was squashed into the corner, its colourful lights on the slow dimmer-flash setting. They had white, shimmery tinsel, like snow, adorning almost every surface and hanging in swathes in the doorways, and Polly had found a sensor on the Internet that made a sound like sleigh bells whenever anyone stepped over the living-room threshold. It made its tinkling sound now, and Cat laughed.

'Nothing much.' She sipped her coffee, trying to adjust her position without dislodging Shed, who was keeping her feet warm by being asleep on them. Owen's 'serious chat' with the pets had, to Cat and Polly's surprise, gone well, and Shed and Rummy now spent most of their time circling uncertainly round each other, like boxers in a ring. 'I'm walking the Westies in a bit,' she continued, 'and taking Disco and Chalky because Elsie's still under the weather.'

'Lights meeting later?' Polly asked. 'I've got the day off, so Owen could come round, we could look at what we've tried so far, what's left to do, and see if we can actually make a decision.'

'Sounds good,' Cat said, grinning. Over the last few weeks, without Mark, and now that Polly was qualified and had no studying to do, they'd spent most of their evenings together. Polly occasionally disappeared to Owen's house on the other side of Fairview, but more often than not it was the three of them, and for the first time since moving to Primrose Terrace, Cat felt she was getting to spend time with her best friend – and she didn't mind sharing her with her new boyfriend.

'Oh, and here's the paper.' Polly turned back to the hallway, pulled *The Fairhaven Press* out of the letterbox and placed it in front of Cat. Cat looked up at her friend, watched as she disappeared into the kitchen and, feeling suddenly nervous, turned the pages.

She looked for the familiar title, and read the cartoon, focusing on one frame at a time.

The first showed Curiosity Kitten asleep in bed, while above her, Santa and his sleigh were landing on the roof. The second frame showed Santa in the kitten's bedroom, standing next to the stocking on the hearth, his sack turned upside down, his expression horrified as he realized it was empty. The third frame saw Santa's leg retreating up the chimney, Curiosity Kitten with one eye open.

Cat laughed. It was just the kind of thing she'd do. She had never been able to leave her stocking untouched until Christmas morning when she was little, and in this cartoon, Curiosity Kitten was going to look early and be disappointed with no gifts.

She looked at the last frame.

Santa was on the roof, heading back to the chimney with a full sack, while below, Curiosity Kitten's eyes were wide and sad as she looked in her empty stocking. But Cat's heart was thumping, because at the top of Santa's now full sack was a tiny model house, a miniature doll's house. That in itself wasn't significant – she was sure lots of children would love to get doll's houses in their stockings – but this one had an attic window and a number nine on the front door.

Was that simply a nod to home, or did it mean he was coming back?

Polly sat opposite her and blew on her coffee.

Cat resisted asking her friend. In Polly's mind, there was no reason for Cat to be overly interested in Joe's movements, and Cat knew she couldn't feign nonchalance any longer. Of course she wanted to tell her best friend, but she had no idea if Joe still felt the same, or if he was even returning to Primrose Terrace. She glanced at the cartoon again, looking for more signs that she knew wouldn't be there. Was he coming home for Christmas or was there too much – complicated feelings, the beauty of Portland – to keep him away?

'Right,' she said, 'I'd better go and walk some doggies.'

'Do you know what Elsie's dressing Disco and Chalky up as for the fancy dress?' Polly asked.

'No,' Cat said, grateful for the distraction. 'Or Jessica's Westies. Or the Barkers' retrievers. Everyone's keeping schtum.'

'I wonder if Shed would like to go as Lassie. That would be fun, a cat dressed up as a famous dog.'

'What would be *even more hilarious* is putting Shed into a whole room full of real-life dogs. I don't think they'd all be as accommodating as Rummy.' Cat stood, grinning down at her friend.

'Oh yeah,' Polly said. 'Maybe not.'

'Come on, Chalky,' Cat said, 'it's not that cold, and look – sunshine!' She pointed to the sky, which was the pale, watery blue of a winter's day. Chalky sniffed and stopped walking, and Cat crouched, the leather of her boots cracking. 'Come on, poppet, we won't be long, and we're getting the Westies.' She ruffled the fur under his chin and stood, slowing her steps as she made her way up to number one, waiting for Chalky to perk up.

Jessica opened the door and kissed Cat on the cheek. She was wearing black trousers and a rose-coloured jumper that looked impossibly soft. Her blonde hair was tied back from her face, and she looked stunning even make-up free.

'Please excuse the state,' she said, 'I'm in editing mode.'

Cat glanced down at her dark-green wool coat and chunky purple scarf over jeans and jumper, and thought she'd never be as stylish as Jessica's editing mode in a million years. 'Is it going well?'

'Yes!' Jessica clapped her hands together. 'I've thought of some fantastic new recipes. I'm going to trial some of them at the party, and I still have time for Christmas lights planning. I won't let you down.'

'I'm kind of hoping you will, so that we have more chance of winning.'

They both laughed, and Jessica called to her dogs. 'Coco, Valentino, Dior! Walkies! Look, Cat,' she said, her expression suddenly serious. 'I've been meaning to say something, about you and Mark.'

'Oh?' Cat felt her throat tightening. Jessica and Mark were close – she'd told him about Fairview in the first place – so she wasn't surprised that Mark had confided in her. Only Polly, Owen and Elsie knew from Cat, and she suddenly felt like her friendship with Jessica was under threat. 'What is it?'

Jessica gave her a sympathetic smile. 'He told me what happened. He was upset, understandably. You're gorgeous, a total catch – I don't think he realized quite how much until you'd ended it. And I think deep down he knows – but won't admit – that he treated you unfairly, and can't blame you for letting him go.'

Cat frowned. 'Unfairly?'

Jessica nodded. 'Spending so much time with Sarah.' She bent and clipped the leads onto her dogs' crystal collars.

'Sarah?'

'Sarah. His wife.'

Cat tried to swallow but found she couldn't. 'Mark has a *wife*?'

Jessica stared at her. 'Oh my God, he never told you?'

'Mark is *married*?' Her voice sounded loud in the cold, quiet air.

Jessica rubbed Cat's arm. 'Well, they're on and off, but – this is awful, Cat. You really didn't know?'

Cat shook her head, thinking of the guilt she'd been carrying over her feelings for Joe. 'He still saw her?'

Jessica nodded slowly. 'From what he's told me, their relationship has always been tumultuous, but the last few months, while you were together, I think he's just been helping her with a dispute.'

'You *think*?'

Jessica dropped her gaze. 'There's been a long-running feud with their neighbours in London. She's in the house on her own now, but he was there when it started, so he's been supporting her, attending mediation, and when that didn't work, organizing lawyers. I – Cat, I honestly thought you knew. I thought that you broke up with him because you realised he hadn't properly let her go.'

Cat stared at the floor, thinking of the letters she'd seen him looking at. 'So all those trips to London, the phone calls? I thought he was working on his film.'

'He was doing that too, although recently it's been put on hold, so I think he's writing something else now.'

No producer meetings via Skype, no phone calls. They were all to Sarah, his wife. 'But why—?' she started, then crouched down to stroke Disco and Chalky, to hold their warm bodies against her. Chalky pressed the tip of his nose into her chin. Cat's anger surged. 'You think he could have been doing more than just helping her?'

'Do you want to come in?' Jessica asked. 'Come and have a cup of tea, bring Chalky and Disco.'

Cat shook her head. She stood up, a sense of indignation firing through her even though she and Mark were no longer together. 'You think he was with her every time he went back? That they were still together? He was keeping me interested down here, and then going back to his wife every time he was in London.'

Cat thought of the photo of the elegant woman she'd seen on Mark's fridge, thought of the months they'd sidestepped around each other, the time it had taken Mark to take her out to dinner, his spur-of-the-moment trips back to London, dropping Fairview – and her – in a heartbeat.

'He never gave her up, did he?' she said slowly. 'He never stopped loving her.'

Jessica closed her eyes and let out an almost imperceptible sigh.

Cat knew she was right.

Despite the cold, it was a beautiful December day, exactly two weeks until Christmas, and the dogs were enjoying the park without sideways rain or a violent, spinning wind. Cat let them off their leads, grateful for the time to be alone with her thoughts.

Chalky walked ten yards and sat down, looking out across the wide expanse of grass. Cat crouched beside him. 'Hey,' she whispered, 'what is it, old boy? Don't fancy a run today? Want to go home and crawl under the duvet?' She wrapped her arms around him, listening to his breathing, fast and slightly uneven.

'Are you all right, Chalky?' She looked down at him, and the mini schnauzer dipped his head, resting it on her knee. 'Are you?' She stroked his ears. 'Are you cross with Mark, too? Do you think he's a shithead like I do?'

How could she have got it so wrong? Throughout their relationship, Mark had been spending time with his wife and hadn't once mentioned it to her, though he'd told Jessica everything. He hadn't even told her he had a wife, however ex she might be – he'd told her he'd been single for nearly a year – and surely that, in itself, proved that there was something about the relationship he wanted to hide from her.

Cat wondered if she was overreacting; after all, she wasn't with him any more. But it felt like a big deal. It tainted her memories, made her feel used. From what Jessica had said, it sounded like he hadn't made the decision to leave Sarah, and had, ever since he'd known Cat, been hedging his bets, leading them both on, confident that those two parts of his life would never overlap.

Cat had been Mark's seaside girl, someone to keep him amused when he wasn't in London. A consolation prize when things were difficult with Sarah. She thought back to their first, flirty meetings, her excitement when she saw him, Jessica's party, their first nervous, delicious date. She was stunned, her thoughts dancing around her, unsure whether she was more upset or relieved.

Cat sat on the cold gravel and Chalky climbed onto her lap.

At least it proved to Cat that she'd made the right decision. It would have been so much worse if she'd stayed with Mark, and found out while they were together. But it hurt that he'd been stringing her along so completely. She'd ended their relationship once she knew her feelings for him weren't enough, but – given the chance – would he have carried on spending time with her, sleeping with her, and returning to London whenever Sarah clicked her fingers and asked him back?

'What an asshole,' she murmured into Chalky's fur. 'Can you believe him?' She hadn't spoken to Mark for a month, and she'd been the one who ended it, but she still felt a sense of outrage. Cat waited for the tears to come, but there were none. Despite her anger, she knew that he didn't have her heart. The winter air wrapped itself around her and she shivered.

The Westies and Disco ran across the grass towards them. Coco put his front paws on her shoulder, and Disco tried to climb on top of Chalky. Cat was bundled by dogs, and their warmth and loyalty brought a smile to her lips. She dished out treats and clipped them onto their leads. She held a treat out to Chalky but he turned his head away. Cat frowned, running her hand over his fur, touching his nose.

'Maybe you've got Elsie's cold,' she murmured. 'Shall we take you home?'

Chalky looked up at her with solemn eyes.

Gently, she lifted him off her, clipped his lead on and stood up. He was standing still, as if waiting for instructions. Cat's chest contracted with worry. Polly wasn't working today, but the vet's wasn't far. She started walking, keeping her pace slow, Coco, Valentino and Disco bounding on ahead, Dior walking alongside Chalky, keeping pace with him. Cat took the path around the side of the park, glancing down at the dogs every few seconds.

And then there was resistance on the lead and Cat cried out as Chalky collapsed onto the concrete. She fell to her knees and Dior started barking, then the other dogs joined in, Disco whimpering and yelping in turn. Cat put her hand in front of Chalky's mouth. His breathing was shallow and irregular.

She fumbled for her phone, pulled it out of her pocket and dialled Polly's number. It rang and rang and went to voicemail. She hung up, scrolling to see if she had the vet's switchboard number, but it wasn't in there.

'Chalky,' she whispered, 'come on. Please don't do this.' She held in a sob and looked around the park. They were too far away to get the attention of George at the Pavilion café, and she didn't want to leave Chalky for even a moment.

She put her arms under the old dog and tried to lift him. He was heavy, his body trembling, and Cat swore under her breath, not wanting to hurt him with her clumsiness. 'Shit, shit, shit.'

'Hello, Miss Palmer. Bit cold for sitting around, isn't it?' She looked up to see Mr Jasper approaching, giving her his best, insincere smile.

Cat pushed her pride aside, prepared to do anything he said if he helped her. 'Mr Jasper, please help me. Chalky's collapsed and I don't know what to do.'

His smile fell and he bustled across to her and knelt down, putting his hand on the stricken dog.

'I need to get him to the vet's. I don't think I can do it on my own.'

'OK, OK. Don't worry. It's not far.' Mr Jasper took his coat off and laid it on the ground, then gently moved Chalky on top of it. He wrapped the dog up, lifted him in his arms, wobbling slightly as he found his balance, and started walking. Cat checked on the other dogs, bent to give each of them a quick stroke and followed Mr Jasper, who was striding towards the park's exit, his face red with exertion.

They were all distressed, the dogs whimpering and staying close to Cat's heels as if they couldn't be without her, Cat keeping up with Mr Jasper, her breaths short with panic, trying not to think of Chalky never opening his eyes again, of Disco playing alone in Elsie's house, of Elsie without her beloved old guard.

Eventually they reached the vet's, and Mr Jasper walked up to the counter, Chalky still in his arms. A moment later a man with grey, receding hair and Polly's friend Leyla rushed out of a room at the back of reception. Cat watched, dazed, as they took Chalky away, her gaze drawn to his paw flopping out from underneath Mr Jasper's coat, and his limp, unwagging tail.

Mr Jasper wiped the sweat off his forehead, his dark eyes wide.

'Thank you so much,' Cat managed. 'I don't know what I would have done.'

Tentatively, he rubbed her arm. 'He's in the best place now. They'll do everything they can.'

Cat turned her head away, the emotion welling up inside her.

'What do you need?' Mr Jasper asked. 'Who do these dogs belong to?'

Coco, Dior, Valentino and Disco had settled uncertainly at her feet. 'The Westies are Jessica Heybourne's, but Disco is Chalky's—'

'I'll take them back to her. You stay with Disco, call who you need to call. Don't be here on your own.'

Cat nodded, stunned, as Mr Jasper gathered up the Westies' leads. He caught her looking at him and gave a quick, embarrassed smile. 'Don't worry, I promise I'll return them safely. We have our differences, Miss Palmer, but I'm not a monster.'

'Thank you,' was all Cat could manage.

Mr Jasper walked up to the reception desk as Cat sank onto one of the hard waiting-room seats and pulled Disco onto her lap. The younger dog was whimpering, aware that everything was wrong, that Chalky wasn't with them.

'Could you get that young lady a cup of tea,' she heard Mr Jasper say, and then, to her, on the way out, he said, 'Call someone.' Before she had a chance to reply he'd gone, taking Coco, Dior and Valentino with him.

A moment later, a cup of tea was placed in her hand, and then, only seconds later, it seemed, it was cold when she took a sip. Disco had settled uneasily on her lap, whimpering softly into Cat's coat, and Cat slowly became aware of the weight of the dog, of the chill of the nearly empty waiting room, now adorned with Christmas decorations, of an old couple with a cat basket giving her pitying looks.

She had to call someone. She should call Elsie, but she didn't want to tell her over the phone, and she didn't want to leave the vet's in case they had news. Placing her mug on the floor, she dialled Polly's number.

'Hi, Cat.' She sounded chirpy, happy.

'P-Polly,' Cat stammered, 'it's Chalky. I'm – I'm at the vet's. Can you get Elsie? Can you bring her here?'

'What?' Polly whispered. 'What's happened?'

'I don't know. We were in the park and he collapsed. He looked so –' The words caught in her throat.

'I'm coming. I'll bring Elsie. Are you OK, Cat?'

But Cat could only manage a mumbled 'mhmm,' before she hung up.

23

People came and went around her, cold blasting in every time the front door opened, making the foil paper chains rustle. Cat kept her eye trained on the door they'd taken Chalky through, wishing with every fibre of her body that a smiling vet would emerge and tell her it was just a scare, or, even better, that Chalky would trot out, his dark eyes looking up at Cat from under his bushy eyebrows. She was taking deep breaths, trying not to give into her emotions, holding onto Disco for comfort and warmth.

But then the front door burst open and Polly ran in, green scrubs on, followed by Elsie, her face pale above a dark-grey coat, and then Joe.

Joe. Back in Fairview.

Cat stared at him. At his blond hair, slightly longer and scruffier than when she'd last seen it, his skin, browner than it should be in December, his jawline fuzzy with stubble, his eyes creased at the edges. He was wearing a pale-grey hoody, the colour of day-old snow. Her heart contracted and tears stung her eyes. She inhaled and tried to keep her composure.

'Cat.' Polly crouched in front of her. 'How is he?'

Elsie sat next to Cat, putting her hand on her shoulder. Disco moved from Cat's lap to Elsie's, and Cat shuddered at the loss of warmth. She shook her head. 'Nobody's come out, I don't know anything.'

'You've done the right thing,' Elsie said firmly. 'You've got him here.'

Cat turned to her friend, hearing the stoicism in her voice, the pain underneath it. 'It was Mr Jasper,' she whispered. 'He helped me, he brought Chalky here. I'm so sorry, Elsie. I should never have taken him out, I—'

'Tush, girl,' Elsie said, squeezing her shoulder. 'You've been a marvel.'

'I'll see what I can find out.' Polly stood and hurried into the treatment room.

'He was fine.' Cat glanced at Joe, then turned back to Elsie. 'Quiet, but fine. And then he didn't want a treat, he seemed a bit off, so I thought I'd bring him here. He was walking OK, and I was going slowly, but then he just crumpled.' She covered her face with her hands, bent forward and pressed her elbows into her knees.

'Hey,' Joe said, suddenly beside her. 'Hey, come on. There's nothing more you could have done.' His gentle, solid voice was instantly comforting. She nodded but didn't sit up, wishing she could hide in the dark space behind her hands and listen to him forever.

But then a door opened and a man cleared his voice. 'Mrs Willows? I understand Chalky is your dog.'

'Yes, that's right.'

Cat heard the tremor in the older woman's voice. She sat up and blinked at the tall, greying vet.

'How is he?' Elsie continued.

'He's very sick,' the vet admitted. 'He's suffering from acute pancreatitis. His pancreas is inflamed, and so it isn't working properly.'

'Oh my God,' Cat murmured. 'Is he going to be all right?'

The vet gave them a hesitant smile. 'I'm afraid I can't answer that just yet. We'll need to keep him in. We have to withhold food and water, reintroduce it slowly, help settle the pancreas down. If that goes well over the next seventy-two hours, and with a few changes to his diet, then he does stand a chance of making a good recovery.'

'But he might not?' Elsie asked.

'We really have to wait and see how he responds to treatment. At this point, I can't guarantee anything.'

Elsie sighed and pressed her face into Disco's neck. 'I understand. I can't see him?'

The vet shook his head. 'Not now, I'm afraid. We'll call you first thing in the morning to update you on his progress, and I can assure you he's in the best hands. You should go home and get some rest.'

Elsie nodded, and Cat could see that her hands were shaking. The vet left them, and a moment later Polly came out of the treatment room. 'Did he tell you?'

Cat nodded. 'It sounds bad, but he – he could still recover.'

'We're doing everything we can,' Polly said. 'Elsie, we're looking after him for you.'

'I know, my love,' Elsie said. 'I know.'

'I'll take you back.' Joe stood and waited while Elsie put Disco on the floor and walked out of the surgery, her head held high as always.

Cat heaved herself up, her limbs stiff from hours sitting motionless, and hugged Polly. 'Thank you,' she whispered.

She couldn't believe how calm Elsie was being, how much she was holding it together.

'You should go home, Cat,' Polly said. 'You look exhausted. I'm going to stay here with him.'

Cat climbed into the back of the Fiesta and sank into the seat. Nobody spoke on the journey home, and when Joe pulled up outside Elsie's house, she got quickly out.

'Elsie,' Cat fumbled for the door handle and followed her. 'Let me come in, let me make you some food.'

Elsie put her arms round Cat. It was something she rarely did, usually offering a quick hand-pat or an arm-squeeze, and Cat was taken aback. 'I'm just going to go in and be quiet, Cat. You've been amazing today, looking after my lovely old boy. There is nobody I would rather he'd been with, and if he survives now, if he pulls through, it'll be down to you.'

'You shouldn't be alone,' Cat said.

'I'm not.' Elsie smiled down at Disco, still quiet and uncertain at her owner's feet.

'Are you sure I can't—'

'Tomorrow,' Elsie said. 'Come and see me tomorrow.' She gave her arm a squeeze, the familiar gesture forcing a smile out of Cat. She watched as the older woman climbed the stairs and went inside, for once looking every bit her age.

'Come on,' Joe said. 'Let Elsie deal with this in her own way. You've had a shock, and you're freezing.'

'You're back,' she murmured.

He gave her a quick, tired smile. 'I am.'

'It's not the best homecoming.' Cat squeezed her hands under her elbows, trying to stop them shaking.

'God, Cat. I wasn't expecting balloons and party-poppers. Just come inside, get warm.'

'Did you have a good time?'

Joe nodded and took her arm, and, despite everything, she felt a spark at his touch. She let him lead her up the stairs of number nine, drinking him in, weary happiness rushing through her at his closeness, reminding her how much she'd missed him.

He glanced at her. 'What?'

'Nothing,' she murmured.

'You're staring at me.'

'I'm glad you're back.'

He frowned and stood in front of her. Slowly, he undid her coat buttons, not meeting her eye, concentrating on his fingers as if it was the most difficult task in the world. Cat's breath stalled in her throat. He slipped her coat off her shoulders, walked her to the sofa and lowered her gently onto it.

'You're trembling,' he said quietly.

'I'm alright.' Cat swallowed, waiting for her heart to slow down. 'It's Chalky that's lying on the vet's table, being poked and prodded and manhandled.' She closed her eyes, her emotions seesawing between happiness at Joe's return and despair over Chalky.

'Hey,' Joe said. 'Hey, it's OK. The vet will look after him, Polly's there, and so is Leyla. You just need to rest now, let them deal with it.' Cat felt a warmth surround her and realized he'd put a blanket round her shoulders. She turned to face him, looking straight into his serious blue eyes.

She inhaled, shakily. 'Joe.'

'Cup of tea?' He gave her a quick smile and went into the kitchen. Cat wrapped the blanket tighter around her, pulled her feet up and closed her eyes.

Joe was back. Chalky was gravely ill, close to death, but surely, *surely* he would get better. Everything had to be all right now that Joe was home.

*

She was woken by a cold, wet nose pressing against her cheek, and for a second she thought it was Chalky. She opened her eyes. Shed was sitting next to her on the sofa, purring loudly, his face close to hers. The light was artificial, and Cat saw that beyond the open curtains, beyond the rainbow glow of the Christmas tree, the winter night had already arrived.

'How are you feeling?' Joe was sitting on the sofa opposite her, an empty beer bottle on the table, a magazine closed on his lap.

'OK, I guess.' Cat rubbed her forehead and sat up. 'What time is it?'

'It's nearly five pm. In Fairview, anyway. I've no idea what time it is inside my head.' He sat forward, discarding the magazine, his elbows on his knees.

'Bad jetlag?'

Joe nodded. 'As if I've been hit by a bus. But it'll pass.'

'But your trip was as good as you thought it would be?'

'Yeah, it was great, thanks. Just what I needed.'

'The course?'

'And the break. A holiday away from here, away from everything.' He frowned, shook his head quickly. 'Now, how are you really feeling?'

Cat couldn't look at him. She felt worn out, and her emotions were in a tangle, the news about Mark's wife overshadowed by Chalky and now, Joe's return. She sighed.

'That's what I thought,' Joe said softly. 'But you have to try and stop worrying, even for a few hours.'

'What if it's my fault?' Cat stroked Shed's fuzzy ginger fur. 'What if I could have noticed earlier, got him to the vet's sooner? I was so preoccupied, I—' She could hardly believe

390

Jessica's bombshell had been earlier that day; it had paled into insignificance. 'What if Chalky dies?'

'Listen to me,' Joe said calmly, coming to sit beside her. 'You have done everything. You have looked after Chalky, treated him as your own, loved him. You have been the best walker and friend that lovely old dog could have hoped for. The vet thinks he can pull through, and I've met Chalky, he's a dude, he's stubborn. I'm sure he will. But,' he continued, his voice dropping, 'if it's time for him to go, if he doesn't survive this, then you will get through it, believe me. You've got me and Polly and Disco. You and Elsie will look after each other, and it'll be hard, you'll struggle. You might find it difficult walking other dogs, being reminded of him. But Chalky will always be a part of your life. You'll always have your memories.'

Cat stared at Joe, her eyes stinging with tears. His face was unsmiling but full of compassion, and his words were making her head swim.

'You know,' she murmured. 'You know what it's like.'

Joe inhaled, nodded gently. 'I know.'

Cat felt shock and realization engulf her. 'You had a dog,' she whispered. 'You lost a dog. It's why you won't – you haven't let me—' She swallowed. 'Tell me.'

Joe ran his hand through his hair. 'I had a chocolate Labrador called Truffle. I – we got him as a puppy, just over three years ago. He's ridiculous, really. A huge, soppy thing, friends with everyone. Never chewed a shoe in his life, but collected the post, hid it in his basket. Ran for miles. A proper fire-and-slippers dog.'

Cat tried to take it in. Joe didn't hate dogs at all. He'd had one, one he had clearly loved. All this time, and Cat hadn't guessed. 'What happened?'

'Rosalin took him. I tried to fight. I fought harder than anything else for Truffle, to keep him here with me. Can you get custody of a dog? I don't know, but I—' he rubbed his jaw and Cat could see the pain in his eyes, could see how hard it was for him to tell her. But he kept looking at her. 'In the end I couldn't, I was so—' he shook his head. 'After what they'd done I – I couldn't deal with any more angry phone calls. I let them take him, I gave up on him.'

'Oh my God, Joe.' Cat thought of her confusion at the Pooches' Picnic, when he'd been so friendly with Chips. She thought of the occasions Joe and Polly had skirted round the subject, trying to tell her something but not quite managing it. The lead and tennis ball she'd found in the cupboard under the stairs. 'You had a dog, and you never told me.' She wasn't accusing, she just felt upended.

'I'm so sorry,' he said. 'I was so down after it happened. And you came along, you cheered me up, you were warm and funny, so kind. But then the whole dog-walking thing brought it all back. I just – I knew that if you found out about Truffle, you'd try and fix it. You'd come up with a plan to get him back, or get me a new dog. I didn't want to deal with it. I wanted to try and forget everything. I was still too hurt.'

'Heartbroken,' Cat said.

Joe nodded, shrugging. 'And I asked Polly not to say anything either.'

'Because I interfere,' Cat said. 'And I would have made it worse.' Cat closed her eyes, remembering all the times she'd come up with some hair-brained scheme, and Joe had challenged her, reminding her to look at the bigger picture, the effects of her actions. Of course he hadn't told her about this – it was too much of a risk to confide in her.

'But you always have good intentions. Look what happened with Frankie, with the Barkers, with the cove. I trust you, Cat, but back then I just needed to try and move on from the whole thing. And then, once I started to feel better, it just – it seemed so hard to tell you after I'd kept it from you for so long. There was never a good time. Polly feels the same – she hates me for making her hide this from you. But I just wanted to start again.'

'With a big grumpy cat?'

Joe smiled. 'Shed was a rebellion against everything that had happened. He seemed the ideal companion for me then grumpy, claws out. He's growing on me, though.'

'Me too,' Cat admitted, stroking Shed, who was still curled up next to her. 'I think he's mellowing along with his owner. Wow,' she whispered. 'Joe Sinclair, dog lover.'

'And occasional idiot. I'm so sorry, Cat, for keeping it from you.'

Cat tried to look away, but she thought she might stay lost in Joe's blue eyes for ever. 'I think I'm beginning to realize that the more curious I am, the more people are likely to hold things back from me.' She thought of Mark and the secret he'd hidden from her the whole time they were together.

Joe winced. 'Cat, that's really not—'

'I'm not upset.'

'You're not?'

'You love dogs,' she said, her voice shaky. 'There's no rule that says the moment you move in with someone you have to know everything about them. And you've told me now. You've helped me so much, Joe, with the Pooches' Picnic, the protest. And now I know that you were getting over losing your own dog while I was throwing them at you, talking about nothing else, it makes everything you did even more significant.'

'Yeah, well.' He gave her a lopsided smile. 'Your ideas were ambitious, you needed help. It wasn't just me, anyway. There was Polly, Elsie, Jessica. Most of those things were a joint effort.'

'True,' Cat said quietly, her stomach churning, suddenly uneasy. 'Jessica said she got in touch with you while you were away, about some new work?'

'Yeah,' Joe said, frowning slightly. 'She wants a whole new rebrand, for her website, marketing, personal stationery. It's a big contract, and she's determined to get me to do it.'

'You have just spent the last few weeks honing your skills.'

'I have. She's very chatty, on email at least.'

'She's a bubbly person,' Cat admitted, her heart sinking.

'Well I don't really know her that well,' Joe said, catching her eye and then looking quickly away. 'But I'll nip down and see her later, organize a proper debriefing for this work.'

Cat wondered what else Jessica would want to debrief him on. She thought of her insistence that she had to get mistletoe for her party. By then, it might not be necessary. Joe had kissed her at the last one, after all, and if they were going to be working closely on the rebrand of Jessica Heybourne, then . . .

'Shall we have some food?' Joe asked, cutting into her thoughts. 'I'm starving.'

Cat realized she hadn't had any lunch, her stomach growling now the shock of Chalky's collapse was lessening in Joe's company. 'How about a Thai takeaway? We could find a film to take our mind off things.'

'Good plan,' Joe said. 'I'll get the menu.'

When Cat woke, the room was in darkness save for the pulsing lights on the tree. Her neck was stiff, and the right side of her body was warm, the sound of breathing close by. She shifted, her legs suddenly cold as a furry lump jumped off them and onto the floor. Shed. She blinked, growing accustomed to the gloom, and realized she was still in the living room.

The television was off but the DVD player was still on, winking at her. She jumped as the front door closed, and then suddenly the living room was bathed in light. Cat tried to sit up, feeling weighted down and sluggish, staring at Polly as she took her coat off, her green scrubs still on underneath.

'What time is it?' Cat asked, and it was Polly's turn to jump.

'Shit! Sorry, Cat, I had no idea you'd be in here. I thought you'd be in bed.' Polly gave her a watery smile, her eyes widening as she took in the whole scene, a scene that Cat hadn't fully grasped in her half-asleep state. She was on the sofa, fully clothed, and Joe, still asleep, was lying against her, his head on her shoulder. They were both under the blanket. Cat gave an involuntary shudder.

'Has my brother been looking after you?' Polly asked, her eyes narrowing slightly.

Cat could only nod. 'We were watching *Prince of Thieves*, but I guess with Joe's jetlag, and . . . we must have drifted off. What time is it?' she asked again.

'Just after six,' Polly said, the sleigh bells jingling as she came into the room and sat on the sofa opposite.

'In the morning?' Cat squealed. Joe shifted beside her, groaned and opened his eyes.

'Morning, jet-setter,' Polly said.

'Hmmm?' Joe lifted his head off Cat's shoulder and sat up quickly, dislodging the blanket. Cold air wrapped itself around her, replacing the warmth of Joe's body. He stared at her, and then at his sister. He looked as bemused as Cat felt. 'What's going on? I heard sleigh bells. It's not Christmas, is it?'

395

'I stayed at work,' Polly said. 'I – I couldn't leave Chalky. I wanted to stay with him, to see if he—' Her voice dropped to a whisper. 'If he made it through the night.'

Cat froze and she heard Joe's intake of breath. They stared at Polly.

'A-and did he?' Cat asked. 'Did he make it through?'

Chalky was hanging on.

Cat accompanied Elsie to the vet's as often as she wanted to go, though Cat found it hard to look at the loving, loyal mini schnauzer so weak and unresponsive. She couldn't imagine how Elsie was coping. Polly did extra shifts, keeping a close eye on him, her brows often knitted together when she returned home, the shadow of worry not quite leaving her face.

Cat frequently went with Elsie and Disco to the park, walking slowly despite the bitter cold, the grey sky heavy with winter. They didn't say much, but threw a stick for Disco, laughing at her antics, their levity forced but their love and appreciation for the younger dog heightened, aware that she, too, must be feeling Chalky's continued absence.

But while part of their lives was on hold, all around Fairview, Christmas had taken over. Christmas trees and light displays winked at them from every house, festive songs filtered out of shops and cafés, groups of school children burst into loud, tuneless song, carol singers door-knocked and filled the air with 'Silent Night' and 'We Wish You a Merry Christmas'. Cat couldn't help but be swept up in the good cheer and excitement of the festive season.

Polly and Owen were always together, the ice cream expert now a semi-permanent fixture at number nine, bringing different lights with him every time he came, trying new combinations, searching the web for inspiration. He and Joe spent hours at the large Mac in Joe's office, trying to come up with the perfect display, leaving Polly and Cat to keep an eye on Shed and Rummy's tentative truce downstairs.

And of course there was Joe. Joe who was back in Primrose Terrace, in his rightful place, wearing his winter hoodies. They'd settled back into an easy rhythm, as if he hadn't been away, and as if he hadn't called her his muse in the back of a van filled with surfboards. She knew he'd been spending a lot of time with Jessica, and had seen his designs in sketchbooks on the coffee table, most of them as striking and glamorous as she was. She tried not to read anything into it, but she couldn't blame Joe if he'd decided to move on.

'They're good aren't they? Probably some of his best.' Polly said, bringing a bottle of wine and two glasses into the living room as Cat leafed through one of Joe's notepads, her wrapping abandoned.

Cat nodded. 'That course was obviously a good investment. I bet Jessica's ecstatic.'

'Do I detect a hint of sarcasm, Cat Palmer?' Polly poured wine into her glass and handed it to her.

'Of course not,' Cat rushed. 'Jessica will be genuinely delighted with what Joe's done.'

Polly pulled her legs up under her. 'I think Joe could do an ugly charcoal scrawl and Jessica would be over the moon. She's blinded by the man, not the work, although of course his designs are incredible.'

'You really think she's got a thing for him?' Cat held her breath.

'Don't you remember her at our first Christmas committee meeting? She was almost purring. I would *love* to see the emails between them while he was in the States.'

397

Cat winced. She couldn't imagine anything worse. 'And what does Joe think? Has he talked to you about it?' Her voice came out as a squeak, and Polly gave her a sharp look.

'Oh, you mean after what happened at the protest? The way he feels about you?'

'What he said to me then, about his cartoon, it just seemed that . . .' Cat shrugged. 'He's had some time away now, though. It's great. If he's moved on, I mean. The best thing.'

Silence filled the space between them, and though Cat kept her gaze focused on Joe's sketchbook, she could feel the weight of the Sinclair stare on her. 'I don't want to speculate,' Polly said eventually, 'and I can promise you that he's not said anything to me. But I don't think that Jessica's enthusiasm is entirely reciprocated. Though Joey could just be trying to keep things professional between them, for the sake of his business.'

'You really don't know how he feels, then?'

'Feelings don't just disappear like that,' Polly said, her voice dropping to a near-whisper. 'Even when you try and cancel them out by putting an ocean in the way. It's good that you're worried about him, Cat, but this isn't your fault. You can't help it that Joe fell for you. He may be moving on, he may still be working through it, but he'll get there. Part of me wishes he would talk to me, but then . . .' she took a sip of her wine. 'That might be a bit awkward.'

'Piggy in the middle?' Cat asked.

Polly nodded. 'My brother likes my best friend. My best friend isn't interested, and we all live in the same house. Not awkward at all! But it might be worse if you *did* like him. Then I'd really be stuck in the middle of something.'

She laughed, and Cat tried to join in, but it fell flat. Polly's laughter died out, and her smile disappeared, her brows furrowing.

'Cat?'

'Yes, Polly?' Cat sighed, her shoulders dropping.

'You don't like him do you? Not like that.'

Cat held her gaze and took a long sip of wine. 'I've wanted to tell you about it for ages, but I knew it would make things more complicated. With me living here, with the way things have . . . have happened. It's not straightforward.'

Polly gripped her glass as if it might jump out of her hands and fly out of the window. 'S-since when?'

'Since that day, really. In the surf van. I mean, it must have started before, but I was with Mark and I – I wouldn't let myself believe it. Then Joe said what he said, and I realised that the reason I was annoyed about the cartoon was because I didn't want him to see me as a calamitous stuff-up, I wanted him to like me. I mean properly like me. He told me he did, and then he went to America. I already knew that it wasn't working with Mark, we limped on for a bit, but I knew I couldn't keep stringing him along.' She laughed. 'Ironic, really, considering what he'd been doing.'

'So you really care about Joe?'

'I do,' Cat said, glancing at the doorway, aware that Joe and Owen were somewhere in the house, messing about with lights. 'I do, but if he's getting over me, if he's got feelings for Jessica. I can't . . . I don't know what to do.'

In the spring she had been worried that Mark might have feelings for Jessica, and now she was looming, albeit elegantly, between her and Joe. Cat's first fears had proved unfounded – it was simply Jessica's glamour and confidence playing on her pre-existing insecurities – but this time she wasn't so sure.

'I never thought that you –' Polly said. 'Bloody hell. Are you going to tell him?'

399

Cat looked at the table. 'I have to do *something*. But I don't know what.'

'Is talking to him too radical a plan?' She gave Cat a gentle smile.

'I just . . . not yet,' Cat said. 'Right now, that feels too difficult.'

'So sing to him,' Polly said.

'Don't be flippant, Pol.'

'I'm not! I've heard you practising your guitar, and so has Joey. He even complimented you the other day.'

'He did?' Cat frowned. She'd not had nearly as many lessons with Frankie as she'd intended, and the news that Joe had heard her practise, never mind comment on it, was a shock. 'Sure he's not being sarcastic?'

'I think his exact words were "she can serenade me any time",' Polly said, laughing.

'I can only play half a tune!' But Cat felt the flush of the compliment, however unlikely it seemed. She'd been practising a Christmas song, wondering if she'd be brave enough to try it. 'And I'm not sure it's the right way to declare my feelings for Joe.'

'Why not?' Polly asked. 'Why not take your inspiration from the festive season, and show Joe how you feel with a grand gesture?'

'You're serious? You, Polly Sinclair, think I should serenade your brother? What if he and Jessica have started something? What if he doesn't feel that way about me any more?'

'Cat.' Polly sighed and sat forward on the sofa. 'You always have these big ideas for other people, schemes to help them and rescue them and make things better for them. You always throw caution to the wind and go for it, and more often than not, it works. Why not, for once, take some of your own advice?' She raised her eyebrows, and Cat looked at her

400

friend, her heart thudding, wondering if she had the courage to do what Polly was suggesting.

They drank their wine in silence until the sound of cheering from the floor above drew them upstairs.

'What's going on?' Polly asked, pushing open the door into Joe's office, Cat following closely behind.

'Come and look at this,' Owen said, racing towards Polly and dragging her towards the computer screen. Joe grinned and beckoned Cat over, and her insides did a little dance. 'We,' Owen continued, 'have found the light display to end all displays. No way anyone else has a chance of winning. What do you think?'

Cat and Polly followed Owen round to the other side of Joe's desk, and Joe maximized the window on his Mac.

They both gasped.

24

It was two days before Christmas, and all through the house, not a creature was stirring, because Shed was wiped out on the sofa, oblivious to the operation that was going on around him, and Rummy was asleep under the window. Cat looked at him, thinking about Chalky, who was showing slow signs of improvement. Polly had told her that his pancreas had settled down, but because he was old, his recovery would be slower than most, and not without danger. Cat had seen him at the vet's two days ago He still looked weak, and Cat's faint glimmer of hope that he might be able to finally come home and spend Christmas with Elsie and Disco seemed hopelessly optimistic.

Cat turned away from Rummy and shook her head at the state of the living room. Lights were strewn everywhere, Joe and Owen intent on turning their competition entry into a military operation. Cat had wondered whether it was even possible for them to win, as they had been part of the committee that had planned the event, but Phil from the *Fairhaven Press* was promising to be an impartial judge, so they had to give it their best shot. Cat could hardly remember a time when there hadn't been a string of lights draped across every carpet just waiting for her to trip over.

'We're having these ones along the roof and the window-sills,' Joe said for the hundredth time, holding up the white icicle lights.

'And these on the walls.' Owen gathered together their Arctic creatures – a polar bear and reindeer, and a penguin that Cat wasn't about to tell them was actually only found in the Antarctic – and the fastenings which would secure them onto the wall. The whole front of the house would be covered in a mesh of snowflake lights that pulsed different colours. If it worked, it would be spectacular. But it seemed like there was still quite a lot to do to get it ready for that evening.

'How are we going to attach it all?' Polly asked. 'How will we fix the lights along the bottom of the roof? We don't have a ladder.'

'I'll do it out of my bedroom window,' Joe said.

Polly looked sceptical. 'You won't be able to reach all the way along.'

'Sure I will,' Joe said. 'You can hold my feet while I dangle out.' He took the icicle lights and, grinning, headed up the stairs.

'No, Joey.' Polly followed him. 'Be serious.'

'I'm deadly serious.'

'Come on,' Owen said as Cat stared wistfully up after Joe's retreating form. 'You can help me with the animals. Ground level, much safer.'

'Good-oh.' Cat followed him out, trying to banish her fear at Joe risking danger by dangling out of the top floor window.

She was glad that there was no awkwardness between them, but they still avoided certain subjects, such as what had happened with Mark, whether Joe's trip had given him the space he needed to resolve his feelings for her, and his current project with Jessica. Cat had been mulling Polly's idea over in her mind, while also trying to focus on Christmas. But Christmas made her happy, and when she was happy she thought of Joe.

It was bitterly cold outside. The sky was heavy and pink and, Cat was sure, full of snow. Would they have a winter wonderland for their competition, real snowflakes falling past the fake ones on their wall? Or would it hold on and give them a newly minted white Christmas? The pavement was slippery with ice, and Cat's fingers were soon red and numb, but together she and Owen attached the penguin and polar bear to the front of the house, checked the wiring, made sure everything was secure and ran to their large outdoor extension plug.

'Guys,' Joe called down, and Cat looked up to see him leaning out of his window, waving at them. The row of icicles ran along the bottom of the roof, dangling prettily down.

'How did you do that?' Cat asked.

Joe spread his arms wide. 'I'm a genius. We just need to sort out the snowflakes and then we're ready to turn them on, see the full effect – in daylight, at least.'

Owen applauded and Cat joined in, watching as Joe bowed out of the window, bending far too low. She bit her lip and resisted the urge to call out to him to be careful.

'Right,' Owen said, 'snowflakes. They're in the living room.'

Still looking at Joe, Cat went to climb the front steps and missed her footing. She slipped, and her ankle twisted under her. She cried out and grabbed hold of the wall.

'Are you all right?' Owen asked, rushing over to her.

'I'm OK,' Cat winced. 'I jarred my ankle, that's all.'

'Come and sit down.' Owen put his hand under her elbow and led her slowly inside. Cat flopped onto the sofa and clamped her lips together against the pain. Rummy, woken by the commotion, trotted over and sat next to her.

'Thanks, Rummy,' Cat murmured. Owen disappeared upstairs and Cat unzipped her long leather boot and slowly pulled it off, closing her eyes at the pain that shot through her ankle. She rolled up the leg of her jeans, and then came the sock, the woollen fabric grating against her tender skin.

'Cat,' Polly said, 'what have you done?'

'I stumbled.' Cat looked up and then away again, her cheeks burning as Polly and Joe followed Owen into the living room. Polly was carrying her first-aid bag – as vigilant about human health as animals', if not quite so expert. 'I'm fine,' Cat added, looking down at her ankle, which was definitely thicker and pinker than it had been first thing that morning.

'And you think leaning out of an attic window is dangerous,' Joe said softly. He went into the kitchen and returned with a bag of frozen peas wrapped in a tea towel. 'Ready?' He gave Cat an appraising look and she nodded.

Joe crouched next to her, and, putting his hand under her leg to support it, placed the peas against her ankle, watching her face closely. As her ankle got colder, the heat of the sprain dissipating, she felt herself get hotter. His fingers against her bare skin were a welcome distraction, his stare almost intoxicating.

'Better?' he asked.

'Much.'

She saw him swallow, his Adam's apple bobbing. 'Hope you weren't planning on wearing heels tonight.'

Cat had spent a long time planning the perfect outfit, but at that very moment Jessica's party seemed like the least important thing in the world. She shook her head.

'I've got flats I can wear. I'm not sure where my patent heels are anyway.'

'Well,' Polly said, leaning forward and breaking their eye contact, 'we need to get this strapped up or you won't be moving much further than this sofa.'

Cat sat back as Polly wrapped her ankle up, and thanked Owen as he got her a glass of water and some painkillers. Joe, still holding the peas, didn't move from Cat's side. Rummy put his head on Joe's lap and he stroked the dog absent-mindedly. Every time Cat looked at Joe, he was looking at her, so she shot him a quick smile and turned away.

'Right,' Polly said, glancing between them, fighting against a smile, 'you're done. Stay here, elevate it and keep putting the peas on it. We need to get this house finished, and then we need to get to Jessica's for the dog fancy-dress competition. Owen, have you got Rummy's outfit sorted?'

Owen saluted. 'Yes, ma'am.'

Polly giggled. 'Sorry. I'm just trying to take control of the situation. We've got a lot to do and not much time.'

'Not to mention one clumsy idiot,' Cat said.

'Exactly.' Polly grinned at her friend. 'Now, Joey, you can either sit there and ogle my best friend all day, or you can come and help us win this competition. What's it to be?'

Joe gawped at his sister, flashed Cat a quick, embarrassed look, then got to his feet and hurried out of the living room. Polly watched him go and, when he was out of sight, leaned in towards Cat. 'I hope you've tuned your guitar,' she whispered.

Cat's ankle was sore, throbbing mercilessly despite the painkillers, but being supported up the street by Joe, she felt it was almost worth it. She leaned into him, glancing down at Rummy, resplendent in a Superman costume complete with red cape, trotting alongside Owen. As they walked, Emma and Lizzie raced up to join them.

'Cat! Joe! Polly! Gooey-eyes!'

Cat looked behind her and waved at Frankie, who was pushing Henry in a pushchair, Olaf sitting in the basket underneath. Cat couldn't see what he was dressed as.

'Why are you walking in a stocking?' Emma asked, pointing at Cat's leg.

Joe and Owen had thought that, in the Christmas spirit, Cat should protect her shoeless foot against the cold by wearing an oversized Christmas stocking. They had tied it to her leg with gold Christmas ribbon.

'Cat was clumsy and fell over,' Joe said, smiling at Emma, amusement in his voice. 'She's got a bandage on her leg, and we thought we'd make it as Christmassy as possible.'

'Well,' Emma said, 'it looks silly.'

'And Santa won't be able to fill it with presents if your foot's in it,' Lizzie added.

'I'm hoping I get to take it off before Christmas Eve.'

'I wouldn't be so sure,' Joe said seriously.

'And why aren't you wearing two?' Lizzie asked. 'Your trainer looks funny on its own.'

'And you're walking in a silly way,' Emma said.

'Hey,' Cat laughed. 'You're meant to be commenting on what the dogs are wearing, not me.'

'You'd win the pretty competition,' Lizzie said.

Cat smiled. 'I wouldn't stand a chance with both of you in your dresses.' They were wearing long party dresses under their coats, thin strands of pearlescent tinsel woven through their long hair. 'What's Olaf dressed as?'

With Cat's limp, Frankie had soon caught up with them and, eager to say hello to Rummy, Olaf hopped out of the basket. Spying the cocker spaniel's outfit, Cat descended into laughter. She wasn't alone.

'Of course,' Joe said, shaking his head. 'What else could Olaf come as but Olaf?' The little dog had a perfect snowman outfit on, and looked unnervingly similar to the Disney character he was named after.

Frankie narrowed her eyes. 'You've seen *Frozen*?'

Joe's laughter stopped abruptly. 'I was forced to.'

'Oh yeah,' Polly said. 'We held you down.'

'Tied you to the sofa,' Cat added.

'Loving *Frozen*'s nothing to be ashamed of,' Owen said. 'Doesn't everyone love it?'

'I'm not saying I loved it, I'm saying I *had* to watch it.'

Polly and Cat looked at each other. 'He loved it,' they chorused.

'All these lights look pretty spectacular.' Frankie stared up at the houses as they passed them. 'I can't wait until it gets dark and we can see the whole street lit up.'

'Looks like it might be lit up with snow too,' Owen added.

'Snow!' the girls squealed, running up the street, arms raised in the air.

'Just in time for Christmas,' Polly said dreamily. Owen wrapped his arms round her and pulled her close. Cat thought it might have been her imagination, but did Joe tighten his grip on her arm just a little?

Jessica's house was resplendent with Christmas cheer and barking, snuffling dogs. Inside, her decorations were simple and elegant: pure white lights, red tinsel, glitter and stars, a simple, real tree with silver and red baubles. Outside, the lights were hard to make out. There were no bold shapes, just strings of tiny fairy lights and, not yet turned on, it was impossible to know what they'd look like. Jessica had been threatening something impressive, and Cat was itching to see what it was.

Cat could see some more dog costumes that had taken inspiration from their namesakes. Boris and Charles's Frenchies were dressed as Bob Dylan and Bruce Springsteen, leather jackets on both, sunglasses on Bossy, and a tiny, adorable flat cap on Dylan. They both had miniature guitars velcroed onto them.

There were a couple of Border terriers that Cat thought were called Huey and Harry, dressed to look like they were being eaten by dinosaurs: gaping jaws made to look like the dogs' heads were sticking out, long costume tails dragging on the floor. Letting go of Joe's arm, Cat slowly limped around the room, saying hello to everyone she knew, bending to stroke the dogs and congratulate them on their efforts.

Jessica appeared, wearing a black jumpsuit and killer heels, her three Westies skittering at her feet as if they knew it was time to perform. Cat had been imagining some fashion-show outfits, but the West Highland terriers had gone back to their roots and were dressed in full Scottish regalia with tiny kilts and berets, Coco, Dior and Valentino each in a different tartan.

'Do they mean anything, the different tartans?' Cat asked.

'Just that they're splendid, individual dogs,' Jessica said, beaming. 'What have you done to yourself?'

'I had an accident with a step. I'm an idiot.'

'Party outfit?'

'Modified,' Cat confirmed, realising that, in the glamour stakes, she wouldn't be any kind of competition for Jessica that evening. Her fears were compounded when, giving Cat a quick air kiss to the cheek, Jessica spotted Joe chatting to Owen and went over to him, wrapping her arms around him in the most sultry hug Cat had ever seen. Cat turned away, determined not to prolong her misery, and decided that she wouldn't be tuning her guitar after all.

Everyone mingled, waiting for Phil from the *Fairhaven Press* to arrive. He'd agreed to judge both competitions, as Cat knew most of the residents on Primrose Terrace and couldn't consider herself entirely unbiased.

The front door opened and Cat turned towards the icy blast. Elsie and Captain walked in with their pets, and she felt the tears spring to her eyes.

'Chalky,' Cat squeaked, hobbling as fast as she could to greet the new arrivals. Because although Paris looked magnificent dressed as a tiny Santa Claus, and Disco was wearing an outfit made out of silver panels that made her look like a walking glitter ball, Cat was more overcome by the fact that Chalky was there too, well enough to leave the vet's, firmly on the road to recovery. He wasn't dressed up, other than the large fleecy blanket he was wrapped in, but had been carried up the stairs and over the threshold by Captain, who now lowered the old dog into a small cart that Elsie had hauled into Jessica's house.

Cat dropped to her knees, ignoring the pain in her ankle, and embraced the old dog. He lifted his head, eyed her from beneath his fuzzy eyebrows, and put his paw out, touching her arm. Cat grinned up at Elsie through her tears, and the older woman smiled back, her own eyes bright with emotion.

'We can't stay long,' she said. 'It looks like it's going to snow, and I can't risk Chalky getting cold.'

'It's so lovely to see him,' Cat said. 'He's back on Primrose Terrace, where he belongs. Hello, Chalky. Happy Christmas, my poppet.' She kissed him on the nose.

She didn't notice Phil arrive, and jumped when Jessica rang a bell that momentarily whisked all the dogs into a fervour, calling them all to attention.

'Right then, ladies and gentlemen,' Phil said. 'This is the first part of the Primrose Terrace Christmas Spectacular, and I'm going to ask all the competing dogs – and their owners, of course – to do a circuit of this room, so I, and everyone else, can get a good look at all the costumes. After that I'll be judging the winners. There are two prizes, one for effort and one for inventiveness. Are you happy to start us off?' he asked a woman with a Chihuahua dressed as a Christmas pudding.

Cat sat on the floor next to Chalky's cart, one hand tenderly stroking his soft fur, and watched with glee as the dressed-up dogs took turns at centre stage. Polly and Owen were getting Rummy ready, fussing around him like proud parents, but she couldn't see Joe anywhere. She forced herself not to check whether Jessica was absent too.

All the dogs were magnificent – everyone had made a fantastic effort. The lights competition was restricted to Primrose Terrace, but there were lots of people here she didn't know, or recognized from elsewhere in Fairview. Jessica's influence, and perhaps maybe that of Pooch Promenade's protest, had spread interest in the competition far and wide.

In the end, Phil gave the 'effort' award to a cockapoo dressed as a mermaid, with a hand-crafted tail made up of shimmering, individual scales, its curly russet hair perfect for the flowing locks. Cat approved of the selection, and then had to resist the urge to hug Phil when he awarded the inventiveness prize to Disco.

'Disco dressed as a Disco ball,' he said, handing Elsie a hamper full of doggy goodies. 'It's epic. Only beaten, possibly, if she'd been dressed as a salt-and-vinegar crisp from the nineties.'

'I did consider that,' Elsie said, handing the hamper to Captain.

'Oh, and –' Phil touched the older woman on the shoulder – 'this award is for Christmas Spirit. Nobody else was in contention, but all the residents of Primrose Terrace wanted to recognize what a special and loved dog Chalky is, and how pleased they all are that he made it through. So this is from everyone.' Phil reached behind him and lifted up a luxurious dog bed that they'd all clubbed together to get. It was shaped like a mini chesterfield chair, with a fur lining for comfort.

Elsie actually squealed, her hands clamped against her cheeks. 'Really, everyone,' she gasped, 'you didn't have to do that. But he will love it, I know it.' She hugged Phil, and then did the rounds, thanking everyone.

'Cat, you lame old thing.' She embraced her. 'I have a feeling you might be behind this.'

'It was all of us,' Cat said. 'I know we couldn't be sure, until now. But we all kept hoping, and I thought if we did this, if we were confident about his recovery, then that might help in some small way. We're just so glad he's back. Primrose Terrace wouldn't be the same without him.'

'I know,' Elsie murmured. 'I know it more than anything. Listen, I should get him back.'

'I'll bring this, if you like.' Phil held up the mini chesterfield. 'There's a bit of a break before the party and the other competition.'

'I'll pop round on Christmas Day,' Cat said. 'Maybe tomorrow, too. I want to see how Chalky gets on with his new throne.'

'Come on.' Captain held out his arm for Elsie. 'Let's take old Chalky back.'

Cat watched as they left, the other competitors filtering out behind them. There was a commotion from the front door, squeals and cheers, and she felt Joe beside her, smelt his subtle aftershave. She inhaled.

'It's snowing,' he said softly.

'A perfect winter wonderland.' Cat peered out, watching the thick flakes as they fell gently to the ground.

'You're welcome to stay here,' Jessica said, putting her hand on Joe's arm, 'if that's easier than trying to get back again.'

'Oh no,' Owen said. 'We've got lights to turn on.'

'Outfits to change into,' Polly added.

'And I can always give her a piggyback if it's too treacherous for swollen ankles out there.' Joe grinned, and Cat's insides did a little shimmy. 'Let's go, hopalong.'

They walked slowly back to number nine, lifting their faces up to the sky, tasting the snowflakes on their tongues, catching them on their eyelashes. The cold helped to numb Cat's ankle, and by the time they'd reached home, she could hardly feel it. She went into the kitchen to make tea, ignoring the entreaties of the others to sit down. She wasn't going to let a sprained ankle render her useless.

'I've got to nip out,' she heard Joe tell Polly.

'What,' Owen said, 'in this?'

'It's not far. I'll be back in a jiffy.'

'Where are you going?' Cat asked, wondering if, after all, he was returning to Jessica's, making the most of the quiet time between the fancy-dress parade and the party. 'The snow's getting heavier.'

'I promise I'll be back soon. But don't wait for me – go to the party and I'll meet you there.'

They watched him zip up his black Jack Wolfskin jacket, pick up the Fiesta keys and leave the house, and then Polly, as if sensing Cat's disquiet, said, 'Sod tea, we're opening a bottle of prosecco. It is a Christmas party, after all.'

Polly looked amazing. She had styled her long blonde hair into springy, bouncy curls, and was wearing a floor-length dress the colour of the midnight sky, with subtle silver sparkles sewn into the fabric. Owen, dressed in a black suit and white shirt, could barely take his eyes off her, and Cat could see why. Even Rummy, no longer in his Superman outfit, and not even invited to the second party, looked smart.

Cat, on the other hand, felt distinctly underdressed. Because of her bandage and her need for flat shoes, she had abandoned the short coppery dress she had planned on wearing and opted for black, wide-legged trousers and a dusky-pink halterneck top with sequin details. She'd squeezed her bandaged foot into her cream pumps, but they were mostly hidden beneath her trousers anyway.

'You look gorgeous, Cat,' Polly said.

Cat screwed her face up. 'It's not what I'd pictured when I got up this morning.'

'I'm going to second Polly's words,' Owen said, topping up their glasses, 'and take one step further, from gorgeous to stunning.'

Cat laughed. 'Thank you. I know who's going to be the best-looking couple at the party, though. You are the belles of the ball.' She held up her glass and Polly and Owen grinned at each other, a look of pure happiness passing between them.

'Should we get going,' Cat said, 'or wait for Joe? Do you know where he's gone?'

Polly shook her head and chewed her lip. 'I don't,' she said softly. 'But he said he'd meet us at the party, so I don't think we should worry.'

Owen peered out of the curtains. 'The snow's pretty relentless.'

'Then I'm sure he'll get in touch,' Polly said. 'Come on, we need to turn our lights on and get going.'

'Now,' Owen said, crouching down in front of the sofa where Shed and Rummy were sitting passively at either end, like bookends. 'I hope this is really how you feel, and you're not just pretending until we leave the house. I want no disruption, no fighting, from either of you, understood?' He ruffled

Rummy's fur and then gave Shed a long, thorough stroke until he was purring loudly, eyes closed.

'It's magic,' Polly whispered.

'It means that maybe,' Cat added, 'we can have an addition to our family sometime next year.' Cat had told Polly that she knew about Truffle, and had spent a long half an hour trying to stop Polly apologizing for keeping it from her. It was finally out in the open: number nine Primrose Terrace was a dog-loving household.

'Maybe.' Polly squeezed Cat's arm. 'But now we need to go.'

Cat hobbled into the hall and looked at her guitar, leaning against the wall, safe from the snow in its bag. She turned away from it.

Polly narrowed her eyes and gave her the Sinclair stare. 'You're not taking it?'

'It's not the right time,' Cat said softly.

'It's Christmas. Of course it is.' She picked it up and hefted it over her shoulder, teetering on her heels.

'Give it to me,' Cat said. 'I've got flats on. But I'm *not* doing it, unless . . .'

'Unless the timing's right,' Polly said, 'got it.' She grinned and gave Cat back the guitar.

'You go outside, and I'll press the button.' Owen opened the front door.

Polly took Cat's arm and they walked slowly down the snow-covered front stairs, turning to look up at the house. In moments, their hair and coats were covered in snowflakes: a thin layer had already covered the roofs and the cars and the pavement.

Along Primrose Terrace, lots of the lights were already on. Frankie's animal-themed display, the songbirds dangling beautifully down the side of her house, Boris and Charles's white and gold fairy lights shining with understated elegance, and Elsie's house resplendent with a boat-shaped design covering the space between the lower and upper windows, blue lights below it for the sea, stars along the roof. That, Cat thought, had to be Captain's influence.

Jessica's house was still unlit, except for the windows, which were glowing invitingly.

'We need a countdown,' Polly called.

'It's a shame Joe's not here to see this,' Cat said.

'He'll see it when he gets back. There's nothing we can do about my brother's bad timing.'

'Right!' Owen shouted.

Cat held her breath.

'Three. Two. One!'

He flicked the switch and their house lit up, the winter menagerie along the bottom, white icicles shimmering from the roof and windowsills, and the soft, pulsing snowflakes turning blue, then pink, then green, then yellow.

'Wow,' Polly murmured.

'That,' Cat said, 'is stunning.'

Owen locked the door and made his way carefully down the stairs. 'It was worth all the effort.'

'Look at Primrose Terrace,' Cat said. 'I mean, look at ours, but look at the whole street.' They took a moment, standing in the snow, huddled into each other, the glitter and colour of the lights magical in the winter darkness. The air around them was quiet, the snow blanketing any sounds, adding to the effect. Cat found herself breathless at the beauty of their little road. The only thing that was missing was Joe.

'What time's Phil judging it?' Polly asked.

'In a couple of hours,' Cat said, blinking herself out of her reverie. 'And it might take us that long to get to Jessica's with our various impairments.' Polly had completed her outfit with beautiful navy heels, which Cat knew were treacherous to walk on at the best of times, let alone in an inch of snow. 'We'd better get going. Put your hood up, Polly, or your curls will die.'

They arrived at Jessica's house, stepping out of the winter scene into the glow and merriment of a Christmas party, and the warmth and laughter hit them like a wave. Cat resisted the urge to throw her guitar out into the snow, dashing it into a hundred pieces. Of all of the things she'd conjured up since she'd moved to Primrose Terrace, this was the most deluded idea. There was no way on earth she could serenade Joe at this party, not even if she was sure he still had feelings for her. Silently cursing Polly's faith in her, she snuck the guitar into the hall cupboard, where Jessica kept the spare dog leads, and returned to her friends.

25

Jessica greeted them wearing a white dress that Cat was sure was actually Valentino. She had straightened her blonde curls, and looked sleek and glamorous, like a snow leopard.

'Well done on the outfit,' Jessica said, hugging her. 'You look positively glowing, and nobody would guess you were flat-shoed and limping.'

'They will the moment I move from this spot.' Cat smiled.

'But no piggyback from Joe this time? I have to say, I was almost tempted to twist *my* ankle.' Jessica looked at the door, her groomed brows lowering slightly.

Cat gave a hollow laugh. 'He'll be here soon. He didn't . . . come back for anything, after the fancy dress parade?'

'No,' Jessica said, turning back to Cat. 'Did he say he was going to?'

Cat shook her head. 'Why isn't your house lit up? Have you seen the rest of the road?'

Jessica gave her a sly grin. 'The other houses are impressive. Is yours on now too?'

Cat nodded.

'I thought,' Jessica said slowly, 'as we'd all have to go outside for the judging, I could wait until everyone was there and then turn my lights on.'

'A-ha,' Cat said, 'hoping to make an impact?'

'Oh, I guarantee it.' Jessica tapped the side of her nose. 'Now, come and get a drink, all of you. My new canapés are circling, and I'd love to know what you think. Bacon and Christmas pudding is my personal favourite, but you'll have to decide for yourselves.'

Polly looked horrified, but Owen rubbed his hands together. 'Sounds delicious.'

'Yes,' Polly said, 'but you like horseradish ice cream.'

'I promise, once you try it, you'll be sold.'

'So you'll have to take me to that hotel then,' Polly said, leaning in to him.

'I will. I'll take you for the weekend. It'll be incredibly romantic, and you won't even notice when I sneak off to talk to the chef so I can start making my own.' He kissed her on the nose.

'I'm not sure Fairview's ready for it.'

'I think Fairview's ready for anything,' Owen said seriously.

'Nearly anything,' Cat added, thinking of her guitar.

'Ah, Miss Palmer?' Cat turned towards the voice. She tried not to gasp at Mr Jasper, resplendent in a claret-coloured suit, white shirt and Christmas bow tie.

'Mr Jasper! How are you?'

'I'm good thank you, very good. How is – uh – Chalky? Is he OK?'

Cat grinned, feeling a glow of happiness. 'He's much better now, on the road to recovery. But it was touch and go for a while, and I really don't know what would have happened if you hadn't been there that day. I tried to find a way of getting in touch to let you know, but I drew a blank. Thank you.' She gave him a hug, and Mr Jasper, stiff and resisting at first, patted her on the shoulder. 'It's lovely to see you here.'

'Miss Heybourne invited me, after I brought her Highland terriers back here. They're very well behaved,' he said uncertainly.

Cat laughed. 'Most dogs are. Maybe you've just had a couple of bad experiences – my first dog walk included.'

Mr Jasper nodded seriously. 'I'm not sure anyone could have foreseen the squirrel. But you – you seem to be doing so much, for the community. With this . . . competitions and things.'

Cat bit her lip. 'And the cove?'

Mr Jasper's mouth twisted as if he was working out what to say. 'It's a fair decision. People still have the main beach.'

'People and dogs can survive together, you know,' Cat said lightly. 'They have done, for thousands of years. And lots of the time, it's a perfect match.'

Mr Jasper looked at the floor. 'They're not that bad.'

'See?' Cat rubbed his arm. 'And you're a hero among dog lovers now. You've completely reinvented yourself.'

'I wouldn't say that. But my mother died.'

'Oh, Mr Jasper, I'm so sorry.'

He waved her sympathy away. 'You see, she wasn't that fond of dogs. No, that's an understatement. She brought me up to believe they were evil, unwanted pests and I kept the pretence up while she was alive. And now I've got to know Chalky, and those little white terriers.'

Cat nodded. 'I'm glad they've helped change your mind,' she said softly. 'Maybe you can convince Alison.'

'Oh, Alison won't be convinced. Dogs are messy and dangerous, in her opinion. That's not likely to change. And to be honest, I think her involvement was as much about attacking you as it was dog walking in general. She has a lot of vitriol for such a small person. Don't take it to heart.'

'I won't,' Cat said. If it hadn't been for Alison's vitriol, she would never have become a dog walker in the first place.

Coco appeared at their feet, barked up at Mr Jasper and put his paws on the claret-coloured trousers.

Cat laughed. 'He remembers you. That is one happy dog – and look, mistletoe!' She pointed up to where Jessica had hung a large branch of leaves and white berries from the hall's central chandelier. She gave him a peck on the cheek. 'Merry Christmas, Mr Jasper.'

'It's Terry,' he said, bending tentatively to pat Coco on the head. 'Merry Christmas, Cat.'

Cat left them to it and hobbled away, looking for an exotic canapé and perhaps a seat. Her ankle was starting to throb, and it wasn't long until the judging started. Jessica's elegant, spacious front room was crammed with people, no inch of sofa free. She turned, slowly, looking for somewhere to perch, and bumped straight into Mark.

She stepped back and, putting all her weight on her bad ankle, almost fell. Mark grabbed her arm. 'Steady.'

Cat waited for the flash of attraction, but it didn't come. He was in his customary outfit, sharp black suit and black shirt and, while he seemed relaxed, as confident as ever, there was no hint of a smile.

'How are you?' he asked.

'Fine, thanks. You?'

Mark nodded. 'Not too bad.'

'I didn't realize you'd be here.' It was a stupid thing to say, but Cat hadn't even considered that she might see him that evening.

'I wouldn't miss one of Jessica's parties. We're good friends.'

'Of course you are,' Cat said, inwardly cursing herself.

Mark broke eye contact, glancing round the room as if Cat was the least interesting person there. She bristled and planned her escape, aware that, unfortunately, it would have to be slow and laboured.

'Listen, I should get—'

'I hope there's no bad feeling between us,' Mark cut in, giving her his full attention. 'We said a few things, there was some anger flying around, but you have to admit that we're good together, Cat.' His hand traced its way up her arm and Cat shrugged it away.

'We had fun,' she admitted. 'But it's not—'

'You don't have to apologize. We all make mistakes. If, after this,' he leaned into her, his lips brushing against her neck before whispering into her ear, 'you wanted to come back to mine, wish Chips a happy Christmas . . .'

Cat flinched and stepped back. 'No.'

Mark gave her a bemused smile. 'No?'

Cat shook her head. 'No, Mark. I made my decision, and I don't regret it. Why did you think I did?'

'Seeing each other again. It's bound to stir up old feelings. I'm as irresistible as I ever was.' He flashed her a grin.

Cat folded her arms. 'And still as married?'

His grin vanished.

'Don't forget that I'm friends with Jessica too.' Cat swallowed. 'You're pretty unbelievable, do you know that?'

'That's what everyone says about me.'

'You were spending time with Sarah the whole time we were going out, trying to resurrect your marriage, keeping me dangling like some kind of poor injured fish on a rod –' she frowned, wishing she had managed a snappier insult – 'and then, when we broke up, you accused me of doing the same.'

Mark shrugged. 'Takes one to know one. How is Joe, anyway? I haven't seen him tonight, strutting around in his Top Man suit.'

Cat rolled her eyes. 'God, Mark, is that all you care about? I'm not denying that we had fun, but good looks and charm will only get you so far.'

'They got me quite far with you.'

'But they haven't won Sarah round completely, have they? Not if you felt the need to amuse yourself with me at the same time.'

Mark's smile fell, and irritation flashed in his eyes.

'Happy Christmas, Mark,' she said, turning on her good heel and limping back into the hall. Glancing behind her, she saw Mark was still standing there, his wit and charm muted, if only momentarily.

Cat's relief was overwhelming when the Christmas music paused and Jessica called for everyone to go outside. It was time for the pièce de résistance.

If anything, the snow had got heavier. They all traipsed outside, pulling on coats and hats and scarves, and filled the pavement, turning to face the glittering, shimmering house fronts.

Cat found Owen and Polly, and linked arms with her best friend, watching snowflakes land on the collar of her coat and on Owen's tight curls.

'Everything all right?' Polly whispered. 'You're clenching your jaw.'

Cat nodded. 'I bumped into Mark.'

'Are you OK?'

'I am. It was actually a relief to tell him I knew about Sarah, that I knew what we had wasn't real. It was cathartic.'

'Laying the past to rest?' Polly whispered.

'Something like that.'

'Right,' Phil called, standing on the top step of number one alongside Jessica. 'I've made my way up and down the terrace several times, admiring all the hard work everyone's put in. I'm sure there isn't a more beautiful or Christmassy street on the whole south coast. Primrose Terrace residents, you have outdone yourselves, and I'm finding it hard to judge. But there's one house left to reveal itself, so I want you all to join in with the countdown for Jessica's switch-on. Are you ready?'

'Yes!' Their chorus rose up to meet the snow.

Phil counted them down. 'Five. Four. Three. Two . . . ONE!'

Jessica pressed the button, and the front of number one Primrose Terrace lit up.

The air filled with gasps and coos, a single scream.

'Holy shit,' someone murmured.

'How did she do that?'

'Bloody hell,' Owen said, mesmerized. 'So much for our snowflakes.'

Jessica's entry was more like a laser show than Christmas lights. Starting out in red and green, the tiny lights that covered her house made small squares that looked like a chess board, then the colours chased each other from left to right, then the whole house flashed green, then red, then white. Little snowflakes appeared and seemed to fall to the ground, hypnotic against the real snow. Everyone stood in awe, numb toes and noses forgotten as they watched the lights turn from falling snowflakes into a colour show, from gold, to silver, then purple. The LED lights transformed the front of Jessica's house into a screen, filled with pattern after pattern, colour after colour.

'Wow,' Polly murmured as the lights began flickering white against blue like stars in the night sky.

Then a loud bang filled the air and the house went dark.

Cat blinked and rubbed her eyes, pushing melted snowflakes off her cheeks.

'What happened?' Owen asked.

Cat looked around, tried to pick out Jessica or Phil or even Polly. But she couldn't, because all the lights had gone. Not just Jessica's, but the other Christmas displays down the street, the warm glow of lit rooms, the orange reach of the streetlights. Primrose Terrace was in complete darkness.

The crowd started murmuring, voices gradually getting louder.

'What happened?'

'Was that part of the show?'

'Charles, are you there? I can't see a thing!'

'People!' a voice called, louder than the others. 'People! It's Phil.' Cat turned towards the voice and saw he was trying to light his face with the torch on his phone. 'It seems we've had a technical difficulty, so if everyone could just go back into Jessica's house, get out of the cold while we try and sort it out, that would be fantastic.'

'But it's dark,' Polly said.

'Candles,' Jessica shouted. 'I've got lots of candles!'

After an evening so full of bright, sparkling lights, the next twenty minutes were how Cat imagined it might feel like to live in a black hole. She followed her friends back inside as fast as her throbbing ankle and the slippery snow would allow her, and helped Jessica, Polly and Owen, Boris and Charles collect candles. They lit up the downstairs of the house, while other guests, less familiar with the property, hovered about uncertainly, anxious not to knock things over in the dark.

'What did you do?' Cat asked.

Jessica shook her head. 'I knew my lights were powerful,' she said, 'but I thought that the extension cord was good enough. Clearly not.'

'Aren't they LED? They're meant to be low energy.'

'Maybe it's the whole street? Maybe all together we've used too much electricity and my lights were the final straw. Phil's gone to investigate.'

'It does look lovely, though, doesn't it?' Cat said, lighting her last candle and standing up, taking in the soft, romantic beauty of Jessica's house filled with flickering light, picking out her elegant decorations, the sparkle of party dresses. Valentino and Dior rushed up to their owner, and Cat bent to stroke them, burying her chilled face in their warm fur. 'Are you having fun?' she asked. Valentino licked her chin, and Dior dropped a half-eaten bacon and Christmas pudding canapé at her feet. 'Of course you are. It's an adventure, isn't it?'

'But,' Jessica said, hands on hips. 'We have no music.'

Cat thought again of her guitar, and how idiotic she'd been to believe that she could ever have gone through with it. She'd had such promising plans for the whole day, all of which culminated in showing Joe how she felt about him with the big, romantic gesture that Polly had suggested. But she'd injured herself and ruined her party outfit with an inelegant limp, and then Joe had disappeared and possibly got himself stranded somewhere in the snow, and now the whole street had been plunged into darkness.

'Cat,' Owen said, 'what about your guitar? Didn't you bring it with you?'

Cat's stomach swooped. 'Oh no, that was a mistake.'

'You put it in the cupboard in the hall. I'm sure we can find it in the dark.'

'And we could all join in,' Jessica added, clapping her hands together. 'You wouldn't be singing on your own, just starting us off. Which songs do you know?'

'Oh, not many.' She shot a terrified glance at Polly, and Polly shrugged helplessly, her eyes wide with an unspoken apology. 'Look, really, I don't think I can—'

'Come on, Cat.' Jessica gave her a warm smile. 'We've got no lights, everything's a bit flat. A sing-song would be perfect.'

Owen nodded. 'It'll be like a festive campfire. Flickering flames, a guitar, singing.'

'I've got lots of mulled wine,' Jessica added. 'I'm sure it's still warm, even though the heat's gone out under it. What do you say, Cat?'

Cat tried to swallow past the lump in her throat. What could she say? That she only knew one song, and that she'd been practising it for just one person; that she'd imagined a perfect scenario where she serenaded him, showing him how she felt while everyone at the party looked on in awe.

Except she couldn't do it. There wasn't enough light to check her finger positions – and she needed to do that, at least at the beginning – and she'd known all along, in her heart, that she didn't have the confidence to sing in front of her friends, let alone a whole partyful of people. And all this was pointless anyway, because the song was for Joe, and Joe wasn't here. He'd disappeared somewhere without telling anyone where he was going, for all Cat knew he could have been planning a romantic gesture of his own for Jessica, and had got stuck in the snow on the way to fulfilling it.

Jessica took her panicked silence for assent and strode into the hallway. 'I'll get your guitar,' she called.

'No!' Cat lurched forward but missed Jessica by a few inches. She hobbled after her, wincing as pain shot through her ankle, skidding on the melted snow brought inside on people's shoes. In the flickering light, she picked Jessica out amongst the other guests chatting quietly in the sizeable hall, coming back towards her with the guitar. 'Jessica, please stop!'

She reached out and took her guitar.

'I can't do it.' Polly and Owen had followed Cat out into the hallway, and others had latched onto Cat's urgency and were now paying full attention.

'But you brought it with you specially,' Jessica said. 'You just need to be a bit more confident, everyone will love it.'

'I only know one song,' Cat whispered, aware of their audience.

Jessica frowned. 'Well, that's OK. We can do that one first, and then we probably won't need the guitar, we can all just sing. Which song is it?'

Cat looked at the floor. '"All I want for Christmas",' she mumbled.

'Is my two front teeth?' Owen asked, laughing.

'No,' Cat sighed, 'not that one. The Mariah Carey one.'

'"All I want for Christmas is you"?' Jessica said. 'That really schmaltzy one?'

Cat felt her cheeks burning and was grateful for the gloom. She nodded.

'Why?' Owen asked. 'I mean, each to their own, but if you were planning to sing here at the party, then—'

'But I wasn't,' Cat rushed. 'I mean, I was, but not – not as part of some big Christmas sing-song.'

'Well, what then?' Jessica asked.

Cat looked at the shadowy faces around her, at Owen and Jessica frowning, and Polly, her best friend, aware that she was partly responsible for the mix-up.

'I'm sorry,' Cat said to Polly, 'I don't know why I thought I could do it. There's just no way.'

'You are a wonderful person, Cat.' Polly embraced her. 'I know you're not confident, but it would have been amazing. I'm sorry it hasn't worked out.'

'Will someone tell me what's going on?' Owen asked.

Jessica raised her hand. 'Me too. I'd like to know too.'

Cat glanced around the room at the figures she could half see, a few turned in their direction. Boris and Charles were watching, intrigued, and Juliette and Will were pretending to be deep in conversation, their eyes shooting furtive glances towards her.

'Cat wanted to sing to someone,' Polly started, looking at Cat while she spoke. 'She wanted to sing that song, "All I want for Christmas is you", to one person in particular. But sadly, that person's not here.'

'Mark?' Jessica asked, her frown deepening.

'Ah!' Owen slapped his hand to his forehead. 'Of course!'

'What "of course"?' Jessica asked. 'Who?'

'Not Mark,' Cat said, shaking her head. 'Definitely not Mark. It's . . .'

'It's someone who you think would be great to bump into under the mistletoe,' Polly said.

Cat didn't think now was the best time for cryptic clues, but it took Jessica only moments to figure it out.

'Joe?' she screeched. 'You want to sing Mariah Carey to Joe?'

Cat resisted the urge to hide where the candles couldn't find her. She heard one of the Westies barking in another room.

'Yes.' She whispered it loudly. 'Yes, that was my stupid plan.'

'You and Joe are . . .' Jessica clasped her hands together in front of her.

'N-no. I mean, I had hoped . . .'

'You care about Joe?' Jessica asked again, her voice carrying over everyone else.

Cat closed her eyes, shivering as a blast of icy air wrapped itself around her shoulders, the candle flames bending and flickering. 'Yes,' she said. 'Yes, I do. I have done for ages. I'm sorry, Jessica, I know that you like him, too. I never meant for things to work out like this, and if there's something between you—'

Jessica shook her head. 'There's nothing between us, the flirting's all been mine. I applaud your good taste, but I certainly don't fancy him enough to risk all my dignity by singing for him. You must really like him.'

'A lot,' Cat confirmed.

'You, Cat Palmer, *really* care about Joe Sinclair? And you were going to serenade him here, tonight?' Jessica's eyes were wide, her smile gleeful.

Cat frowned at Polly but she just grinned back. 'Yes, Jessica. Yes to all of that, except I can't. Why, what do you—'

'Do you love him?' Jessica asked softly.

Polly gasped, and Owen looked at the floor, but Jessica stared at Cat without embarrassment, waiting.

Cat swallowed, felt her whole body tingle with nerves, down to her fingers, her throbbing ankle, her toes.

'Yes,' she said, her voice surprisingly clear. 'Yes, I am in love with Joe Sinclair, and I had planned to serenade him, undoubtedly very badly, with a Mariah Carey song tonight, and see if he still had feelings for me, if he still felt the same. But it's all gone wrong, and he's not even here, and I—'

The lights flickered back on, everyone blinking and murmuring, Cat's friends coming into full, brilliant view in front of her. She saw that Polly was red-cheeked, Owen's eyebrows were raised, and Jessica was looking not just happy, but positively triumphant.

'What?' Cat whispered.

'Yes,' said a voice behind her. A voice she knew so well, a voice that made her breath falter.

Slowly she turned and found she was looking straight into a pair of blue eyes beneath damp, blond hair, snowflakes melting quickly onto a Jack Wolfskin jacket.

'Joe,' she managed, the tingling increasing, tears burning at the corners of her eyes. 'Joe, I—'

'Yes,' he said. 'Yes, I do feel the same.'

Cat felt the space grow around her, sensed everyone else drift away, leaving her, and Joe, and the candles still flickering, even though the lights were back on.

'I've got something for you,' he said. 'But first, I think you've got something for me?' He raised an eyebrow, a smile on his lips, and pointed at the guitar, which Cat was still holding.

She looked down at it, wondering how she could possibly do this now, when she could barely speak. Slowly, she lifted the guitar and put her fingers on the fret board, finding the right position. Checking again that they were alone, she tentatively played the first note, and then opened her mouth, her voice reedy and shaky and not at all up to the task.

But she kept her eyes on Joe, and he held her gaze, showing no signs of embarrassment or shame, just the depth of feeling and compassion she'd seen so many times before. This time she knew that it was aimed solely at her, and it gave her the confidence to make it through the first verse and the chorus, before her fingers slipped, and her voice faltered on the last line and the words came out in a whisper.

'All I want for Christmas is you, Joe.' She leaned the guitar up against the wall and took a step towards him.

'That,' Joe said, 'was pretty special. You're the most incredible, bonkers, passionate person I have ever met, and I love you. Happy Christmas, Cat.'

Cat smiled, still not quite able to believe what was happening. 'It was hopeless. But it seems my Christmas wish might have come true, after all.'

'Are you talking about me? Or this guy?'

Joe reached inside his coat and pulled out a familiar turquoise handbag, one that Cat hadn't used since the spring, but now had tinsel tied round the handles. He held it out to her, and as Cat took it, a little black nose, followed by scruffy caramel and white fur and two large dark eyes, peered out.

Cat gasped and pulled the puppy out of the bag, clutching it to her. 'A puppy,' she whispered, her tears falling freely now, the tiny, warm body burrowing against her, whimpering softly.

Joe gave her a lopsided smile. 'I found the piece of paper on the coffee table when I got back from America. I phoned, and she still had one puppy left. I was meant to pick him up tomorrow, but when the weather got bad I arranged to go tonight. I thought, seeing as Shed's done so well with Rummy . . .' He shrugged his coat off and hung it on the banister. Underneath he was wearing a fitted dark-grey suit, his white shirt open at the collar. 'He doesn't have a name yet.'

Cat stared at the puppy, at Joe, thinking her heart might burst with love for the man standing in front of her and the tiny creature clutched against her chest.

'Mistletoe,' she whispered.

Joe looked up at the bunch above them dangling from the chandelier. 'That's an excellent idea.' He stepped forward and kissed her, taking her breath away. His skin was cold against hers, but his passion, the certainty of his feelings, warmed her, and every fibre of Cat's body knew that this was it. This was right. Her and Joe, the puppy enclosed in the circle of their embracing bodies. Melted snowflakes dripped from Joe's hair onto Cat's face, mingling with her tears.

'Joe,' she said, breaking away. 'Joe Sinclair.'

'Yes, Cat Palmer?'

'I meant the puppy.'

'You want to kiss the puppy?'

She couldn't stop grinning. 'I meant as a name for the puppy. Mistletoe.'

'Oh.' He smiled at her, then laughed. 'You want to call him Mistletoe?'

'Don't you think it's a great name? Don't you always want to be reminded of this moment?'

'Say it again.' He stroked the mongrel's fuzzy, puppy fur.

'Mistletoe,' Cat whispered, looking up at him, not quite believing that her perfect Christmas dream was coming true, despite all the obstacles.

'Do you know what?' Joe said. 'I think that's an excellent idea.'

He kissed her again.

Christmas Day on Primrose Terrace

Cat couldn't stay asleep any longer.

She looked at her alarm clock and saw that it was only five seventeen. But it was Christmas morning, her first on Primrose Terrace, and she had more to look forward to than she ever had before. She flung the duvet back and padded to the window. It was dark outside, but the streetlights highlighted the fresh snowfall, everything topped with a dusty, icing-white coating. She grinned and hopped to the bathroom, her feet dancing on the cold tiles.

Above her, Joe was asleep in his attic bedroom, and downstairs, in his puppy pen, was Mistletoe. She'd known him just over twenty-four hours, and already the tiny dog had as much personality as the other dogs she knew and loved. Joe had bought a pen when he'd picked Mistletoe up, and while Cat had been desperate for the puppy to sleep in her room, she knew they had to bring him up to be the happiest, healthiest dog on Primrose Terrace, teach him rules and boundaries.

Washing her face and hurrying back to her bedroom to get a thick, woolly jumper, she tiptoed downstairs and into the living room. The sound of sleigh bells filled the air as she stepped over the threshold.

She switched the light on and there were the stockings hanging up near the television. Each member of the household – including semi-permanent fixture Owen – had agreed to fill one for someone else. By default, that had meant her doing Joe's, and him hers. But right now, it wasn't stockings that she was interested in. She tiptoed over to the puppy pen and crouched down, next to Shed, who was snoozing gently with his nose close to the bars.

'Have you been terrorizing our new addition?' she whispered, stroking him. But she wasn't worried; she thought the cat might even be protecting Mistletoe, as if saying, *stick with me, kid, I'll show you the ropes*. Rummy had been a trial run, the fox terrier and ginger cat taking a while to get used to each other, but now Rummy was curled up on their sofa, and when they'd brought Mistletoe home, Shed had been intrigued and not at all aggressive. It had, Cat thought, as she sat in front of the pen, been one of the weirdest Christmas Eve's ever. But the thought of it, and of the Christmas day to come, brought a smile to her face as she peered through the bars.

Mistletoe was asleep, curled up on the blanket, half hidden from view inside the crate at the back of the pen. She knew that sleep would be fleeting for a while, that he would take a long time to settle down, as he had done the night of the party and last night, but Cat was prepared for all of it – she'd been waiting long enough. She left Mistletoe to snooze, put the coffee machine on, and gave Shed, who was now fully awake, some breakfast.

'You're a dark horse, aren't you? Grumpier than a dog chewing a wasp when I first moved in, and now best pals with two of them.'

Shed meowed, and Cat nodded in agreement.

Coffee in hand, she opened the living-room curtains, turned the main light off and the Christmas tree lights on. She sat cross-legged on the sofa, the sole of her foot against Rummy's warm fur, listening to his gentle snores and staring out at the winter darkness. The stillness and beauty of it made her shiver.

Christmas Eve had been frantic, with last-minute food shopping in a supermarket groaning under the weight of panicked people, everything extra complicated, and cold, and damp, because of the snow and her slowly healing ankle. Then they'd all disappeared to separate corners of the house to wrap presents, and Cat had shut herself in the kitchen to make a savoury mincemeat roll and some mince pies.

It was her first day of being with Joe, and they'd hardly seen each other, exchanging brief moments – holding hands, kissing – as they passed in the corridor or supermarket aisle, both still slightly disbelieving that, after all this time, they had made it.

That's how it felt to Cat: she had made it to where she needed to be. She'd gone on a long, rocky journey, taken wrong turns, made mistakes, had to backtrack and apologize and rethink, but finally, she had got to him. She thought back to the night of the party, to the passion in his kiss, the desire and love and wholeness she'd felt in his arms. The memory wrapped itself around her like a delicious cloak, and she closed her eyes. She opened them again at the sound of sleigh bells.

Joe was in the doorway, wearing a white T-shirt and boxer shorts, his blond hair scruffy, his eyes crinkled with sleep. To Cat, he looked more gorgeous than ever.

436

'Happy Christmas, Joe,' she said quietly.

He padded over and knelt in front of her. 'Happy Christmas, Cat.' He put his hands on her knees and she leaned forward and kissed him, wrapping her hands round the back of his neck. They looked at each other, his smile infectious, everything about him filling her senses, firing her nerves.

'There's coffee in the pot,' she said.

He nodded and went to the kitchen, crouching down at the puppy pen on the way. 'How's our little evergreen?'

'Sleeping.'

'He clearly hasn't realized it's Christmas.'

Cat left Rummy sleeping and moved to the other sofa so she could sit next to Joe. When he came back with coffee, she turned sideways, putting her legs over his and kissing him again.

'We should wait for the others, shouldn't we?'

'I'm not sure this is a team sport,' Joe said, pulling her closer.

Cat laughed. 'To open the stockings. We should wait.'

'I'm happy to.' He stood and pulled her to her feet. 'But not here.'

They had stood like this, facing each other in this room, so many times before. But now, everything had changed. Her hands in his, she kissed Joe, her lips lingering, letting the feel of him wash over her body, and then wordlessly followed him out into the hallway, and up the stairs to his bedroom. Outside, the first traces of Christmas sunrise began to appear on the horizon.

Later, they sat on Joe's bed and, sure that Owen and Polly wouldn't mind, opened their stockings, watching the winter sun make the snow glitter like a carpet of diamonds. Cat's stocking had chocolate, fruit, a cute dark purple puppy lead and collar, slipper socks with poodles on, a mini bottle of limoncello and a book of modern guitar tunes. Each gift was carefully chosen, and Cat hoped that the artists' pens, new running headphones, iPad speakers and chocolate orange she'd got him were as thoughtful. From Joe's expression, she thought she hadn't done too badly.

Cat realized there was something still lodged in the bottom of her stocking. Frowning, she dug her hand in and pulled out a tiny model of number nine Primrose Terrace.

She stared at Joe, and he smiled back. 'From the cartoon,' he said.

'I know,' Cat whispered. 'I saw it and I thought, then, that it meant you were coming home. Well, hoped more than thought.'

'I set it up to come out on the day I returned. I didn't know if you'd get that, or if – well, things went a bit mad the day I got back.'

'With Chalky,' Cat confirmed. 'I loved your cartoons. I waited for the paper every Thursday. And the one on the beach, with the shark.'

Joe winced. 'Was that a bit too close to home? I didn't know then, about you and Mark. I didn't think you'd end it with him. I hoped, but I . . .' He shook his head, 'It was kind of a silly apology. I didn't really know how to say what I wanted to.'

'I loved it,' Cat said, moving closer to him, clutching the small model house. 'It's taken us a while but I'm so happy that we're here.'

'I don't think it could have happened in a better way.' Joe put his arm around her. 'This, Christmas, it's perfect. But I have more for you than just stocking fillers.'

'Me too,' Cat whispered.

She felt more nervous about this than any other part of Christmas day. She'd bought presents before she could be sure that she and Joe would be together and was worried they might be over the top. She watched, her heart pounding, as he unwrapped the new hoody she'd bought him. It was bright blue, with EARTH written across the front. The E and H were white, the ART in the middle yellow, a paintbrush splashing colour onto the letters.

'Too corny?' Cat asked as Joe stared at it.

He shook his head. 'I love it. And this is yours, though it's from all of us, not just me.' He handed Cat a small red envelope.

Cat frowned and took it. She opened the envelope and pulled out the card. It was a beautiful drawing – this time in colour – of Curiosity Kitten. She was tiptoeing forward towards a button marked 'Push' next to a house covered in Christmas lights. On the other side of the card, a handsome-looking cat was standing under a bunch of Mistletoe, a tiny puppy in his arms.

'I didn't cause the power outage,' she said, laughing. 'And you've drawn yourself as an incredibly buff cat.'

'Artistic licence,' Joe said, 'in both cases.'

'It's perfect. And when you're famous, it's going to be worth a lot of money. I'd better hold onto it.'

'Open it,' he said softly.

She did. Inside was another envelope, and inside that was a voucher. Cat read the words, unable to take them in.

'Is this a joke?' she asked.

'Nope,' Joe shook his head. 'And you can take whoever you want. Polly or Elsie or Jessica. Maybe not Mistletoe.'

'But it's ridiculous,' Cat said. 'It's so over the top that I can't even get my head round it.'

Joe shrugged. 'I had a great time in America. Just being in a different place, getting a new perspective. You've had a busy year, and I thought that maybe you could do with a break. And this one seemed like it would suit you down to the ground. You like Christmas – you seem to like snow – and you like dogs.'

'It's crazy,' Cat murmured. 'Dog sledding and Northern Lights tour in Norway. You did this, for me?'

'Happy Christmas, Cat.'

'Will you go with me? If – I mean, I'm sure Polly won't mind.'

Cat leaned back against the pillows, staring at the tickets. She and Joe were going to Norway, to be driven across the snow by a pack of beautiful, strong huskies, and to stare up at one of the most spectacular sights the world had to offer. She had no idea what to say.

'You really don't have to take me, you know,' Joe said. 'I didn't get it so I could come too.'

'But you will come with me?'

'Of course, I'd be honoured to.'

'Do we have to stay in an igloo? Keep each other from freezing to death with our body heat?' She squeezed his thigh.

'I think they're luxury igloos,' Joe said, moving closer to her, kissing her neck. 'Heating's included. But we could always pretend.'

'I'd like that,' Cat murmured. 'Hang on, I'm not done. This doesn't come close to a trip to Norway, but . . .' She reached down the side of the bed and handed him another present, complete with gold wrapping and glittery red string.

Joe put it on his lap and unwrapped it slowly, his brows narrowed in concentration. When he saw what it was, he whispered something under his breath that Cat didn't quite catch.

It was an A3 leather journal, the pages crisp and white, a tiny Curiosity Kitten, wobbling on her stack of crates to try and see into a window, embossed in the bottom corner along with the initials *JS*. She'd got the idea from her parents' present, and had found someone in Fairhaven town centre who could do the embossing.

Joe stared at her as if he'd never seen her before. 'Cat, this is—'

She shrugged, suddenly embarrassed. 'It's a cheat, really. My parents got one for me, so that's where the idea came from. I thought it would be perfect for you. Look at the first page.'

Joe opened the front cover, and read the words that Cat had written there.

To Joe, who can see beyond my curiosity and who, despite everything, loves dogs. I hope you always find inspiration, and that you fill this book with your wonderful creations. Thank you for being my inspiration. Happy Christmas, I love you. Cat. xx

'You're incredible,' he whispered, taking her hand.

'Maybe that could be your next cartoon – Incredible Iguana or something.'

'Don't tempt me. You're far too tempting, Cat Palmer. I'm just lucky that now I get to give in.'

When Cat and Joe finally made it downstairs, Polly and Owen were sitting cross-legged on the floor, watching Mistletoe demolish a box that had once contained a set of snowflake Christmas lights. Shredded cardboard covered the carpet like a snowstorm.

'Happy Christmas,' Joe said, setting off the sleigh bells. Rummy padded in from the kitchen and went to inspect Mistletoe. Cat followed closely behind, biting her lip as the dogs tentatively sniffed each other, and Mistletoe whimpered softly. She crouched and stroked his tiny body, and he buried himself in her jumper.

'You'll get used to him,' Cat whispered. 'He's a pretty cool dog. And wait until you meet Olaf and Disco, and Chalky will be able to tell you what's what – he knows everything. Do you need to go outside? I bet you do.'

While Polly and Owen made scrambled eggs, Cat put on boots and took Mistletoe out into their snowy courtyard. A robin hopped along the fence, disturbing the snow on top, singing its cheerful, pealing song. She knew, though her puppy was tiny, and despite the cold, he could be outside for short amounts of time. Mistletoe took two steps, sinking up to his tiny belly, and started to eat the snow.

'No, no no,' Cat said softly, 'do your business, puppy. Don't eat that.' She tried to encourage him, tried to get him to stop eating the snow, but in the end gave up and took him back to the litter tray in his crate.

'Doesn't he like the snow?' Polly asked, putting fresh coffee on the dining table.

'He does, but not in the right way.'

They ate their breakfast, and thanked each other for their Christmas presents.

'We'll look after Pooch Promenade while you're gone,' Polly said, when Cat gave her and Owen a hug, thanking them for the tickets to Norway.

'You don't mind if I take Joe?'

'Go, have a romantic getaway. Besides, I'm not sure that leaving Owen and Joe in charge of the new menagerie is entirely sensible. One of us is definitely needed here.'

'I don't think that's fair,' Owen said.

'Oh, you know it is.' Polly laughed and squeezed his hand, while Owen did a good job of looking crestfallen.

'But now, we have to get the turkey in if we want to eat before midnight.'

While Cat and Polly prepared the Christmas meal, Joe and Owen tried to puppy-proof the living room so that Mistletoe could explore.

'Christmas lights?' Joe asked.

'He'll destroy them,' Owen said. 'Let's tape the flex to the wall, out of his reach. And maybe move the tinsel that's dangling down by the window.'

'We've already lost a bit of it,' Joe said. 'We caught him just before he swallowed it. I'd forgotten all this, about having a puppy. It's bloody hard work.'

'It's a full-time job,' Owen agreed.

'It takes military precision.'

Cat and Polly, listening from the kitchen, grinned at each other, and Polly rolled her eyes.

'Do you know what,' Cat said, 'if I never get another Christmas present, I won't care. I've got everything I could ever hope for. I'm living with you, you're happy with Owen, I've got Joe, and we've all got Mistletoe. I've got my perfect job and Primrose Terrace. It's like a dream.'

'You worked hard for it, though,' Polly said, 'even with me and Owen.'

Cat punched her playfully on the arm. 'Yeah, well, you needed the push.'

'I did,' Polly agreed. 'And you could find worse people to love than Joey. He's a pain-in-the-ass brother, but he's quite nice when he wants to be.'

'Mmmmm,' Cat said, the smile automatically returning to her face.

'However,' Polly said, chopping up parsnips while Cat wrapped mini sausages in streaky bacon, 'it does mean that

443

we won't be able to tell each other any juicy details, because I definitely don't want to hear about my brother's sex life.'

Cat laughed, feeling the heat rise to her cheeks. 'That's a fair point,' she said. 'So I should probably apologize—'

'Blah blah blah.' Polly clamped her hands over her ears, parsnip peelings flying everywhere.

'Sorry!' Cat peered into the living room, but Joe and Owen were crouched by the window, examining something that might turn out to be a target for puppy-destruction.

'Pigs in blankets ready?' Polly asked, changing the subject.

'Last one ready . . . now.'

The turkey went into the oven. The vegetables were prepared, and all they had to do was wait for it to cook.

'Do you think Joe and Owen need help?' Polly asked.

'Do pigs live in blankets?' Cat replied, laughing.

After they'd eaten too much food, and drunk champagne followed by wine followed by Irish coffees, Polly and Owen announced they were taking Rummy for a walk. It was dark outside, but the Christmas lights along Primrose Terrace sparkled happily, without fear of future blowouts.

'I could do with the fresh air,' Owen said. 'And Rummy would like another walk.'

Cat nodded. She'd been round to visit Elsie and Captain, and Chalky, Disco and Paris before dinner, and had stayed in with Chalky while the other dogs went to the park. 'I have to wait in for Mum and Dad to get in touch. They're due to FaceTime in the next half-hour.'

'Do you want me to go with the others?' Joe asked.

Cat shook her head, trying not to laugh as Joe looked at her seriously beneath his red party hat. 'Stay,' she said. 'I'd like you to say hello, if – if you want to?'

'I'd love to,' he said.

It was nine o'clock in the evening in Fairview, just after lunchtime where they were in Canada.

When her parents realized what was going on, her mum shrieked, and Peter beamed from ear to ear. The mountains were visible through the window of their camper van, behind their happy faces.

'You two,' Delia said, 'I *always* knew you'd be perfect together. Oh, Joe, I wish I could pinch your cheek.'

Joe laughed. 'I'll look forward to that, Mrs Palmer.'

'Delia! Don't be so formal. You're practically part of the family.'

'You're happy, munchkin?' Peter asked.

Cat glanced at Joe. 'No,' she said, 'I'm pretending because Joe's sitting next to me.'

She listened to them tease her and tell her off for being cheeky, they showed her and Joe the view all round the camper van, and gave them a dramatic account of a recent bear sighting. Cat introduced them to Mistletoe, who had provided them – or more accurately their carpet – with two Christmas presents since breakfast.

'I'm quite impressed you've got Wi-Fi out there on your camper van,' Joe said.

'Oh no,' Cat whispered quietly. 'Mistake.'

'What?' Joe frowned, 'I—'

'Well,' Peter started, 'it's actually a very interesting set-up, Joe. Let me tell you how it works. When we got here, there was absolutely no chance—'

'Merry Christmas!' Delia called. 'Love to you both! Better go, our dinner's going to burn!' She blew them a multitude of noisy kisses, drowning out her husband, and leaned forward and ended the call. The iPad returned to a selfie

445

of Cat and Joe sitting on the sofa, Joe's face clouded with confusion.

'What happened there?'

'She saved you,' Cat said. 'From an hour-long explanation of how they've managed to get Wi-Fi on their camper van in the middle of the mountains. We're pretty lucky. That would have been Christmas over.'

'I'll have to thank her next time.' Joe stroked Mistletoe, who was asleep on his lap. 'We should toast them.'

'And I have the perfect thing,' Cat said, going into the kitchen and returning with the mini bottle of limoncello.

'Where did you get that?' Joe asked.

'Someone pretty amazing gave it to me.'

'Santa Claus is a special guy.'

They toasted Cat's parents, and then Polly and Owen came back, red-cheeked and exhilarated from their walk in the snow, and they found lots more things to toast: Polly's new job, Owen's plans for exotic ice cream flavours, Curiosity Kitten and Pooch Promenade. New relationships, new four-legged companions, and living on Primrose Terrace. Soon the bottle of limoncello was empty and Polly couldn't stop giggling.

'I think it might be time for bed,' Owen said.

They said goodnight, wished each other a final merry Christmas, and Owen and Polly climbed the stairs to her room.

'I need to stay up for a bit,' Cat said, putting her hand on Joe's chest. 'I want to try and take Mistletoe outside again.'

'I'll stay,' Joe said. 'I was kind of hoping we might spend the night together.'

'Oh, you were, were you?' Cat raised an eyebrow.

'Yeah,' Joe said. 'Pretty much. We could finish Christmas Day off the way we started it.'

Cat giggled. 'Are you drunk, Joe?'

Joe shook his head. 'Nope, not drunk. Bit fuzzy, maybe.'

'Ah. Well, you're cute when you're fuzzy.'

'Cute enough to go upstairs with?' Joe asked.

'Cute enough,' Cat murmured, kissing him. 'And sexy enough.'

'But first,' Joe said, 'Mistletoe. Not for kissing under, we seem to manage that quite well by ourselves.'

They stepped out into the cold, Christmas night, and watched the puppy take a few tentative, sinking steps, then turn the snow yellow. Cat gave a quiet cheer and they brought him back inside. She wrapped and warmed him in a towel, and then kissed him, held him out to Joe to say goodnight to, and put him inside his pen. He padded around it, sniffing the corners, then settled inside the crate on the blanket.

'Think he'll sleep through?' Joe asked.

Cat shook her head. 'No. That's OK, though. I'll come back down in a bit.'

Joe looked at her, his blue eyes creased at the edges. 'What if you fall asleep?'

'I don't think that'll be a problem.'

She put her hand in his and led him out of the living room, the chink of sleigh bells sounding as they stepped into the hallway. Cat paused at the front door and then opened it. The cold blasted in, along with fresh snowflakes.

She walked down the front steps, her ankle throbbing slightly, pulling Joe with her until they got to his car. Cat turned and leaned against it, wrapping her arms around him and looking at Primrose Terrace, the lights still blinking merrily on most of the houses.

Frankie's animals were still sparkling, and she wondered if Frankie was having a quiet drink after the girls – and Olaf

447

– had gone to bed, overtired from so much Christmas excitement, and whether Leyla was with her or with her family. Did Charles and Boris have guests staying over Christmas, or was it just the two of them, Dylan and Bossy?

Elsie and Captain had seemed snug and happy when Cat had visited earlier, and she was so pleased that her friend had a companion, as well as her old dog on the way back to health. Juliette and Mark might have their daughter back from university, maybe even their son from Australia, filling their house with laughter. She wondered briefly who Jessica was with. The lights were on at number one, her LED display a subdued shimmer of white and blue. Did she have family visiting? Mark's Audi was there, but his house was dark. Maybe they were together, friends enjoying a quiet Christmas with their dogs.

Cat loved living here. She had never felt more at home, never felt more excited or positive about the future. She was sure, at that very moment, as the lights twinkled and the snow fell, that she was the happiest person on Primrose Terrace – probably in the whole of Fairview. She hugged Joe tighter and he squeezed her back.

'Thank you for making my Christmas so perfect,' she said.

'It was nothing,' Joe said. 'It was easy. Everything's easy with you.'

'Even watching *Blade Runner*?'

Joe was quiet for a moment. 'OK, maybe not that. But everything else.'

'Putting Christmas lights up?'

Joe sighed. 'You're a bit of a liability there, too. Maybe if you didn't have ankles . . .'

'Getting on with things without interference?'

'Right. That's it.' Joe picked her up and hoisted her over his shoulder. Cat couldn't help it – she squealed.

448

'Put me down!'

'No.'

'Joe, it's snowy and slippery, and you're drunk.'

'Fuzzy,' Joe corrected, walking back to the house. 'Not drunk.'

He climbed the front steps, went inside and locked the door. With Cat still over his shoulder, squirming to be let down, he checked on Mistletoe, gave Shed and Rummy, asleep on separate sofas, a quick pat, and then turned the Christmas lights off.

'Please, Joe,' Cat said, laughing. 'Let me down.'

'Nearly,' he whispered, 'shush.'

When the house was in darkness, inside and out, he carried Cat out into the hallway.

The sleigh bells jingled a final time, signalling that Christmas day on Primrose Terrace was drawing to a close.

He climbed up to the first floor, bent his knees and put Cat down, brushing her hair off her forehead as he faced her. It was dark on the landing, but as she got accustomed to it, she could see the intensity in Joe's eyes, the warmth, the kindness that had slowly cast its spell on her, that had shown her how easy, how right it was to love him. She realized, then, that it had been inevitable. A case of when, not if.

Joe took a step up onto the second flight of stairs and held his hand out.

Cat took it.

What gets your tail wagging?
Find your Inner Doggess with this fun quiz!

 Where would you most like to go on a romantic weekend away?

A   A chic, skiing mini-break in Courchevel

B   A big old manor house in the country

C   A lovely little cottage in the Highlands

D   An active, adventure holiday in the Lake District

 You're making a speech at your friend's wedding. What style do you go for?

A   An easy blend of sentiment and humour

B   Loyal to the end, compliments aplenty

C   Short and sweet, always works a treat

D   What's a good speech without a few jibes and fun-poking!

You're feeling bored at a party. What would you do to liven it up?

A   Hit the dance floor and show these people your natural talents

B   Blossom into the social butterfly that puts everyone at ease – circulate, oozing warmth and intelligence

C   Find a comfy seat with an old friend

D   Sniff out somewhere else to go, you can't flog a dead horse

You spot the bar, what's your poison?

A   A burgundy red wine

B   Can't go wrong with a no-nonsense pint

C   A nice Scottish whisky

D   Tequila slammers, why not!

You're trying to get on a really full train. Would you:

A   Subtly edge past people

B   Smile and ask if people would mind making some space

C   Stick out the wait till the next train – it's not worth the rush and aggro

D   Bustle your way in, surely there's room!

A friend wants to organise a blind date for you. Your response?

A   Only if they meet my standards

B   Sounds good. Who knows what might come from it?

C   I'd run a mile, what's wrong with the traditional method?

D   As long as it's not a sit down dinner

MOSTLY A's – Spaniel

You're a cool, classy customer and love maintaining your well-groomed demeanour. You manage to get through the most stressful of situations without a hair out of place. Cheerful and breezy, you ooze innate likeability, and you probably have quite specific tastes – but who wouldn't want the finer things in life?

MOSTLY B's – Retriever

Totally affable, bubbly and at ease in any social situation, you're the life and soul of the party and are always sniffing out new friends. Never one to make a fuss you'll go along with most plans – although you're truly in your element in the great outdoors!

MOSTLY C's – Westie

You're not the most gregarious, but also never to be underestimated. You know your own mind and can hold your own, and even though you're not the most adventurous, people can't help but admire your steadfastness – and you usually lure them into your comfort zone, with chocolates and a blanket!

MOSTLY D's – Terrier

You're a whirlwind of energy and know exactly how to keep people on their toes! You love to keep moving (couch potato day, eh?) and are always seeking out new adventures and activities. You'll latch on to an argument and won't give in easily, but when it comes to poking fun you'll take as much as you dole out!

A Q & A with Cressy

What was the inspiration behind Primrose Terrace?

I love dogs and, while I've never had one of my own, I have met lots of affectionate and hilarious ones. They have huge potential to be characters in their own right, and the idea that my heroine could be a dog walker evolved out of wanting to write about lots of dogs, not just one. Cat loves dogs, but – like me – her circumstances mean she can't have one at home, so instead she takes care of other people's pooches.

Of course, as well as all the westies and terriers, dog walkers get to meet their owners on a regular basis, finding out about them along the way. Cat's curiosity, combined with a close-knit, picturesque community full of pet owners felt like the perfect recipe for a heart-warming, romantic and pooch-filled tale.

Can you tell us about some dogs that you have known and loved?

When I was younger, my parents agreed to house sit for a friend while they were on holiday, which included looking after a menagerie of six rabbits, two cats, and a beautiful border collie called Wags. She was so friendly and well behaved, and my sister Lucy and I relished having a dog for a week. Then on the last morning, while my parents were packing the car, Lucy and I took Wags for one last walk.

Far from trotting along at our side as she had been doing, she went straight to the pond, dived in and then raced back to us, showering us with water. She knew that without my parents there, she could do whatever she wanted, and she rebelled! Wags was such a clever, mischievous dog, and the memory of getting a soaking will always stay with me.

Pete, my friend's cairn terrier, also deserves a mention. He is sweet and friendly, but a little on the ditzy side, and always makes us laugh. He has a hilarious, ongoing battle with a wooden hippo ornament – he barks and runs in circles round it whenever they're in the same room!

Just to be sure, dogs or cats?

Dogs! But I love cats too – can I have both? (My main character is called Cat, after all). I think dogs are very straightforward and loyal, but cats can sometimes be misunderstood. Shed, Joe's cat in *A Christmas Tail*, is a bit misunderstood I think. He's not as grumpy as Cat thinks he is, just a bit solitary, and not always openly affectionate. But you can't take a cat (or a goldfish) for walks.

Do you have a personal favourite pooch in Primrose Terrace?

Don't make me choose! I feel slightly disloyal to Chalky saying this, but I think it has to be Disco, Elsie's young mini schnauzer and Cat's partner in mischief. My parents' neighbours have a mini schnauzer called Humphrey, who is super bouncy and puts his front paws on my knees to greet me every time I see him. He's the inspiration behind Disco, and is utterly lovable. But Chalky has to get a mention too, and little Olaf, and I love Chips. Can I pick them all?

Who is your favourite romantic hero/heroine?

My favourite romantic heroine is Catherine Morland from *Northanger Abbey*. She's young and naïve, she loves reading and she lets her imagination run away with her. But she's adventurous too, and throughout the book she grows and learns from her mistakes, becoming a real, rounded heroine by the end of the novel.

It's harder to narrow down my favourite hero, because there are so many! I love John Thornton from *North and South* by Elizabeth Gaskell, and Julian in *The Unfinished Symphony of You and Me* by Lucy Robinson is gorgeous and completely believable.

But most recently, and like so many others, I have become mesmerized by a scythe-wielding, tricorner hat-wearing, horse-riding Cornish hero called Ross Poldark. He's the perfect mix of moody and tender, dashing and principled. He might just be romantic hero perfection.

Where's your favourite writing place, and do you have a particular routine?

I have a little office in my house in Norwich where I do most of my writing. My desk is surrounded by books, my lava lamp, a glass board with neon pens for all my scribbled ideas, and a view of our back garden – of grass and trees and the washing line.

I'm a morning person, so I like to be at my desk by 8am, and generally read through my previous day's words before I start writing – though I'll try not to get caught up in editing until the first draft is done. I always have a coffee and biscuit break about 11 (currently chocolate digestives if you're interested) and a late lunch, but I try to keep going until 4. It's not always as organised as this, and if I'm in the writing zone I'll keep going until my brain is completely scrambled.

Do you have a favourite doggy film? Perhaps *Beethoven* or *Marley & Me*?

I've never dared to watch *Marley & Me*, because I think it would be too sad. Having said that, my favourite doggy film is also a tearjerker. It's going back a few years now, but I still love *Turner and Hooch*, with Tom Hanks as a by-the-book detective, who inherits French mastiff Hooch after his friend is murdered. Hooch is the only witness, and while it's complete chaos, the two of them form a bond as they solve the murder together. It's a lovely, romantic story, but have the tissues handy!

What were you, Westie, Spaniel, Retriever or Terrier? (We asked Cress to find her 'Inner Doggess' in the fun quiz on the previous page!)

I was overwhelmingly a spaniel, which I'm very happy with! Who wouldn't want to be seen as cool and classy? And I know that Olaf, the spaniel that Cat befriends, has had a lot of love from readers so far. I'd love to know which dog you get, so get in touch via Facebook or Twitter if you'd like to!

What was your favourite book when growing up that you would still read now?

My TBR pile is huge, but I always find time to go back to *Tiger Eyes* by Judy Blume. It's about a teenage girl, Davey, who's grieving after her father's murder. Her mother decides they're going to move to Los Alamos, and whilst there she meets an older boy, Wolf, in the canyon. It's heartbreaking and uplifting and mysterious, and I remember being completely captivated by it. It still affects me now, and I never tire of rereading it.

Tell us what you will be writing next?

My new book is called *The Canal Boat Café*, and will also be serialised in four parts. I'm really enjoying writing it, exploring new ideas and places, and immersing myself in the idea of living life on the water. I can't wait to share my characters and their stories. I'm pretty sure I have the best job in the world!